PRAISE FOR THE NOVELS OF

Emma Holly

"Emma Holly, known for her torrid tales, treats her readers to an equatorial heated romance." —*BookBrowser*

"Fans of bolder romances will relish [Emma Holly's] potent combination of heady sexuality and intriguing characterization." —*Publishers Weekly*

"Emma Holly once again pens an unforgettably erotic love story . . . A wonderful tale of creative genius and unbridled passion." —*Affaire de Coeur*

"Ms. Holly is a rising star who creates tantalizing tales . . . Delicious." —*Rendezvous*

"Steamy sex, interesting characters, and a story that offers a couple of twists . . . A page-turning read." —*The Romance Reader*

"The love scenes were an excellent mixture of eroticism and romance and they are some of the best ones I have read this year." —*All About Romance*

"I was captivated . . . and fascinated . . . powerful erotic overtones . . . that will fulfill readers' desires for Holly's signature erotic love stories." —*Romantic Times*

STRANGE
Attractions

EMMA HOLLY

BERKLEY SENSATION, NEW YORK

THE BERKLEY PUBLISHING GROUP
Published by the Penguin Group
Penguin Group (USA) Inc.
375 Hudson Street, New York, New York 10014, USA
Penguin Group (Canada), 10 Alcorn Avenue, Toronto, Ontario M4V 3B2, Canada
(a division of Pearson Penguin Canada Inc.)
Penguin Books Ltd., 80 Strand, London WC2R 0RL, England
Penguin Group Ireland, 25 St. Stephen's Green, Dublin 2, Ireland (a division of Penguin Books Ltd.)
Penguin Group (Australia), 250 Camberwell Road, Camberwell, Victoria 3124, Australia
(a division of Pearson Australia Group Pty. Ltd.)
Penguin Books India Pvt. Ltd., 11 Community Centre, Panchsheel Park, New Delhi—110 017, India
Penguin Group (NZ), Cnr. Airborne and Rosedale Roads, Albany, Auckland 1310, New Zealand
(a division of Pearson New Zealand Ltd.)
Penguin Books (South Africa) (Pty.) Ltd., 24 Sturdee Avenue, Rosebank, Johannesburg 2196, South Africa

Penguin Books Ltd., Registered Offices: 80 Strand, London WC2R 0RL, England

This is a work of fiction. Names, characters, places, and incidents either are the product of the author's imagination or are used fictitiously, and any resemblance to actual persons, living or dead, business establishments, events, or locales is entirely coincidental.

First edition: October 2004

Library of Congress Cataloging-in-Publication Data

Holly, Emma.
    Strange attractions / Emma Holly.— 1st ed.
      p. cm.
    ISBN 0-425-19821-9
    1. High school dropouts—Fiction. 2. Young women—Fiction. 3. Sex customs—Fiction. 4. Physicists—Fiction. I. Title.

PS3608.O4943S77 2004
813'.6—dc22

                               2004049024

PRINTED IN THE UNITED STATES OF AMERICA

10 9 8 7 6 5 4 3 2

To Kerri Sharp,
for giving me my first chance.

Author's Note

FOR those of you who, like me, aren't science geeks, here are the relevant basics of B.G. Grantham's field.

Quantum, or subatomic, particles possess many strange qualities. Nobel prize–winning physicists have verified that they can: a) spin in different directions simultaneously, b) behave as waves (like water) or particles (like teeny-tiny bullets), and c) move faster than the speed of light—something Einstein's theory of relativity supposedly forbids. Nonetheless, entangled particles have been shown to communicate with each other instantaneously over great distances. Finally, quantum particles exist in a "fuzzy" state where they inhabit all possible positions at once, creating what are known as probability waves.

These qualities contradict the equally proven laws of Newtonian (or large body) physics. In other words, a photon appears not to obey the same rules as a planet. The quest to reconcile this paradox has been called the search for the Theory of Everything.

Back in the 1920s, German physicist Werner Heisenberg formulated his famous uncertainty principle, which states that by the very act of observing a thing, you change it. To measure a particle's momentum, you must alter its location. To pin down its location, you must alter its momentum. When you are not looking at a particle, its true status can only be guessed. To make matters more mind-boggling, recent experiments support some physicists' belief that consciousness itself is capable of collapsing the particles' many "fuzzy" states into one. In other words, our thoughts may truly create our reality.

—To learn more, try *Time Storms* by Jenny Randle or *In Search of Schrodinger's Cat* by John Gribbon.

One

"Come closer," B.G. Grantham said to his employee.

Though Eric Berne was dressed, his boss was not. The notoriously reclusive physicist lay facedown on a black leather massage table—his long, lean body gleaming with oil. Eric knew it didn't bother B.G. to be naked. His employer's reserve had never been physical. It didn't need to be. From his broad, straight shoulders to his narrow feet, his every sinew was perfectly conformed. Had B.G. wished, his image could have been used to hawk men's cologne.

He's the Greek ideal, Eric thought, flashing back to his days at U.C. Berkeley—*mind and muscle both at their peak.*

Because he was an avid swimmer, B.G. had taken to removing his body hair. As Sylvia, the pretty blonde masseuse, pushed her hands slowly down his spine, nothing spoiled his sleek, athletic lines.

Eric fought an urge to lick his lips.

"Yes?" he said, shaking himself from his fugue and stepping within arm's reach. "You have an assignment for me?"

"Of a sort," B.G. said, then groaned as Sylvia took his butt in her hands and squeezed.

The masseuse was his latest find, hired away from an

exclusive spa in nearby Victoria. Though B.G.'s staff usually went through a longer vetting process than Sylvia had, Eric could understand why he'd made an exception for her. Her hands were magic, her gift for intuiting what sort of touch would spur the greatest pleasure formidable. It was as if she'd been born to please. Naturally, this fascinated B.G., whose lifelong study of pleasure—what caused it, what heightened it—neared obsession.

Now his legs shifted slightly, languorously, betraying his enjoyment as much as his groan. The change in position bared the lower bulge of his balls, full and sexually flushed. For the last three months, B.G. had withdrawn from everyone on his staff, devoting himself to mental labors until he had to be reminded to eat and sleep. Eric could tell that phase was over and that B.G.'s appetite for sensual indulgence—always considerable—had been heightened by abstinence.

Once again, B.G. was taking his place as the erotic fulcrum around which Mosswood revolved. Once again, he'd decide who would be pleasured and who would not. Sylvia seemed to sense the change, her body humming softly with interest. She stood at the head of the table, and her front brushed B.G.'s back as she reached down.

She was a lovely woman—naked, of course—with slight, high breasts and nipples as tight as pencil erasers. Her hair was so short it clung to her head like a feathered platinum cap. Eric had reason to know those locks were just as soft as they appeared. She was an odd creature in bed, more comfortable with giving pleasure than in taking it. The few times they'd had sex—while B.G. was caught up in work— she'd given the impression that she wasn't completely there, as if she were perpetually waiting for someone else to appear. The effect was disconcerting, and explained why her status had been so quickly changed from plaything to staff. Competence was what B.G. valued most in an employee. In a sexual partner, however, a desire for the rewards he meted out was all important. Ironically, Sylvia wasn't greedy enough to suit B.G.—a problem Eric suspected he'd never have to worry about.

He did wonder, though, if he'd ever get used to being able to desire a woman even as his mouth was watering for a man.

Eric had been attracted to both sexes since he was young, a quirk in his makeup he'd been lucky enough to accept almost as soon as he'd figured out what it was. His parents had been open-minded, his circle of friends liberal. Before taking this job as B.G.'s sexual major domo, he'd thought attraction ought to be a one-gender-at-a-time affair. Serial mono-sexuality, so he thought, would keep his feet on the ground.

He should have guessed his old friend would be beyond any rules at all. The world of the quantum, B.G.'s favorite playground, knew few limits. Consequently, B.G. saw no reason why he should invent limits for himself.

"You've been here, what, three years now?" B.G. asked, his voice altered by a combination of sensual enjoyment and the pressure of stroking hands.

"About that," Eric agreed.

"And we've met in this chamber at least twice a year."

Reflexively, Eric looked around. The room in which he stood was shaped like a pyramid, great blocks of softly polished greywacke narrowing rank by rank to a central point. Blue pinprick lights underlit each level, enhancing the impression that this place was both old and new, a juxtaposition B.G. loved.

The quantum realm, he liked to say, *can't tell the difference between all times and none at all.*

Then again, since some of his employer's beliefs verged on the crankish, he might have been trying to test the validity of "pyramid power."

"Yes," Eric said, fighting a smile, "we always start our adventures here."

Despite the chamber's familiarity, or perhaps because of

it, merely opening its heavy door had the ability to disengage Eric from his normal self. His inhibitions fell away, along with his preconceived ideas of what sensible people did. Here, where each new round of play began, his desires spoke to him in the clearest possible tones.

Though it disturbed him sometimes, he was beginning to think the person he became within these walls was the real him. Regardless of whether that was true, his skin tightened in anticipation as his employer drew breath to speak.

"I want you to choose," B.G. said, startling Eric enough to rock him back on his heels.

Abruptly, he was aware of what hung beneath the lining of his trousers: the thickening weight of his cock, the tensing power of his legs. Eric was bigger and stronger than B.G., not stupid, but more of an athlete than a brain. B.G.'s mental charisma was the force that kept him in check. On his own, Eric wouldn't have had a fraction of the experiences B.G. made possible. Because of this, as well as his debt of loyalty, Eric chose to indulge the other man's whims, to wait however long it took for permission to sate his desires—which didn't mean the reins never chafed.

That was the idea, of course: that no one around B.G. be able to predict when release would come, that the possibility it would be withheld would make them desperate. In that state of suspended frustration, the smallest erotic reward gained intensity.

Blinking sleepily, B.G. turned his head on his folded arms. His face was as attention-grabbing as the rest of him—quirkier perhaps, narrow and olive-skinned, with a long, curving nose and a mobile mouth. His hair was straight and black, cut short except for a shock that hung over his dark-brown eyes. On anyone else, these features would have been expressive. On B.G., they gave away virtually nothing. His emotions were hidden, as was usual, behind a wall of lazy calm.

Only a long-time associate like Eric could tell how jazzed he was.

"Did you hear me?" B.G. asked patiently. "I said I want you to choose our next candidate."

The candidates' files sat open on the granite tiles beneath the table where B.G. lay. One candidate was male, the other female. These reports were part psychological profile, part personal history. Eric had not only directed their compilation, he had summarized them for his boss. It wasn't standard procedure, but Eric himself had taken the long-lens photos for one. That being the case, he knew the files' contents intimately.

"I heard you," he said to B.G. "I'm just not sure which option you'd enjoy more."

This spurred a reaction. Like a leopard waking from a nap, B.G. rolled onto his back and pushed up on his elbows. His chest bore creases from the table's leather seams. Though the marks cut enticingly across his nipples, Eric's eyes drifted farther down. B.G.'s cock was swollen and straight, flushed like his scrotum but not lifted yet. Because his hips were slender, his shaft seemed larger by comparison. With painful clarity, Eric recalled the silkiness of its skin.

As B.G. undoubtedly intended, remembering the pleasure they could share made the waiting worse.

B.G. and Eric had known each other since they were boys, thrown together by well-meaning parents who thought the odd-ball genius needed a friend his own age. Eric sometimes wondered if the Granthams and the Bernes had suspected what they'd begun. From the time he and B.G. were teens, it had been like this between them, a game of do-we-dare and Lord-I-can't-resist. Losing touch for a while hadn't changed their chemistry. B.G. was still the partner Eric couldn't get out from under his skin.

Similarly drawn, if not for the same reasons, Sylvia reached for her client's burgeoning erection. To see a need and not satisfy it went against her nature. B.G. held her off by spreading his hand across her diaphragm. Though his touch was gentle, it made her flinch. No more than that was needed to make her stop. Sylvia might believe in instant gratification, but like everyone at Mosswood, she knew who was boss.

"I want you to choose the candidate *you* would enjoy," B.G. said, his gaze intent on Eric's face. "I want you to consider no one's desires but your own."

"My desires?" Eric repeated. The hair at his nape prickled in a wave. He had to take a step to keep his footing, more off-balance than he could account for by the surprise. Without exception, B.G. always set the rules. He bore the ultimate responsibility for the end result. Changing that seemed vaguely dangerous, as if the haven Eric had found here could be threatened by what he chose.

Why B.G. would want to do this was beyond him.

Watching him, B.G.'s fingers played idly across the shaven skin of his own abdomen. "Yes," he said. "I want to know which of these people you could get most enthused about having. Who would frustrate you more to be deprived of? Who do you wish to help me drive to their brink?"

Eric knew the answer, and had known it even before he passed the name to their investigator to start the file. He'd never had such a strong reaction to a candidate. The thought of having this person here, at B.G.'s estate, under their conjoined control, thrust through his body like a velvet hammer blow. Goose bumps swept his scalp as he hardened with a swiftness B.G. seemed mysteriously able to suppress.

"You know you can't lie to me," B.G. said at his hesitation. "I've known you too long, and I'm too good at reading how you feel."

The knowledge that this was true freed him to respond.

"This one," he said, stooping to pull a picture out of the pile. His hand shook slightly as he held it out.

B.G. nodded, smiling faintly as if the decision was expected. "Good," he said, settling back against the table. "I appreciate your honesty."

B.G. beckoned to Sylvia, who moved eagerly forward and took his shaft between her well-oiled fingers. B.G. was human enough to shudder at the first contact. Given her personal predilection, the reaction encouraged her to even more exquisite care. She stroked him hand over hand, from root to rim, the rhythm slow and hypnotic while his cock wavered back and forth at each pull—the tides of his blood a force both Eric and she could see.

This time B.G. didn't stop her, though his eyes, glittering within the spikes of his dark lashes, remained on Eric. As if he'd given himself permission to be aroused, he rose to full erection, his veins filling darkly, his untouched crown as taut as a drum.

The visual he presented was tempting in the extreme—and not only to Eric.

"Do you want me to suck you?" Sylvia asked breathlessly.

B.G. reached out but not toward her, the back of his hand brushing the front of Eric's thigh. Trembling now, Eric tried to breathe as steadily as his friend. His own erection felt like a club, hot behind the cloth B.G.'s feather-light caresses tugged. His employer was always gentle, always careful not to hurt. It was the only complaint Eric ever had. Right now, Eric wanted a good, firm grip so desperately he could have screamed.

Images streaked through his mind of taking someone against a wall, of pounding recklessly into them until he came. Who it was he hardly cared, though he couldn't deny the phantom had a face.

The guilt this specificity inspired didn't weaken the fantasy.

"What do you think?" his old friend asked. "Shall I have her take me in her mouth?"

Eric shivered, his inner vision seeing someone besides the masseuse performing the task. Unused to having the power to choose, he took a moment to decide. He had no doubt what Sylvia wanted the answer to be. "Yes," he said, "but don't let her bring you to climax."

B.G.'s hand shifted sideways, his palm closing gently over Eric's crotch. "If I can't come, neither can you."

Eric gritted his teeth. B.G. was already rubbing his erection, probing for vulnerabilities, stretching him impossibly inside his skin. When his longest finger dragged toward the nerve-rich flare, Eric couldn't repress an anticipatory twitch.

His zipper was a barrier he wished his heat could melt.

"Agreed," he gasped, knowing his employer—his rescuer, truth be told—would make it as difficult as possible to comply.

"I want us all to wait," Eric added impulsively. "Nobody gets off until our candidate arrives."

B.G.'s brows quirked in surprise—this edict more his style than Eric's—then relaxed as his eyes briefly closed. Sylvia had bent to surround the upper half of him in her mouth. She held him for a moment, her tongue working against the cap, before beginning to move up and down. As before, her pace was languid, her suction strong. A sheen of sweat broke out on B.G.'s face as his now-rigid cock grew wet.

Sylvia would get him off if he wasn't careful. Then again, "Careful" was pretty much B.G.'s middle name.

Despite the battle for control he must be going through, when he spoke, his voice was only a little husky. To Eric's relief, he did not seem angry at his demand. "This," B.G. said, "should prove more entertaining than usual."

Eric got the distinct and somewhat unnerving impression that, in addition to making his own choice, he had vindicated B.G.'s.

Two

Charity Wills was late. Slipping hastily into her nice ergonomic chair, she set her cardboard cup of Seattle's Finest beside her keyboard, far too frazzled to worry about flashing thigh. She had a lot of thigh to flash, as it happened, her legs being long and her skirt being mighty short. She bit her lip as she caught a look at the clock. *Damn.* Four months on this job and she'd yet to make it to her desk on time.

She'd been certain she could be punctual if she tried. She'd rolled out of bed on time for once, then spent the morning checking her watch every other minute and making a determined mantra of *Don't be late.*

Despite her efforts, it seemed the universe was against her. Right up until the end, she'd been fine. The line at her normally speedy coffee kiosk had only looked slightly longer than usual. Unfortunately, the woman in front of her, a Californian with blazing red hair, had changed her order three times. When the woman had finally turned away with her half-skinny, half-fat caramel macchiato, she'd had the nerve to smile at Charity as if this were the pleasantest morning in the world. Maybe for her it was, but Charity was beginning to think her mother was right. Maybe no

Wills woman was destined to set the world on fire.

Exasperated, she blew her dark wavy bangs out of her eyes.

"9:22," noted the guy in the next cube over. "You're getting closer."

His skinny arms were folded on the low dividing wall. He propped his chin on them as he grinned. He was her age: mid-twenties, although his glasses—not to mention his aura of responsibility—made him seem older. He was cute, she supposed, in a geeky sort of way. She just wished he didn't find her imperfections so entertaining. She couldn't help it if she wasn't cut out to be a suit.

Of course, she hadn't been cut out to be a waitress, either. That job had only lasted a month.

"The coffee place was packed," she said, hating that she felt the need to explain. He wasn't her boss, and who cared about twenty-two measly minutes?

His grin took on a gleam of interest as she tugged the hem of her tight black skirt. Generally speaking, she wouldn't have been self-conscious. Charity liked being a girl in every possible way. She liked being ogled, liked having doors held, liked when cars let her cross ahead of them rather than wait. To her, being female was a lovely perk. Sadly, the other women in this office didn't agree. Few Seattleites knew the meaning of dressing up, but here they took it to extremes, wearing serious trousers and plain, button-down shirts—as if working for a high-tech firm required them to dress like men. Though Charity refused to go as far, she had decided to leave her belly-baring tops at home.

Which was a shame, really. Her cubemate would have gotten a charge out of her navel ring.

"You know, Charity," he said, "if I may be so bold as to call you by your name—seeing as how you keep forgetting mine—people at Future-Tech are pretty laid back. No one's going to yell at you as long as your work gets done."

"I know," she whispered back, taking hold of the wall to

roll her chair confidingly closer. "I haven't been repri-
manded once. But everyone else is on time. In fact, everyone
else is early. It's completely freakish. Nobody should be that
eager to get to a job. And anyway, I know your name is
Dan."

"Dave," he corrected, laughing softly.

"*Dave.*" She knocked her fist against her forehead. "Tomorrow I swear I'll tattoo it on my arm."

"I can think of more interesting places than that," he
said, then flushed and cleared his throat. "You should find
work you like. Then you won't mind getting out of bed."

His big-brother air was ruined by the fact that the thought
of her in bed made him blush as well. Charity immediately
felt better about being late. Freakishly punctual or not, her
co-worker was human. She was about to razz him when she
heard her name being called over the PA.

"Charity Wills," said the smooth female voice. "Please
proceed to Human Resources as soon as you're free."

Charity cursed under her breath. This job had been relatively tolerable, but it looked as if her luck had expired. Resigned but defiant, she headed out.

"It's probably nothing," Dave called after her, but she
was already stalking grimly down the aisle.

The best thing about working at Future-Tech had been
the location. Unlike Microsoft, which had a creepy, overly
manicured "campus" out in Redmond, Future-Tech was
housed in one of downtown Seattle's sleekest buildings, a tall,
round tower with different departments arranged in wedges
around a central shaft. As offices went, it was swank. Pale
wood floors. High ceilings with exposed struts. Plenty of
plants and windows all the way around. The cube walls were
low enough that you could actually see the outside world. At
the moment, given the city's typical summer morning fog,
the view was three hundred sixty degrees of gray. The Space
Needle floated to the west of them like a ghost, and Elliott

Bay might as well have been Neverland. By afternoon, when the clouds burned off, Charity would be able to see Mt. Rainier . . . assuming she was still here.

She assured herself she couldn't be fired yet. That, after all, generally required a warning.

She fought a wash of depression that she was getting this familiar with being let go. She didn't think she was a bad employee—just one who danced to her own tune.

As she neared Human Resources, her heart jolted unexpectedly in her chest. A familiar figure sat leaning over his knees in one of the waiting area's chrome-framed chairs. Eric Berne, a vendor who sometimes took her boss out to lunch, was a solidly muscled stretch of good-looking man. Tall and outdoorsy, with squinty gray eyes and sunstreaked hair, he looked like he should be sailing out on the bay. Instead, he poured his broad-shouldered physique into beautifully tailored Saville Row suits that would have cost her a couple months' rent. The first time she'd seen him—on her first day here, interestingly enough—she'd nearly swallowed her tongue. At the moment, his shapely hands were clasped between his knees. His gaze was on the carpet, his brow a pucker of serious thought.

He shouldn't have appealed to her; he wasn't her type at all. Charity liked fun guys, guys who maybe didn't shave every day, guys who knew a Chili Pepper from a Stone. Maybe her boyfriends weren't prizes. In fact, maybe something was wrong with any guy she could get. What mattered was that they were comfortable to be with. That was what counted when the lights went out.

Despite knowing this extremely well, every time she saw Eric Berne—or smelled him, for that matter—her pulse began to patter between her legs. She was so obsessed she was beginning to imagine she saw him everywhere. At the grocery. In the park. Hanging around the tattoo parlor, of all places. Every time she thought she saw him, he'd be gone when she turned to look—which didn't keep her hormones in check at all. He was just so hot and yummy, so totally out of her league. A guy like Dave she could probably coax into unbending over a beer. This man would spend five minutes with her and know she needed to grow up.

"Um, hello," she said, because they hadn't been introduced and it would seem odd if she knew his name. "Are you waiting to go in?"

He looked up, slowly, with no expression that she could read, though his furrow remained where it was. She felt an embarrassing zing when his eyes met hers.

"No," he said in what she thought of as the voice of East Coast privilege. "I'm here to speak to you. Mr. Green was kind enough to lend me his office. I thought I'd wait for you out here."

She caught her breath without meaning to. The way he spoke, the way he held her gaze, suggested he knew perfectly well who she was. It crossed her mind that this might be some kind of weird setup for asking her on a date—though even she knew that would be out of line. *Had* he been following her, or was she finally going around the bend? Confused, she jerked her thumb over her shoulder. "I'll, ah, just go in."

She nearly tripped on her heel as she turned. *Geez,* she thought. *Way to convince Mr. Hot you're completely spastic.*

As if he was too much of a gentleman to notice, Eric reached ahead of her to hold the door. He followed her in and closed it behind them, then took the seat behind Mr. Green's keyhole desk. He didn't look at home exactly, but as if he had the right to take over whatever space he liked. He straightened his tie, shot his expensive cuffs, and spread his hands like starfish on the file that sat dead center on the green felt blotter. All thoughts of inappropriate dating scenarios fled her mind. No way could that file be hers. It was almost two inches thick. Even she couldn't have collected that many complaints in a couple months.

"I thought you were a vendor," she blurted out.

"I work for one of Future-Tech's advisers. Occasionally I deal with personnel. Why don't you take a seat, and I'll tell you what this is about."

"Hoo boy," she said. "It's never good when they tell you to sit down."

To Charity's relief, he smiled. She was used to the suits not getting her sense of humor, not that this made her stop joking.

"I assure you, Ms. Wills," he said, "I haven't called you here for a scold. No one has any complaints about your work."

"They don't?"

He laughed at her automatic doubt. "No, Ms. Wills. In fact, your boss says you're quick, accurate, and let's see—" He referred to the top page of the file: hers, apparently, despite the brevity of her employment. "He mentions you're especially good with visitors."

"That's because they're mostly science guys," Charity said. "They like it when I flirt. A little, you know. Strictly a little businesslike sort of flirting." Sensing she was digging herself a hole, she tugged her too-short hem. "I could buy longer skirts. Money's been kind of tight, but I wouldn't mind keeping this job if dressing more conservatively would help. I never worked anyplace where I rated an ergonomic chair."

Eric seemed to think this was funny, though her offer was genuine. "You're not being fired! I suspect the people who work here like your skirts just as they are. They're . . . festive."

"What's this about then? If I'm not being fired or told what to wear . . ."

He folded his hands on top of her file. Coupled with his suddenly serious expression, the gesture made the skin tighten on her nape. "I hope you'll bear with me," he said, "while I explain the proposition we have in mind."

"'Proposition'?" Charity's tone was sharpened by the bright red flag that had started waving in her head.

For the first time since they sat, Eric's composure slipped. Wincing briefly, he waved his hand. "We thought you might enjoy a position that utilized your talents a bit more than filing."

Utilizing her talents didn't sound much better than a *proposition*. Plus, why was he saying *we?* Charity knew she had the kind of looks that made men jump to conclusions—some of which were true. She was curvy and soft and wide-eyed, proud of her glowingly pale skin and her lush, shoulder-length hair. She loved her femininity, seeing it as a stroke of luck that was fun to share. What she didn't love was the suggestion that, because of her looks, she ought to be anybody's fool.

Drawing herself up to her full five foot, five inch height—or as close to it as she could get while sitting down—she prepared to nip this assumption in the bud. "Forgive me if I'm misreading you, but if you're hoping to set me up as some kind of 'escort' to shmooze prospective clients, you can think again. I've left jobs over less than that. And I'm not afraid to sue."

Eric grinned at this, a disconcerting response, to say the least. "I know. That's why we think you're perfect for this position. You're friendly, you're—if you'll pardon my saying so—sexually adventurous but also capable of saying no. Emotionally, you present evidence of being resilient. You seem, so to speak, the captain of your ship. It's all in the file, Charity. Mr. Massey and I were very careful to ensure your fit."

Charity shook her head to see if she could clear it. It was a measure of her befuddlement that his calling her by her first name sidetracked her ability to think most of all. "*Dave* Massey? The guy who has the cube next to mine?"

"Mr. Massey has a degree in behavioral science," Eric said, as if this excused everything. "And a private investigator's license. Believe me, this file was compiled for your benefit."

"You *were* following me. You're, like, Nutty Stalker Guy."

A hint of color crept up his neck. "I prefer to think of it as being responsible, as you'll see once you hear me out."

Before she could make the crack she sincerely hoped would cut him down to size, he began slipping papers from the file and passing them across the desk. Charity was reminded of a card shark's sleight of hand. Maybe he hoped to distract her from her anger. In truth, she couldn't deny a touch of fascination. This was like a bad girl's *This Is Your Life.*

"Here's the bit he found about your childhood," he said, tapping a neatly typed report. "Mother unmarried. Father unknown. Various 'uncles' joined your household and moved out. Lived in six states before you were twelve. Mr. Massey theorizes this is the source of your adaptability." A copy of old report cards joined the pile. "Didn't finish high school, but got your GED. Three separate teachers mentioned you were bright but didn't apply yourself. You attended secretarial trade school while working as an exotic dancer. Successfully took one employer to court for sexual harassment. Waitressed briefly. Took assorted clerical positions where you performed well but refused, in your words, 'to become a corporate drone' and showed, in their words, 'a noticeable lack of interest in moving up.'"

"Those were really boring companies," Charity said in her own defense. "They weren't worth moving up in."

"Exactly." Eric uttered the word with a sincerity and an approval she didn't expect. "What you need is the means to convince someone to hire you to do a job you'll enjoy. For that you'll need a decent education and someone to foot the bill. A Harvard-type education, where your brain will be challenged, where you can find an ambition that will engage you enough to build some security. I think you'd be tired of living like a gypsy."

Charity was too floored to be polite. It took a moment for her to do more than gape. "Are you nuts?" she demanded once she caught her breath. "Maybe you grew up believing you could be anything you want, but women like me can't get into Harvard."

"You can," he insisted. "Everything I've seen in your record suggests you're not lacking in intelligence. Yes, you'd need help, but Future-Tech can arrange that. You'd have tutors, mentors, people who could guide you through the different disciplines you might choose."

"And they'd do this because—?"

Eric sighed and put her papers back in a stack. He seemed reluctant to answer. "Are you familiar with the work of B.G. Grantham?"

"I think so. He wrote that *Quantum Quirks* book about time travel and multiple universes, the one everybody bought and nobody read."

He grimaced at her description, but acknowledged she'd remembered right. "What matters to you," he said, "is that B.G. Grantham is the Future-Tech adviser for whom I work. He consults for them—a one-man think tank, you could say. You might not know this, but true creative geniuses, the kind who spur revolutions, are extremely rare. Most scientists need someone else to spark their greatest thoughts. We stand on the shoulders of giants, as Newton said."

"And B.G. Grantham is a giant?"

"To put it bluntly: yes. Were it not for his contributions to the fields of medical technology, to engineering and computer science, Future-Tech wouldn't have been able to develop half the instruments that make them big profits. Without B.G. Grantham, Future-Tech would be one more victim of the high-tech crash."

"Bummer," she drawled, ignoring the cloud that crossed

his face, "especially for the patients who need those pricey doo-dads."

"Better a pricey doo-dad than none at all when it's your only hope. I mean no offense when I say this, but B.G. Grantham has helped more people in the last five years than you or I will in our whole lives."

Charity couldn't argue the likelihood of that. She gripped the arms of her chair. "Let me get this straight. You want me to sleep with this Einstein whose brain is saving the world."

"No." Eric's graceful hands flattened on the blotter. "If that were all there was to it, we wouldn't require a candidate with your spirit."

"O-kay," said Charity, feeling like Alice down the rabbit hole. "Then what do you want me for?"

"I want you to cede to my boss the responsibility for fulfilling your sexual needs—or deferring them, as the case is likely to be. I want you to let him rule your pleasure." Eric leaned earnestly over the desk to explain. "B.G. is obsessed with the lure of things that seem out of reach. The Theory of Everything. The meaning of life. The mysteries of the human soul. Most of all, he's fascinated by the way denial whets longing, especially in people with well-developed erotic imaginations."

"I might have *imagination,* as you put it, but whatever you might think, I haven't been swinging from the chandeliers!"

"It's your potential to swing that interests him. If you'd been everywhere he hopes to take you, he'd miss half his fun."

Such passion to convince suggested—to Charity, at least—that Eric was hiding a catch. "Is he hideous?"

"Not at all. He's quite attractive. My age. Perfectly fit." His discomfort at admitting this snagged Charity's interest. Was the golden boy secretly bent? With a tug at his collar, he continued hurriedly. "He couldn't play these games as well as he does if he weren't appealing. Your desire is his prize, Ms. Wills. However he can elicit it, he will. He finds the challenge refreshing, says it clears his mind of scientific obsessions. Then, when he returns to work, he's renewed."

Charity rubbed her face, wondering how a silver-spoon prince like Eric came to be selling this patch of swamp. Unless she missed her mark, his world was maids and polo ponies and holidays in the Hamptons with an ever-so-tastefully screwed-up family. She squashed the temptation to ask if his parents knew about his job. His background was none of her business. She might be pretty, but a girl like her would never be more than a walk on the wild side to a man like him.

Sighing, she sagged back in her chair. "This is the craziest thing I ever heard."

"I expect it seems that way," Eric agreed. "But think of the adventure. Plus, you really might be saving the world. It's not every twenty-four-year-old who can say that."

Charity's laugh was only half dismissive. "What if I don't like him? What if he does something that scares me?"

"I doubt he would. B.G.'s not dangerous the way you mean. But if you wanted, we'd cart you back and pay you just like I said. Tuition to wherever you like, plus all the bells and whistles. You wouldn't have to study science, either. I'm sure Future-Tech would like to hire you, but they have jobs for all sorts of skills."

"Harvard, huh?"

"Yale's nice, too, or Stanford . . . if you can stand the Californians."

Charity suppressed a smile. East Coast transplant or not, Eric Berne was enough of a Seattleite to enjoy bashing their neighbors. "You really think I can do this?"

"I think the chance to turn your life around is worth a very serious try."

He probably didn't realize he was insulting her by suggesting she hadn't been trying all along. He probably thought she ought to be flattered by this offer. She was flattered, but that didn't mean she couldn't also be mad.

"Stupid rich kids get through college all the time," he said more persuasively. "Their parents' money and clout ensures it. Why shouldn't a smart girl like you claim their advantages for yourself?"

That this was more flattery, she had no doubt. When she thought about it, though, why shouldn't she go to college? At the least, she'd prove she wasn't afraid. So she'd have to play footsie with some eccentric brainiac. For all she knew, it might be fun.

She'd never met a genius before.

"All I have to do is meet this guy?"

"All you have to do is meet him. We've even put it in writing." Smiling, Eric pulled a contract from beneath her file, then set a slim silver pen on top. "Just sign your name and claim a new future."

The fact that he was prepared gave Charity pause.

"Huh," she said. "I think I'd better read this first."

The rules seemed simple enough. She'd have a keeper— an erotic manservant, it sounded like—who'd relay the wishes of the mysterious Mr. Grantham and keep her in sensual tune. Punishments would be imposed for infractions, but no harm—physical or otherwise—would be done. She'd be given pleasure or refused it at a whim. If at any time she became uncomfortable with what was asked, she had only to tell her keeper and he'd whisk her home safe and sound and, most important, paid in full.

The same confidentiality agreement she'd signed on joining Future-Tech finished out the contract. That was fine with her. With her past, Charity understood the value of not blabbing everything.

"So basically," she said, rubbing her temple in bemusement, "we're talking chains but no whips?" When Eric nodded, she released her breath. "You know, your boss really has this company over a barrel, getting them to facilitate all this stuff."

"They consider it part of his benefits. Plus, I doubt you'd take me seriously if I approached you anywhere but here. It's a measure of trust, Charity, that we make this offer without knowing what you'll say. Potentially, you hold not only B.G. Grantham's reputation hostage but Future-Tech's as well."

She liked the low-key way he put this. He'd made his pitch, and now he was leaving the choice to her. The only sign that he might be impatient was his tapping the pen on his thigh.

"Ever been burned by someone you picked?"

"Never," he said. "We pride ourselves on how well we choose our candidates. For the last three years, each and every one has honored their agreement."

In this day and age, that was practically a miracle.

Go ahead, said the inner voice she never knew whether to trust. *Open the door. This is the way you want to go.*

Never mind her mother had all too often followed her hunches straight to Stupidville. What else did Charity have to go by? Whatever Eric said, she knew she wasn't the biggest brain in the Western world.

"All right," she said aloud, putting out her hand for the pen. "I guess I can give this a shot." She signed with a flourish she was proud of, then looked up. "Who's my slave boy?"

"Excuse me?" Eric said.

"My keeper. The guy who's supposed to keep my motor revved."

"Um." Eric's face looked as if he'd taken too much sun. "That would be me."

"You!" She supposed her reaction was rude, but she was too surprised to keep it in. The last thing she'd expected was that he would take a job like that.

"Yes," he said, "unless you have some problem with my assuming that position . . ."

Charity's snort of laughter was directed at herself rather than him, but he pressed his lips together anyway.

"Oh, no," she assured him, unable to resist. "I have no problem with you assuming any position at all."

"Good," he said, ignoring her double meaning. Still stiff, he rose from the chair and once again shot his cuffs. His small gold cufflinks flashed exotically. "I trust you'll remember that I don't answer to you. I am not, strictly speaking, anyone's *slave.*"

Charity was forced to swallow back another snicker. Though she suspected he wasn't someone to play with, she couldn't contain her giddiness.

"I trust you'll forgive me," she said, "when I say that's a freaking shame."

Three

E<small>RIC'S</small> boss had accused him more than once of being a worrier, but Eric hadn't felt this overwound since his previous employer's stock underwent a dot-bomb implosion.

Let her make the right choice for her, he thought as she looked over B.G.'s contract. *Even if the choice is no.*

Somewhere inside him, his libido laughed. It knew the only answer it cared to hear.

He couldn't help staring at her while she read. She was the most naturally feminine female he'd ever met: soft and curved from head to toe. Her eyes were Liz Taylor violet, her lips a bee-stung pout. She'd been biting them the first time he'd seen her typing at her desk. Something about the unconscious habit had sent an instant jolt of possessiveness through his veins. Ever since, he'd been unable to keep his cool. How could he, when any man with half his lizard brain intact would find her attractive?

B.G. would have explained Eric's reaction with a quip about his particles having known hers in a previous life. *You're entangled,* he would have said. *A pawn to the laws of physics.* Eric himself had a simpler reason.

Charity Wills was Woman with a capital "W."

What really got him, though, what had him nervous as well as enticed, were the things he saw in her eyes. For all their sooty-lashed bedroom appeal, the soul that swam behind them was no siren. This girl was the walking wounded, tough in her way, but bruised. Once he'd perceived this, nothing Dave Massey dug up surprised him.

Her eyes couldn't hide how much she yearned to be loved.

He wanted her to have every advantage Future-Tech could give her, wanted her to meet the kind of man she should really be shooting for. B.G. could give her a taste of that. Maybe so could he.

This bit of ego faltered when she expressed her shock at him being her keeper. Of the many results he'd pictured, that wasn't one. Caught off-balance, he bristled at her joke about him assuming the position, enough that he made her uncomfortable—which wasn't in the least how he'd meant to start.

He'd wanted—no, needed—her to trust him if this game was going to play out successfully.

Doing his best to unstiffen, he stuck his hand across the desk to shake. "I'm sorry if I've disappointed you, but I'm glad we're going to be colleagues."

His good manners seemed to rattle her. Her hand fluttered to the neck of her snug blue top before coming out to join his. To his surprise, given her smart-assed comments, when he gripped her fingers they were cold. He brought his second hand up to warm them without thinking twice.

Maybe she wasn't as fearless as she seemed.

"Don't worry," he said, his voice instinctively dark and soft. "It's our responsibility to see that you enjoy yourself, not the other way around. You can't fail, no matter what you do."

"That'll be a first," she said with a raspy laugh.

"It's *your* desire B.G. hopes to rouse. Really, Charity, you can't go wrong."

At his use of her name, color rose like wine to her

cream-pale cheeks. Too late he realized he'd betrayed the more personal component to his interest.

"You can call me Eric," he said, dropping her hand as his own face threatened to heat.

His awkwardness seemed to cure hers. She cocked her head to the side, a smile playing lightly around her lips. "That sounds mighty informal," she said, her voice revealing the slightest twang. "Are you sure you wouldn't prefer Master Eric? Or Mucky-Muck Number Two?"

"Those aren't quite the kind of games we play."

"No?"

He shook his head. "You'll see how it works when we begin."

"I thought we had begun."

He smiled at her teasing tone. "Not yet."

"In that case, there's something I'd like to clear up first."

He tensed, but she didn't have more bargaining in mind. Instead, she came around the desk and stepped toe-to-toe with him. Taking hold of his lapels, she pulled his head down for a slow, openmouthed kiss. It wasn't a coy kiss by any means, more like a declaration of intent, full of tongue and wetness and—underneath—an unexpected tenderness. To Eric's dismay, her mouth was as irresistible as the rest of her. Though he didn't grab onto her the way he wanted, he was gasping by the time she let go, his heart pounding as if he'd run the circumference of the floor.

All she had to do to feel it was uncurl her hands.

When her tongue came out to lick the taste of him from her lip, he thought he'd burst.

With a smile of feminine pleasure, she fastened the buttons of his suit. "There," she said, giving his chest a pat. "That was off the clock, cowboy, to let you know I'm genuinely interested."

He tried to speak through his hoarseness. "Wow. Um. I'll just, uh, call the driver and tell him to bring the car around."

He had to unbutton his coat again to reach his cell. Charity laughed, taking her chance to ogle what she'd been kind enough to cover up. "Not bad," she said, one judicious finger to her chin, "unless you're filling that out with socks."

Her suggestion—definitely a first—made him fumble the phone. "I'll put you on the clock," he warned once he caught it. "Then you'll have to behave."

If anything, her grin grew broader. Two deep dimples appeared on her cheeks. Seeing them, Eric's stomach did an alarmingly pleasant flip.

He was beginning to suspect Charity Wills had a bit more spirit than any of them were ready for.

In no mood to talk to Dave, the "private" investigator, Charity asked Eric to retrieve her purse while she waited by the elevators. He handed it to her when he returned.

"Dave didn't mean any harm," he said. "Researching you was his job."

"Hah," said Charity. "He's a snoop."

The elevator dinged shut, enclosing the two of them. Still buzzing from the kiss, which had seemed like a good idea at the time, Charity tried to pretend she couldn't smell Eric's woodsy cologne. Bad employee or not, she knew it wasn't smart to get too stoked by your co-worker.

My keeper, she corrected, a long, warm thrill slipping down her spine. She pressed her thighs together in self-defense, but that couldn't keep her body from going wet. What would Eric do to her, she wondered, and what would she be able to do to him?

She stood a bit behind him as they rode down, her gaze drifting from the slightly rumpled pleat of his linen trousers to the breadth of his athletic back. The little curves of hair at the base of his haircut were sticking darkly to his neck. As if he felt her eyes, he ran one finger around his white collar. She was certain he hadn't been sweating before they kissed.

"Here we are," he said as they hit the black marble lobby. From this, Charity knew she'd ruffled him. He didn't strike her as a man who talked just to make noise. She would have reveled in her victory if the knowledge hadn't sent a fresh pulse of excitement between her legs.

At this rate, she was going to be begging for it within the hour. While his boss might like the begging, she had a feeling it would bug her.

"We'll go to your apartment," he said, "so you can pack."

The car—a limo, actually, and a welcome distraction—was waiting on the street outside. Freeway Park rose behind it, a man-made green space straddling Highway 5 on a concrete bridge. Charity liked to eat her lunch beside its waterfalls. It felt peculiar to think she wouldn't go there today.

As if to underscore the unexpected shift in her fate, the limo's uniformed driver emerged. He was built like a wrestler, the World Wrestling Entertainment kind, right down to his mane of shaggy blond hair. The style was out of place with his shining cap and professionally sober expression. Behind his mirrored sunglasses, she sensed him watching her approach. She wondered if he, too, were a player in Grantham's game. For sure he was giving off some kind of vibe, as if how she looked and who she was might have relevance for him.

He wore a headset, the kind receptionists used to save them from having to hold the phone. Charity considered the contraptions a form of bondage, but this guy didn't seem to mind. "Subjects approaching," he muttered into the mouthpiece, like maybe he watched too much TV.

But that was okay. Whatever it took to get into your job. And he did make his look kind of sexy.

"Wow," she said, pretending she hadn't noticed his attention as she slid her hand admiringly down the limo's hood.

Left running, the motor purred beneath the black expanse. "Must be nice to take this to work every day."

"It's a Rolls," Eric informed her. "A custom Phantom. Direct injected V12 with self-leveling air springs. It'll float you right around a corner. Cars are kind of a hobby of mine."

She allowed herself a private smile for boys and their toys, then obeyed the chauffeur's gentlemanly gesture to get in back. The seat was leather, of course, squeaking nicely and smelling good. Her hip-hugging skirt slid right across it. Eric followed her with the reluctance of a man who would rather drive. He sat just far enough away that their knees didn't touch. Charity rectified this oversight by turning sideways, causing her hose to rasp his linen pants. As if he couldn't help it, his gaze flicked to her thighs.

Gratified, Charity put her elbow on the seat back and propped her jaw on her hand. True to Eric's promise, the limo glided silently from the curb. Seattle's hills could be a challenge to pedestrians, and never mind to cars, but the limo didn't labor once. She sensed more than saw the driver glance in the rearview mirror. That he knew the way to her house without being told was no surprise. Like the Rolls, this adventure was a well-oiled machine.

"He's not a regular chauffeur, is he?" Charity asked.

"No," Eric admitted, seeming fascinated by her eyes. His had a ring of blue around their stormcloud gray. "Maurice was hired because he's good, but not so long ago, he came to B.G.'s estate just like you."

"Were you there?" Her body tingled as a possibility rose in her mind. "Were you his keeper?"

"I was."

"I guess you, uh, swing both ways then."

"I do." Apparently not offended, he turned on the seat, his fingers mirroring her jaw-supporting pose. "Both men and women push my buttons, so to speak. I hope that doesn't bother you."

She pretended to think as she fought the urge to squirm. Not hardly it didn't bother her! "I think that's fine," she confessed when she thought she'd hesitated long enough. "I've always wondered what boys get up to with other boys. I just wouldn't have guessed. Looking at you, you seem kind of straight-laced."

"If I were exactly what I appear, I couldn't do my job."

"Are you good at it?"

His smile was slow and scrumptious. "That question is for you to answer in due time."

The way he looked at her, the lust he was able to convey with just his eyes, made a wash of heat rush out from her core. Those eyes held all the things he wanted to do to her but wasn't allowed, things she couldn't begin to dream of, things she might not dare to do with anyone else. He hadn't even touched her, and she was soaked.

Charity had a feeling she was even more out of her league than she'd feared.

"Phew," she said, laughing nervously as she leaned back and fanned her face. "Remind me not to doubt you again."

He ran a gentle finger across her lower lip. "Doubt me all you like. I enjoy exceeding expectations."

Charity refrained from admitting he already had.

Eric was grateful he could unnerve her. The advantage almost restored his sense of being in charge. Because "almost" was probably the best he could hope for, he held his peace for the rest of the drive. It was a brief one, just a cruise up Highway 5 in the big Phantom, then east to Capitol Hill.

Understandably, considering her economic constraints, Charity's apartment was on one of the neighborhood's seedier streets. Halfway down the block, the popular Apocalypse Tattoo—whose shadowed doorway Eric had used during his surveillance—did nothing to increase confidence. Without being told, Maurice stayed with the car while Eric walked Charity up. The chauffeur muttered under his breath about *Mr. G* not liking this. Eric wasn't fooled. He knew Maurice adored every aspect of his job, from his uniform to being wired for surveillance. Even setbacks, such as being separated from Eric and their charge, were simply fodder for his rich fantasy life. This, as much as his excellent driving skills, were what had led B.G. to keep him on.

Smiling to himself, Eric followed Charity up a stairway full of stains that appeared to go back to the state's founding.

At least the apartment was an improvement. Inside the third-floor studio, Charity had made her own small oasis, with bright Indian hangings and thrift-shop furniture. A tinkling beaded curtain separated the galley kitchen from the single room. Her bed was a boxspring and mattress stacked on the floor.

She must have had a knack for making things grow, because the window held an impressive array of cacti, a monstrous asparagus fern, and a view of the distant bay. Eric knew better than to let his gaze linger there. Too forceful a reminder of how high up he was would make him dizzier than her kiss. He turned away with gritted teeth. Contrary to his expectations, the rest of the apartment was neat.

"Turn your attention this way," Charity suggested with a fey smile, "and I'll show you why I'm renting this heap."

She thrust open two folding doors to reveal a big walk-in closet, jammed from floorboard to rafter with clothes and accessories. From the looks of them, very few of the contents qualified as sensible. He marveled that she'd found anything conservative enough to wear to work.

"I may not be good at much," she said, "but I'm a regular bloodhound for a sale."

"My," he breathed, unable to withhold a grin. "An embarrassment of riches to choose from."

"Not your usual challenge, eh?"

"No, indeed." Overwhelmed but entertained, he sat on her makeshift bed, already racking his brains for how he could top what she owned herself. "Tell you what: choose your favorites—whatever makes you feel sexy and comfortable."

"I'm comfortable in most anything."

Her tone held a warning that made him smile. "No worries," he assured her. "You can't shock anyone at Mosswood."

This caused her to laugh with genuine delight. He was glad to hear the sound, then uncomfortable. He kept forgetting that this was business, that it wasn't—not truly—for his pleasure alone. Being out of range of B.G.'s mechanical eyes and ears was making him reckless.

Too antsy to sit while she made her choices, he paced around the orderly clutter, taking inventory of her possessions. His mother, a born snob rather than a schooled one, would have been horrified by such love of sparkle and flash. Eric was charmed. The place was pretty for all its cheapness. Because no one else would do it for her, Charity had made herself a home.

A shock awaited him at her bookshelf. Next to a stack of fashion magazines, he spotted B.G.'s name. It leapt out from the spine of a former library copy of *Quantum Quirks,* mildewed and minus its dust cover—the type of book you could pick up at a rummage sale for a dime. It seemed the last thing a girl like Charity would find intriguing, yet here it was.

Nonrandom synchronicities, B.G. would have said. *Our minds forge meaning out of chaos.*

Eric was about to ask her if she'd read it when a photo studded with purple rhinestones drew his eyes away.

The picture showed a slightly younger Charity standing on a ramshackle boat dock, arm-in-arm with a woman who could have been her sister. Dressed in matching shorts and halters, they were laughing wildly as each held the opposite end of a fish the size of a sardine. It was a happy picture, but something about it made Eric sad.

"Is this your mother?"

"Yes," she said, closer than he realized. She had come up behind him without a sound. She smelled of orange-scented shampoo and hot woman, the combination instantly branding itself on his brain. Her hand brushed his where it held the sparkly frame. "She's in L.A. now, I think. I cut off contact between us. Mom's last boyfriend was a drug dealer. Just a 'rave organizer' according to her—as if those bags of pills he toted around were candy. I love my mother, but that was too much for me. I'd had enough of watching her prove how stupid Wills women are when it comes to men."

"You aren't stupid."

"I have been, as you must know if you've read my file." She sighed and touched her mother's laughing face. "I try to be smarter. It just never seems to work out."

He set the picture back and turned to face her. "Charity, if you don't feel comfortable doing this, if you have any doubts at all, we can call it off. You don't have to worry about the money. I'd pay you out of my own pocket."

She smiled, the expression tilting her violet eyes. "I'm not afraid of taking risks. I've done plenty of dopey things in my life, and I've come through them all. If going with you turns out to be stupid, I'll survive that, too. I mean, all I have are my instincts. Even if they're wrong, they're all I have. A person has to decide which road to take based on something. I don't want to miss out on an experience that could be good."

Her attitude inspired admiration and a pinch of fear. To think of her going on as she was, year after year, losing jobs and hooking up with slacker boyfriends, never even trying to play it safe . . . *You've got your mind,* he wanted to say. *Your reason.* But that was presumptuous. Who was he to lecture anyone about their life? He'd done a few colossally dopey things himself.

"I'll make sure this is a good experience," he said, brushing her silky waves from her face. "No matter what, I'll make sure."

For a moment her eyes were wide and starry. Then she laughed, a throaty chuckle that set off fireworks inside his groin. "Galahad," she teased.

He kissed her even as she laughed. Because he wanted to. Because no one was here to stop him. Because she'd said the name he wished he could really claim. Tilting his head for access, he slid his hands down her lush little body and pulled her giving flesh tight against his front.

His cock thrummed like an engine, but she didn't fight. Instead, she wound her arms behind his neck and melted, squirming against him when his hold wasn't close enough. One thigh climbed and wrapped the side of his hip. Unable to resist, he slid his hand slowly down its slope to cup her rear. Nothing but her lay beneath her hose. Her cleft was wet. When he brushed his fingertips along it, her pleasured hum made him long to toss her onto the bed. He didn't care that B.G. expected him to wait. He didn't care that this job had saved not just his pride but his sanity. At that moment, he would have traded everything he had to be an average Joe about to get laid.

"Mm," he said, unable to restrain the sound as he carefully pushed her off. Once again she had him panting. "Okay. We're not doing this now. We're going to follow the rules."

Her gaze narrowed, and she folded her arms across her chest. He saw he had chosen a less-than-fortunate word.

"You agreed," he reminded her, "unless you want to renege."

She rolled her eyes at him and stalked back to her red canvas carryall, preparing to zip it shut.

"Wait," he said. "I want to dress you for our trip."

"You want to dress me."

"Yes."

She stared at him, her face stubborn and closed. He thought she was about to protest, but she surprised him. Without warning or ado, she pulled off her top and wriggled out of her mini-skirt. Her bra was classic Victoria's Secret, sheer and blue with fussy embroidered flowers that covered next to nothing at all. In spite of his desire to keep the upper hand, Eric's breath went out of his lungs. Her figure was really something, making his blood feel suddenly sluggish within his veins. The hose, however, had to go.

Before he could open his mouth to say so, she peeled them off and threw them in his face. He caught them, plus a whiff of her arousal. Though the scent shot through him, he did his best to sound calm. He promised himself that her neatly trimmed pubis, now delightfully exposed, wasn't going to be his personal Bermuda Triangle of lust. "Do you own the panties that match that bra?"

"It's a thong," she snapped—as if he, or any man, would consider that anything but a plus.

He smiled and, after a heartbeat, she did, too. "All right. I'll find it."

Digging the scrap of blue out of a drawer, she pulled it on with more finesse than she'd yanked off the rest of her garments. Eric appreciated the show, as well as the end result when she turned around. Her navel ring twinkled like a star. He'd been looking too low to notice it before.

"Very nice," he said, adding an irrepressible male sigh.

For that he earned a peck on the cheek.

"Well." She spread her arms, obviously enjoying his bemusement. "Do I go like this, or is there something in particular you want on top?"

He knew the answer already. He'd spotted the perfect thing as soon as she opened her closet door. Going straight to it, he removed a demure pink knitted dress with a retro-looking fold-down neck. He spread it gently out on her bed, then added a pair of off-white pumps. All the outfit lacked was a pillbox hat and a pair of gloves.

"That's my interview dress," she objected. "It's, like, totally boring good girl's clothes."

"Please," he said. "I'd enjoy seeing you in it."

She raised one well-plucked brow. "I thought you wanted me to wear what made me feel sexy."

"Wear it to make *me* feel sexy."

"Right. Ever hear about the silk purse and the sow's ear?"

"You already are a silk purse. Clothes can't change that either way."

She had her fists dug into her waist and her feet set wide. She wasn't terribly tall, but the length of her legs made her seem as if she were. Her thighs had a bit of muscle, just enough to call to mind an X-rated version of an Amazon. "I want a bribe before I'm wearing that."

"This isn't a negotiation."

Unimpressed, Charity flashed a grin. "Dude, you've thrown a boner the size of Texas, and you've had it since before I took off my clothes. You want me to go along with you. You know you'll be disappointed if I don't. Therefore"—she made a drama of the word—"I strongly suggest you compromise."

He was forced to concede her point. "What do you want?" he asked warily.

She padded to him, barefoot in her bra and thong, jiggling the way women were born to jiggle from the dawn of time. She stopped with her peaking nipples brushing his shirt. "I want you to show me what you would do to a guy. In bed. If you had your choice of favorite things."

He blinked, startled. No one had ever asked him to blur his preferences this way. He wouldn't have guessed the request would pack such a punch.

"It's your job," she pointed out when he paused. "Maybe you're not allowed to get me off, but you're supposed to keep my motor revved. I guarantee this will do the trick."

He wished he could argue but couldn't quite form the words. He was supposed to be in charge here. On the other hand, if she decided she liked male-on-male action, they'd have more erotic options down the road, options he very much wanted to explore. What he did now could ensure he'd have the chance—as long as he didn't give up all semblance of authority. With his jaw bunching in frustration at the reality of that risk, he jammed his hand through his hair.

"You want to," she said, the statement shocking through him as if they were connected by electric wires. "You want to hump me like a man."

He felt the flush scald across his face, then saw its echo in the darkening of her eyes. This idea was turning her on.

"All right," he said, his body deciding for him. "Take off your clothes. I want you facedown on that bed with your bottom in the air."

Her mouth went slack with surprise, with arousal, and then—without a word of debate—she did what he asked. She slipped off her bra and thong and climbed into bed. A candy-pink bolster held her hips at just the angle he wanted. The smooth curve of her haunches made his mouth water.

He hesitated, then did what he was craving, smacking one side of her bottom with the flat of his hand. He did it just hard enough to make her jump, to test how firm she was. She rubbed the pinkened flesh as if it stung.

"Every favor has a price," he said as she sucked a breath to protest. His voice was not as steady as it should have been, but it silenced hers. "You have to pay even if no one sees except us."

When she looked at him, interested and alert, her eyes were too bright to bear, her curiosity very close to innocence.

"Don't watch," he ordered, pressing her head back down. "I don't want you seeing what I do."

She shivered, but the reaction seemed more like excitement than nervousness. Eric could claim both himself. His fingers were stiff as he wrenched down his zipper, his current state inviting accidents. He only released his breath when he swelled free. His shoes were next, then his trousers and briefs. He hadn't the patience to remove more than that. When he climbed over her, his arousal hanging hot in the open air, her shoulders tensed.

For a second, he thought of doing what he guessed she feared.

"I have oil," she said, clearly trying to sound game. "Plus a box of condoms. They're in the nightstand drawer."

"Sh." He blew her hair aside and kissed the back of her neck. When he dragged his tongue along her vertebrae, he tasted salt. To his relief, she wriggled pleasantly at the touch. While she might be nervous, she wasn't truly scared. "I won't do anything you're not used to until we're both sure you'll like it. I'd never hurt you, honey. I only want you to feel good."

"If that's the case, you should have taken off your shirt."

He laughed and reached for the oil. "Right now, there's only one part of me you need to feel."

"I could guess which one," she said, her words muffled by her tie-dyed coverlet. "But I think I'd rather let you demonstrate."

Four

Charity heard him oil himself. He was on his knees behind her, straddling her hips. She wanted to look but managed to hold back. The sound was extremely personal—like masturbation—his slippery hand rubbing up and down the contours of his hardened cock.

He was slow about it, as if he couldn't help liking what he did.

"I could help," she offered huskily.

"Wait," he said, which she was beginning to think was his favorite word.

He oiled her, too, massaging her buttocks until all that remained of his single spank was a pleasantly warm spot. She doubted she felt much like a guy to him, but he didn't seem to mind. The pads of his thumbs rubbed lingering circles over her tailbone, the pressure skillful and welcome. She felt as if he were stirring some unsuspected pool of sexual energy, one that went deeper than she had guessed. Sensation flickered inside her like swimming fish.

Apparently, the folks at Mosswood got all sorts of training.

She bit her lip as he lowered himself gingerly. Supporting his upper body on his elbows left the weight of his hips to press her down. His thighs turned slightly outward to bracket hers. Beneath their covering of hair, his muscles were strong. *Bet he's a rower,* she thought, picturing him and his college team skimming down a river with ivy-covered buildings rising from the banks. As if to draw attention to the sensuality of the image, his erection settled perfectly between her cheeks. His heat made her roll her head from side to side.

She felt too good to be still.

"Don't move," he warned, "or I'll have to stop."

Her arousal didn't lessen when he moved himself, one gliding millimeter at a time. The first well-oiled thrust pushed him upward, while the next pulled him slowly down. His shaft was so stiff she suspected going faster would make him come. By the sixth protracted stroke, her hands were fisted in her bedspread. She could feel both his tension and her own, his arms beginning to tremble, his breath growing loud and harsh.

She wanted him inside her with a toe-curling ferocity.

He must have sensed this, because his head dropped down to whisper in her ear. "Don't move," he repeated, though she didn't believe she had. "You feel so nice, honey. Smooth as silk. I can't risk letting go right now."

"Tell me about your first time," she whispered back, hoping to distract him enough to last. She didn't want this to end a second sooner than it had to.

His motions paused, but he didn't pull away. "You mean my first time with a man? That would have been when I went away to college. Experimenting, I guess, out from under parental eyes. I'm afraid my first few experiences aren't worth a story. Mostly fumbling, if you know what I mean."

"I remember those days."

"I expect everybody does." He shifted his weight onto one forearm and let his other hand meander up her side. His knuckles caressed the swell of her breast. "People get more comfortable as they go along."

It occurred to her that he probably knew most everything she had done. She didn't have to agonize over whether to hide or divulge her sexual history, didn't have to worry about scorn or shock. The realization was peculiar but kind of nice. It made her muscles relax all at once, sinking her deeper into the bed. The change in her eased something in Eric. He groaned with enjoyment, not rubbing any more, just pressing his hips back and forth.

It might have been her imagination, but she thought his cock was fuller than before. When he pushed the tip to the small of her back, it left a trail of dampness behind.

"Tell me about your first *exciting* time," she said, her request coming out lower than normal. "The first time that really rocked you out."

"Ah," he said. "That would have been B.G."

Eric had returned from his first semester at college extremely full of himself. Once he'd concluded neither lightning nor social censure would strike him dead, he'd screwed his way from one end of U.C. Berkeley to the next. Boys, girls, even a hot professor of philosophy fell to his charms. Eric might have left Southampton a kid, but he'd definitely come back a man. Who cared if his grades were tanking? He'd proved himself a stud to be reckoned with.

With all these triumphs to keep him busy, he hadn't realized how much he was looking forward to seeing his boyhood pal. He'd been home a day and a half when his mother ordered him across their yard to the Grantham's.

"Benjamin will want to see you," she said, puckering her face at the duffle bag of laundry he'd left for the maid. "Since you went to school, he's been stopping by once a week. To talk. To me! You know he must be missing you if he's doing that."

The idea of B.G. missing him had a strange and flattering appeal. Eric's old friend had reasonably good social skills—as long as the person he was dealing with was willing to take him as he came. He wasn't shy, at any rate, not like people tended to assume prodigies would be.

Pleased, but preferring his mother not see it, he shrugged on his beat-up bomber jacket and crunched across the leaves the gardeners had yet to rake. In spite of his desire to come across as cool, anticipation buoyed his step. Yeah, seeing B.G. would be good. Eric could show off his new sexual credentials, maybe even get up the nerve to finally test which way the boy genius swung.

He smiled at the thought as he shoved his hands into his pockets, then stepped onto the gravel path that curved up to B.G.'s door. B.G. was living in the matching Stratford-on-Avon cottage behind his parents' house. He was too lazy to move farther and unlikely to be inconvenienced by the older Granthams' absentmindedly permissive ways. He paid rent, according to Eric's mother, and was working on some hush-hush project with the physics geeks at the State University of New York.

Recalling this, a bit of wind sagged from Eric's sails. Not only had B.G. long since finished college—including graduate school—he was gainfully employed in a job that was probably more important than anything Eric was ever likely to do.

Luckily, the self-doubt he might have wallowed in was cut short by B.G. poking his head out the front window. His narrow, slightly mournful face split in one of his rare smiles.

"Hey!" he called. "I've been hoping you would stop by."

They didn't hug when B.G. opened the door, but B.G. did squeeze Eric's arm as he walked through. The weird, zinging power his touch had always had was heightened by Eric's recent and more empirical knowledge of the fun men could have in bed. The inhibitions that kept him safe when they were younger had been erased.

He could make a pass at B.G. if he wanted. B.G. might turn him down, but Eric knew him well enough to be convinced he wouldn't let a temporary awkwardness ruin their friendship. B.G. simply didn't have the same prejudices as other folks.

I could do it, he thought with dawning wonderment. *I could be kissing B.G. tonight.*

His mouth went dry from a sudden upsurge of nerves. Unaffected by his jitters, his cock thrust longer within his briefs, thickening and hardening until, within seconds, the cotton clasped it tight. Eric had always been quick to rouse, a trait he occasionally found inconvenient. He was glad B.G. had his back to him. Oblivious to Eric's response, he led him through a predictable maze of books and periodicals to the cottage's airy kitchen, the only part of the house he did his best to keep neat. B.G.'s mother's decorator was responsible for the gingham curtains, B.G.'s dad for the hand-built white cabinets.

"I'm trying to develop a concept of 'now,'" B.G. explained, "for a book I'm planning to write. Unfortunately, I'm not sure how well I'm communicating my idea. I think I need a better analogy."

"Uh-huh," said Eric, listening with half his ear, trying to recall if B.G.'s butt had been this cute before. His friend wore a pair of faded jeans, snugger than he remembered. Maybe, like Eric, B.G. had had a little growth spurt left.

Thoughts of where else he might have grown made Eric's palms go wet.

"There," B.G. said, pointing triumphantly at the counter of the breakfast bar.

Recovering his focus with an effort, Eric scratched his head. "Your concept of 'now' is a pair of placemats?"

" 'Now' is the little macaroni I've employed to form a bridge between the placemats. The quandary is that the pasta shell is too large. 'Now' may be the connector between past and future but, in truth, it's so fleeting that, given the limits of our brains' capacity to register events, it's virtually nonexistent. As soon as you're aware of it, it's the past. Personally, I'm not convinced the present exists in a real, measurable way. 'Now' could be similar to a neutrino, a particle so small it might as well have no mass."

"I don't think macaroni comes as small as neutrinos. I mean, if macaroni were massless, it sure wouldn't fill you up."

"No," B.G. agreed, "and where would you put the cheese?"

As always, B.G.'s jokes were delivered deadpan and came out of the blue. It took a second for Eric to laugh. "Only with you," he teased, "could I be having this conversation."

"But you see my dilemma?"

"I do." Smiling, Eric accepted a bottle of beer from his friend. He didn't recognize the label, but it tasted cold and expensive—probably the product of some arcane brewing process B.G. admired.

B.G. downed half of his in two swallows, then turned to Eric with a more customary sober face. "I missed you," he said, calm but watchful, seemingly prepared to let Eric read whatever he wished into what he said. Because he might mean anything, Eric strove not to blush.

"I missed you, too, man."

"Hm," said B.G. as though he doubted this. His thumbnail tore a strip from the label of his beer, after which he drew a breath and let it out without speaking. For B.G., this was practically a nervous fit.

"What is it?" Eric asked, leaning next to him on the breakfast bar. "Did something happen while I was gone?"

B.G. grimaced, apparently impatient with his own hesitation. A wave of his hand swept it away. "I lost my virginity," he said. "Afterward, I discovered I wanted to discuss the experience with you. I studied the process beforehand, of course. Psychologically. Physiologically. I used the most statistically reliable methods of prophylaxis. I'm reasonably confident my functioning was adequate."

There was no point in asking B.G. not to talk about this so dorkily. B.G. talked the way that made sense for him. If anyone didn't like it, that was their problem. Rather than waste his breath, Eric pulled a kitchen chair from under the table, turned it backward, and sat.

"So . . . how was it?" he asked. "For that matter, *who* was it?"

"Remember the theater arts student I tutored in calculus a few years back?"

"The redhead with the rack?"

"I ran into her at the SUNY bookstore. Because we no longer had a fiduciary relationship, and because she was interested in initiating me, we went to her apartment and had intercourse."

"Wait a minute." Eric set his beer on the table with a thunk. "You didn't *tell* her you were a virgin."

"Of course I did. If I hadn't, she would have noticed my inexperience. It seemed only fair to inform her beforehand." Troubled, he pulled out the chair next to Eric's. Unlike his friend, he sat in his facing forward. "Was telling her the wrong thing to do?"

"It wasn't wrong," Eric said. "Though most guys wouldn't have admitted it. I trust, uh, everything went all right?"

"It was . . . quite enjoyable."

He had a look on his face—a combination of pleasant memories and regret—that made Eric wish he could run back a film of the great event. He shifted in his seat at a sudden increase in his erection, realizing he really, *really* would have liked to watch.

"But?" he prompted, his voice just a little thick.

Lost again, B.G. paused to grip the top rung of Eric's

chair. Like his newly mature physique, his hands were sexier than Eric recollected: long and flexible, with a light
sprinkling of dark hair. Eric held his breath for B.G. to go
on. After another restless resettling of his fingers, he did.
"When we were finished having sex and I was dressing to go
home, I realized—it came to my awareness that what I'd
done wouldn't have been my first choice for a first time."

His dark eyes lifted and held Eric's, shadowed by insecu-
rities Eric didn't think he'd ever seen in them before. To
save his life, he couldn't have turned away. Every inch of his
skin seemed to have broken out in hot chills.

This was the signal people talked about searching for at
parties, the look that said, *I'm interested. Take your chance.* Eric
had seen it plenty of times himself. He just hadn't realized
how much power it would have when he saw it in B.G.'s eyes.

"Jesus," he murmured, shivering as he broke the spell.
"Wherever I go, you're there before me."

"You're not a virgin," B.G. objected. "You slept with at
least three girls in high school."

"I didn't mean that," Eric said with barely breath enough
for a laugh. B.G. had skipped high school altogether, so
their mothers' gossip mill must have been working over-
time. Touched that B.G. had paid attention, and more excited than he could express, Eric cupped the side of his old
friend's face. B.G.'s skin was gratifyingly hot. "I mean you're
here before me in this. You've figured out what you want
while I'm still trying to get my head around it."

Eric could barely hear B.G. when he spoke. "Do you
want to? Get your head around it?"

Eric's trousers felt tight enough to strangle his pounding
cock. He laid his second hand against B.G.'s cheek, framing
his face between his hands. "My head and everything else."

"I've never done it, you know. Not with a man. I'm afraid
I won't know how to—"

"I'll show you." Patience shredding, Eric cut him off,

pressing his lips, once, briefly, over B.G.'s. "Believe me, I'd be ecstatic to show you anything you want."

"Anything?" B.G. murmured wonderingly.

Eric pulled him forward to kiss again, groaning as B.G.'s mouth opened eagerly. Whatever his slowness at getting laid, B.G. had managed to learn a few other things. His kiss was perfect: hard and greedy but not too fast, wet and generous but not messy. Loving every taste, Eric groaned and turned his head for a deeper fit.

They kissed as if neither dared to stop, as if they'd never get another chance to do this thing they'd been dying for. A long, slow moan marked B.G. breaking for air at last.

"Take off your clothes," he said. "I've been dreaming of touching your skin for years."

Eric moved his mouth to the pulse that was racing in B.G.'s neck, his hands trying to race just as fast down his shirt buttons. "Years?" he said. "You've been wanting to touch me for *years?*"

"Ever since that weeklong camping trip with the Boy Scouts when we were thirteen."

"No," Eric responded disbelievingly.

"I jacked off in my sleeping bag every night."

"Jesus, so did I."

"I couldn't even ejaculate yet. I just rubbed myself and thought of you lying next to me until I couldn't bear how good it felt. It was the first orgasm I was sure about."

Eric couldn't stand not to be touching him an instant longer. He kissed him again, eating at B.G.'s mouth, not even caring about technique. This time he was the one who broke for air. As Eric swung out of the chair that had formed a barrier between them, B.G.'s eyes glittered with interest. Willingly, he lifted his arms so Eric could peel his sweaty T-shirt over his head.

His passivity was as exciting for Eric as what stripping him revealed.

"Hey," Eric said, finding a well-built chest and an unsuspected set of washboard abs, "you've been working out."

"Some," B.G. admitted shyly. "I liked the way your muscles looked on you." Eric shuddered as B.G.'s hands slid between the tails of his open shirt, caressing his stomach with his fingertips. "I like the way the way you feel, too. I want to kiss you here, Eric. I want to do everything our bodies can."

"We'll work up to 'everything,'" Eric panted, tearing his arms out of his shirt. "Some things take a little prep work."

They rose simultaneously into each other's arms, kissing hungrily again even as they tried to wrench each other out of their remaining clothes. B.G. nearly nicked something crucial as he yanked down Eric's zipper.

"Sorry," he gasped. "Oh, God, you're *big*."

The exclamation made him swell even more, as did the admiring clasp of B.G.'s hand. Eric cursed at how close the unschooled touch brought him to climax. They sank onto their knees as soon as B.G. kicked off his jeans.

"My bed," B.G. said as Eric started to pull B.G. over him on the floor.

"Here."

"But I need—"

"I can't wait." Eric ran his hands hard down B.G.'s back. They were naked now, and the press of skin and muscle felt heavenly. The tiny lick of hair over B.G.'s tailbone demanded licking of its own. Eric mouthed his neck instead and struggled not to bite. God knew what B.G. would think of that. "Rub yourself against me. I want to feel it on me when you come."

"Wait," B.G. pleaded, fumbling to open the refrigerator door.

"Damn it, B.G. This is no time for a snack!"

"Wait," he said more softly. "Wait for me. Just a little longer, and we can do whatever you say."

He grabbed a container of Crisco from the bottom shelf.

Seeing it, Eric's brain refused to compute anything at all. He shook his head to try to get some of his blood to move farther north. He hoped B.G. didn't mean for him to take him in the ass right now. It wasn't that Eric didn't want to; he just didn't think his fuse was long enough to do it as gently as he should.

His shoulders shook with a little spasm as B.G. pried up the lid.

"I like it slippery," B.G. explained. "And I want to touch you. I want us to touch each other."

" 'Kay," Eric said, swallowing back his eagerness. "Lay it on me."

"Enough?" B.G. asked, scooping up a fingerful.

It was a truly pitiful amount. Eric reminded himself that this was B.G.'s first encounter with a man. Eric needed to treat his pride carefully. Then he thought, *To hell with it*. This was B.G., who hated when people handled him with kid gloves. Eric would treat him the same way he did when they were arguing over whose big sister was stupider.

"Don't be stingy," he said. "You said you liked it slippery. Give me enough to grease you up like a pig."

B.G. laughed, and suddenly everything was okay: the wait, the awkwardness, the fact that Eric wasn't quite the expert B.G. thought. They smeared the shortening over each other, laughing and gasping and squeezing anything squeezable in long, tight strokes. Straining penises flipped through shiny, admiring fists, while nipples grew taut beneath pinching thumbs. Eric discovered B.G.'s balls were hypersensitive, enough that he jumped whenever Eric cupped them. For his part, B.G. demonstrated a rather amazing facility for leaving hickies. The hand play went on longer than Eric would have guessed he could stand, and surprisingly, B.G.'s tolerance was the first to break.

"Lie down," B.G. said abruptly in a strange, breathless tone.

"Oh, now you've gotta have it. Now that you've held me off and teased me for half an hour."

"Fuck it," B.G. said, his face going dark. "Fuck it, I want you now."

He pushed Eric back with a strength and an aggressiveness Eric hadn't known he possessed. Braced on one straight arm, B.G. gathered their thickened shafts together in a well-greased fist.

"Hold me," he ordered. "Wrap your hand next to mine."

Eric did as he demanded, then groaned when B.G. began to thrust through the channel their fingers formed. Their dicks were like dueling swords, one going up while the other was dragging down. Because B.G. was angled up from his knees, it was possible to witness every inch of the drama, though it was a struggle to keep his eyes from drifting shut with bliss. The most sensitive parts of their penises squeezed together, growing redder and stiffer with the repeated sliding back and forth. It wasn't long before Eric was about to burst.

"Two-minute warning," he rasped, then shuddered as B.G. took this as a signal to speed things up. The oiled rims of their erections made an insanely erotic clicking sound. "All right. Thirty seconds . . . maybe. God." The top of his skull was threatening to lift off, and his balls felt as if they were filled with steam. Despite the near-blinding sensations, Eric couldn't take his eyes off the head of B.G.'s cock. His slit was leaking a rivulet of pre-come. B.G. glanced down to see what Eric was looking at, then blushed tomato-red.

"I want to kiss you," he said.

"Later," Eric put off, grinding his teeth for a few more seconds of blessed agony. "Later. I want to see you shoot. I need to watch it to know it's real."

"I love you," B.G. said.

No one else could have made that declaration sound matter-of-fact. Eric's gaze flew up, burning with emotions too big to hide. B.G.'s eyes tilted with his gentle smile.

"Watch," he said softly. "Watch if that's what you want."

"Kiss me first," Eric countered, half growling out the words. "Hold off coming until I'm done."

B.G. grinned at the compromise, then ducked down and kissed him deeper than he'd ever been kissed in his life. For the first time, Eric knew what a soul-kiss meant. Sensation roared outward from his groin, bigger, sharper, until he came with a strangled sound that was barely human, his spine arching off the linoleum as his seed shot from him in a long, hot burst. As if from a distance, he heard B.G. grunt.

Amazingly, he didn't come, though it must have been hard as hell to hold on.

Still shaking, Eric flipped an unresisting B.G. onto his back. Too greedy to ask if it was okay, he shoved B.G.'s hand out of his way, bent to his crotch, and sucked his brutal hard-on into his mouth. The head was melting soft, enchanting him as no other cock had done. It bucked at the sudden pressure of lips and tongue.

"Eric," B.G. groaned. "Yes."

Eric sucked him again, eliciting a quavering moan. Gently, so as not to hurt him, he pushed the heel of his palm against the seam of B.G.'s drawn-up balls.

Given their sensitivity, this was more than his friend could take.

He cried out, instinctively pushing up with his hips. If Eric hadn't been holding onto him, he would have gagged. B.G.'s shaft gave one, hard throb and then he was gone, a pulsing, salty flood.

Clearly B.G. had been waiting for this release; it seemed to go on and on. Eric was happy to let it, milking each spasm with steady tugs. He knew he'd never forget the sound of B.G.'s groans.

As they waned, he let his lips grow softer, licking tenderly upward and across the crown. When B.G. couldn't bear any more stimulation, Eric crawled up his side and collapsed on his back. B.G. lay in the same position beside him, panting and sweating, powerless to move except for reaching out to take Eric's pinky in the hook of his own. Their breathing echoed through the clean kitchen, making Eric wish he had the wherewithal to start again. His chest was still pounding from his orgasm, his cock still twitching with tingling waves. He felt as if he'd been hit by a very pleasurable truck.

"Wow," B.G. finally said with a contented sigh. "I have to admit, that was more in line with my concept of a first time."

"Mine, too," Eric agreed, though—to be honest—it was far better than he'd dreamed.

The end of the story left a hanging silence in her little room. Eric eased away from her as if his body hurt. Charity understood how he felt. What she didn't understand was how he could stop. Disbelieving, she craned her head around. She found herself wishing he looked a little sillier with that raging boner poking from his shirt. Instead, the visual destroyed any hope she had of getting her hormones under control. "You're going to leave me like this? After telling me that?"

"Those are the rules, Charity. You're encouraged to get aroused, but no one takes or gives release without permission."

On his face was the same uptight look she'd seen on every Dudley Do-Right she'd ever met. She wasn't sure what Eric's problem was, but in her experience, the expression generally meant the man who wore it was dying to be led astray.

Huh, she thought. *We'll see who gives permission to whom.*

"Just one question," she said before she swung out of bed to re-dress. "Is your boss really that good a kisser?"

His boyish grin wiped away his primness. "He's all that and more. In fact, the only person I've met who comes close to kissing that well is you."

Five

Eric knew his compliment to Charity would prick as much as it pleased—which was why he'd put it the way he had. What he hadn't guessed was that implying her kisses came second to B.G.'s would exponentially increase her determination to assert her power.

She stewed—very prettily, he thought—during the ferry ride across the sound. The day had cleared until the sky was no more than hazy, making a postcard of the low green islands they chugged around. The Olympic Mountains spread across the horizon like a mirage, their bases blue, their rugged peaks streaked with snow. Despite the drama of the scene, apart from some gulls wheeling overhead on the hunt for fish, every male eye in sight was glued to Charity's knock-out body in the demure pink dress.

She was a dark-haired Marilyn decked out as Jackie O, from her gleaming waved coiffure to her cream-colored two-inch pumps. Despite his extensive experience with women—and good-looking women at that—the subtle shifting of her curves behind the knee-length knit left him mesmerized. Even Maurice, normally careful about getting too close to guests, let her coax him to her side by the rail.

When the former wrestler loaned Charity his jacket to shield her from the sound's cool breeze, Eric's only recourse was to roll his eyes. There was, after all, no rule against being a gentleman.

He was forced to listen, admittedly with amusement, while she twirled her hair and prattled suggestively. Did Maurice enjoy driving stick, she wanted to know, or was it hard to get comfortable? Had he needed time to adjust, or did he plunge right in? Her hand drifted to her bosom as she confessed she couldn't imagine driving that way herself, but maybe if someone showed her—patiently, gently, taking care that she wasn't hurt—she'd get to like it just as much as the normal way.

Simple soul that he was, Maurice blushed and stammered enough to satisfy the most jaded flirt.

"You are so pretty," he finally burst out, despite the fact that B.G. had to be listening through his headset. "I really hope we get to fuck."

Charity laughed at this, seeming pleased by his directness. Whether she'd guessed they had an invisible observer, Eric couldn't tell. Her wink of answer, noncommittal though it was, made Maurice tug at the cloth stretched across his crotch. Eric was impressed by the bulge she'd managed to inspire.

"That's enough," he said, catching her hand before she could "accidentally" brush against it. "Leave Maurice at least a fraction of his brain for driving."

She didn't pout or pull away her hand, but her smile said she knew what her performance had done to him. Predictably, she chose to sit up front with Maurice when the chauffeur drove the Phantom down the ramp at Bremerton.

She made quite a seduction of handing back Maurice's jacket, going so far as to help him button up. Eric wondered if she knew how long she'd have to keep this up. They had a drive ahead of them; Mosswood was deep in the Olympic forest, closer to the Pacific side of the peninsula. Rather than point this out, Eric swung into the back without comment. He told himself he wasn't worried. The car had no window between the seats. Charity couldn't say anything to their driver that he wouldn't hear.

To ensure she also didn't do anything he couldn't see, he slid forward to the edge of his seat. It was a toss-up as to whether this or Charity's simple nearness unnerved Maurice more.

When she slipped off her pumps and crossed her ankles on the walnut dash, the car bobbled in the lane. The incline of her legs made her hem fall halfway up her shapely thighs. Back at her apartment, Eric had instructed her to finish off her outfit with real stockings. Now they shimmered like golden sand.

Maurice heaved a long-suffering sigh.

"I'm sorry," he said at her inquiring smile. "I love the view, but it's been way too long since any of us got off."

Charity twitched the hem to her knees. "What do you mean? I thought the game didn't start until I reached the estate."

"Well, uh—" Maurice darted a quick look into the back, but Eric had no wish to censor his answer. Apparently, his earpiece gave him no direction, either. "Usually that's the case, but Mr. Berne started the proceedings early. As soon as you were chosen, he said everyone had to wait until you arrived. We weren't even allowed to masturbate."

His voice lowered on the word as if Charity were too much of a lady to have her ears defiled. Eric doubted she noticed. Her cheeks were flushed with what might have been anger but probably was not. Her feet came down with a thunk, and she turned on the leather to face Maurice. "How long ago was that?"

"Three weeks," Maurice answered. "Three weeks and twelve horny hours without an orgasm." He laughed at his own doleful tone. "I was starting to pray for a wet dream so I could stop hobbling around."

"Three weeks," Charity repeated, then pressed her tongue between her lips. "What would have happened if you'd disobeyed?"

Maurice's big, square hands shifted on the wheel. "We-ell," he said with a grin that probably surprised her. "If I'd really cut loose, I'd have been kicked out. If I'd just misbehaved a bit, I'd have been punished."

"You say that like it's a good thing."

"Oh, it is a good thing, believe me, even if it does make a person nuts."

Wetting her lips again, Charity shook her head in disbelief. "I don't think I'll ever learn to like following rules."

"You'll see," Maurice predicted. "After you've been waiting a while, after you've been teased until you think you're gonna go insane, when you finally get some, it just about blows your head off. I never had sex like that before I came to Mosswood. Never knew it existed. Once, I actually had an orgasm from the sound of a woman's laugh. To tell the truth, I'm usually sorry when Mr. Grantham goes back to work, 'cause then we do what we want. I don't know about that physics stuff, but B.G. Grantham is a genius at cranking people up."

"But you'd rather I didn't tease you now?"

"I wouldn't stop you," Maurice admitted with a quiet laugh. "Thing is, three weeks is longer than we're used to going without. We're all a little blue-balled now."

Charity blinked, taking this in, then turned to gaze out her side window. They were passing through one of the peninsula's picturesque Victorian towns. When she squirmed slightly in her seat, Eric suspected she couldn't have cared less about tourist charm. She was thinking about how hard-up they all must be, about how hard-up she might be herself in a little while.

Despite the likely reason for her silence, he knew better than to assume she was giving in.

❧⁕❧

She made up her mind before she spoke it, letting them drive deep into the mountains before the words came out.

The trees were thick here: old-growth Douglas firs overshadowing the blacktop with long, shaggy shawls of moss. This was the Hoh Rainforest, one of the biggest and most fertile remaining in the world. Apart from the road and their car—the only one she'd seen for miles—they might have entered a primeval land. Charity had never been to this part of Washington, hadn't known this many shades of green existed. The sun itself seemed an alien substance when filtered through the living screen.

"Not long now," Maurice said, his first words in a while.

His voice held an edge of tense excitement. She looked at him, at his knuckles tight on the wheel, at the solid ridge between his thighs. His erection pounded at whatever fantasies had him in their grip. From what she'd heard of their eccentric host, it seemed unlikely he'd get the release he'd been praying for anytime soon. That being so, his anticipation at nearing Mosswood was worse than cruel.

Speak up, she ordered herself. *Tell them what you want. The worst they can do is refuse.*

"Stop the car," she said with such determination that Maurice obeyed with a screech of brakes.

He turned to her worriedly. "What is it? What's wrong?"

Rather than answer, she looked at Eric. He'd slid back in the seat once he'd realized she wasn't going to grope Maurice while he drove. Now, as cool as he'd been before she kissed him, he crossed his arms and curved his lips in a faint, smug smile.

This, more than anything, set her path. She would not,

under any circumstances, be treated like she was bush-league. Maybe she was compared to him, but she didn't care. She'd demand respect all the same.

"I want this man to take me, and I'm not going any farther until he does."

"What?" said Maurice, obviously shocked.

"Charity . . ." Eric began with condescending caution.

She raised one hand to silence his protest. "I know the rules, but before I decide to obey them, I want proof."

"Proof." Eric's slitted eyes took on a laser gleam.

"Proof that this will be worth it. Proof that letting your boss play games with my libido will create an out-of-the-ordinary experience. If *he* can't prove that"—Charity jerked her thumb toward Maurice—"I doubt anybody can."

"Oh, boy," said Maurice, sounding torn as to what he hoped would happen. Charity didn't consider turning her head. Eric's burning gaze held all the answers she cared about.

"You must have the power to make decisions. You're the one who chose to make your boss's staff wait three weeks."

"I chose for all of us. B.G. and I have been waiting, too."

His voice was graveled, lower than his usual tone. The sound touched her inside like a stroking hand. She wanted to kiss him then, wanted it with a deep and ferocious ache—to press her lips from his stern, fine mouth to the tip of his hardened cock. She knew from the flush on his face that he was as ready to rock as Maurice. With that in her consciousness, she waited for him to decide. After a minute, he did.

"Give me your earpiece," he said to Maurice, confirming her suspicion that more than a flunky was on the other end. She was disappointed that Eric wouldn't choose on his own, but intrigued that the mysterious Mr. Grantham was probably listening in.

Sadly, Charity couldn't hear a word he said. The only evidence that he was speaking was Eric's serious face and nods.

At last, he handed the headset back to Maurice. "Here's

the deal," he said. "You"—he pointed to Maurice—"may climax at my discretion. You"—he pointed to Charity— "may not. And both of you must agree in advance to pay the penalty B.G. and I set."

"Penalty?" Charity said, disinclined to give him carte blanche.

"Nothing that will harm or frighten you," Eric assured her. "But I won't tell you now what this will cost you later."

Charity rubbed the groove beneath her lower lip. "If I agree, I want you there. I want you close enough to see and hear every stroke. And"—she continued before he could speak—"I don't want you consulting your boss for permission."

Eric grinned like a cat. "Permission isn't necessary. He's already insisted on my presence to facilitate."

Her excitement surged at the heat in his eyes. The energy between her and Eric had the air humming.

Almost forgotten, Maurice mumbled a curse. "You two are gonna kill me. I think I'd rather watch you do it than get off myself."

"That offer isn't on the table," Eric said, still not looking away from her. "At least not today. So Charity, do you agree to pay our price?"

Charity's skin tingled violently. "I do," she tried to say, but all that came out was a whisper.

"Good," he said. "Maurice, pull the car onto the shoulder and get out."

Maurice performed this maneuver smoothly.

⁂

"You get out, too," Eric said to Charity.

Charity obeyed wide-eyed. She'd put her shoes back on, and her ankles wobbled on the mixture of gravel and grass. No doubt she'd expected getting her way would require more of a fight. She was lucky B.G. allowed room for spontaneity.

To Eric's relief, the road was as quiet as if they'd parked in the wilderness. The rustle of pine needles was the only sound that added to their own. Since they'd stopped at the top of a hill, if any cars did come, they'd be able to spot their approach. Eric hadn't planned this, but it was just as well. B.G. wouldn't like it if his private games became a matter of public talk.

B.G. left me in charge, he thought, the knowledge giving him a thrill. *I say what happens now.*

"Start with his belt," he said, pointing to Maurice.

Maurice was breathing heavily, his big wrestler's chest going up and down, his chauffeur's hat clenched in one hand. His erection pushed out the front of his pants, lines of strain radiating out from it all around. When Charity reached to pull the tongue of his belt from its buckle, his eyes closed in longing.

"Watch her," Eric ordered the chauffeur. "I know you want to see her take it out."

Maurice gasped as he obeyed.

The sound of the belt clanking free was loud. Despite the bounty that swelled—barely covered—before her, Charity's eyes slipped to Eric's when she was done.

"Zipper?" she asked helpfully.

His nod had her easing it down, peeling the halves apart like the wrapping for a present. More of Maurice's boxers appeared, gray to match his uniform. They were loose enough that his erection didn't breach the placket. Length wasn't Maurice's most distinguishing attribute. Instead, his cock was as thick around as a beer bottle—and as hard to work into a tight space. Remembering made Eric a little too excited for comfort.

Knowing he wasn't the only one in this state made the excitement worse. When Charity sank her teeth into her cushiony lower lip, his arousal went straight from urgent to pained. He struggled to pull himself together as she paused for instructions.

"Reach into his pants," he rasped, unable to sound unmoved. "Bring him out in the air."

"Wouldn't you like to do it?"

A shiver crawled down his nape. Her voice was as rough as his. "I already have," he said. "Now I want to watch you."

They might have been alone, the way her gaze locked onto his. Abruptly he was dizzy, as if the earth beneath his feet had rocked. A dragonfly darted out from the ferns, but his brain barely took note. Her eyes were mirrors. He saw himself in them, the times he'd felt just as fascinated and unsure as he sensed she was. Admitting to the echo frightened him, but he didn't know how to stop the slide he sensed they were on.

I'd fall with her anywhere, he thought, *no matter where the plummet led.*

Suddenly feeling too dressed, he shook off his jacket and tugged his tie. This partial disrobing inspired her to go on.

" 'kay," she said, one breathless syllable, then turned back to Maurice. The driver's shaggy blond head was lowered, his attention avid on her burrowing hand. The mouthpiece on the headset quivered with his excitement.

"You ever done this before?" he asked, sucking in air as her palm wrapped skin.

"Touched a man?"

He laughed at her confusion. "Had sex for an audience."

"Ah." She smiled. "No, actually. This is going to be a first."

"Mr. G can see you, too," Maurice blurted out. "There's a miniature camera in this thing."

"Is there?" Charity tipped her head to the side. "Of course you're assuming he won't be too busy watching you."

Maurice grinned in response to her flattery. Before he could counter with a compliment of his own, he shuddered and went speechless.

She had him out. Eric swallowed at the sight. Maurice's shaft looked even thicker in her slim feminine hand. Its color glowed in the soft green light—angry, maybe, at the three long weeks it had done without. Maurice's knees were shaking in his trousers, his humor exhausted, his fists clenched white-knuckled at his sides. His hat, which he'd prized since he received it, had fallen to the grass. Though Eric knew Maurice would do his damnedest not to embarrass himself, the signs of imminent explosion were clear. Eric let Charity push her hold down a single time before he put his hand on her wrist.

Even with the halt, Maurice twitched and groaned.

Charity squeezed him for good measure.

"Let him go," Eric said. "He's too far gone for a long hand job."

"What about a kiss?" Charity suggested archly, her eyes heavy-lidded with enjoyment at what she'd wrought. "I've been thinking I need a broader sampling for comparison."

She was only twitting him, but Eric answered with a firmness that took him by surprise. "Your kisses belong to me."

Her irresistible mouth parted on a breath. "To you?"

"To me and B.G."

The amendment was reluctant, the edict out of character. She smiled, and he knew he'd inadvertently stroked her ego. The drawl that occasionally colored her voice came thick. "All right, cowboy. My kisses belong to you and your boss. Tell me what I'm allowed to do for Maurice."

For this, Eric needed no consult. "Lean over the hood as far as you can. I'm going to pull up your dress."

* * *

The hood was warm as Charity stretched herself over the metal, her hands going instinctively up and out. Her curves flattened against the car, the effect strangely comforting.

"Good," Eric said. "Hold just like that."

Air tickled her legs as her dress slipped up. Eric tucked the cloth beneath her hips to secure it. She was vulnerable then, in the best possible way. The tiny blue thong didn't cover much of anything. She couldn't help wondering what sort of eyeful his boss would get.

"Jeez," Maurice murmured, obviously enjoying his view.

Like any sensible girl, Charity had worn the thong on top of her garter belt. Now Eric took advantage of this convenience, easing down the scrap of fabric until it hit the ground.

"Shall I stroke her?" he asked Maurice. "Would you like to know if she's wet?"

Maurice's *yes* was strangled.

Eric's hand curved over her skin, first caressing her buttocks before sliding warm and gentle between her legs. He hesitated at what he found, then pushed one long finger slowly inside her. He didn't rub, just held at the deepest point, the pressure subtle but pleasant. Charity pressed her cheek to the car.

"Is she tight?" Maurice whispered, apparently concerned.

"She is," Eric confirmed. "But I think you'll manage with a little work. She's very warm, after all, and very wet."

Charity heard a sound that might have been Maurice's teeth beginning to chatter. His left arm free, Eric reached around her and through the passenger window, popping the glove compartment with an expensive snick. She turned her head toward the sound. He was removing a box of condoms and a small glass jar of lubricant.

"I'll help you," he said to Maurice. "Lube you good. You shouldn't have a difficult time at all."

His finger stroked her once before pulling out.

"Stay," he said to her when she would have turned to watch him prepare Maurice. She felt so sensual and relaxed she couldn't argue. Whether or not Maurice's claims were true, she'd never had an experience like this. This encounter

involved no guesswork and no pressure. She didn't have to
fret about freaking out her partner with some trick she'd
learned in the past. She didn't have to worry if the guy was
good enough to make her come. Coming was not expected
or allowed. All she had to do was follow orders.

She wouldn't have guessed she'd take pleasure in being
this passive, but her body didn't know how to lie. She was
creamy with arousal, as lazy as a cat dozing in the sun. Maurice's muffled moans at being dressed in the condom, his
curses at the careful addition of the lube, merely made her
smile. Neither man was paying her any mind. Free to suit
herself, she tipped her bottom higher for her own pleasure.

"Ready to start?" Eric asked Maurice. "I want you to last
a while."

"So do I," Maurice responded breathlessly. "Look at her!
She's flushed up just like a rose."

Charity grinned to herself but didn't bother to shake her
tail. She didn't want to make her watchers laugh. She liked
how serious they were. This, it seemed, was a Very Important Screw.

"Come closer," Eric said. "Let's see how your heights
match."

Footsteps crunched on the gravel, and the heat behind
her increased. A brief discussion ensued during which the
men decided to slide her body higher on the hood until her
feet dangled off the ground. The position made her feel in-
triguingly helpless.

"I want to touch her," Maurice said.

"Go ahead," Eric allowed graciously.

A big, hot hand cupped her gently between the legs.
Maurice's palm was callused, but his grip was nice. His
thumb roved backward, giving her a tingle she kind of liked.

"That's enough," Eric said before he could get far.

A noise she'd had no intention of making escaped her
throat, a noise that—if she were honest—probably qualified

as a whimper. Determined not to make another, she pressed her lips between her teeth. She might have saved herself the bother. Eric wasn't focusing on her.

"Spread your hands beside hers on the hood," he said to Maurice. "And keep your weight off her back. I don't want you holding her hips or thrusting hard."

"But . . . how am I supposed to do this if I can't grip her? You know I'm too big to slip in easily."

"I'll guide you. I'll hold her steady enough."

"I want to drive all the way," Maurice said, clearly struggling against making it a plea. "I want to feel her around my root."

"You will," Eric assured him. "You just won't be able to do it right away."

She was close enough to hear Maurice's headset buzz. To judge by Maurice's groan, his boss wasn't overruling Eric. Just imagining what he might be saying had arousal trickling down the inside of her thigh. She knew when Maurice saw it because he groaned even louder.

Eric took this as his cue to guide the other man into place behind her. That done, Eric's fingers spread her for entry. She heard gasps, pants, and then an impossibly broad, hot glans pressed against her gate.

She knew Eric held it in place.

"There," he said. "Feel how ready she is." The huge tip waggled up and down, either because Eric moved it or because Maurice was that excited. With her hips hanging at the edge of the sunwarmed car, Charity was even more dependent on help than Maurice. Luckily, Eric squeezed his second hand beneath her to support her mound. His hold felt lovely, even if he did avoid her best spots.

"Push," he said to Maurice. "Slowly. I don't think her body will stop you now."

Maurice's palms fogged the hood as the pressure against her increased. He went in all right, but with a closeness that made him groan. Charity fought to swallow back a cry. The stretch she felt inside was amazing, on the very pleasant edge of too much. She tried to widen her legs, but her dangling position didn't allow it. Maurice was left to work back and forth as best he could.

"Deeper," he moaned when he finally got halfway in.

Eric obliged him by crooking one of her thighs to the side.

This proved to be the crucial aid. Suddenly Maurice slid in all the way. "Oh, man," he said, his cock jolting inside her. "Oh, man, that is really good."

Charity thought so, too, her sex twitching hungrily around his. She almost didn't care that the back-style entry didn't provide the proper friction for her to peak. The evidence of his gratitude was reward enough.

"You can move," Eric reminded him. "Just not fast."

A quick intake of breath marked Maurice dragging back, followed by a pleasured grunt as he pushed again. The satin strip that lined his trousers brushed her hose. Charity knew she'd never look at a chauffeur the same again.

"Slower," Eric cautioned. "I want a hundred strokes before you come."

"A hundred!" Maurice's muscles knotted as if he was already on the verge. All the same, Charity noticed he didn't refuse.

His fingers pressed beside hers on the gleaming hood, his slab of a chest curling closer with Eric's count. At twenty, his arms ran sweat. At thirty, his breath began to whistle. At forty, he panted like a freight train and had to stop.

"Can't," he pleaded, quivering from head to toe. "I'm about to blow. My balls are so ready I think they're trying to crawl up my gut."

"I can tug them down," Eric offered. "Help you back off the edge."

"I've come from that," Maurice said with more than a

hint of panic. "I've come when people were trying to help me stop."

"I'll be careful. I won't handle you any more than I have to."

Maurice moaned at the words, his cock swelling ominously inside her. "Just let me come," he said raggedly, and Charity didn't know if he was begging Eric or the invisible B.G. "It's been three fucking weeks, and she's as hot as that engine she's lying on. We've never been asked to wait this long. Believe me, I can prove to her how good it is here and now."

"No," Eric said. "If you don't think you can last a hundred, you should pull out."

The names Maurice called Eric then were hardly appropriate for a subordinate. When the tirade ended, Charity spoke up.

"Try," she said, her spine arching slowly with the tension that filled her limbs. "I'd love to have sixty more."

Maurice groaned, but she knew it was a surrender. Eric performed whatever trick he'd been describing and, one by one, huff by huff, she got her remaining strokes.

She couldn't have imagined how much she'd like them. Her pussy felt like it was getting a slow massage.

"All right," Eric said when he hit a hundred at last. "The ride to the end is yours."

Freed, Maurice gripped her fists in his and set his teeth lightly on her neck. Though this surprised her, she didn't object. His thrusts lengthened, growing stronger, faster, until she almost thought they could make her come. She had to remind herself to relax.

"Fuck," she heard him say against her nape. "Pull her legs wider. Yes. *Yes!*"

A flurry of hard, quick strokes marked his desire taking control. Pushed way past its limit, his body was doing exactly what it wished. A sound like a sob wrenched from his chest. "Fuck," he said again, tight and desperate, and then nothing came out but a hoarse, long cry, as raw a noise as she'd ever heard. At that instant, she knew she was little more than a receptacle, a soft tight passage to take the jolts of pleasure streaking through his flesh.

He came in swift, strenuous contractions, pulses that went on far longer than she would have believed a man could experience—as if every week he'd waited must have its own minute. When the spasms finished, Maurice collapsed. The only part of him that moved was his hand petting weakly over her hair.

"Thanks," he mumbled as she tried not to feel too squashed. "That"—he sucked a weary breath—"was the best ever."

Charity would have said he was welcome except she wasn't the least convinced he was thanking her. For her part, she was shaking like a leaf with unrequited lust. Going without release had, illogically enough, been easier when Maurice was working toward his. Now she had nothing to distract her from Eric's promise of a penalty.

"I should make you wait," he said as he helped her slide off the car, "but I suspect you need your punishment now."

Charity didn't know how to argue with this and lacked the breath for it in any case. She watched as Eric pulled an elegant leather valise from the trunk. Inside it was a stiff leather swimsuit sort of affair that was part warrior princess and part *Playboy* bunny wear.

"If that comes with ears," Charity managed to gasp, "I'm going home."

Eric laughed and, once she'd peeled off her dress, he held the suit for her to step into. When it was on, he laced it snugly up the back.

"It fits perfectly," she said, liking the feel of it clasping her.

"Of course it does. It was made to your measurements. No one's ever worn it but you."

"Excuse my ignorance, but how is this a punishment?"

"It's a chastity corset," Eric said. "If you'll notice, the gusset between the legs is stiff and thick, as are the breast cups. It's nearly impossible to stimulate you while you're wearing it—at least by way of standard erogenous zones."

His finger skated across her bare shoulders, demonstrating where else she might be teased. A shudder of unusual strength chased his light caress. Whatever Eric claimed about her needing this punishment, it didn't take a genius to figure out that this contraption was going to increase her frustration—especially since it was inherently sexy.

"Very ingenious," she said, choosing pride over protest.

"The chastity corset is also impossible to get out of without help," he added pleasantly.

The glint in his eye was very close to rubbing it in.

Six

Charity had the odd sensation of not being settled into her body when she returned to the car with the men. Her leather undergarment, covered now by her dress, might have been part of the reason but not all. The men's clothing was set to rights, the flush of sexual excitement fading from their skins. The car was exactly as it had been. Still, it seemed wrong that Maurice would simply get behind the wheel and start driving, as wrong as Eric shrugging into his jacket and straightening his tie.

Charity sat in back with him, a choice that came more naturally than it should. Even though—strictly speaking— Maurice had been the one to take her, it was her connection to Eric that seemed stronger now. She didn't think this was a good thing. In her experience, her love life tended to run smoother when she didn't want the guy in question too much.

As if he sensed her mood, he laid his hand atop her thigh, tightening his fingers just enough to be possessive. The touch was so welcome she couldn't help rolling her sex against the seat. That was when she discovered the corset's true devi- ousness. She hardly felt a thing through the stiff gusset.

"You all right?" Eric asked, his habitual furrow threatening to appear again between his brows.

"Fine," she said. "I'm just . . . restless."

His eyes darkened at her admission. "You won't be left unsatisfied forever. B.G. wouldn't waste your sensuality that way."

At the moment, Charity was more interested in what Eric would do than B.G., but she kept the thought to herself. "I'm satisfied about one thing at least," she said with a rueful grin. "Waiting for gratification does seem to have dramatic effects."

Eric made a noise of agreement, a cross between a groan and a growl, one that said their little episode outside the car hadn't left him unmoved. If that hadn't convinced her, the tentpole behind his zipper would. She laughed, patted his hand, then turned her gaze to the safer scenery outside. She noticed the instant he removed his hand from her leg, though she tried to pretend she did not.

They rolled up to the estate soon after—or at least to its formidable looking gate. The barrier was black forged iron, complete with curlicues and spearheads and lightning bolt warnings that it was electrified. Two stone pillars anchored it on either side. The right one held a modest bronze plaque asserting that this was Mosswood. The left sat in the shadow of a small guardhouse.

The uniformed man who came out of it looked like the real deal—as opposed to another player in Grantham's game. With his hand on the butt of his holstered gun, he leaned down to Maurice's open window, exchanged a few words with him, then peered into the back at Eric and her. She felt as if her corset must be screaming its presence beneath her clothes, but his expression, or lack of it, was all business. After he'd stared long enough to memorize her face, he put two fingers to his mouth and blew a sharp whistle. An eager-looking German Shepherd, seeming happier than his master but no less efficient, bounded out of the bushes to sniff around and under the Rolls.

"Wow," said Charity, "that's some security your friend's got."

"It's just a precaution," Eric said, obviously used to it. "Some of the projects B.G. works on are sensitive."

"Well, all I can say is, I'm glad I left my stash at home."

Maurice chuckled as they drove through the opening gate. Charity was glad someone got her joke—although, from the half smile Eric rubbed with his hand, maybe he did, too.

Eager to catch a glimpse of where she'd be staying, she moved to drape her arms over the front seat. Ahead of them, the drive curved gently through dense green trees. Its surface was paved in mossy cobbles arranged in fans. As fancy as the roadway was, Charity didn't expect it to continue far. To her surprise, minutes passed and she still saw nothing but old-growth forest on every side.

"There is a house, right? Mr. Grantham doesn't live in a cave."

"There's a house," Eric assured her, humor coloring his voice. "It's a few miles from the gate."

Not wanting to betray her lack of sophistication, she kept the rest of her questions to herself. Eric had to know she didn't hang with the upper crust, but she didn't have to remind him. Despite her resolve, she couldn't contain a gasp when the trees thinned out to reveal the residence.

"Holy cow," was all the exclamation she could manage. She'd been expecting a dreary Victorian manse: turrets, curtains twitching at the attic windows, shrubbery cut into persnickety Gothic shapes. What she got was a spread from *Architectural Digest,* with soaring modern lines and windows that glowed gold within the leafy murk. Parts of the complex were underground, leaving glassed-in domes and pyramids to poke through the earth.

Flummoxed, Charity sat back.

"Cool," she said, forgetting to move again until Maurice came around the car to help her out.

To her secret pleasure, Eric claimed her arm after that.

"This way," he said, leading her to a heavy, brushed-steel door that was sheltered by a wing of glass. A camera whirred to life as Eric rang the bell. She thought of asking him why he didn't have a key, then figured this was another layer of security.

"State your names," said a disembodied computer voice.

They didn't get a chance, because the silvery entrance swung open, the door making a sound like a refrigerator breaking its vacuum seal. Charity suspected it could have sealed a vault at Fort Knox.

She guessed at once that B.G. Grantham stood behind it. He was tall and slim, younger than she expected, with a swoop of dark hair brushing his eyes. The individuality of his face struck her immediately. His long, thin nose gave him the slightest air of geekiness, though he really was too beautiful to qualify as a nerd. He was dressed casually in tan cotton trousers, bare feet, and a white linen shirt. His posture was casual, too, one arm propped on the open door. In spite of this, his spine seemed straighter than most people's.

"Welcome to Mosswood, Charity," he said formally. "I'm so pleased to meet you in the flesh."

"Uh, likewise," she said, trying not to blush.

As they passed inside, their host squeezed Eric's shoulder. Then he faced Maurice. His expression was hard to read: not stern, not angry, not fake authoritative. Mostly, he just seemed watchful.

"Mr. Grantham," said the chauffeur, his cap pressed to his breast in an oddly old-fashioned way.

Grantham inclined his head in acknowledgment. "Maurice. You'll spend the afternoon in the mystery room. Please freshen up, then report there and wait for me."

This sounded innocent enough, but from the way Maurice shuddered, Charity knew he'd just been told the nature of his penalty. The threat was enough to harden him again.

Grantham didn't watch to see if Maurice complied but turned to her. He looked, if possible, even more benign than before. "Charity," was all he said, just as he had to his chauffeur.

Regal as a king, she thought amusedly. The Fates must be having a laugh at a girl like her turning up in a palace like this. The atrium in which she stood was a rise of more steel and glass—a cubist greenhouse, except that the greenery was outside. Opposite the door, two funny-angled squares formed wide arches. Rooms swept out behind them, similarly washed in light. The furnishings were the colors of sand and sea, each perfect works of art. In what appeared to be the living room, a V-shaped, green-glass catwalk hung suspended halfway up the space. Charity couldn't begin to calculate what a place like this would cost. Probably more than she could earn in her whole lifetime.

It doesn't matter, she told her wavering self-confidence. *If you didn't have something these Ralph Lauren poster boys wanted, they wouldn't be making you their next plaything.*

"If you're going to call me Charity," she said, her gaze on the sinuous, abstract lines of a glass sculpture, "you'd better be prepared for me to call you B.G."

When she turned back, she saw she'd startled him. He was rubbing the edge of one hand across his lean, sharp chin. Eric set down her bag—as if he might need his hands to protect his boss. For now, Charity ignored him. This was between her and B.G.

"You're younger than me," B.G. said, more like he was curious than arguing. "Why shouldn't you address me respectfully?"

"I'm old enough to vote, old enough to drink, and—as

far as I'm concerned—old enough to call a fellow adult by his first name."

"You called me Mr. Grantham in the car." His eyes alive with interest, his face and body remained still.

"I hadn't met you yet. Now I have."

"You believe that calling me B.G. will put us on an equal footing. You think our statuses need leveling because I saw you unclothed."

"You more than saw me unclothed."

"I suppose I did. Maurice put on quite a show." He stepped toward her into a patch of dappled sunlight, nearly close enough to touch. His lips had a lovely delicate cut. "I don't always watch, Charity, but I always reserve the right. There are few rooms in this house into which I can't see."

"Does anyone ever watch you?"

Eric sucked a breath, but B.G. smiled for the first time, an expression that had an unexpectedly goofy sweetness.

"That could be arranged," he said, "for an appropriate trade. To be honest, however, I don't offer anything like the entertainment value of my guests."

"You'll excuse me if I doubt that."

He laughed softly and, without even looking, she felt Eric relax. "Will Maurice be all right?" she presumed to ask.

B.G.'s coffee-brown eyes didn't just warm, they heated. "I have no doubt in the world he'll enjoy his penance, especially if you'd be kind enough to assist."

She couldn't respond to that, the prospect of tormenting the recently satisfied chauffeur making the air go thick in her lungs. Submission might not be her natural state, but teasing men very nearly was.

"Why don't I show you to your room?" B.G. suggested. "Then you'll see how open every area is to everyone."

To her surprise, Eric didn't follow, but there was too much to see to worry about that. B.G. hadn't lied about the house being exposed. At least half the walls were clear glass. A long

Turkish runner led them along the center of a wide lime-
stone hall. As they proceeded down the off-kilter angles, she
could see into every room. Only the bathrooms and those
walls necessary for load-bearing were made of weightier stuff.
They were composed of huge sandy-looking blocks.

"Rammed earth," B.G. said. "Very good insulator."

"Tree hugger?" she asked, razzing him a bit.

B.G. answered calmly. "I've been known to embrace a
trunk now and then."

Her room overlooked a small courtyard with a fountain
in which a weathered cherub was pouring water from a vase.
The space was shady but inviting—certainly to the birds.
They twittered in and out of the pool like it was party time.

"Pretty," she said, though it didn't match the house at all.

"It's from an estate in England. I had the stones shipped
here and reassembled. I prefer that the place I live reflect
varied architectural periods."

This was precisely the sort of conversation Charity didn't
know how to contribute to. Clothes she could talk about.
Television. The latest Hollywood romance. But anything remotely intellectual left her at a loss. It wasn't that she knew
nothing, just that she was afraid of looking stupid. By the
time she decided what was safe to say, the topic had changed.
Frankly, she would have been more at ease if B.G. had
moved straight to jumping her bones. She wasn't used to
being this nervous.

"I know this can't compare to being home," B.G. was
saying, "but I hope you'll be comfortable."

"I wouldn't worry about that. My whole apartment could
fit in here twice."

She was glad B.G. hadn't seen it. By comparison to this,
her things could only look cheap. Everything here was the
epitome of good taste: pale wood floors, a low queen-size bed,
a graceful chair and console desk, plus a Japanese-style screen
behind which she supposed she could change if she were

feeling shy. Dark wood beams stretched across the ceiling, easily twelve feet above her head. In spite of its simplicity, the room conveyed a sense of luxury beyond any place she'd lived. A bathroom led off to the left, which she decided to explore once she was alone.

"I restarted that for you," B.G. said, pointing to the plasma screen that hung above her bed. The squiggles that moved inside it made her think of an Etch A Sketch made of light. "There's a camera behind it, of course, but the picture, or what's going to be a picture, is a computer model of a complex system playing out in a chaotic way."

"Well, hey," Charity said, "how silly of me not to guess!"

B.G. neither laughed nor took offense. Instead, he stepped to her left and put his hand on her shoulder. A zing moved through her at the touch, followed by a wash of warmth.

Whoa, she thought, unsettled by the effect. *Two guys with more than their share of chemistry.*

"Weather is an example of a complex chaotic system," he explained. "It obeys the laws of classic physics, but there are too many variables interacting with one another to do more than guess what the future holds. Worse, the science is only accurate in the short term. The smallest change can cascade unpredictably. That's why you get the old adage about a butterfly beating its wings in Brazil and causing a typhoon in Hong Kong.

"Some people," he added, "claim that chaos is a metaphor for life. Although unpredictable, life obeys certain rules: genetics, psychology, things like that. Presumably, each event is part of a grander scheme, as is the case with chaos. However, it's difficult to see life's pattern until it's complete. Humans are *in* the forest rather than above the trees."

"So if that blip of light were me, that jump to the right it just made might be my decision to come here rather than stay home?"

"It might," B.G. said and smiled angelically. "Dare I

conclude that you're accepting our invitation? You understand, I trust, that the same rules that apply to the others apply to you. You are forbidden to achieve release unless I say."

"I understand. I'm pretty sure I can handle it."

Abruptly more devil than angel, B.G. rubbed his hands
palm to palm. "In that case, I should share the rest of the
rules. First, when your presence is not required, you are free
to wander the house at will. Any area that is barred to you
will be locked, with the exception of the other residents'
rooms. Out of politeness, I ask you not to enter them."

"Will do," Charity agreed. "Can I ask, am I Mosswood's
only guest?"

"We have additional *residents*," he said. "People like Maurice who perform useful jobs. You, however, are the only guest
per se. Consequently, all our focus will be on you. Everyone is
dedicated to seeing that you, above all, have an extraordinary
experience."

"Because you like studying desire."

B.G. gave her his courtly nod. "Speaking of our residents: Should you happen to meet a pretty blonde in the
hall, and should she inquire about the nature of your desires,
be sure you don't answer her. Sylvia is a marvelous masseuse,
but not well suited for playing games. I try not to let her
participate unless she's under my or Eric's supervision."

"Okay," Charity said, mystified. "I won't tell any pretty
blondes what I want."

"Thank you," B.G. said, "and now, if I might make a request of you?"

She used a shrug to cover an inexplicable shiver.

He stepped around to face her, one hand on her shoulder
while the other came to rest gently on her hip. For a second,
she thought they were going to dance. Though the hand
that touched her hip was little more than a weight on her
leather corset, the double contact made her feel as if a strong
sexual current were coursing across her body.

Seeming oblivious to the effect, B.G. bent to look into her eyes. "May I kiss you, Charity?"

She had to shake her brain before it would work. "You're asking permission?"

"I believe in choice."

"When it suits you, you mean."

His lips curved faintly. "Even when it doesn't. The sweetest gifts are given freely."

"You're the strangest physicist I ever met."

"I'm the only physicist you've met, but that doesn't answer my question."

"Well, I'm supposed to say *no,* aren't I? I'm supposed to play hard to get."

"Only if playing hard to get is a personal kink. We want to rouse *you,* Charity, to intensify your longing to its highest pitch."

The hand that had warmed her shoulder rose to stroke her cheek, the caress as light as if she were made of glass. His eyes held a keenness she didn't understand, a hunger she suspected had nothing to do with her. She was willing to bet he had a personal kink, or a hidden agenda. That was the watch spring that wound him up.

As if he had all the time in the world, he swept the tip of his index finger across the upper lashes of her left eye. The tickle made her shiver again.

"A kiss," he said, "is merely an aperitif. It whets the appetite rather than sates it."

"And if I don't want a kiss?"

"Then you should refuse. What you shouldn't do is lie. That puts me out of patience. If you are too eager to please, you cannot be pleased yourself. Of course"—he treated her to another brilliant smile—"I do not foresee that being frank will be a trial for you."

"No," she agreed with a sheepish grin of her own. "I'm pretty much honest to a fault."

"What do you wish then? A sampling of what's to come or a few more hours to prepare yourself?"

She thought—but mostly that a person could get addicted to making him smile.

"What the hell," she said. "Lay one on me."

"I must lift you," he said, "or this won't be comfortable."

She thought he meant lift her in his arms. Instead, he carried her to the console desk and sat her on top. Despite its height, she was still a little short for him. He braced his hands on the polished ebony beside her hips.

With his nearness, his heat became a subtle, fascinating force. She couldn't swear to it, but he seemed warmer than he'd been before.

"Relax," he said like a hypnotist. "You have nothing to prove to me."

His words made her neck unkink. She let him kiss her, his lips brushing softly back and forth. They were smooth lips, sensitive and resilient. She was getting used to the feel of them when his arm came around her back. His palm slid slowly up her corseted back.

"Relax," he crooned again, adding a lick to the whisper of his lips.

Her own lips seemed to part by themselves. The kiss came closer, his fingers kneading her tingling scalp. He pushed his tongue far enough to tickle her upper palate. He tasted good, like a clean spring berry. When her tongue followed his back, he sucked it, gently, but with a delicious, alternating pressure that made her insides steam. It was as if he knew the secret rhythm her nerves answered to. She couldn't care how wet she grew. This kiss was worth getting hot and bothered for.

Just as she decided she had to have more, he broke it off.

"You're very sweet," he said, his voice too soft to tell if he was hoarse. "Next time I'll kiss you deeper. Next time I'll invite you to kiss me in your own style."

She couldn't speak, couldn't do anything but stare into the unwavering intensity of his dark-brown eyes. What went through his head, this former boy genius? What did it mean to him that he could reduce a woman to melted caramel with a single kiss—and a PG-rated kiss at that!

"I would like to tempt you a little more," he said, still within kissing range. "Why don't you pull off that charming dress and follow me down the hall? I'm going to see to Maurice."

"Is that an order?"

He shook his head.

"Then I'd like to."

The way his lips quirked at her answer made her think she'd revealed more than she should.

❧

The mystery room was B.G.'s favorite: a reproduction of the fictional Sherlock Holmes's study. Period novels lent gravitas to the paperbacks on the shelves, a deerstalker cap hung from the coatrack, and an old wooden index file held cards on real and imaginary crimes. The librarian who'd compiled them had been a firecracker. She was married now, but whenever B.G. came here, he recalled her stay with him. He didn't miss her precisely, but he remembered. Sometimes he wondered why he didn't manage to miss more people who were gone.

But he couldn't contemplate that now. Charity had followed him in.

"This is so cool!" she exclaimed as Maurice hopped up from the windowseat where he'd been reading yet another Dashiell Hammett. Maurice loved vintage detective yarns. B.G. suspected Maurice began to pretend he was a private eye the moment he came here. Charity seemed not to have quite the chauffeur's escapist bent, but B.G. was curious to see them interact. Would any handsome man attract her? Or did she have preferences? It was to get these and other answers that he'd put them in proximity.

Now the pair stared at each other, Charity in her fetching leather corset, Maurice in his street clothes. The chauffeur looked ten years younger out of uniform.

Then again, both seemed ages younger than B.G.—an effect due more to mind-set than chronology. Like the blip on Charity's screen, she and Maurice lived in the blinding, beautiful thick of life. B.G. envied them a bit, although he wouldn't have traded places.

"You look different," Charity said, nodding at Maurice's blue jeans and white T-shirt.

"You look great," Maurice answered back.

His grin was more than male appreciation. *Why, he's fond of her already,* B.G. thought. It seemed a good sign that she was likeable. Sadly, psychological profiles could only predict so much. One did have to test the subject in person.

"Chair," B.G. said gently, reminding Maurice why they were here. "It's time to pay for your indulgence."

Maurice knew which chair he meant, a thronelike Victorian with deep-red upholstery. He looked toward it, then at Charity.

"I'm helping," she said cheerfully.

Maurice grunted at that and sat. Her ability to unsettle him seemed promising as well. A woman who made men nervous was a woman hard to forget.

"If you'd be kind enough to do the honors," B.G. said to her, "those leather straps need buckling."

Charity secured Maurice's wrists, then his ankles. She didn't tease or playact, simply fastened him in. B.G. couldn't tell if she was embarrassed to exercise her gift for seduction in front of him, or if she wished to lighten Maurice's penance. If the latter was her wish, she failed. As always, the procedure excited his chauffeur. His face grew flushed and his blue jeans tight. Through it all, Charity's manner remained friendly and casual.

Not a bondage fancier then. At least, not a fancier of binding others.

"Is that it?" she asked, turning to him.

"The last set fastens around the crotch."

This elicited a slight increase in pupil size.

"Okey-doke," she said as if it hadn't happened. She crouched down to find the straps behind the seat, momentarily distracting him with a spectacular view of her ass.

"Third hole," he stipulated once he recovered. "Maurice prefers this one tight."

She hesitated when Maurice's big, blunt hands clenched on the chair. From where B.G. stood, he bore all the signs of full arousal. She must have doubted she could fit the straps around his cock. "I don't want to hurt you," she said worriedly.

B.G. found he liked her for addressing their prisoner, unnecessary though it was. Maurice, on the other hand, wasn't concerned with the finer points of safe sex-play.

"Do it," he urged her hoarsely. "It's what I need."

To B.G.'s pleasure, she looked to him for confirmation.

"He won't be hurt. Maurice doesn't trust his control. He won't be able to enjoy his punishment unless he knows he can't gratify himself."

At this, a full-fledged blush rose in her cheeks. Pretending to ignore the reaction, he filed it away for future study. While Charity finished buckling the last constraint—accompanied by the pleasant music of the chauffeur's groans—B.G. pulled a wafer-thin cell phone from his breast pocket.

"Michael," he said into the phone, "please play tape thirteen in the mystery room."

Nothing if not efficient, Mosswood's head of sexual surveillance took only seconds to have the screen rising from the floor in front of Maurice. The tape would run for an hour, a compilation of the chauffeur's favorite scenes, most of which involved various costumes. By the time it finished, he'd be as frustrated as before he'd indulged himself with their newest guest.

Maurice struggled in his bonds as it began to play, as though the explicit pictures posed a literal danger. Charity stared at him goggle-eyed.

"Let's leave him to his entertainment," B.G. said to her. "His reactions will be less inhibited if he's alone."

"*Less* inhibited?" she said with a little gasp, then shook herself. "You're sure he'll be okay?"

"A member of my staff will come for him the minute he hits the call button on the chair." He curled his hand around her elbow. "Come. I'm sure you'd like to get out of that corset. Maybe rest a bit and settle in?"

She blew out a breath like someone surfacing from a dream. "Yes," she said, "I would like that."

She shot Maurice one last glance before they left. Engrossed as he was, the object of her attention didn't notice. This time she displayed no worry. This time she looked the tiniest bit disappointed that she couldn't stay. Apparently, whatever her feelings on bondage, she very much liked watching others being denied. Wheels turned in B.G.'s head as he calculated how best to exploit that.

So it begins, he thought. *Another slow unfoldment of a human soul.* In spite of all the reasons to be cautious in the execution of his plan, in spite of the many variables that could go wrong, B.G. was looking forward to what lay ahead.

After all, if this girl could touch his stunted emotions, she'd have no trouble shaking Eric's to the ground.

Seven

By the time Eric carried Charity's things to her room, she was gone. He'd purposefully hung back to give her and B.G. time alone, but he hadn't expected both to leave. Charity's absence in particular caused a pang he regretted having to acknowledge. This experience was supposed to be about expanding her horizons and increasing her confidence. It wasn't about keeping her to himself.

He left her carryall on the bed, figuring she'd prefer to unpack her own belongings. Idle then, his feet led him to B.G.'s suite. He didn't necessarily believe he'd find the pair together, but the least evolved part of him needed to be sure.

B.G.'s door was open when he arrived. His private apartment was part of the complex's buried rooms, with a geodesic skylight that let in a soft-edged, magical flood of sun. The atmosphere inside was cozy—sound-proofed, naturally—the sitting room decorated in shades of blue and cream with furniture that was the most traditional in the house. Eric's own mother would have felt at home with this old European charm.

Adding to the ambiance, built-in bookshelves topped with pediments and flanked by columns overflowed with B.G.'s varied personal library. Dog-eared scientific journals, novels, and nonfiction were shoved into whatever space had been closest when B.G. set them down. Here and there a title better suited for undereducated waitresses leapt out, like *Mind Power for the New Millennium!* and *Are Humans Alone?* Because B.G. couldn't be talked—or teased—out of keeping these things, Eric had learned to pretend he didn't see them. Now he rolled his eyes at *Ten Steps to Success* and stepped inside.

B.G. sat beneath the skylight in one of his spindly French-looking chairs. He was alone, which made Eric happier than it should. A desk on a clever mahogany arm was swung in front of him, allowing him to tap out letters on his laptop. Even when he was off-duty, B.G. maintained a correspondence with scientists—including aspiring ones. No high school egghead who managed to obtain his email would hope in vain for a response. B.G. claimed their questions kept him from going stale. Eric was pretty sure he was being nice. It was one of the traits he most admired in his friend.

B.G. going stale was a possibility Eric could not conceive.

After typing a few more sentences and hitting *Send,* B.G. looked up. "Hey," he said with a grin of welcome that gave Eric's conscience another twist. "Come to quiz me about our guest?"

Eric took a seat on the corner of the settee that matched B.G.'s chair. Like all his furniture, it was more comfortable than it appeared. As B.G. liked to say, there wasn't a piece in the place that you couldn't get busy on. He sounded silly when he said it, but he never minded if Eric laughed.

"I *was* wondering what you thought of her," Eric confessed.

B.G. smiled, closed his laptop, and swung the desk aside. "I think she won't disappoint you."

"My concern is that she not disappoint you." The words weren't strictly true—it was Charity's reaction that concerned him most—but the claim came as easily as if he were sincere.

"Eric, Eric, Eric," B.G. scolded. "It's not a crime to put yourself first."

"I do," Eric said. "I have." *At least once rather ignominiously.* Despite the private reminder, he didn't object when B.G. took his face between his hands and kissed him gently to silence. The tension from his memories drained as B.G.'s fingers slid into his hair, his thumbs rubbing soothing circles beneath his ears. B.G. hummed with satisfaction as he relaxed. It might have been Eric's imagination, but when the kiss deepened, he thought he tasted a hint of Charity.

His stomach tightened even as he got hard. He was throbbing by the time B.G. eased away. For the first time since he could remember, a silence felt awkward.

"Do you want me to set up a scene for her?" Eric asked, knowing B.G. would understand who he meant. "Maybe play out something with Maurice?"

B.G. held his gaze a moment before speaking. His expression was mild but intense. Eric didn't try to identify what lay behind it. B.G.'s emotional inscrutability was old news.

"No," his boss said at last. "I'd like to study her a while longer. Investigators are useful, but they can't tell you a person's deepest desires. I want to judge for myself what makes Ms. Wills tick. I suspect she'll be worth the supplemental time." He smoothed his thumb across Eric's eyebrow, coaxing it to lie in place. "You don't mind waiting a bit, do you? Before you play with her yourself?"

"I'm supposed to mind," Eric said, rather than put in words how much he wanted her right away.

"Well, yes, but I don't want you miserable."

"I'm not."

"But you do find her attractive?"

"Of course I do. Who wouldn't?"

B.G. cocked his head. "She's different from the others," he said, and Eric didn't want to ask whether he meant different in general or different for Eric. "You chose well."

He shrugged. "She has a lot of fire."

B.G. made a quiet noise that could have been a laugh. "Yes, *fire* is a fine word. One might also say she's sex on wheels. Maurice was quite inspired by her today." His hand dragged down the center of Eric's chest, down his breastbone, and over his waistband, his fingertips coming to a halt an inch from the straining tip of his erection. "Would you like to take one of the others in the meantime?"

"No," Eric said, perhaps too quickly. "I'd rather wait until Charity's ready."

"Hm." B.G. shifted his hand so the heat of his palm overhung Eric's shaft. "I think you might be too patient. Maybe you need winding up."

"Me?" The word was startled out of him.

Seeing this, B.G. chuckled. "Yes, you. Or did you think your position puts you beyond my personal attention?"

"No, but I hardly think I need—"

"Unbutton your shirt," B.G. said softly, cutting him off. He nodded toward the lidded cardboard box that sat on the small round table beside his chair. Though its wrapping was nondescript, muscles tightened in Eric's groin. He'd seen boxes like this before.

"Scarlet Creations sent me a package today," B.G. said, confirming his suspicions. "A few new products they'd like me to help them tweak. I think they might prove helpful tonight."

Scarlet Creations was a small sex-toy company B.G. had invested in as a lark after they solicited his advice on the best way to reduce torque in a ceiling swing. Given his usual uncanny financial luck—which Eric refused to ascribe to his more sensationalistic reading—it was no surprise that his share of the venture was now worth five times what it had been originally. As thanks for his continuing help, the company sent him periodic gifts—some more welcome than others.

"Just promise it doesn't involve edible underwear."

"It doesn't," B.G. said. "I didn't think much of that of-fering myself. No, they sent the latest version of your fa-vorite cock ring, plus a few custom pieces I suggested they might develop."

Eric paused in pulling his shirt tails out of his slacks. "Custom?"

"Anyone could use them," B.G. said, rising to help him with the buttons. "But they were designed with your tastes in mind."

Eric's shirt was open now, and B.G.'s palms ran savor-ingly over his skin. "I'll never tire of this," he murmured. "The feel of you. Breathing harder under my hands."

This unexpected sweetness had Eric's eyes stinging. Then B.G. brought out his first surprise, a tube of minty-smelling ointment that he rubbed around the outer edge of Eric's nipples. B.G. was right about this shipment catering to Eric's taste. He'd always been susceptible to nipple play.

"Encourages blood flow," B.G. said as he pulled out the tips gently. "This will get them hard and keep them that way for hours. Plus, it's more discreet than wearing a pair of clamps under your shirt. There." His lashes dipped to admire the results. "Nice and rosy and sharp. And no numbness, I presume."

"No," Eric confirmed. "The sensation is very nice." Even without B.G. fondling him, the tingling went through him in peculiar but pleasant streaks. He was so sensitive he could feel each stirring of the air. When B.G. touched the center of one nub, he jumped.

"Good," B.G. said. "You can tell me later if you think we ought to try this on Charity."

Without warning, the image of her in her apartment, stripping her clothes over her head, came starkly back. Her nipples had been pale pink, full and soft except for a stiffening at the tips. He regretted now that he hadn't sucked them. He knew they would have been smooth.

Loyalties torn, he cleared his throat at the sudden jolting of his cock.

He and Charity had been on their own when that happened. Unlike their scene with Maurice, B.G. could neither watch what Eric had done, nor hear the story she'd asked him to tell—a personal one, to say the least. Eric had given Charity a window on his and B.G.'s relationship even as he'd been shutting his old friend out. "I'll, uh, study the effects with her in mind," he said uncomfortably.

"Good," B.G. said again and patted his arm. Unlike Eric, he seemed disgustingly free of the envy gene. "Now drop your trousers and bend over the back of that chair."

Eric hesitated briefly and then obeyed. As he'd expected, B.G.'s eyes widened at the state of his erection. Rather than comment, or decide he didn't need winding up after all, he gestured Eric to turn around. Eric braced himself on the chair arms while B.G. stroked the length of his flank.

Eric knew he meant to put him at ease. A partner's comfort was always critical to his boss.

"We'll use regular lube for this," he said, moving away for a moment behind him. "Until we're sure that mint stuff won't numb you out." He tapped the inside of Eric's thighs. "A little wider please. And relax."

Something slick and cool nudged him from the back. Eric didn't recognize its shape as one of their usual toys.

"What *is* that?"

"A remote-controlled vibrating anal plug."

"Jeez."

"Yes," B.G. agreed. "I wish it had a more aesthetic name, but I suppose this is preferable to something cute."

"I can't even imagine." Eric gasped and struggled not to tense as the thing slid past the nerve-rich inches inside his entrance. The plug was small, no more than thumb-size, with a flaring base and a give that told him it was rubber. The tip didn't quite reach his prostate. Eric suspected that omission wouldn't be much help once its mechanism was turned on. "You're keeping control of the remote?"

B.G. laughed. "Yes. And I don't want you to let on I have it. For tonight, this toy is just between us. Later, however, I strongly encourage you to tell Charity. I've discovered she likes the idea of other people's sexual suffering."

Eric tried to process this information without resenting how B.G. had likely obtained it. Without warning, a buzzing from inside had him gripping the chair. B.G. had turned on the vibrator. Though the sound was low, the feeling was not. As his fingers turned to claws, his hair prickled from his scalp down to his toes, his balls and buttocks shivering deliciously. The sensations were so intense, he thought he was done for. Luckily, even as he huffed out a breath for control, the vibrations eased back to a dull, penetrating throb. His cock felt as if it were stuffed, but not in imminent danger of blastoff.

He found his voice only after the thing switched off. "Damn," he said. "If you want to keep that toy a secret, you'd better stick to the low setting."

"Duly noted," B.G. said. "Now let's see if you can stand."

He could—barely. Four narrow velvet ribbons led from the base of the plug, two of which B.G. pulled forward so they ran between his balls and thighs. He tied them over Eric's hipbones to the ribbons running from the back. The toy felt secure but odd, making him aware of places he usually forgot. Happy to be reminded, his erection jounced against his abdomen.

The arrangement of bows must have looked amusing because B.G. smiled.

"Fuck you," Eric said, and the smile became a grin.

Unfortunately for his pride, his knees weren't steady enough to bend. B.G. retrieved his trousers and pulled them up.

"You're lucky you buy these loose," he said as he zipped them and did the catch.

Eric waited until his friend's eyes came up. "I always feel lucky when I'm with you."

"As I do with you."

Briefly, B.G. touched his cheek. He seemed embarrassed, which wasn't like him, turning hastily away to resume his seat. Once there, he pointed a remote at a length of paneling. The retractable wall slid up to reveal a bank of closed-circuit screens, each liquid crystal display showing a different area of the house. This being B.G.'s idea of surveillance, the pictures were very clear.

"Sit," he said, gesturing to the couch. "We'll see if we can discover where our guest has gone."

⤙⤚⧉⤙⤚

Charity didn't get far in her explorations, mostly because everything she found tempted her to stop and look around.

A string of libraries opened off the hall from her room, each organized around a theme. The mystery room she'd already seen, but the astronomy library was cool, too. When she hit a button by the door, the room turned into a planetarium, complete with constellations spinning on the walls. The romance room—for female guests, she supposed—was a cross between a tea shop and a wedding cake, so crazy over-the-top with ruffles it made her grin. Though she didn't know B.G. well, she could imagine him chuckling to himself while he planned it. She had a feeling he was sillier when he was alone.

Stage sets though they seemed, the rooms showed signs of use. The cushions were squashed, the spines of the novels cracked, but the absence of the people who'd left the wear created the impression of a ghost town. A few times, she thought she glimpsed someone out of the corner of her eye, then turned to find the spot empty. She fought the niggle of fear this caused. No way was Grantham's estate a haunted house. It simply had a sense of presence.

Her first live human showed up in the kitchen, one Señora Alvarez, a motherly Spanish-speaking cook who wouldn't let her leave until she ate a yummy bean-filled snack.

Thus fortified, she wandered down another hall, this one painted in blue and white Greek designs. It led to a sapphire lap pool that stretched across an elegant conservatory. Smooth white marble paved the floor, while potted palms whispered secrets to the fan-stirred air. The most eye-catching ornament, however, was the slim, naked blonde who was swimming the crawl in perfect form—maybe the very blonde B.G. had warned her about. Curious to meet someone who hopefully spoke English, Charity waited until the woman climbed out, sheeting water off her nymphlike form.

She must have been accustomed to being naked. Rather than bother with a towel, she sleeked the drips from her short fair hair with the palms of her hands. Her cool green eyes studied Charity without expression, but Charity had been the new kid on too many blocks to act cowed. Knowing the value of a confident appearance, Charity smiled.

"You're the new guest," the swimmer said with a faint accent. Charity wondered if anyone but another woman would have heard the challenge in her tone.

"That's right. I'm Charity Wills."

At last, the woman reached for a towel, though all she did with it was pat the golden skin between her amazingly perky breasts. "I'm Sylvia, the masseuse."

"Sweet job. Getting to rub your hands all over the hot guys."

Sylvia's mouth pursed and smiled at the same time. "I'm just as partial to hot girls."

"Oh," said Charity, abruptly feeling naive. "Of course you are. Handy being flexible in a place like this."

"Yes, it is, though I was hired as much for these"—Sylvia waggled slender fingers—"as for my eclectic tastes." She lifted one pale brow as if Charity might not know what *eclec-*

tic meant. "You have a lovely blush," she added, causing it to deepen. "So many people just turn red."

"I'm a bit out of my league here," Charity confessed.

Sylvia seemed to like that. It brought a flicker of approval into her eyes. Charity thought she might be the sort of female who was nicer when she felt superior. Sylvia's next question was kindly. "Never been with a woman?"

"No-o," Charity answered slowly, not sure she wanted to go where this was heading.

"Perhaps you don't think it's worth trying." Sylvia's tone had grown chilly. Perhaps unconsciously, her posture was now combative: hands on waist, feet planted wide. The muscles of her shapely thighs were just taut enough to see. Apparently, this Nordic snowfairy liked to work out. Then and there, despite the fact that Sylvia hadn't issued the smallest threat, Charity decided not to get on her bad side.

"Um," she said. "I'm afraid being with a woman has never been one of my fantasies."

"Then what has?" Sylvia almost purred.

The sudden shift in her manner reminded Charity this was exactly the question she wasn't supposed to answer. "Oh, this and that," she said, waving her hand vaguely. "The usual."

"Bondage?" Sylvia suggested. "Corporal punishment?"

If it had been dark, Sylvia's cool green eyes would have glowed. She seemed positively hungry to know Charity's kinks.

"Those are the *usual?*" Charity asked, trying to make it a joke. "I must be more out of my league than I thought."

"I know you are not disgusted," Sylvia said, her certainty unsettling.

Charity wouldn't have guessed she'd be that easy to read.

"No," she said. "But your questions *are* kind of personal."

Sylvia tossed her head disdainfully, her drying locks beginning to float like down. "Everyone is here for something, some dark, secret dream they wish to fulfill."

In spite of Charity's discomfort with this conversation, Sylvia's words, and the passion they were uttered with, sent a flash of heat to her sex. She could see why B.G. had felt the need to warn her. Sylvia was insidious.

"What's *your* secret dream?" she asked, her tone almost as intimate as Sylvia's. She hadn't meant the question to come out that way, but the quick surprise in Sylvia's eyes was a charge.

"I'm submissive," Sylvia said. "I live to please others."

"Baloney," Charity scoffed, as certain as Sylvia had been about her. "There's got to be something you want for yourself, whether or not it pleases anyone else."

Her grin took Sylvia aback. The masseuse looked furtively to either side, maybe searching for watchers. "It's really nothing," she hemmed.

"You can tell me," Charity said. "Heck, I bet you could tell anybody here. It's not like they haven't seen it all."

Sylvia leaned so close Charity could smell the chlorine on her skin. "What I'd really like," she said in a near whisper, "is a good, brisk spanking. Nothing against Mr. Grantham. He's a wonderful employer. But he doesn't have the stomach to turn a woman's bottom red."

"Um," said Charity and rubbed her nose. "That's a dilemma."

Sylvia straightened and laughed. "I've embarrassed you. I am sorry."

"No, no. I'm the one who asked."

Sylvia's expression turned sly. "You look strong," she said. "Perhaps you'd like to give it a try."

"Me?" Suddenly Charity had trouble catching her breath.

"Why not? The bigwigs are probably watching as it is. You know how men are. Why not give the tormentors a taste of their own medicine?"

The idea did hold a certain appeal. Did watching qualify as "supervision"? Could B.G.'s voice boom out of a speaker

to stop it all? She'd always thought if you encouraged someone to confide in you, you shouldn't make them feel bad
about what they'd revealed. Refusing Sylvia now seemed
too close to breaking her own rule. "Is it allowed?" she
asked uncertainly.

"Absolutely," Sylvia declared, "as long as neither of us
climaxes."

"Well," said Charity, "if all you want is a spanking, I guess
I could manage that."

"Excellent," Sylvia responded, promptly laying facedown
on the marble tile. Her skin looked even more golden against
its white. She put her head on her folded arms. "I don't like
giving instructions, so please proceed as you wish. And do
not worry about hurting me. I'm much tougher than I look.
You should also be aware that if you wet your hands first, it
makes a better noise."

"You know," said Charity, "for a person who doesn't like
to give instructions, you do it pretty easily."

"You asked what I wanted," Sylvia said. "If I don't tell
you, when will I have another chance to get it?"

Since Charity couldn't argue with that, she knelt to dunk
her hand in the heated pool, then returned to Sylvia's side.
Her well-toned bottom was slightly raised, whether deliberately or just in anticipation, she couldn't say. Charity had
to admit the position made a pretty curve of her spine.

You can do this, she told herself. *You've wanted to whack your
female bosses often enough.*

"Cup your hand when you spank me," Sylvia said into
her arms. "I like that better than the flat."

"Are you sure you don't want to instruct me? 'Cause I
can wait."

"I am done," Sylvia said, her dignity injured by Charity's
teasing. "You may proceed."

Charity had to bite her lip against a laugh for the first few
strikes, but, true to her word, Sylvia kept any more advice to

herself. In no time she was squirming against the floor and giving out little mewls that Charity found surprisingly arousing. Sylvia's eyes were so tightly closed, Charity thought she must have gone off into another world. For some reason, this made her task easier—not that it was actually hard. To be honest, it was fun to exercise this much power with such a simple act.

It was, in its way, as fascinating as watching Maurice struggle in his punishment chair.

"Tell me," Charity said, treating her victim to a particularly forceful smack. "How does Eric . . . Mr. Berne rate on the spanking meter?"

"He is better," Sylvia gasped, "but he, too, lacks the will to make a spanking sting."

"Hah!" said Charity, readying her arm for another swing. "Lucky for you, Wills is my last name."

Put on her mettle to best the men, she let loose a flurry of quick, sharp blows, taking care not to let either side of Sylvia's bottom get too red. No matter how tough Sylvia claimed she was, Charity had no desire to harm her.

"Oh, oh, oh!" Sylvia cried, but because it seemed like a happy noise, Charity kept up her efforts. In truth, if Sylvia hadn't been appreciative, she might have flagged. This spanking thing took a lot out of a person's arm.

"Oh, Arne," Sylvia groaned, presumably transported to another time. "Do it. Do it as hard as you can. You know I need it. You know I am too wicked to be left unmarked!"

It seemed rude to mention her name wasn't Arne. Sucking up a lung-filling breath, Charity gathered herself for a few last end-of-the-fireworks blows.

As the first one hit, Sylvia groaned and said something that sounded like the Nordic version of *oh, God, yes!*

"Yes," she moaned, recovering enough to speak English. "More, more . . . oh, God, quick stop!"

Charity stopped at once, but Sylvia was quivering on the

floor, grinding her hips against the marble as if she meant to push her body through. It took a minute until the shaking stopped, after which her breath panted out in ragged huffs. Her bottom was blazing pink—a good deal pinker than Charity had meant to make it. As if the discomfort this must entail was nothing, Sylvia sighed euphorically and sat up.

"You brought me to climax," she said, her green eyes wide.

Charity blushed, despite this having been obvious. "I'm sorry, Sylvia. I know I wasn't supposed to do that."

"Oh, no." Sylvia clasped her hands fervently, squeezing them hard enough to hurt. "You are marvelous. That hasn't happened since . . . well, since a boy I knew when I was a teen."

Before Charity's mind could spiral through semi-scary thoughts of a teenage Sylvia, the other woman grabbed her face and planted a big wet one right on her mouth. As kisses went, it wasn't bad, maybe a bit too hard but not bad. Charity's lips were tingling by the time Sylvia let go.

Only then did she remember she'd promised not to kiss anyone but Eric or B.G.—not that Sylvia had given her a choice.

"Um," Charity said, knocked way off her normal balance. "You're welcome, I guess."

Sylvia tossed her head on a laugh, a gesture that made her look like someone who could have once been eighteen. Charity couldn't help smiling back. Obviously giddy, Sylvia scrambled to her feet and skipped toward the door, her teacup breasts jiggling fetchingly. She paused at the entrance like Tinkerbell lighting on a flower. "I'll see you at dinner, Charity Wills. And thank you. That was worth any punishment."

Charity was glad she thought so. For her part, she wasn't yet convinced she wished to pay.

Eight

Maurice collected Charity for dinner. As usual, she would have been late without the help, having lost track of time while painting her toenails pink. Someone—Eric, she assumed—had laid out an outfit on her bed. Chosen from what she'd brought with her, it included her favorite super-low-riding jeans and a baby-blue cropped hoodie.

The underwear was new: real silk stuff that probably cost a mint. Thankfully, it held her up and fit her to a T. Even if it hadn't, she wouldn't have considered not wearing it, not that evening anyway. She'd pushed her luck enough by playing with Sylvia. If she behaved herself for a while, maybe she'd escape punishment. She certainly didn't want to be kicked out. Weird or not, her experiences thus far had been fun. She could stand wearing what someone else picked out for once.

"Lord Almighty," Maurice said, his attention snagging on her navel ring. "You look like jail bait in that outfit."

"Fake jail bait," Charity assured him, giving her chest a wiggle behind the snug velour. She'd slid the hoodie's zipper down enough to show the edges of the ice-pink bra. "Hopefully your boss will enjoy a change from leather and bondage wear."

"Trust me," Maurice said, his hand to his heart. "B.G. Grantham would like you in a sack. He may be Mr. Science, but he's a man."

Gratified by this response, Charity followed him through a series of underground halls, each built of monolithic stones. Because the lights were equipped with motion detectors, darkness preceded as well as followed them. Charity found the effect slightly creepy but interesting, reminding her— as if she needed reminding—that she was having an adventure beyond the norm. At the end of the last passage, an elegant mahogany door with its own spotlight opened onto a combination library/sitting room.

The smell of charbroiled steak made her mouth water.

Behind the door, Eric and his boss sat at a table as fancy as one in a fine restaurant. Lamps shed pools of light here and there, but the main illumination came from an antique candelabra burning on the serving trolley that had been rolled between the men. She couldn't doubt they'd done this kind of thing before. Both looked relaxed—or they did until she came in.

As soon as he saw her, Eric jumped from his seat. She couldn't be sure, but she supposed this was a compliment to her clothes. Either that, or he always stood for women. Cool as ever, B.G. simply raised his brows, his gaze trailing down her body and up again.

His mouth tipped up on one side when he spied her piercing.

To her surprise, Maurice bobbed a small bow and left. His wasn't the only missing face. Despite Sylvia's promise to see her at the meal, the discipline-loving masseuse was nowhere in sight.

"Is it only us?" she asked as Eric pulled out her chair.

"Yes," B.G. said. "I thought you'd welcome the chance to get to know your keeper."

From the way Eric's eyes widened, he hadn't known this

was the plan, though B.G. appeared to think he'd said nothing odd. He smoothed his white linen shirt and filled her glass with water, a politeness that showed off how lean and broad his shoulders were. "I suppose you were expecting Sylvia to join us."

"I'm sorry about that," she said, experience having taught her it was better to admit guilt as soon as you'd been caught. "She kind of took me by surprise."

"Sylvia has a way of doing that. She's being . . . seen to, if not as perfectly as she was by you. You seem to have a knack for bringing out your partners' most passionate responses."

"I didn't mean to," Charity said, remembering to shake her napkin into her lap. "It was more of an accident."

"An accident Eric and I enjoyed observing, even if it did show us up. I expect you've earned yourself a friend for life. But we shouldn't be letting our meal get cold. My cook is quite adept. I believe you'll find this to your taste."

"Am I going to be punished?" Charity blurted out, unable to bear the suspense.

B.G.'s smile was slow, its curve sending a slither of heat through all her secret places. "Oh, no, Charity. You haven't earned your punishment yet. When the time is right, I'll let you know."

They hadn't finished the first course before Eric decided something was seriously up with B.G. They'd dealt with candidates on their own before, but tonight felt personal. This was steak and wine and ordinary conversation, as if Charity Wills were a more traditional sort of guest. Aside from B.G.'s occasional activation of the anal toy—the effect of which Eric did his best to conceal—his boss was ignoring him. He was talking TV with Charity, for God's sake: asking her whether she thought *The Real World* or *Survivor* painted a truer portrait of human life. Eric hadn't known his boss watched these shows. In fact, he would have sworn he did not.

It occurred to Eric, as he gritted his teeth against a burst from the vibrator, that B.G. might have done a bit of boning up precisely so he'd have something to talk about with Charity. If this was true, it was beyond any prep work he'd done in the past. Evidently, B.G. thought it important to make Charity—both the person and the plaything—feel comfortable.

"You are too funny," she said now, her hand shoving B.G.'s shoulder, her cheeks flushed with the wine and some off-the-wall witticism his boss had cracked.

B.G. inclined his head. "I'm gratified to have amused you."

"I read your book, you know," she said, slanting a glance at him as she turned her wineglass in a circle on the tablecloth. "Or part of it. I'm afraid I gave up when you got to the bit about the cat."

B.G. nodded understandingly. "Many brilliant minds have been stumped by Schrödinger's famous thought experiment."

Predictably, Charity grimaced at being lumped in with brilliant minds. "I couldn't get my head around it," she admitted, propping her elbows around her plate—forgetfulness, Eric was sure. Up until then, her manners had been fine.

"I'm sure you understood the premise." B.G. leaned forward to match Charity. He'd gone into teaching mode, his hair flopping in his eye, his focus on his audience. Eric hoped this meant he'd be safe from the vibrator for a while. His erection was starting to pulse in time to its rhythm even with it off.

"You could remind me," Charity said. "In case I forgot."

"Schrödinger's imaginary cat is closed in a box along with a vial of poison whose seal is linked to an unpredictable quantum event, a particle which has a 50/50 chance of decaying or not. If it decays, a Geiger counter triggers the seal on the vial to break, thus killing the imprisoned cat. If the particle doesn't decay, the cat survives."

"That's what I thought," Charity said. "But in your book you claimed that nothing happened until someone opened the box. You said that until there was an observer, the cat was neither dead nor alive. I just can't understand how that could be."

"But you've cut to the heart of the quantum paradox!" B.G. exclaimed. "According to the way people have always understood the world, a dead-alive cat is impossible. This, however, doesn't change the fact that in the quantum world— the world of the very small—contradictory states of reality have been proven, repeatedly, to coexist."

Charity sighed and wagged her head. Seeing how close she was to giving up, B.G. pressed his lips to her cheek. Though this teaching tool would have been inappropriate in a college lecture, it relaxed her enough to listen as he went on.

"Let me try to make it clearer," he said. "Take an electron, which has qualities of both waves and particles: clear, mutually exclusive states. Now say you have an electron gun." To demonstrate, he picked up a fork and held it tines-out. "This electron gun is capable of shooting a single electron at a time. In front of this gun is a wall with two tiny electron-size holes, either of which can be opened or closed on demand." To represent the barrier, he balanced a leftover slice of garlic bread on its side. "In front of this hole-y wall—Eric, if we could borrow your hand here? In front of this hole-y wall is a special electron-detecting screen, represented now by Eric's palm. When an electron hits it, it glows.

"Wanting to see what's what, you open one of the two electron holes and shoot a single electron from the gun. As a Newtonian, or large body, physicist would expect, the electron behaves like a tiny bullet, creating a discrete, particle-size blip on the electron-detecting screen. Seeing this, you conclude that an electron is a particle."

Chin on hand, Charity nodded to show she was following.

B.G. smiled in approval. "Now," he said, "just to be certain you've found the truth, you open both the holes in the wall that sits between the gun and the screen. Again, you shoot a single electron, fully expecting it to go through one hole or the other. Instead, the electron behaves like a wave, going through both holes at once and then interfering with itself on the other side, with peaks intensifying peaks or being cancelled by troughs, until what registers on the screen is not the mark of a single 'bullet' but a pattern of bright and dark bands—classic evidence of wave interference.

" 'How fascinating,' you think, and decide you must observe this waving electron going through both holes at once, just as water would do. So you place teeny tiny electron detectors on each of two electron-size holes. And what do you think happens?"

"I'm sure I have no idea," Charity said with a bemused smile. Eric smiled as well. Some people had favorite jokes. This aspect of the quantum puzzle was B.G.'s equivalent.

"What happens," B.G. said, "when you install the electron detectors on the two open holes, is that the electron reverts to behaving like a particle. Even though you just proved it is a wave, you can never record it going through both holes at once, only one or the other. It's as if the electron *knows* you are watching, and for some unfathomable reason, it's forced to commit to a single choice."

"But . . . how could it know?" Charity stammered.

"That," said B.G., "is a very big mystery. As in the theoretical case of the cat, human consciousness appears to hold the conundrum's key. It may be that we create our world as we observe it."

Charity slumped back in her chair, looking completely baffled but not the least self-conscious about her lack of knowledge. "You're telling me noncrazy people have proved this with real experiments. It's not physicists sitting around in armchairs saying 'Wouldn't this be neat?'"

"I've simplified the process for the sake of clarity, but, yes, perfectly rational scientists have proved this and other things equally as strange. They've proved that our concepts of time and space are human illusions. They've proved that not only do quantum particles exist, but so do their ghostly opposites. Atoms that have appeared in a certain spot create mirages in a second where they had a probability of showing up, mirages a scanning microscope can pick up. It can be argued, in fact, that every possible choice an atom or a person can make exists in a multi-layered quantum fuzz, lacking anything we would call reality until we turn our attention to an event. Most important, scientists have found evidence to support these claims when they were striving to undermine them. To tell the truth, Charity, reality is much more peculiar than the average person is aware."

"Huh," she said. "Cool."

At this, B.G. sat back, visibly pulling his composure around him. He seemed to regret having let his enthusiasm run away. "I'm glad you think so," he said. "But I'm afraid I've monopolized the conversation. Why don't we let Eric tell you about the time he went on tour with the Rolling Stones . . ."

Her I'm-with-the-band fashion sense aside, Charity wasn't the sort of girl to be awed by name-dropping, at least not to the point of skewing her judgment. Still, it seemed polite to express interest when B.G. so obviously wanted her to.

Too, she had to admit it was uncanny that she'd been thinking just this morning how different Eric was from the guys she usually dated, the kind of man who wouldn't know Sir Mick from Sir Galahad.

"Really?" she said, turning to Eric for confirmation. "You toured with the Stones?"

Her question was simple enough, but Eric choked on his water and gripped the table edge.

"Jesus," he said when he'd caught his breath, glaring at B.G. for no reason that she could see. B.G. must have been doing something he shouldn't. He was smiling innocently. Charity wondered if Eric had earned some secret punishment.

"Yes," he said to her with an air of studiously ignoring his boss. "I traveled with the Stones on one of their tours. Nothing glamorous. I was still a suit, as you would say. I handled their PR. That was my field before I came here."

"Well, no wonder you had no trouble convincing me to come!"

"Oh, I'm persuasive," Eric said. "I've had people tell me I could sell sand to Arabia."

He didn't sound as if this pleased him, but Charity didn't get a chance to ask why. She was reaching for the last of her wine when the oddest feeling swept through her head, a sensation of pressure as if her ears had been stopped with cotton balls. An unnatural silence swallowed the room until even the ticking of the fancy mantel clock was blotted out. Then, like a broken film being restarted, the glass she'd been about to pick up jumped clearly and unmistakably at least six inches to the left.

She was too shocked to keep her girlish shriek inside.

Eric was on his feet before the sound faded. "What?" he said, his hands on her shoulders. "Honey, what's wrong?"

"Didn't you see it?" she gasped, craning around, her heart pattering frantically in her throat. "My glass moved all by itself."

"Surely not," Eric said.

Charity turned to B.G. "It's a trick, isn't it? You did something sneaky to make it move."

B.G. smiled and spread his hands, far too complacent for

her peace of mind. "No trick," he said, "although I regret I didn't observe the incident myself."

"It was real," she insisted. "I'm not drunk."

B.G. rubbed the side of her arm. The gesture calmed her in spite of her wish to stay angry. She had seen what she said. She didn't need to be humored.

As it turned out, this wasn't what B.G. was doing.

"I believe you, Charity," he said, shocking her all over again. "People often see things in this house. It's a place where the impossible is invited in."

"Now *you're* talking like a crazy person."

He laughed, not answering her accusation either way.

His reaction made her shiver even harder than the magically jumping glass. No doubt if she asked, he would give her his explanation for what had happened. A genius like him was sure to have one. To him, this freaky stuff probably seemed normal. The problem was, she didn't want to hear what he had to say. If the world wasn't what she thought, who knew what else might be true? Worrying about being punished seemed piddly compared to that.

Maybe there *had* been ghosts following her around.

Abruptly overwhelmed, she pushed back her chair and stood.

"I'm tired," she said. "I need to go to my room."

The moment the words were out, her fatigue doubled, her knees as wobbly as warm Jell-O.

"I'll walk you back," Eric said, wrapping his arm around her shoulders. The squeeze he put into his grip was exactly the comfort she craved. For a while tonight, she'd been thinking maybe his boss was more interesting. Now she wanted nothing more than to let Eric lead her away.

"I'm sorry," B.G. said, sounding like he really was. "Believe me, I couldn't have predicted this would happen. I never meant to spoil your meal."

"The meal was delicious," she said. "Please tell your cook

she's super good." Then, because she truly didn't want him
to be hurt, she pressed her hand to his cheek.

The touch made him blink at her rapidly.

"I'll see you tomorrow," she said.

"Yes," he said. "Tomorrow."

His breath caught as if he'd thought of saying something
else. She didn't stick around to see what it might be.

❧

Eric walked her to her room, glad he was there for her even
if he wasn't sure how aware she was of his presence. She
moved beside him in a daze, only speaking after he'd closed
the door. When she plunked down on the low edge of her
futon, she looked young and lost.

Perversely, this kicked Eric's arousal back into gear.

"I thought quantum theory was *theoretical*," she said, her
hands caught forlornly between her knees.

Eric stepped in front of her and stroked her hair, a pleasure he enjoyed despite his concern. "It *is* theoretical. It's
also very well supported."

"You can't prove those things B.G. said. Ghost particles.
Fuzzy reality. How can you make experiments for that?"

"Well, you probably have to be a physicist to come up
with them. The important thing for people like you and me
to remember is that those theories, proven or not, constitute a
useful recipe book. Just as you don't have to know chemistry
to bake a cake, you don't have to understand Schrödinger's cat
to build a laser. The theories gain legitimacy because they
work."

"So he wasn't messing with my mind?"

"B.G. does have a quirky sense of humor, but it doesn't
lean toward playing pranks."

Charity sighed so heavily a lock of hair fluttered from her
brow. As if searching for something solid to hold onto, her

hands found the back of his knees. The touch was immediately, forcefully sensual.

She laughed at the sudden lurching at his crotch.

"You think this is sexy." She tilted her head up to see his face. "You like watching me fall apart."

"I admit I like being needed, but I wouldn't say you're falling apart. Of course, I may be overly excitable on account of having a remote-controlled vibrator up my, er, nether parts."

"You're kidding." Caught between laughter and disbelief, she patted his rear to see if she could feel it.

"It's not turned on this minute."

Her touch changed to a caressing squeeze, one that seemed to arouse her as much as him. A rose-pink flush had crept up her cheeks. "B.G. was playing with you at dinner. That's why you were jumpy. I thought maybe you really liked me in the clothes you picked out."

"I did," he said. "I do. Especially the way your bra peeks out from that little jacket." She shivered pleasantly as he tugged the tag of her zipper. "You have the sexiest breasts I've ever seen."

"Better than Sylvia's?" Her tone was only half a tease.

"Better than anyone's you could name." Glad to be able to reassure her on this at least, he slid both hands into her hooded jacket, cupping her rounded flesh through the pale pink bra. Her nipples poked seductively behind the silken barrier.

"Is B.G. watching us?" she whispered. "He told me there was a camera behind that screen. Could that remote of his work this far?"

Eric fought a groan as her nails dragged up the back of his trousers. "Don't know," he said. "With B.G., almost anything is possible."

She rubbed her face against his shirt, breathing through the cotton that overlay the skin above his waist. When she spoke, her voice was small. "Could you could stay with me tonight? Otherwise, I'm going to lay here like Linda Blair, totally terrified that my furniture is going to start hopping off the ground."

"You shouldn't worry about that. I've only seen small things happen, things I wasn't sure I'd witnessed afterward."

"Yeah? Tell that to Linda."

He laughed, but humor didn't relieve the pounding urgency at his groin. Unable to resist temptation, his hands pushed her tight baby-blue jacket off her shoulders. Still partially zipped, the open edges framed the swell of her breasts.

"I want to stay," he said. "I want to stroke inside you all night."

"Could you?" she asked, her hopeful tone bringing his erection to a painful state. "Is it allowed?"

"It's allowed," he said grimly. "But only if we don't come."

"You sound like that would be hard." The throatiness of her words reminded him of B.G.'s earlier comment, that she enjoyed seeing others suffer sexual denial.

"It would be very hard," he said. "Maybe impossible." But his mind was already imagining how it could be done, his body craving her clasp as if it were a lifesaving drug. "Maybe I could be inside you for a little while. I have . . ." He hesitated, unsure how she would react, despite B.G.'s insight. "I have a new cock ring."

"A *new* cock ring," she said, laughing softly through her nose. "I can't tell you how that intrigues me."

Relief increased the surging in his veins. "It's not foolproof," he warned. "Cock rings keep blood from leaving the penis, so you stay hard, but when you're as excited as I am, you can still ejaculate."

She laughed and fanned her face. "You sweet-talker, you."

"Sorry, I—"

"No, I mean it," she said with an endearing earnestness. "I love listening to you talk about sexy stuff. Just hearing you say 'ejaculate' makes me hot. And I'd love to have you inside me—even for a while. I remember how hard you were when you rubbed against me at my place."

He couldn't help shuddering at the images her words inspired, at the memory of her oiled-up curves. "You could come if you wanted to," he said rashly. "B.G. will put a price on it, but I wouldn't stop you. I understand if you need comfort. I want you to be happy here, not afraid."

She looked up at him, her whole being aglow. "If you let me come, he'll make you pay, too."

"Yes," he said. "Despite my being his right hand, he'll make me pay, too."

Her wide, star-struck gaze said she couldn't quite accept this idea: that he would put her pleasure before his pride. "Show me," she said softly. "Prove how much you want me happy."

"Too much," he swore, scarcely aware of what he was saying. "Oh, God, I want you too much."

He peeled off her jacket, not wanting to rush the pleasure of unveiling her but unable to keep it slow. He did pause long enough to kiss her perfect pink toenails and belly ring. Then he noticed her bra had left marks he had to nuzzle off, leading him irresistibly to the buttery smoothness of her taut nipples. At that discovery he could only sigh.

She was satin in his mouth, beading up erotically against his tongue.

For the moment, he forgot about her X-rated jeans. The pleasure he felt at suckling her stole the strength from his knees. Rather than collapse, he knelt on the hardwood floor and hugged her waist. For long, delicious minutes, he did nothing but turn his mouth back and forth.

"Mm," she said, her fingers kneading his scalp. "Let me kiss you, too."

Her suggestion broke his tenuous patience. He wrenched off his shirt with a ripping noise.

This made Charity grin.

"Here?" she said coyly, lightly circling his nipples with her fingertips. "You want me to kiss you here?"

His moan of longing was answer enough. She tugged him up and onto the bed, pushing him firmly onto his back. His chest heaved up and down in anticipation while the nail of her index finger slid from his breastbone to his waistband. Her voice came like the rasping of a match.

"Do you want the cock ring yet?"

He shook his head. Right then, he didn't want any constriction on him but her.

"Should I cup you?" she offered. "Should I feel what it does to you when I suck?"

"Yes," he said, too decided in his preference to be polite. "Squeeze my balls."

His demand brought more lovely color into her face. Slowly, she brought her hand to the crotch of his trousers and curled it around the seam. Her hold was warm, one finger pressing gently between the halves of his testicles. She watched his eyes to see how he liked that.

"Oh, yeah," he said. "Now put your mouth on my nipples."

She licked her upper lip and bent, fastening onto one tiny peak. The sensation was so intense the skin of his belly jumped. Feeling it, her palm squeezed a little tighter between his legs.

Suddenly, she broke off with a laugh. "You taste like mint," she said. "And you're so sharp. I think someone's been getting you ready for me."

Her words had as powerful an effect on him as his had on her. Had this been B.G.'s intent? To prepare him for Charity instead of the other way around? His mind was too distracted to answer. When she settled her mouth on his chest again, he felt it even more, lightning streaks that skittered unpredictably along his skin—now to the soles of his feet, now to the tangle of nerves behind his knees. Despite the intensity of his pleasure, he was anxious. He wanted to please her and wasn't sure he could—doubts he thought himself long beyond. Sensing something of his agitation, Charity shifted her hand to his stomach.

"Sh," she said, nuzzling across his chest to the other side. "I'll be careful not to push you over the edge. This won't be like Sylvia."

The reminder of what he'd seen her do was hardly calming.

"I can feel it," he said, his legs shifting restively. "I can feel everywhere you touch me straight through my cock."

She kissed him on the mouth, deep and hungry and hard. Caught up in the sudden change of treats, he didn't immediately notice her tugging off his trousers.

He gasped as the cooler air of the room hit his blazing cock. He'd forgotten about the butt toy's black velvet bows. Charity snorted out a laugh when they appeared. "Very stylish."

"Hey," he said, "they could have been pink."

She crawled back from him and stood, wriggling out of her low-slung jeans. Having seen her naked before didn't prevent her lush, sleek beauty from punching his gut. Plus, she had a tattoo he hadn't noticed, high on the inside of her thigh, a small blue angel with purple wings.

"That," he said from his pole-axed sprawl, "is the next place I'm going to kiss."

She touched it with her fingertips and grinned. "I had a boyfriend who claimed it was lucky."

"I'm sure every time he got to see it, he was."

She laughed outright, the sound a pleasure to his ears. He couldn't remember the last time he'd joked like this with a guest. Still standing over him, she nodded her head toward her bathroom. "Every kind of rubber you could imagine is stocked in there."

"Extra thick," he said to her unspoken question. "I'm feeling a bit sensitive."

"Looking it, too." She wagged her brows at his bobbing shaft, now stretching toward his waist. Its head twitched at the touch of her gaze. "Maybe I better bring two."

He hoped between the cock ring and wrapping up he'd make it through, but part of him didn't care. He wanted to be inside her enough to risk anything, including shaming himself.

When she returned with the condoms, he sat up on the side of the bed and set them out of the way. With thighs spread wide, he pulled her closer by her hips, kissing the tiny angel that guarded her heaven.

"We'll use the condoms later," he said at her tiny murmur of protest. "I want to kiss your pussy before I slide inside it. I want to make you as hot as you can get."

He coaxed her foot onto the bed, the pose opening her secrets, then slid his thumbs up and down the length of her outer lips. Within two strokes, the tip of her clitoris peeped from its hood. Within a dozen, she was glistening.

"Pretty," he said, drawing closer to inhale her scent.

His exhale made her quiver. "Eric . . ."

"Don't come when I kiss you," he warned, loving the way she shook. "I want to save that for my cock. Relax into the sensations. Push them out instead of trying to pull them in."

"Push," she repeated huskily.

He took the whole of her swollen button into his mouth, sucking gently, working his tongue a little against the shaft. Her taste went straight to his spinning head. Apparently, she liked his technique. Her nails dug into his shoulders, nearly pricking right through his skin.

"Boy," she breathed, obviously struggling to relax, "do you ever know what you're doing!"

Even as he grinned, he kept up the motion of his mouth and thumbs, not touching her entrance but massaging over the channels where her sexual nerves rooted deep. Her hips began to push at him in slow, rocking rolls, her button swelling even fuller, her sighs coming long and low. When her nails started pricking him again, he stopped.

"Now you can lie down," he said, his voice gritting out like sand. "Now you're wet enough to take everything I've got."

She shook herself as if she'd been in a dream, then clambered slowly onto the mattress. When he shifted around to face her, her gaze slid from his face to his cock.

He didn't have to look to know how hard he was. Every bursting inch was screaming to his brain. A tiny spot of coolness told him his slit was seeping pre-come.

Seeing it, Charity bit her lip, then licked where her teeth had been. "You need the condom now."

He loomed in front of her on his knees, rolling on the sheath himself, loving the way her eyes followed every motion. "I need the cock ring, too," he said. "Want to put it on?"

She laughed shakily. "I'm afraid my hands aren't working well enough."

"I'll wait, if you want. I'd enjoy having you try."

Sensing acquiescence, he handed her the box he'd slipped into the pocket of his pants. Watching her fumble it open had him fighting a smile and at the same time feeling like a king. He knew how much experience she had. That he could inspire this awkwardness did things to his insides he was pretty sure he shouldn't like so much. His heart was beating fast enough that he could have been racing toward a quickie instead of wanting to linger in her for hours.

"I'm supposed to wrap this around you?" she said, staring dubiously at the flexible snake of black rubber.

"Around my base and testicles. The tail goes around twice and then you push this little protrusion through the hole that fits best, just like a belt. That way, if you need to, it's easy to get off."

"Easy to get off," she muttered, but she maneuvered it on with ease. Whether she realized it or not, she was naturally dexterous. When she was done, his balls were lifted against his shaft and his cock stood nearly straight. The increase in pressure made him feel simultaneously more excited and more relaxed. The relaxation worried him. He knew better than to take his self-control for granted. This was going to be a fight.

"Wow," she said, her hands lingering on the end result. "This ring really makes you thick."

His hips pushed forward without his will, adding pressure to her measuring touch. "Not as thick as Maurice."

"You're longer," she said, her fingers skating upward on his darkened skin. "And fuller around the head. God, I love the way this looks. It's so fucking brutal."

He ground his teeth together as she drew a circle on his crown. "You felt what size he was with him behind you?"

"I felt everything, especially the way you steadied him when he slid in."

He growled, the only possible word for the lustful sound.

"I liked that part," she admitted even as he crowded her back onto the pillows. "I liked knowing how excited you were about helping him get inside me. I wished I could see your hands on his cock, just like I watched my hands on you now."

He couldn't wait, couldn't answer except to grunt. Pulling her thighs apart, he poised his rigid cock at her opening. The moment his crown touched her heat, his pulse doubled.

"It's only us," he rasped, surprised to hear it come out a threat. "No matter who might be watching, it's only us tonight."

"Good," she fired back. "You're the one I've been wanting all along."

The words were more than enough to get to him, but her pupils swelled as he pressed inside her bit by bit, deeper and deeper, until their hipbones bumped and tilted for the closest fit. Holding as far as he could reach, Eric closed his eyes and savored her clutching heat. Every woman felt different inside, and every woman felt good. This, however, was the first time any woman had felt perfect. Charity's fit was magic, a glove-tight harbor to guide and reward his strokes.

Sweat beaded his forehead as he fought the urge to pop off the cock ring and ride her to his finish.

"Aren't you going to move?" she asked, a bit plaintively.

In spite of his inner struggle, he smiled, his eyes opening slowly. "I want you to touch yourself first. I want you to bring yourself off with me rammed inside you. I want to feel you come against the skin of my cock."

"Taking notes?" she said with a humorous lift of one brow.

"You know it. I intend to use every chance I get to learn what you like. Go ahead, Charity." He kissed her temple. "If you're going to be punished, you might as well get the most out of the sin. If I can't make you come half a dozen times, I'll be disappointed."

She laughed, but she didn't argue, squeezing her hand between their close-fit hips. If he hadn't had years of practice holding back, the bumping of her knuckles would have set him off. She came quickly and hard, as if she'd needed the release. Its ripples stroked his shaft like fluttering velvet.

"Nice," he said as she panted in the aftermath. "Now hold my shoulders and let me thrust. I want to push you over again."

She moved her hands as he asked, the embrace adding an unexpected intimacy. Up on his elbows, he was able to meet her gaze. Her expression was so open, so trusting, it made his throat tighten. He regretted he couldn't stay like this, but he knew he had to catch her while she was primed.

True to his expectations, he stroked her to her next climax in seconds.

"Oh, God," she moaned, wriggling beneath him. "Oh, God, it's not enough."

He gave her more pressure, as much as he could stand without exploding, adding the deftness of his hand to his thrusting cock. Even with that, this orgasm took longer. Her body might be eager, but her nerves needed to build to a higher level before they fired. The increase in friction made him want to weep. It didn't help when her hold slid restlessly down his back. He tensed as she found the flaring base of the anal toy, now being clenched and released by his glutes.

"I want to touch this," she said. "I want to move it around."

"Don't," he gritted through his teeth. He might be willing to let her see him suffer, but that extra stimulation would be too much. Bad enough that the thing was such a strong presence.

Her hands pushed at the base when her hips came up, his involuntary shudder making her moan. "I don't know which is worse," she gasped. "Thinking your boss might be watching or wondering if we're free to do what we want."

"Don't talk about that. I'll have to stop."

"But it's exciting." Her hands skimmed up his spine, coaxing him faster in spite of himself. "Maybe he *is* watching. Maybe he's jacking off and dripping like you were before." She grinned. "Maybe he got out the Crisco."

He kissed her to shut her up, but the images stuck in his mind. B.G.'s lubed-up erection. B.G.'s fisted hand. His hold would feel like the cock ring, like the milking grip of Charity's sex. Some crucial barrier began to crack. He pistoned into her harder, recklessly using the sensation to blot out her words.

"Eric," she gasped, clearly on the edge.

The sound of his name went through him in a long quiver. Desperate now, he shifted angles to stroke her upper wall. If he caught her G-spot, he could make her come. If he made her come, he could pull free. Groaning, he pinched the hood of her clit and rubbed it hard.

If she'd been less aroused, it might have hurt. She screamed instead, her neck arching violently with her spasm, her hips cocking up with impressive force. A gush of moisture told him he'd hit her right, but his success was two-edged. The first ball-tightening threat of a climax surged against his constricted base, threatening to burst past the barrier. He stopped it only by biting his lip hard enough to bleed. Even then, he barely stuck with her until the end. The way her sex contracted made every cell in his hard-on ache.

When she finally settled, he sighed in relief.

Charity seemed embarrassed by what she'd done.

"Oh, my God," she said, pressing both hands over her mouth. "No one's ever made me scream. I thought women faked that to stoke their boyfriends' egos."

Because he was—at that moment—pulling carefully out of her body's hold, his laugh shook more than a bit. "Works wonders," he assured her once he was free. "My . . . ego feels quite secure."

The sight of his bleeding lip distracted her from his joke. "You cut yourself!"

"It'll heal," he said, almost as flattered by her concern as he'd been by her screams. He let her touch the injury and cluck, then lowered himself to her side. The cock ring and the rubber were a pleasure to strip off. Despite the continuing frustration of his needs, he felt satisfied. He'd fulfilled one of her secret desires, and he'd done it better than anyone had before.

"Rest," he said as she snuggled her head into his shoulder. "I want another go when you've recovered."

Her breath rushed out in what could have been disbelief or a laugh. "You rest," she countered, her arm draping his waist. "I'll let you know when I need your 'ego' again."

Her mockery didn't bother him in the least. How could it, when her drowsy tone assured him her earlier fears were a memory?

*   *   *

Considering how thoroughly satisfied Eric had left her, Charity had been sure she'd drop off right away. Instead, she drifted while he sank. She was almost afraid to hold him but couldn't bring herself to let go. Worse, she didn't think she could blame the strangeness of being at Mosswood for the feeling's strength.

Eric was really, really good in bed. Good in a way that suited her tastes so perfectly it seemed unfair. His occasional bossiness seemed no threat; he'd let her tease him with impunity. And she could tell his mind was as much a sex organ for him as hers was for her. When she'd started talking about B.G., he'd stiffened inside her like he was stone. Instead of being jealous, she'd wished she had a window to see if the scenario she'd spun was true. At that instant, she'd have thrown out every rebel principle she possessed to get the three of them in one bed. She wanted to watch them do each other. Even more, she wanted them to do her.

Though it scared her to admit it, she was beginning to see why the threat of being sent home was, in and of itself, enough to keep Mosswood's guests in line.

Nine

Charity lifted her head from the pillow and rubbed her nose. The clock glowing on the bedside table said one fifteen. Eric slept like a baby, but for a night owl like her, this was the evening's shank. Careful not to wake her companion, she padded to the bathroom for a quick shower in the slate-tiled stall. Feeling much fresher, she returned to bed.

Eric was blindly patting the mattress as she climbed in, his hair standing out in peaks like soft-serve ice cream. The fact that he'd missed her left a glowy feeling in her chest.

She was pretty sure cuddling his charges wasn't part of his job.

"There y'are," he mumbled, tucking himself against her again.

She could really take in his height when he curled close, the muscular length of his legs and arms. It was a strange sensation, but one she liked. The fur on his chest felt nicer than most men's. She smiled to herself, thinking maybe he groomed it. Maybe bisexual guys had the same fashion instincts as gays.

"Everything okay?" he said into her shoulder. "Not still worried about demonic furniture?"

STRANGE ATTRACTIONS   121

"No." She pulled his near-limp hand to her breast. "That thing at dinner threw me, but I guess a jumping glass isn't as dangerous as plenty of ordinary stuff."

"Not even close." He dropped a kiss half onto her ear. "Driving I-5 at rush hour's far more dangerous than that."

His breathing slowed, but—sleepy or not—she thought he probably wouldn't mind answering the question she'd been reluctant to ask B.G.

Better to hear the response from Eric. Since he wasn't a genius, she could always tell herself he got it wrong.

"Eric?" she said and waited for his prompting hum. "Do you know how B.G. would have explained what happened?"

He took a breath to bring his mind back to consciousness. "A slip of the time track is my guess. B.G. believes that time is only linear from the human perspective, a product of our neural makeup and social conditioning. According to him, humans join an unconscious agreement to perceive this world as one of cause leading to effect, of minute one preceding minute two. But in his and a number of other physicists' concept of the quantum realm, all times are now. Going backward or forward or skipping from point A to point F are perfectly okay."

"But why would time do that for us? Why go along A, B, C, and suddenly jump to F?"

This question obviously required more alertness. Eric pushed himself into a seated position, then refluffed his pillow behind his back. "It's possible that something you were thinking or feeling had such power it compelled your glass to be in a different place. B.G. believes that strong emotion can trigger atypical time events. It's even possible that something you're going to think in the future made it happen. Rather than pop you into an alternate universe—"

"An alternate universe!"

"Let me finish. Rather than pop you into an alternate universe where your glass was already there, your consciousness simply adjusted this one. Only you saw it, so I doubt there's any danger of undermining this reality's consensual rules."

"Eric—"

"I'm only telling you what I suspect B.G. would say. If an event doesn't have a zero probability of happening, many physicists claim it must occur, on some branch of reality. In a different universe, Charity, you and I never met."

The thought of this made her right hand clench the sheets. "Take my word for it," she said tightly, "my little brain doesn't have the power to adjust the world. That's just crazy. Even if quantum theories are true, this is real life."

"Charity, reluctant as I am to admit it, if there's one thing I've learned from living with B.G., it's that the implications of quantum theories are real. They're as real as the friend you haven't heard from in ages calling ten minutes after you stumble across her picture in your kitchen drawer. They're as real as finding your car keys in the very spot you swear you've looked ten times before. They're as real as a woman knowing the minute she gets pregnant because she senses the baby's soul. Just because these things are inexplicable doesn't mean there's anything to be afraid of. The world is the same as it was yesterday."

"I bet your boss would disagree with that. I bet he'd say if I think the world is different, it is."

She'd risen on her elbow to confront him. Now, on the monitor above his head, she saw the scribbling amber blip of chaos wink on and off. The picture—if you could call it that—looked deeper in the darkness, as if it truly were three-dimensional. She had the strongest urge to yank the screen off the wall and let it smash. B.G. wouldn't like her breaking his camera, but the outlet for her anger would have been sweet.

Eric must have sensed her agitation, because he stroked her hair. "You're safe here, Charity. B.G. wouldn't let you come to harm any more than I would."

Sadly, no one could save her from the kind of harm she felt

threatening her. Eric might think he believed these things, but he spoke about them as if they were no more than interesting ideas—with no particular relevance for him. She sat up and faced him, crossing her legs as she tried to get comfortable.

"I want you to understand why I'm upset," she said, surprised to discover how much she did. Usually, she resigned herself to her boyfriends being clueless.

He put one hand over hers where it gripped her knee. "I'm listening."

With her other hand, she dragged her hair from her face. "It's like . . . when I was little, a couple times, no matter what my mother did, she couldn't come up with rent. I don't want you to think she's lazy. Back then, she was constantly getting jobs. But she'd drop everything for a man. Move to Alaska, if he wanted. Living like that wasn't great for her résumé. So a few times, we had to live out of our car."

"That doesn't have to happen to you again."

His tone was so concerned she felt the need to reassure him. "It hasn't happened. Other things, but not that. I've always, always kept a roof over my head. The thing is, the first time we were homeless, it was such a shock I could hardly take it in. I mean, I knew my mom wasn't like other mothers. Other mothers wore track suits. Mine wiggled around in tight jeans. Other mothers taught their kids not to steal. Mine tried to convince me it was okay to take the salt and pepper shakers from restaurants. Even with all that, I never thought she couldn't keep me safe. I thought—like she always said—things would work out. When I realized the promise was a lie, it pulled the rug out from under me. Suddenly, I couldn't be sure of anything. Suddenly, the world was a scary place. These things you're saying . . . thinking they're true makes me feel like I felt then."

He was quiet, his thumb sweeping back and forth across the sensitive inner side of her knee. She could tell he didn't have an answer and, strangely enough, the fact that he didn't try to make her feel better was comforting.

"How old were you?" he asked after a bit.

"Eight or so the first time. We were in Houston that summer, because I remember the car was really hot."

He shook his head. "The worst thing that happened to me when I was eight was my mother forcing me to teach B.G. how to ride his bike. He read the encyclopedia when he was three, but ask him to balance on two wheels and he couldn't cope."

"B.G. was reading when he was *three?*"

"Two, actually. But because he didn't talk until later, nobody guessed. Once he did, my big sister, who baby-sat for him now and then, started calling him Rosemary's baby."

Charity laughed, glad for the chance. "That was mean of her."

"Yes, it was, but Dana grew out of it, and it was a little creepy to hear a toddler talking like a Ph.D."

"He must have had a tough time growing up."

"He did, though you'll never hear him admit it. He refused to let anyone make him afraid."

She touched the hand he'd put over hers, tracing the line of a vein. "You really love him."

"Yes," he said with unexpected ease. "He's the person I most admire in the world. When I was eight, of course, he was the person I most resented. Nothing like having a parent order you to make a friend. Mom was . . . is a stickler for doing the right thing. According to her, being born to privilege means you have more of an obligation to pay back. Nobody can stand up to her when she's on a mission." He grinned with a flash of orthodontically perfect teeth. "We have a saying in our house, that Mom wears the pants in the family and Dad wears the whoopie cushion."

"He likes to joke?"

"He likes to be obnoxious. He drove my sister to tears of

mortification once when he festooned her boyfriend's car in toilet paper. He's an officer at a bank, which means he has to save most of his jokes for us. I promise you, there were times when I would have traded both my parents for your mom—salt shakers and all."

He didn't sound like he meant it. He sounded like he loved his folks, like he forgave them all their flaws—further evidence that he was more grown up than she was.

She tried to shift the conversation to safer ground. "I guess you got over your resentment at being forced to be B.G.'s bud."

He laughed, memory warming the sound. "Even then he was impossible to resist. After a while, I realized I was never bored when I was with him."

"My mom wasn't boring," she admitted. "A lot of times she was fun."

He seemed to read the cloud on her mood. He took her hands, gathering them to his heart. "Since I'm up now," he said with a coaxing grin, "want to fool around?"

Charity smiled, silently thanking his mother for raising him to be nice. She was amazed at how open he'd been, sharing stories as if they were making friends. "Let's just sleep," she said, "that is, if you don't mind staying?"

"I live to serve," he said—which wasn't quite the answer she was hoping for.

The creak of Charity's mattress pulled Eric from sleep. His cheek was in her hair, and the sun from the little courtyard shone warm on his bare shoulders. Because Charity was in his arms, someone else must have lowered their weight onto the foot of her bed.

Eric really, truly didn't want to see who it was. His cock was stretched to its limit, routine enough for morning except for how badly it ached. It might not be physically possible to stay hard all night, but the way the ache reverberated in his balls and thighs made him think he had. He wanted nothing more than to bury himself in Charity. He didn't even want to wake her more than a little, just enough to drape her arms around him, just enough to push in and out of her sleepy softness until he shot her full to dripping with his pent-up seed. As far as he was concerned, she didn't have to move. She could lay beneath him like it was a dream.

Her husband would have had the right, he thought, the idea coming to him out of the blue.

Groaning, he rolled onto his back and opened his eyes.

Crisply dressed and shaved, B.G. sat with his arms crossed over his loose shirtfront. When his gaze caught on the tent Eric's erection made in the sheets, his cluck of mock disapproval roused Charity.

"Mmph," she said, struggling up on her elbows. "And here I was thinking I'd give anything to have the three of us hit the sheets."

Her froggy comment sent a perceptible jerk through B.G.'s frame. The flush that followed intrigued Eric. He marveled that his boss hadn't considered this possibility before. They'd taken guests together many times.

"You broke the rules," B.G. said with his trademark mild sternness. Despite his outward calm, a muscle ticked in his jaw. "As you are aware, both of you have something to answer for."

Eric suspected habit had Charity explaining, or maybe it was that B.G. actually did look ticked. Maybe it bugged him that his trusted keeper had encouraged the transgression. If that was true, Eric wasn't sure how to handle it. He couldn't remember the last time B.G. had been angry with him.

"Eric was comforting me," Charity said. "After I freaked out."

"The first climax was comfort. The others were indulgence."

"Fine." Charity thrust out her wrists so the sheet fell to her waist. "Slap on the cuffs."

Her breasts were bare and lovely. To Eric's relief, B.G. shook his head and smiled faintly at the show. It seemed their guest could coax anyone into a good mood. "At present, Eric requires my attention. His was the greater offense. You I'm handing over to Sylvia and Maurice."

"Fine," Charity said, feigning indifference as she swung naked out of the bed. "I hope I'm allowed to brush my teeth and all that first."

"You are," B.G. conceded, "but please don't dress."

He watched her flounce into the bathroom, obviously appreciating the twitch and bounce of her smooth young flesh. When she shut the door and burst into a defiant snatch of "Born to Be Wild," he cracked a grin.

Eric found her reaction less humorous. To him, it looked like bravado to hide hurt pride. "She'd respond better to a punishment that came from you," he said quietly.

"Perhaps." B.G. stroked the length of Eric's thigh through the rumpled sheet. The touch made his hard-on jump. "But I'd rather show her what I can do before I work on her directly. Specifically, I'd rather demonstrate on you."

"Lucky me," Eric said with a shiver he could not suppress.

"She'll see everything," B.G. promised. "Every shudder and bead of sweat. She'll wish she were you in no time at all."

By the time Sylvia and Maurice arrived at Charity's room, the masseuse had recovered from her earlier fit of gratitude. She also seemed not to have enjoyed whatever "seeing to" B.G. had arranged for her. The expression on her elfin face was petulant.

"I hear *someone* is due special treatment," she said, her fists digging into her waist.

"Stow it, Syl," Maurice said, a hint of steel beneath his amicable tone. "You had your turn in the spotlight when you were a guest. Now it's time to get with the new program—at least if you want Mr. G to keep letting you stay on."

"Do not imply that I'm a bad employee."

"Of course not. You live to please. That's why we're dressed like escapees from a beach movie." He rolled his eyes at Charity. "In case you hadn't guessed, she chose these things."

Their outfits were unusual: snug banana-yellow surfer gear. Sylvia looked lean and sporty in her bikini, while Maurice bulged pretty much everywhere in his clinging knee-length shorts. The rubberized cloth made his package seem even fatter.

"I don't know." Charity put her finger to her chin. "You look kind of hot."

"See!" Sylvia crowed. "In case you weren't aware, Mr. I-Want-to-Live-in-a-Pulp-Novel, some people have fetishes for this sort of clothes."

"And if they didn't," Charity put in, "they might develop one after getting a load of you two."

"Yeesh," Maurice said. "Women always stick together."

Sylvia turned her back on him. "Come on if you're coming. I'm not going to keep Mr. Grantham waiting."

"I know you're not," Maurice retorted. "You think he'll fall in love with you if you jump whenever he says boo. It's just too bad you don't jump as well when he's not watching."

Sylvia's answer to this was to smack his head.

"Exactly what am I in for?" Charity asked, trying not to sound uncertain.

Sylvia's face softened. "Nothing to frighten you. Mr. Grantham has a theory as to what will push your buttons best."

Unsure what to make of this, Charity followed with no more questions. She thought they were in the part of the complex that held B.G.'s room, because the halls were the same blank stone, free of the voyeur-friendly windows that distinguished the rest of the house. Thankfully, her escorts had stopped squabbling. After a short turn to the left, Sylvia flung open a thick steel door. She gestured toward something on the ceiling.

"The idea," she said, "is for you to feel secure."

The room she'd brought Charity to was a black, windowless cube with soundproofed walls and a marble floor. A huge flat TV took up one wall. What caught Charity's gaze most, however, was the object Sylvia was pointing out.

"Secure," Charity repeated, eyeing the contraption her caretakers were now lowering from the black ceiling. It was a complicated arrangement of leather straps and buckles, attached to hooks on the ceiling by silver chains. The thing looked like an S&M spider web. The leather, in particular, seemed well used.

"Very secure," Sylvia assured her. "We hook you up so your body weight is perfectly distributed. Even though you can't get free, you'll be comfortable. But maybe you don't trust the second string to do it right?"

It was a comment Charity herself might have made: self-deprecating humor used as a cover for bitterness. "I trust you," she said aloud. "I'm just wondering how I'll react. I've never done bondage this elaborate before."

"Tied to the bedpost with the boyfriend's shirt?"

Charity chose to take Sylvia's archness as a friendly joke. For all she knew, that's how Sylvia meant it. "Once or twice," she said. "With his tie."

"Whew," said Maurice, his imagination clearly running away with him. "Is it getting hot in here, or is it me?"

His humor cheered Charity. "Why don't you strap me in?" she teased. "And we'll see if the temperature goes up or down."

"I will turn up the air," Sylvia announced loudly, as if she didn't want Maurice to have even a moment of Charity's attention. "When Mr. Grantham starts his show, I'm sure everyone will need cooling down."

"There's going to be a show?"

Maurice had no chance to do more than open his mouth.

"Let her enjoy the surprise," Sylvia scolded.

She returned from the controls to help her grumbling partner buckle Charity into the restraints. One by one, padded leather loops were slipped around her joints, down to her finger bones. As the bonds began to bear her weight, the sensual languor she'd felt when she'd been stretched across the limo returned. This time, it was stronger. Charity might have stepped into this harness of her own free will, but now it held her prisoner. As she recognized this, her nipples hardened enough to hurt.

Quick to recover from his annoyance, Maurice grinned. "You good, babe?"

"She's excellent," Sylvia clipped out.

Without warning, she pressed the button for the winch that wound the central chain. Charity gasped as her feet were swung off the marble tile. The distance was at most a foot, but the psychological effect was great. She was helpless now, at the mercy of her caretakers. A stab of almost painful pleasure surged between her legs. It was hard to remember this was supposed to be a punishment when it felt so good.

"Careful," Maurice said. "The harness isn't supposed to leave marks."

"I'm fine," Charity assured him, her voice unavoidably husky, her body swaying slightly in the web.

"Well, you look fine," he murmured, his gaze sliding over her trussed-up curves.

Sylvia clucked like a mother hen. "Of course she's fine." Despite her caring tone, she adjusted the buckle behind

Charity's waist with a bit more force than required. "Who wouldn't be after spending the night receiving multiple orgasms from Mr. Berne?"

"It wasn't all night," Charity said.

"No, no," Sylvia agreed. "Not all night. Mr. Berne gave you only enough pleasure to help you recover from your shock. Terrible things, those quantum phenomena—though I have to wonder why *other* people aren't privileged to witness them."

"You're welcome to the privilege if you want it. I could have done without."

"Forgive me," Sylvia said, waving her hand in front of her eyes. "I didn't meant to suggest differently. I'm sure that, given a choice, you would have shared the experience."

Her gaze was now warm enough to disconcert Charity, beaming at her as if the two shared a secret.

"Uh, yeah," said Charity. "Why should I be the only one who gets freaked?"

Uncomfortable with Sylvia's sudden buddy-buddy vibe, she turned her head to Maurice. He looked mystified by Sylvia's complaint, which made Charity wonder how the masseuse had learned what had happened at B.G.'s dinner. Even if B.G. did have cameras in his private rooms, surely he didn't give Sylvia access.

The puzzle would have to wait. A flick of static marked the activation of the closed-circuit screen, followed by the soft mechanical whir of a camera. Charity did not doubt its lens was trained on her. Apparently, this "show" was going to be two-way.

She liked that thought as much as she liked the leather's clasp. This might be a punishment, but Charity's sexual enthusiasm had always been her best weapon.

*   *   *

Eʀɪᴄ guessed what was coming as soon as B.G. led him into the gray viewing room. It was a plusher version of the black room. It had furniture, for one thing—a chaise, a table, a small chess player's clock that many a guest had found cause to curse—all painted or upholstered monochrome gray. The shapes of the furnishings were exaggeratedly simple, like an artist's installation for a museum: *Study in Ash* by Pierre Moderne.

When they entered, the screen that displayed the room beyond was already on. Eric halted before it, his breath rushing unavoidably from his lungs. Big as life, the screen showed a real-time feed of Charity suspended, wide-eyed and naked, from a web of leather and chains. The restraints splayed her limbs and lifted her breasts while pulling her slightly off vertical. Tilted forward, she looked as if she were swimming up through the air. Her nipples were sharp and red, the inner curves of her thighs gleaming pale in the clear bright light. The curls of her pubic thatch clung together in wet little spikes.

Eric's toes curled on the silk-wool rug, knowing just by looking that she hung at the perfect level for a man of his height to slide in. His knees wouldn't even have had to bend.

Undoubtedly aware of this, B.G.'s hands settled on Eric's shoulders from behind. "She seems to be adjusting to that harness. No fight, but definite signs of increased arousal. I imagine you're sorry you didn't take your pleasure with her last night. If you had, you wouldn't be wanting her so much now."

"If I had, you might be punishing me even more. You might have excluded me from seeing this."

"I'm glad to hear you'd regret the loss." B.G.'s hold slid from Eric's shoulders and down his arms, ending to cuff his wrists just like Charity's were cuffed. His mouth pressed near Eric's ear. "Are you sure, though, that any of this is really punishment?"

"B.G.," Eric pleaded without a hope in the world for mercy. True to form, B.G.'s caress shifted to his back, his fingertips playing along the channels of Eric's spine. They had stripped before coming here, an intimacy Eric always liked, even if it left him exposed. Taking advantage of their undress, B.G. settled his erect shaft between Eric's buttocks, filling their division with pulsing heat. Positioned then as he pleased, he wrapped Eric in his arms.

Despite Eric's frustration, despite his sense of disloyalty, the embrace was as welcome as if he hadn't been touched for years. He hoped whatever B.G. was about to do wouldn't backfire.

B.G.'s lips came close enough for his breath to tickle Eric's hair. "I'm turning on the camera for our side," he warned, causing Eric's nape to shiver with delight. "Charity's going to see what happens when you're pushed too hard to hold back. She's going to realize how far she ought to be pushing you."

He stepped away as Eric fought a moan, hitting the switch that brought their room out of private mode. Then he drew a pair of leather shackles from a small gray box on the gray table.

It would have been easier on Eric if he hadn't watched B.G. move. His friend was at his most seductive when he was unclothed. Nothing else did justice to the elegant harmony of his limbs. Against the backdrop of gray, the colors of his skin were vivid. His cock, rising from his clean-shaven abdomen, throbbed hard and high. He was as stiff as Eric had ever seen him, certainly stiffer than he usually was this early in a game.

Eric grinned—wolfishly, he supposed, because his old friend faltered and frowned.

"What?" he demanded as Eric offered his wrists.

"I was thinking I'm not the only one who finds Charity's presence inspiring."

B.G.'s frown deepened. "Climb onto that chaise," he said, deliberately ignoring the comment. "I'm going to strap you to its legs."

The chaise was an L-shaped angle with a low back and no arms. Eric could rest his upper body on the end without the camera's view of him being blocked.

"You'd better oil me," he said, obediently stretching into position on his knees. His arms were long enough to flatten his hands on the floor. "I'm not sure you'll be able to squeeze that monster in without a ton of lube."

B.G. swatted his haunch with the leather cuffs. "You know I'm immune to flattery. Now behave, or this will go harder."

"I love harder," Eric said, some devil making him tease. "In fact, one day I'm going to tie you down so you can see how good harder is."

B.G. actually gasped. In all his and Eric's erotic adventures, he'd never given up formal control. Eric might have been on top now and then, but never with a true whip hand. To Eric's pleasure, B.G. didn't recover immediately. His lingering shock showed in his jerkiness as he stepped around to where Eric's arms draped the head of the chaise. Three tries were required to secure his first wrist.

His superior's discomposure made Eric laugh. B.G. had to kneel and kiss him before he'd stop. As always, the magic of his mouth reminded Eric who was boss. His hands strained automatically at the bonds, wanting to touch B.G., wanting to pull him close.

"Sh," B.G. said, laying calming fingers over his wrists. "Don't hurt yourself."

"Kiss me again," Eric demanded, gripping the wood instead.

"She'll be watching," B.G. warned.

"She wants to see," Eric came back.

B.G. hesitated only a moment before kissing him long and slow. Eric didn't think it was his imagination that his old friend put a bit more into it than before. Eric was breathless when he pulled away, and B.G.'s cheeks were pink. "Turn your face to the camera," he said as if to deny Charity might also be watching him. "I want our guest to see everything."

The camera was installed directly above the screen. To look at it was to look at Charity. Her lips moved, but the audio was turned off. *Sorry,* she might have said. Eric smiled and shook his head. No apology was needed. He was, very nearly, exactly where he wished to be.

⁂

B.G. watched his oldest friend lock glances with their newest guest and thought it ironic to be resorting to these false windows when a foot of solid wall was all that stood between the rooms.

Not really solid, of course. Matter was predominantly space, volumes upon volumes of it, far beyond most laymen's imagining. Comparatively speaking, if the nucleus of an atom were the size of a tennis ball, the height of the Empire State Building would be needed for its orbits, of which there might only be a few. That was space you could drive more than trucks through. Considering how empty "solid" matter was, human beings might as well be ghosts—or at any rate ghosts to him. B.G.'s understanding of the world was enough at odds with the general public's that he sometimes felt bereft of a tether to connect him to them. Eric made him feel real, and—oddly—so did Charity. She was lush and tousled in her web, flushed and fuckable. She mouthed something to Eric at which Eric smiled reassuringly.

Considering the warmth that shone from his old friend's eyes, B.G. wouldn't be surprised if he were half in love with her already.

His stomach clenched and a prickle of heat swept his face. Hormones, no doubt, and possibly a surge of stress. If it was stress, B.G. ignored it. Eric was supposed to fall in love this time, supposed to find the partner with whom he could finally live in a stable, committed relationship. Lately, Eric had been exhibiting the signs of a man unsatisfied with his state. There were recently married friends he didn't feel like seeing, long wistful minutes spent staring out of windows, sighs when he thought no one could hear. B.G. had seen these symptoms before. Wonder was, they hadn't developed sooner. In any case, he knew well enough what they meant.

Eric needed a white-picket, knight-in-shining-armor fence. He might deny the need in order to protect his bond with B.G., but without it, he could not be happy. As Eric's oldest friend, and a very poor candidate for white pickets—as previous partners had learned—B.G. had an obligation to do what he could to facilitate his friend's desires.

Desire was, after all, a formula he knew how to manipulate.

With this in mind, he slid his palm along Eric's back. Their guest could see Eric in all his glory. The fanning muscles of his shoulders, glowing now with sweat, were those of a keen athlete. He had a rower's arms and a cyclist's legs, both crying to be caressed. Disinclined to resist, B.G. smiled at the pleasure stretching Eric's toes. He'd never understood why Eric's strength called up his tenderness. Certainly, it shouldn't have today—not with his threat to tie down B.G. still ringing in his nerves.

That had been an unanticipated erotic shock.

Pushing away the memory, B.G. gathered his supplies and swung one leg to either side of the long gray chaise. He was behind Eric, a heat and a threat that made his friend tense up. Maybe he would be difficult to take without generous lubrication. Tense or not, he noticed Eric's gaze never wavered from Charity—not even when B.G. tipped a stream of oil over his tailbone.

Whatever the emotional underpinning of Eric's

fascination, B.G. knew he shouldn't waste this opportunity. He had, after all, planned it from all angles.

"Here's the agreement," he said. "Every minute you last past fifteen without coming is a minute you can spend, unsupervised, with Charity. No rules. No limits. No watchers. You can screw yourselves senseless if that's what you wish."

The offer was not what Eric expected. He bit his lip, either because the idea was so appealing or because B.G. had begun to rub in the oil. B.G. didn't have to remind him to spread his legs. Eric knew very well what B.G. required. He was, however, still using his brain.

"Ten minutes," he countered on a burst of air. "And every minute with you past that is worth two with her."

"Flattering." B.G. slid his hand around to cup Eric's balls. His scrotum was full and warm, already pulled up with excitement. A noise broke in Eric's throat. Gratified, B.G. ran a gentle thumb over his perineum.

At this, Eric gasped and squirmed.

"While I respect your determination to improve the terms," B.G. went on, "I'm afraid I really must insist on a minimum of fifteen. On the other hand, I am willing to concede that every successive minute is worth five with her."

Eric took a trembling moment to think.

"Agreed," he said, "but no hands or kissing below the waist. You're only allowed to use your cock."

B.G. smiled to himself. It was a hard bargain, but one he could live with.

"Done," he agreed and reached past Eric's shoulder to start the chess player's clock.

~~~

Charity held her breath in wonder. B.G. was stroking himself, working the oil into his erection with long, tight pulls that drew his shaft up and out. In front of him, Eric knelt on the couch, quivering with repeated shivers like a rain-soaked dog. His cock was even harder than his boss's, fighting gravity as it curved red and thick beneath his abdomen. The ache of wanting slid through Charity in rolling waves. To be there . . . To be touching them for herself . . .

Her bonds held her too securely to do more than twitch. She couldn't even curl her hands into fists.

"Aren't they beautiful?" Sylvia murmured, her fingers feathering coolly down her captive's hip. "You can see how much they want each other, how much they love to tease. It's hard to imagine anyone ever coming between that."

Charity didn't waste her breath answering. She suspected she wanted to come between them in a different way than Sylvia meant.

For Eric, the moment B.G. first pressed inward was always powerful. He didn't know how to guard against the sensation of surrender, the way it made him feel lost. His nerves buzzed with pleasure as his muscles tightened and then succumbed. Sweat rolled down arms that were bound too well to do more than tense.

B.G. had lubed the hell out of them both. Though the fit was tight, he made it in.

Relax, Eric told himself. *You can do this for Charity.*

B.G. grunted as he hit halfway, a pleasured sound that was as arousing as it was familiar. Slowly, letting Eric feel every inch, he dragged out again. They both shuddered as B.G.'s crown tugged Eric's tightened rim. When B.G. spoke, the words grated.

"I'll give you a handicap," he said. "I won't go for full penetration until we hit the five-minute mark."

*   *   *

Eric swallowed at whatever B.G. had said. Charity saw his
Adam's apple bob. He had closed his eyes, screwing them
shut even as his face remained stubbornly toward her. At
every thrust, the muscles in his legs went taut. The sound
was off, but she knew he had to be moaning. The thought
made her own throat sore.

It was hard to believe he could stand that much stimulation.

"Damn," Maurice cursed admiringly beside her. "Those
two give new meaning to slow torture."

The chauffeur's hand was between her legs, softly, almost
idly, stroking her labia. His erection, trapped by the stretch
of his yellow shorts, pressed the skin above her hip. Despite
the harshness of his voice, the roaring of her blood nearly
drowned it out. When Sylvia pinched her buttock, it just
felt good.

B.G. knew the moment he hit Eric's prostate, even without the rub of the little swelling beneath his tip. Eric's
moan went up half an octave and his back arched hard. B.G.
doubted Eric meant to do it, but the shift in position slid
him in so deep he was completely held. His own excitement
spiking, B.G. mouthed the solid muscle by Eric's neck.
Eric's skin was fevered.

"Easy," B.G. murmured, pulling out and sinking in again.
"If you try to fight the pleasure, you'll feel it even more. Let it
run through you. Let it fill you and then flow out."

"Can't," Eric gasped. "Can't be like you."

No one could be like B.G. No one could rub just the spot
that needed rubbing the minute it needed it. No one could

make the slightest pressure divine torment. Eric didn't
know what the clock said, nor could he say when he'd
started breathing in time with B.G.

"That's it," his torturer soothed. "That's it. Just relax."

But Eric didn't feel relaxed. Eric felt as if he were going
out of his mind.

"I want her," he said, gritting his teeth against a perfect
stroke. "Don't make me come too soon."

Apparently, both of them were drunk on lust. B.G.'s answer made as little sense as Eric's demand.

"You'll have her," he said, one hand sliding down Eric's
chest with the fingers spread like a starfish. "You'll have
everything you want."

True to their agreement, B.G. didn't touch him below
the waist. He left his hand on his sternum and held him up.
Untouched though it was, Eric's cock felt like lead, each
pulse a punch from inside. All at once, the weeks of waiting added up. He couldn't concentrate on anything but
holding back, and his mouth ran away with him as a result.

"I want you, too," he said. "I want to take you with her. I
want to tie us all together and fuck you from behind while
she fucks you from the front. I want you helpless between
us. I want you to come and come until you cry."

His body clenched in reaction to his own words. The
looming pressure of climax increased.

"Damn it," B.G. snapped, suddenly moving faster.

The change took Eric by surprise, enough that he didn't
guess why it had happened for another three jolting strokes.
Then he knew: B.G. had lost control. Undoubtedly trying
to regain it, he reached around Eric's shoulders, his hands
sliding bruisingly to Eric's wrists. The ploy would have
worked if Eric hadn't recognized what was going on and
taken heart.

"I'll give *her* control," he said, grabbing his chance. "I'll
give her a dildo and suck you off. I'll let her spank you like

Sylvia. As soon as you come, we'll bring you up again."

"Fuck," B.G. snarled, pounding harder, each stroke deliciously rough. His cock was like heated stone. "Don't—"

"Tied," Eric insisted, cutting off whatever B.G. had meant to say. Hanging by a thread, he dug his nails into his own palms. "Trapped. Nothing to do but take what we give. Fucked over, Benjamin. Fucked over from head to toe."

Eric didn't know if it was the threats or hearing his given name, but B.G. smashed through the edge. His breath rushed out as his hips jammed forward, his body quaking with the long climax.

The only thing that saved Eric was B.G. completely losing his finesse.

"God," he gasped against Eric's neck. He held there a limp, sweet minute before pulling free. Even with the pause to catch his breath, his first attempt at standing failed. Eric grinned as his decimated boss was forced to sit on the chaise's end.

He looked at the ticking clock, then at Eric, obviously stumped by how this had turned out.

Eric tried not to look too smug about the fact that he was still hard as hell. His attempt at modesty must have failed, because B.G. laughed.

"All right," he said. "For that performance, I have to invent a whole new reward."

Ten

No man had ever looked at Charity the way Eric was, as if he'd walk through hell itself to have her. Maybe he had walked through hell. She wouldn't have guessed he could resist someone he had as much chemistry with as B.G.

He hadn't climaxed. The flush on his face and chest was evidence of that—even without the ram-hard state of his cock. Here was a man who looked ready to blast off at a breath. Though she didn't know the reason, she knew he'd held back for her.

Despite this, he remained at the threshold.

She thought the condom he'd rolled on before stepping in was a nice touch.

"Out," he rasped to Sylvia and Maurice. "And turn off the camera on your way."

Sylvia looked like she wanted to argue, but Maurice took the matter out of her hands. "Don't blame you," he said cheerfully, opening and closing a camouflaged panel that held controls. "Have some extra fun for me."

He winked at Charity, mimicking shooting a gun a little lower than people usually did. When Sylvia failed to move, he dragged her out by the arm.

"Why does he care?" the masseuse hissed on the way. "It's not as if either of *us* can watch what's recorded in the system. Charity needs someone to look out for her."

Charity didn't listen for Maurice's answer or spare one ounce of worry for Sylvia's concerns. She knew she was safer with Eric than anyone. Her gaze was magnetized to him as he locked the door. The shape of his back was a classic muscled wedge, his legs as graceful as a running back's. Best of all, he had the strongest butt she'd ever seen.

"What's this about?" she asked as he turned around. "Why are you here?"

His chest rose and fell twice before he could speak. "We have an hour."

"An hour?"

"An hour to do whatever we want without witnesses."

"Oh," she said, his words not quite getting through her haze of lust. She couldn't stop ogling him up and down. She wasn't sure a man should be allowed to have sexy knees.

"I won it," he explained. "Because I made B.G. come first."

Her body understood a second before her brain, going hot and liquid. Her involuntary quiver made her sway in the chains. *"Oh,"* she said. "Please come kiss me then."

He came to her in three long strides, clasping her against him harness and all. Flattened by the tight embrace, his cock pressed her belly like a rod of living steel.

"I want you," he said between desperate kisses. "I don't think I can wait to get you out of this."

"Don't get me out of it. Pull me right onto you."

He'd tasted so good she had to kiss him herself. He moaned, then cursed, but the harness moved enough to swing her legs around his waist. In spite of both their impatience, she had to laugh. The height the restraints held her at might be perfect, but her arms were sticking out like a scarecrow's.

"Okay," he said, echoing her grin. "Maybe I have to undo you a bit."

She purred as soon as she was able to plunge her fingers in his thick, warm hair. A second later, a tilt of her hips put her where she wished.

He jerked as his burning tip met her opening. "You're really wet."

"Well, I was watching, big guy. You and B.G. were hot."

She could tell he liked hearing this. "God," he said, his hands tightening on her bottom between the straps. She thought he would kiss her, but instead his forehead bumped hers. "Look down at us, Charity. Watch me go in."

A hot flash swept her body as she did. He was barely in her, the edge of his crown swelling just outside. His veins were dark and distended on the thickness of his shaft, moving visibly with his pulse. Her body tightened and then relaxed as if it couldn't wait for him to push inside her. She'd never seen a man this hard. She was so excited she could hardly speak.

"Wow," she managed to breathe. "I'm kinda guessing this will be fast."

"Yes." He set his jaw and shoved halfway in. Charity gasped at the sense of fullness. "Can't do it any other way."

His growl of entry was true music to her ears. Wanting to ease him more than she wanted her own release, she tightened her legs and took the rest of him. They shuddered in unison when he pressed home.

The connection felt incredibly good, but there was no way he could stay as he was for long. Sure enough, a heartbeat later, his grip shifted on her hips.

"Hold on," he said, easing her carefully up his length. "I know I can't last. Just let me . . . take what I need, and I'll get you next."

But, for her, *next* was now. She was as primed as she'd ever been in her life, as soft and wet and on the aching edge. He didn't rush the way she expected. With amazing deliberation, he drove inside her: deep, soft blows, perfectly aimed to tantalize every part of her sex—and likely every part of his.

"Boy," he gasped. "Sweetheart. Yes. Tighten on me like that."

She couldn't warn him. She had no breath. But six thrusts had her coming, or maybe it was the sexy rumble in his chest that did the trick. When he felt her stiffen, that was it for him. Cut loose from any need to control himself, he went wild and pumped. The chains clashed furiously together above their heads.

"Yes," he cried. "Now, Char, ah—"

He sucked in a breath like he'd been burned, coming in bursts hard enough to shake his frame. The only sound he made was a forceful exhalation, but he did it again and again, counting out the throes of release. The final breath was long and silent.

"Charity," he sighed, his knees tottering.

He braced and heaved her up, making her gasp, but he was only slipping some crucial loop off the harness's main hook. The apparatus was arranged so that this released the tension in the other straps, allowing her weight to be lowered to the floor. This Eric did, following her down without once slipping from her body's hold.

She'd barely settled against the marble before he began to move between her legs.

"Mm," he said, as hard as most men would have been for their first go. "Yes, put your knees up by my ribs."

She could tell he was easier despite his hardness, enjoying the journey rather than racing desperately toward its end. She rocked in time with him, matching him thrust for thrust. He was tall for her, but somehow they seemed to fit. He made them fit, pushing up on his arms so he could bend his gaze to hers. He smiled every time her hands played along his back.

Their rhythm rolled like it was oiled.

"You are so pretty," he said. "I love the way your face telegraphs everything you like."

"I love the way you do everything I like."

He laughed softly and dipped to kiss her, a dizzying suck and draw of tongues. The sound had her flushing and newly wet. When he rose straight-armed again, his biceps bulging, he shifted his angle to catch a more sensitive pressure spot.

"Show off," she teased with a definite hitch in her breath.

His response could only be called preening.

She let him finish on his own this time, the matter settled with a raised eyebrow on his part and an urging nod on hers. She was glad he didn't insist on her going first, because she savored every second: watching his face go dark, feeling him tense, seeing his eyes grow heavy with sensation and then squeeze shut.

This is trust, she thought. *This is nakedness.*

He moved off her when he was done but not very far, propping his head on one hand while the other stroked her hair from her face. As his fingers trailed over her breast, the curve of his mouth was fond. "You know I'm going to make certain you get yours."

It wasn't a question, but she reassured him anyway. "I do. From what I've seen, your sense of fairness is highly evolved."

He toyed with the buckle that cinched her thigh. "Are you ready to get out of this?"

"Yes. I'm thinking the straps might get tangled when I'm on top."

"What makes you think I'll let you on top?"

Clearly joking, he undid her bonds good humoredly. When the last was free, she pushed him back and crouched over him like a cat about to pounce. His storm-gray eyes glowed up at her, not the least offended by being caged. She knew it wouldn't be long before he stirred again.

"You relax," she instructed, her fingertips gliding down his sweaty chest. "I'm going to explore all your not-so-little secrets until you feel more yourself."

"Good plan," he said, then stretched from tip to toe like he was the one who'd been released from bondage.

*   *   *

Some time later, a shrill, repeated ringing brought Charity's head an inch off Eric's fuzzy chest.

"If that's your cell phone," she said, her voice slurred from extreme satiation, "I don't want to know where you've been hiding it."

Eric laughed and helped her off him. She had to admire his ability to rise. She could only sprawl on the pleasantly cool black floor. Even more impressive, he strode to the panel where Maurice had shut off the camera. This time, she got a better look at what the soundproofing slid aside to reveal. When she did, she had to suppress a snort. The complicated touchscreen looked like something out of a James Bond film.

Fortunately, the missiles in this adventure were a lot more fun.

Eric bent closer to see what the computer said. "It's Mosswood's communication system. An outside caller. Someone's trying to reach me."

"I could have told you that," she said, one arm slung lazily over her eyes. "I'm ashamed to admit I didn't tell anyone I was here."

His quick inhalation told her this surprised him, but he didn't scold. With all the background checking he'd done, he must have known she didn't have the kind of friends who could do much to help her if she got into hot water.

"Call someone," he said with a touching seriousness. "If only to water your plants. You can let them know where you are without breaking your agreement. In the meantime, B.G. can arrange to have your calls forwarded. He's got a service that takes messages. No one expects you to be completely cut off." He smiled down at her where she lay, obviously felled by his sensual expertise. "Since you're out of camera range, do me a favor and don't sit up."

This wasn't a problem. The best Charity could manage was rolling onto her side to watch.

When Eric pressed a control, the screen flicked to life with the image of a woman in an expensive Ann Taylor suit. Its understated khaki green brought out the red in her sleek cropped hair. Her makeup was just as subtle, and just as flattering. The only jewelry she wore was a string of pearls. Charity was willing to bet they came from real oysters.

Despite the tension that gripped her neck, she didn't have much chance to be jealous. One look at the woman's face said she and Eric were related.

"Good Lord," were the first words out of the woman's mouth. "What happened to your shirt?"

"And *hello* to you, too, Sis," Eric muttered under his breath.

"Don't mumble," she said. "This is an important call."

"I'm shirtless," he enunciated, "because you called me unannounced."

Her perfectly put-together face frowned at the camera. She seemed to be peering at his surroundings suspiciously. "Is this line secure? I need to speak to you privately."

Eric sighed and dragged his hand through his hair. "This better be good, Dana. You are currently interrupting the best sixty minutes of my life."

"It's two-thirty on a Wednesday!"

"Your point being?"

"For goodness sake, Eric. Can't you keep it zipped at all?"

The way Eric balled his hands tempted Charity to squirm across the floor and comfort him.

Clearly struggling for control, he uncurled his fingers and pressed one palm to the spot between his chest and gut. "I assume you really do want to talk to me and aren't trying to make me hang up."

"Call me back," his sister said sharply. "At work. When you're alone."

She cut off the signal without a good-bye.

"Hm," said Charity, trying to sound light. "I'm sensing a bit of sibling rivalry."

"Try sibling infuriation, and you'll have it right. Fuck. I wanted our last ten minutes."

His expression was flatteringly close to a sulk. Charity put her hands out, letting him help her up. The smart thing then seemed to be to hug him. She was right because he immediately put his cheek in her hair.

"I'm sorry," he said. "I really should call her back. Dana may be rude, but it probably is important. B.G.'s switchboard makes everyone jump through hoops to get through."

"That's okay. I'm not sure I could have moved again anyway."

"You wouldn't have had to. I was enjoying just lying there."

She smiled at that, and he tilted her head for a kiss.

"Later," he said. "I promise."

She waggled her fingers in parting, but her mood had already dropped. She'd heard those words many times before. Only rarely had they been true. If that weren't bad enough, Eric had exactly the sort of sister she most dreaded, the sort of sister who viewed girls like her as sweater lint—not hideous, exactly, but definitely an embarrassment to be plucked off.

It was just as well Eric had asked her to stay out of sight. She didn't want to imagine what Dana would have said if she'd seen who her brother had unzipped for.

Eric's quarters were almost as private as B.G.'s. Though his were located above ground, the windows opened onto the surrounding woods rather than the hall. The room was peaceful, but after having spent the last hour with Charity, it was also way too empty.

"Jeez," he said aloud, pushing his hands through his hair.

He knew better than to do this. She was a guest. B.G.'s guest. In spite of this, his mind—no—his skin replayed her touch as he made love to her that second time. Her hands were tender and caring. The feel of them had slid through him as deeply as any orgasm.

He tried to tell himself she was too vulnerable. He knew her history. She must have touched men like that before. Charity would leap first and look later. Love wouldn't break her, but it also wouldn't make her smart. She needed it too much to wait until she was sure. This day's caring could disappear tomorrow.

His logic, inarguable though it was, didn't help. Even in the cool-blooded quiet of his room, he knew he wanted more of what they'd shared.

"Crap," he said, then reached determinedly for a shirt and jeans. He couldn't deal with this now. He had to get his head sufficiently together to call his sister back. Whatever she'd phoned him about, speaking to Dana tended to require more than half his wits.

Since she'd graduated from Georgetown, she'd worked for the government—the Treasury Department, to be exact. He'd never been certain precisely what she did, except that it involved accounting. He did know she was better at it than her peers. More than once, she'd been promoted, each advance marked by switching out her wardrobe and her car to more expensive versions of the same conservative items. Eric didn't understand this mode of celebration, but it seemed to satisfy her. If she had a personal life, she thought it too personal to discuss with him.

His personal life, on the other hand, she thought herself eminently qualified to pronounce about. He knew she'd be happier if he were straight, but the only sin she objected to to his face was his "flightiness"—B.G. being, according to her, the embodiment of that trait. Everything she considered wrong with Eric she blamed on him.

Or that's why she told herself she disliked B.G. The real truth was that Eric's older sister had never gotten over her teenage intimidation by the boy genius. Dana needed to be the one everyone turned to with respect. Dana needed a world where order and responsibility were valued above all else. B.G. broke every rule she believed in and was, as she put it, rewarded obscenely.

Reminders that the world wasn't as she wished would never be an easy pill for Dana to swallow.

Knowing this, Eric schooled himself to patience as he dialed her on his cell phone. Her snippy response didn't make keeping his cool easy.

"About time!" she said as if he'd made her wait hours. "What the hell is your freak of a boss up to now?"

Phone to his ear, Eric lay back against his bed's pillows. "You know something, Dana? You're not thirteen anymore. It's time to stop referring to your brother's lover as a freak."

"Sorry," she said, sounding it at least a little. "I'm just rattled. The men in suits paid me a visit. CIA, I think. They flashed their ID pretty fast. They were asking all sorts of questions about your boss—as if *I'd* know anything about *him*."

"That doesn't make sense." Eric ignored the implication that merely knowing his friend was cause for shame. "B.G. has ties to the government. Loose ones, but he does. If they had questions, his contacts could have taken them straight to him."

"All I know is they were very suspicious about something he worked on recently, presumably something with military applications. The weirdest thing was, they wanted to know if you'd mentioned seeing anyone in old-fashioned clothes."

Eric snorted through his nose. "You're going to have to be more specific than that."

"It's so ludicrous I hate to repeat it, but they seem to believe Mosswood has ghosts."

"Ghosts?"

"Don't ask me why they think so or why they care. I sincerely doubt paranormal activity was their central concern. As for what is, they wouldn't explain any more than I've told you—which is ridiculous when you consider it was *me* they were talking to. If they were smart, they'd beg me for help. No one's better at following money trails than me. But they just kept asking if I thought your boss was a loyal American."

Eric switched the phone to his other ear. "What did you say to that?"

"I said the last time we'd discussed politics he was six years old, and I certainly didn't bother to take notes. Eric, if B.G. is involved in something, anything, please tell him to be careful. These men were serious."

"I'll tell him," Eric said, "but unless they're concerned about his lifestyle, I can't fathom what they're bugged about. The work he does is primarily theoretical. Other people turn it into technology. On top of which, he's very cautious about security. Even I don't know the details of his projects."

"You be careful, too," Dana insisted. "I know you love the little freak, but there's no point letting him drag you down."

It was times like this when Eric wondered what alien ship had dropped his sister into the family nest. Despite the lessons of compassion their mother had tried to inculcate, the thought of putting affection above or even equal to following the rules didn't occur to Dana.

"Thanks," he said through gritted teeth, knowing that in her own ass-backward way she was concerned. "I'll call you back if I hear anything."

He didn't mean it, but the promise would reassure her. That, he'd discovered, was frequently the best way of dealing with difficult sisters.

Eleven

Charity was hardly the poster girl for Eddie Bauer. The plants she felt most comfortable with came in pots. All the same, she felt a sudden need to get outdoors. Everything had happened so quickly. Leaving Future-Tech. Coming here. Sleeping with Eric. Charity might be "adventurous," but any girl would need to clear her head after all that.

Eric's shirt and trousers were still in her room from the night before. Resisting the temptation to borrow, she dressed in her comfiest jeans and T-shirt. She was glad she'd had the foresight to pack them. No one could be a sex kitten all the time.

Happily, she had no trouble leaving the house. Security, it seemed, was most concerned with Mosswood's perimeter. The weather outside was a mist verging on a drizzle, cool enough to warrant shrugging on her blue hoodie. She followed a smoothly beaten path past the conservatory pool, across a short stretch of grass, and into the woods. The presence of planted beds and wooden benches told her she wasn't likely to get lost. People were supposed to walk here. The trail probably made a loop through the trees.

This assumption and the quiet had a welcome effect on

her nerves. So what if she was too attracted to Eric? For the first time in she couldn't think how long, she felt tranquil.

I'm all right, she thought. *I can handle this game.*

A break in the trees up ahead revealed a long, pine-blanketed valley. The mist was thicker at its bottom, a cloud condensing near the earth. Sheltered until now by forest, she'd forgotten a whole big world stretched outside. The reminder encouraged her to keep her head on straight. Her problems were small in the greater scheme of things. Electron-small, B.G. might have said.

When she spotted her host sitting on a stump in front of the view, it didn't even give her a start. Of course he was here. His presence was like what Eric said about thinking of someone moments before they called. However the coincidence happened, B.G. had his back to her and was wearing headphones. He wasn't moving to the music as she would have been. Instead, he looked like he was analyzing whatever played, too focused to remember to enjoy. That, more than anything, prodded her to intrude.

She touched his shoulder lightly, then sat beside him when he twisted around. The stump was plenty big enough for them both.

"Charity!" he exclaimed, pulling the earphones down around his neck.

Because he seemed pleased to see her, she leaned close enough to hear the tune. Sheryl Crow was trying to tell him that every day was a winding road. Charity smiled to herself. Her recent life was certainly proving that.

"I don't know, B.G., I wouldn't have guessed you were down with the rocker girls."

"Eric gave me this CD," he said as if he didn't want her misled. "I appreciate a taste of what other people listen to, but I'm afraid the eighteenth century is more my speed."

"M-M-Mozart?"

He laughed at the way she said it. "Yes. And thank you
for refraining from playing stupid."

"Yeah, well, just don't ask me to name any more
eighteenth-century dudes." Pleased with herself for getting
one right, she bumped his shoulder with hers. "You come
out here because Eric and I were together?"

"You're very direct, aren't you?"

"Yes, I am. It's hard to find out what you want to know
unless you ask."

He met the challenge in her gaze, decision moving behind his eyes. "Perhaps I was avoiding you and Eric," he
said. "Generally speaking, however, I find it more arousing
than uncomfortable to watch Eric perform. If you two enjoyed yourselves, I'm satisfied."

"Thank you for giving us the hour."

Rather than ask how it went, he patted the faded patch
in the denim over her knee. "You know, Charity, you have a
gift for making yourself at home with people—and for
making them feel at home with you."

"Yup, us sex kittens turn everybody warm and fuzzy."

"That isn't what I meant, and I think you know it. Speaking as a person who lacks a common touch, I can attest to
the value of that knack."

"You seem to do all right."

"Here maybe," he said. "Here no one expects me to be
normal."

Charity flipped her hand dismissively. "Normal is
overrated—and pretty rare. I've had bosses out in the real
world who were nutso compared to you."

He smiled at this, a private curving of his lips with his
eyes lowered. "Tell me, Charity: You like Eric, don't you?
You feel comfortable with him?"

She wasn't prepared for this change of tack. "Sure, I do.
He's—" She hesitated as she realized she had no idea how Miss

Manners would advise answering the lover of a man she'd spent the last hour getting sweaty with. "He's a good guy."

"A *good* guy."

"A really good guy. But I wouldn't, you know, fall for him."

"You wouldn't."

"No. That'd be dumber than my usual."

B.G. was peering at her now, and she wished he'd go back to keeping his thoughts to himself. As if this conversation demanded even more attention, he removed the earphones from his neck and shut off the music. He leaned forward over his knees.

"What?" she said, fiddling involuntarily with the zipper on her jacket. The stump beneath her felt very hard.

"I'm wondering why you say falling for Eric would be dumb."

"Well, duh, he's like Summer-in-the-Hamptons Boy."

"And you're . . . ?"

"Practically trailer trash. I mean, Mom and I never actually owned a trailer, but a few of the places we lived were almost as bad."

"Isn't that mode of thinking archaic? Don't you believe good-quality people can come from any background?"

"It's a cultural difference. It's knowing which forks to use, and trust funds, and being able to drive a yacht."

B.G. pursed his lower lip between his middle finger and thumb. Charity didn't understand how she could feel this defensive when she was totally convinced she was right.

"I'll concede the forks," he said after a pause, "and the yacht, although I don't see what bearing either has on the appropriateness of falling for someone."

"Fine," she said. "It's inappropriate because I'm a mess."

This comment required him to perch his chin on his hand. He looked like a skinny version of *The Thinker.* "Why do you say you're a mess?"

"Now who's playing stupider than he is? You read my file."

"Yes, and it reads like the account of a twenty-four-year-old with energy, intelligence, and not enough direction."

"Yeesh. You sound like my high school guidance counselor when I dropped out."

"You object to our age disparity then?"

The question startled her even though he had been acting kind of stuffy. "No way. You guys are, what, thirty?"

"Two."

"Big deal. I've dated men older than that—not that you could tell. That stuff about younger women going for father figures is a crock. Half the time, the older they get, the bigger babies they are."

"I'll take that as a cautionary warning."

"I didn't mean it that way. I don't think you'll ever seem like any particular age."

This seemed to amuse him. "You believe me to be immune from time?"

"Or out of it . . . That was a physics joke, in case you couldn't guess."

His eyes crinkled enough to remind her he was a sexy man—not that she could forget! "I appreciate your effort to communicate across our great divide."

"Haha," she said. "You're pretty funny when you want to be."

Without giving her a chance to see what was coming, he cupped her face, stared straight into her eyes, and touched his lips to hers. "Sweet girl," he whispered against her mouth. "No wonder no one can resist you."

His hands were the gentlest she'd ever felt, and his kiss pulled at her so softly she shivered, a response that doubled when his mouth trailed slowly down her neck. She fought to concentrate enough to speak. "So that's the way to win you over: tell you I get your jokes."

"Do you want to win me? Do you want to be intimate?"

His fingers snuck beneath the hem of her T-shirt to trace a tingling circle at the base of her spine. Despite the pleasure this inspired, her sense that he'd just slipped her under his microscope made her pull back.

"Why are you asking me that?" she demanded.

"Do you doubt I want you?"

They'd turned to face each other during the kiss, their legs automatically rearranging to get closer. What her knee bumped now told her he was perfectly capable of taking her then and there. Normally she would have let him. Here was a perfect distraction from Eric. Plus, she wanted B.G. back enough to think it would be fun. Of course, *normally* she wouldn't have been kissing two guys on the same day, and definitely not when she had kind of a serious crush on the first.

No matter how dumb her feelings were, and never mind the rules of the game, Charity believed in serial fidelity.

Most confusing of all, she wasn't sure how B.G. wanted her to answer. She'd never met anyone as hard to read as him. While emotion gleamed in his bitter-chocolate eyes, she couldn't have said what the emotion was. Instinct was all she had to go by, and instinct told her his question was more of a test than a come-on.

B.G.'s left brow lifted as her silence grew.

"I don't know what you want me to say," she confessed. "If there's a right and wrong answer, I have to tell you I've never been good at tests. Yes, I'm attracted to you, and yes, I think I'd like making love, but you seem most interested in that when your partner is desperate."

"You're saying you're not desperate for me." Like his friend, B.G. had a way of not quite asking a question. Unlike his friend, he could ask a question like that without seeming hurt.

"Well, how could I be after spending the morning with

Eric?" she asked reasonably. "That is what you want, isn't it? For me to be as desperate for you as I was for him?"

B.G. laughed, but it seemed to be at himself, some private irony she doubted he'd share with her. He rubbed his hand across his mouth as if to erase the loss of control. "The answer to that is *yes* and *no*. Appropriately quantum, you could say."

His evasion should have annoyed her. Instead, her chest squeezed with sympathy. It didn't matter that he was eons smarter and more sophisticated than she was. In that moment, with that rueful smile, he seemed the lost boy genius he must have been years ago. Belatedly mad at Eric for having disliked him, she smoothed the single shock of hair from his brow.

"We could turn the game around," she suggested tentatively. "See if I can make you as desperate for me as you are for him."

She flushed as soon as she said it, surprising herself, and surprising him into coloring up in turn. Was it wrong of her to suggest that he was desperate for Eric—especially when she was pretty sure it was true?

"Lord." He laughed again breathlessly. "Forget what I said about you making people comfortable."

"I could work on it."

"Making me comfortable?"

She had to grin as she swung onto his lap. "No," she said. "I was thinking I'd work on making you desperate."

B.G. didn't know how she'd turned the tables this handily, nor could he explain why he allowed it. He'd sincerely meant to keep her focused on Eric, to present himself as no more than the gatekeeper between her and him. In his experience, obstacles whetted interest. Could an hour they'd been given gratis mean as much as one for which they'd fought?

It troubled him that he wasn't sure of the answer anymore.

B.G. wanted her, and he was the rule maker. There were no obstacles to whet his interest. He wanted her simply because she was kind and warm and kissed from the heart. He knew she *could* play games. He'd seen her do it. But she wasn't playing them with him. When she wrapped him in her arms and kissed him, he would have sworn she was only doing as she wished.

Then again, maybe he wanted her because, in his mind, she belonged to Eric.

Unable to make sense of his responses, he slid his hands down her back and cupped her bottom close. The beat of excitement between her legs throbbed in counterpoint to his. Amazingly, at least amazingly to him, he was as hard as he'd been that morning before taking Eric. The only factor that prevented her from achieving her goal of making him desperate was that Eric had wrung him dry.

Was she magic, he wondered, to seduce him with no more than honest enthusiasm?

"Oh, you are a good kisser," she said, breaking free to nuzzle his throat, the tip of her tongue sending inexplicable skips through his pulse. "Every bit as good as Eric said."

He claimed her mouth again, afraid to go where her words were leading his mind. Clasping her tight, he rolled her off the stump onto the matted leaves and moss. He wanted to press her into the ground, to overpower her with physical strength alone—the simplest, and the oldest, game in the world. She was strong herself, her body sturdy beneath its curves. When she locked her shapely calves behind his thighs, their squeeze made sensation spike through his groin.

It felt better than it had any reason to.

Cursing, he pushed his hand under the waistband of her faded jeans, working it past her bottom to find her sex. She made a new kind of noise when his finger reached her slippery bud. She was swimming with arousal. Enchanted by the discovery, he drew an exploratory path around the small swelling, finishing at the tip of the shaft. Not knowing how sensitive she was, he didn't rub it, merely pressed it lightly with his finger's pad. Her breath rushed out against his cheek.

He wanted to feel that rush again when she came.

"Oh!" said a voice he didn't immediately realize wasn't hers. Charity beginning to squirm for escape gave him a clue.

Reluctantly, he broke their kiss and looked up. "Sylvia," he panted, too vexed at seeing her to pretend otherwise. "Why are you interrupting when you haven't been invited to?"

The masseuse turned almost as red as she had when Charity spanked her. "I . . . I was just taking a stroll." She wet her lips, her gaze going to the spot where his buried hand was touching Charity. Whether she wished she owned the hand or the pussy was debatable. "I could help."

"We're fine," he said as mildly as he could. "Go stroll elsewhere."

She nodded and backed away, appearing more stricken than his tone warranted, cowed in a way that triggered annoyance. He let her leave despite a twinge of guilt he knew he'd earned.

He'd recruited her himself from a spa in Victoria, dazzled by her hands of gold and her obvious submissive streak. She'd seemed to have plenty of spirit to offset it, and he'd thought her delicate beauty would inspire the rest of his staff.

Unfortunately, as soon as Sylvia's game began, she'd proved sullen and uncooperative with anyone but him and

Eric, rebelling in ways that led to no one's pleasure—least of all her own. She seemed to think she was too good to play with underlings. Even more problematic, she had a fondness for pain beyond what he felt comfortable administering. In the end, they couldn't please her, and she couldn't please them. She even bickered with Maurice, who could be relied upon to get along with almost anyone.

Because B.G. had felt bad about the failure of her experience, he'd given in to her request to stay on. Now he wondered if that had been wise. He sympathized with her awkwardness, but unless he or Eric watched her like a hawk, she seemed determined to put her foot wrong.

Maybe, he thought, *I ought to exclude her from our games. Maybe I ought to restrict her to the duties of her official job.*

When he returned his attention to Charity, she was biting her lower lip. Although he found the gesture erotic, he could see the mood was lost. Sighing, he pulled his hand from her and let her up. Even if his body argued, he knew he shouldn't have let his lust race out of control. That could only complicate his matchmaking. Irritated with himself, but still aroused, he watched Charity brush what leaves she could reach from her hair and back.

"Sorry," he said, recovering his manners enough to help. "I should have been more considerate of your comfort."

She looked adorably flustered, her cheeks bright rose and her hair tousled. Her lips were swollen from kissing him so hard. Seeing them, his own mouth buzzed. When her head lifted from her cleanup efforts, her eyes gleamed like polished amethyst.

"It's all right," she said. "Rolling around like that was fun. I'm just concerned about Sylvia. Eric sent her away this morning. Between the two of you, I think she's feeling snubbed."

"Sylvia knows the terms of her employment. She's free to leave any time they grow onerous."

Charity snorted. "Somehow I doubt quitting would make her feel better."

B.G. suspected this was true, but didn't want Charity worrying. "As I said, she knows what to do if she's unhappy." The way Charity furrowed her brow at him made him uncomfortable. He seemed to have disappointed her. Maybe she was right. If Sylvia didn't fit in, it was his fault for choosing her. Reluctant to discuss it, he held out his hand. "Shall we walk back to the house?"

"Sure," she said, the answer riding out on a sigh. "I think I've had my dose of the great outdoors."

Offering his assistance was a mistake. Her hand was distractingly small and warm, remaining in his even after she rose. The simple clasp had him tightening inside and out. He couldn't help thinking of other places she might hold him, places that would feel far superior if neither of them wore clothes.

He couldn't help wondering what it would be like to make love to her with no games at all.

"I've been wondering," he said, clearing his throat as he strove to get his mind back on track, "if you'd be willing to engage in an experiment."

She wagged her brows. "That depends on what sort of experiment." Suddenly she halted in her tracks, a look of horror replacing her amusement. "Oh, God. I hope you don't mean more freaky-deaky stuff, because I'm really not up for that."

"No." He put his hand on her shoulder, oddly moved by how slender it was. Women were fascinating creatures, their nature as elusive as the tiny particles he studied. Men were easier to be with, at least for him, but women possessed an allure nothing else could match.

"No," he said again, his voice soft to his own ears. "No more time displacements. Those phenomena, interesting as they are, are not something I'm able to produce on demand."

She turned her face up to his. "You sound as if you wish you could produce them."

"If I could . . ." His gaze blurred on a distant line of moss-veiled trees. "If I could, it would mean I understood more than I have thus far. It would mean I was getting closer to controlling a state of affairs with the potential to be hazardous."

"Eric swore it wasn't."

B.G. shook himself. Why was he talking about this? This was precious close to discussing his most private work. "It's only *potentially* hazardous," he said out loud. "Not actually, so far as I know."

"Boy." Charity gave her little snorting laugh. "Way to be reassuring."

"Trust me, you're in no danger of being accidentally sucked to the Middle Ages. I will admit, however, that when the time displacement occurred in your presence, coupled with the fact that you happened to witness it, the idea to suggest what I'm about to occurred to me."

He took a breath to keep his enthusiasm for the topic under control. Calmer then, he went on. "It's my theory that certain minds are more open to, and quite possibly conducive of, anomalous quantum events. Some unidentified quality in their brain waves prods the phenomena into happening."

"Oh, great."

He smiled at the way she rolled her eyes. "As I said, the condition isn't dangerous. It simply means that you may, *may,* do what every human being does more efficiently."

With her fingers shoved into her front pockets, Charity leaned one shoulder against a tree, looking—thankfully—more dubious than fearful. She might not know it, but she really was a born student. "What does every human being do?"

"Change their reality with their thoughts."

He said it gently, but that didn't help.

"Oh, jeez," she said.

"It all boils down to electromagnetism," he pressed on, knowing his next few sentences would be crucial. "Electromagnetic energy is the basic force-stuff of the universe, the same basic force-stuff of our thoughts. Our brains, you could say, speak the language of quarks. Before you ask, I'm not the only one who thinks this. Since the late seventies, many physicists have believed that consciousness plays a role in forging physical reality, that attention—for lack of a better term—can manifest as matter or events through the action of a focused EM field. As William James said, the power to move the world is in our subconscious minds."

"Yeah, well, you science guys stick together."

"William James wasn't exactly a— Oh, never mind. The question is, should you discount a potentially life-changing theory without testing it for yourself?"

She sighed, and he hoped he hadn't been so fervent he'd put her off. He held his breath as she dragged her fingers back through her hair. He had a strong suspicion the success of his ambitions for her and Eric depended on this moment's choice.

"What would I have to do?" she asked cautiously.

He strove to keep his excitement out of his voice. "Merely practice thinking about yourself differently."

"Differently how?"

"You'd have to stop calling yourself stupid, for one thing. You'd have to stop thinking of yourself as a mess. You are a quantum being, Charity. That means you contain all possibilities, including the possibility of being wonderful."

"Uch," she exclaimed with an intensity of disgust that took him aback. "That's positive-thinking crap. My mother was always doing that stuff, and let me tell you, it didn't work at all."

"Are you sure?" he said. "Maybe she wasn't actually—"

"I do it myself," she interrupted angrily. "Despite knowing it's a bunch of hooey. 'Don't be late,' I tell myself. 'Don't

be late.' And am I ever on time? I don't think so. Instead,
I'm the Queen of Late."

"Unnaturally late?" he said, his heart picking up a beat.

"Huh?"

"What you say to yourself is only part of the equation.
Where your true belief lies, where you direct your emotional energy, matters most. Wolfgang Pauli—he was a Nobel prize–winning physicist—and psychologist Carl Jung
collaborated on this very theme. They concluded that the
emotional component of thought—love, grief, fear—packs
more of a wallop than thought alone. It is our emotions
that cut through the sea of probability waves, collapsing
them into what we experience as reality. If you fear a thing too
intensely—like being late—you may well bring it to pass."

"Come on. Just because the guy won a prize doesn't
mean—"

"Isn't it true you're late more often than seems statistically possible? Aren't you late even when you've done everything a reasonable person would in order to be on time?
Doesn't it occasionally seem as if the universe is in league
against your success?"

"I—"

Her confusion was priceless, the way her expression
telegraphed how precisely he had hit the nail on the head.
He smiled to himself, knowing he had her now.

"I use these methods," he said quietly. "No one under-
stands how, time after time, I come up with solutions other
brilliant people miss. I understand, though: I do it because I
believe I can. Emotionally, I feel as if I have the answer before I do."

"But you're a genius," she said, her objection weak.
"That's what geniuses do. They think up smart stuff."

"If you knew more geniuses, you'd know that wasn't the
case. Some of us are virtually useless." He brushed his fingers

down her dove-soft cheek. "Just say it for me once: 'I am a quantum being, and I might be wonderful.'"

She threw up her hands. "Fine. I am a quantum being and, who knows, in some alternate universe, I might be wonderful."

He chuckled at her idea of compliance. "All right. I'm less than dazzled, but you can progress from this starting point."

He offered her his arm. With a grimace, she took it and began to walk beside him again. Triumph made his steps as light as air. Her next comment didn't bother him in the least.

"You have got to be the strangest genius there ever was."

"I've heard that before."

"I bet you have. Of course, since I like you anyway, it could be my taste in men isn't as sucky as I thought."

"Now *that's* an improvement."

"I wasn't doing anything!"

"Yes, you were." He was enjoying himself too much to hide his glee. "Face it, Charity. You can't stop the process now. The moment you said the words, your life began to change."

Twelve

B.G. Grantham was a freaking Svengali.

Without any assistance, Charity made it to lunch on time, where she participated in a conversation about world events. The meal was once again just the three of them, and B.G. and Eric were knowledgeable. All the same, not once did she betray her ignorance. Whatever topic came up, it seemed she had, coincidentally, happened to pay attention to it on the news. Facts that usually escaped her popped into her mind.

It was enough to make a pessimist eat her hat.

At one point, B.G. winked at her grumpy expression. "First flush of success," he said. "Keep it up."

Because Eric squinted at him, perplexed, she assumed B.G. hadn't told him about their experiment. She was tempted to deny she'd done anything but was too embarrassed to bring it up.

Besides, she had to admit she'd enjoyed not looking dopey for once.

To add insult to noninjury, even though she dawdled and refused to watch the clock, she was early for the appointment B.G. had scheduled for her with Sylvia. Considering

how awkward she felt about seeing the masseuse after their
woodland encounter, her punctuality was perverse.

"Bastard put a hex on me," she mumbled under her
breath.

Hexes seemed like perfectly rational explanations with
the weird pyramid room rising around her. The walls followed the shape of the underside of a flight of steps, with
subdued modern lighting beneath each rank. The glow increased the strange atmosphere. Eric's boss sure liked his
surroundings exotic.

When Sylvia arrived to set up her table, her disposition
wasn't any sunnier than Charity's. In short order, Charity
learned B.G. had talked with the masseuse since morning,
ordering her to perform her duties without "extras."

"You'd have thought walking up on you was a crime,"
she huffed as she pushed her magical hands up the slope of
Charity's back. The oil she used smelled like jasmine tea. It
amazed Charity that a person as uptight as Sylvia could
make someone else mellow. "He didn't even listen when I
said it was an accident."

"His decision might be temporary," Charity said. "He
doesn't seem like the kind of person to hold a grudge."

"He's a boss," Sylvia declared, as if she hadn't nearly cried
when he sent her away. "Not to mention a man. Give him a
taste of power, let him discover a few secrets, and he forgets
all about the little folks. You and I have to stick together,
Charity. Bigwigs like B.G. Grantham can't be trusted to
care about us."

Charity wasn't sure she agreed, but because Sylvia was
doing something spine-meltingly marvelous to the back of
her legs, she didn't waste energy on debate.

"Well, he certainly won't fire you," she said into the pillow of her forearms. "He'd never find another pair of hands
like yours."

"Hah!" said Sylvia, but the bark sounded satisfied.

*   *   *

When Eric found B.G., he was in his private suite. He barely turned at Eric's entrance, his attention occupied by a delivery from his personal shopper that was spread across his French-style, four-poster bed. Considering all the people on B.G.'s payroll, he never had to leave Mosswood. Everything he wanted came to him. With an inner nudge of worry, Eric realized he couldn't recall the last time his boss had traveled off the grounds. That couldn't be good. B.G. used to go out at least once a month.

True, B.G. seemed perfectly content. Maybe this sudden worry was nothing but Eric stalling. He couldn't help his reluctance to share Dana's news—not when it threatened to disrupt their latest game. Whatever the conflict in his feelings for their guest, Eric didn't want their play cut short.

"What do you think of this dress for Charity?" B.G. asked, lifting a brocaded cream-and-gold sleeveless sheath from a tumble of pink tissue.

It was a fancy thing—stiff and shaped by darts, suitable for anything from the theater to dinner at an embassy. The tailoring combined sexiness and class in one package. B.G. was often eerily intuitive, so Eric shouldn't have been surprised, but this was exactly the sort of dress he pictured Charity wearing in his fantasies.

He struggled to answer casually. "I think Charity brought her own clothes."

"Yes, but she didn't pack any similar to the outfit you picked for her. I know you like that ladylike retro look." B.G. turned from the bounty on the bed with a long, flat box balanced on one palm. Lifting the lid revealed a length of cream-colored satin. "Raoul tells me evening gloves are back in style. I think I'd enjoy seeing Charity in these myself."

Eric would enjoy it, too, especially if he stripped her down to nothing but.

"Dana called," he said abruptly. "There's been some trouble at her office."

B.G. set the glove box behind him, suitably serious. Dana would probably be surprised—and vaguely offended—to discover her old nemesis bore her no ill will. "Is she all right?" he asked. "Can I do anything to help?"

With a sigh, Eric related his sister's conversation. To his dismay, his boss was not as surprised as he should have been.

"Central Intelligence Agency?" B.G. mused. "I don't know anyone who works for them."

"But you do know what they're concerned about?"

"I *might* know," B.G. clarified. "But if it's what I think, they're wasting their time. No more than a dozen people in the world would even suspect I'm working on this project. You know how I am about security."

Eric knew. He also knew no system was foolproof. "Even the White House has leaks."

"There's nothing to leak. Thus far, the results of my research have been unpredictable, impossible to replicate, and are—as far as I can see—bereft of practical applications."

B.G. looked so frustrated by this, Eric couldn't doubt he believed what he said. Hoping he was right, he put his hand on B.G.'s arm. "They're not investigating you over nothing. They're not afraid you might be a traitor because they believe whatever this is has no practical use."

"I hope *you* know I'm not a traitor."

"Of course I do." Eric touched B.G.'s mournful face. "I trust you to protect this country's interests—hell, this world's interests—more than anyone I could name. That doesn't mean I think your safeguards, however good, are impossible to crack. Human error is always a factor, as is human curiosity. Rumors get around, B.G., even among scientists."

"Especially among scientists," B.G. said with a muffled laugh. Despite his amusement, he seemed a little startled by the strength of Eric's faith in him. "I'll give the security team a heads-up. Have them nose around the staff, maybe double-check Dave Massey's profiles for our last few guests. If they find anything, I'll call your sister myself."

The crooked grin that accompanied this offer said B.G. had at least a suspicion of Dana's attitude.

⊷≺∾⊱

Charity wasn't late, but she was lost. Though she'd found the pyramid room just fine, reversing the directions was a bigger challenge. Now she stood in an underground passage paneled in dark wood that made her feel like she'd stumbled into Queen Elizabeth's country manse.

Had she been in a better mood, she might have marveled at the expense of shipping all this junk from ye olde England. She couldn't doubt it was the real deal. Two suits of dented armor challenged her from either side of a cold fireplace, while the head of a long-dead stag cast gloomy shadows down its mantle. The deer's tapestry twin hung, moth-eaten, on the opposite wall. The lords and ladies who chased him displayed none of Charity's doubts about where to go. To make matters worse, the lights only turned on when she was beneath them. Charity needed to see farther to get her bearings.

Too bad B.G. hadn't put a quantum hex on her for this.

"It's okay," she murmured to herself, resisting the urge to curse. "Just retrace your steps. You'll be fine once you get back to halls that are lined in stone."

She bit her lip, gazing reluctantly into the darkness from which she'd come. She'd been having creepy feelings ever since leaving Sylvia—skin-crawly sensations like she'd had the first time she explored Mosswood, as if someone kept slipping just beyond her field of view. Back then she'd thought it was funny. This afternoon, she'd have been grateful for even Sylvia's company. When something skittered across the parquet ahead of her, she let out a shriek.

Mouse, she thought through her jumping nerves. A rodent seemed preferable to most of the "anomalous phenomena" she could imagine happening in B.G.'s house. She couldn't calm herself, though she knew she was being too suggestible. No way was her supposedly freaky brain creating real monsters.

Warily, she turned back the way she'd come. If she'd had her druthers, B.G. would have been banned from sharing his theories with people like her.

She froze a second later, every cell trembling. What was that swishing noise? Didn't it sound like a dragging skirt and petticoats? B.G. said she shouldn't fear being accidentally sucked into the Middle Ages, but that didn't rule out the chance of ghosts.

Maybe they'd been shipped right along with the furnishings.

"Sylvia?" she said—or tried to. The name came out a whispered croak.

Anyway, it couldn't be Sylvia. If a real live person were making that noise, the lights where they stood would have come on. Damn B.G. anyway for being so concerned with saving energy.

I'll go the other way, she thought, spinning on her heel. Sooner or later, she'd end up somewhere she recognized.

She walked faster in her nervousness, trying not to run on legs that felt as stiff as two-by-fours. She wasn't sure if she still heard the swishing or just the panicked rush of her blood. She had long since clutched one hand to her breast.

Stupid, she scolded herself. *If anyone saw you, they'd laugh their asses off.*

The scold couldn't soothe her, but a strip of light from an open door in the darkness up ahead had her sighing gustily in relief. She prayed there'd be a person to go with it.

Or a phone, she thought with a surge of hope. Even if the room was empty, the switchboard could call Eric to lead her back.

The room wasn't empty, but its occupant was too engrossed to notice her arrival. He was a tall lunk of a guy:
cute, but more like a football player than a techno-geek. For
sure a techno-geek was what he was, though. He sat in a
chair that put her ergonomic number back at Future-Tech
to shame. It was shiny stainless-steel mesh with gas suspen-
sion, a tilting seat, and motorized wheels. Plus, it had a
cupholder. Awed, Charity came to a halt as he cruised a
horseshoe-shaped console topped by a huge monitor. From
side to side, the guy played the controls like a record pro-
ducer in a studio, splitting the screen, then quadrupling it,
then zooming in on different areas.

With a start, Charity realized all the pictures showed
Sylvia. Sylvia massaging various members of the household. Sylvia pouting while being tied to a column stark
naked. Sylvia—here Charity flushed—being spanked to orgasm by the pool. Finally, like a TV addict finding his favorite show, the techno-geek allowed an image of Sylvia
riding Maurice to fill the screen. The chauffeur, whose
hands were shackled to a mission-style headboard, looked as
if the masseuse was doing a particularly inspiring job. His
face was twisted, his legs twitching spasmodically.

If this drama was happening now, Sylvia was either dis-
obeying B.G.'s new orders, or she'd been set free from them.
Charity noted how determined the masseuse appeared. *Don't,*
her lips very clearly said to Maurice, the order succeeded by
a slap. Charity assumed he must have given some sign he
was about to come. Whatever rules Sylvia was or wasn't following, she wasn't "living to please" Maurice.

She was surprised Maurice let her treat him like this, but
maybe he'd been left tied up by someone else and hadn't had
a choice. Maybe, now that Sylvia was barred from the game,
she took satisfaction from wreaking havoc on those still allowed to play. Maurice did have the look of a man being
forced to enjoy something against his will.

"Is that live?" Charity asked.

The techno-lunk's jerk of surprise sent his coffee flying out of its holder. Now that he'd turned toward her, Charity eyed him curiously. A minute longer and he would have spilled more than coffee. His fly had been gaping all along, revealing an erection as stiff as it was high. His cock wasn't as thick as Maurice's, but it was an impressive shade of purply red. Charity noticed he was uncircumcised. His foreskin was stretched around the middle of the head as if he was so swollen it was stuck.

Blushing fiercely, he spun his chair away to zip up.

"You're not supposed to be here," he said over his shoulder, obviously struggling to get everything back in. "Mr. Grantham didn't approve it."

"The door was open. I was told I could go anywhere that wasn't locked."

"It should have been locked," he huffed. "And you should have knocked."

He'd turned back to face her, his finger wagging at her face. His erection seemed not to have relaxed, pressing behind his zipper like a curving pipe. The bulge was at odds with his self-righteous pose, and she couldn't resist teasing. She tilted her head at the silent screen where Maurice's image was gasping like a fish. No matter what consequences he faced, the chauffeur was about to blow.

"That Sylvia sure is hot," she commented casually. "I can see why you'd want to watch her work."

"I was checking files," said her accuser, his gaze clearly wanting to follow hers to the screen. "To test if they'd been recorded right."

Charity smiled at the flimsy lie. She put her hand on his shoulder, feeling how close his sport shirt was to being soaked with sweat. At her touch, his breath came faster, maybe with fear, maybe with excitement at being caught. She was kind of aroused herself, the inseam of her jeans digging insistently between her legs. She didn't think this man was one of B.G.'s players, but she had no doubt she could have seduced him. He was too turned on to choose a careful path. Oddly enough, she had no urge to take the risk. Keeping him in suspense seemed equally interesting. She imagined this was a shadow of the thrill Eric and B.G. experienced.

"Tell me," she said, her voice sultry. "What's your name?"

"Michael," he answered suspiciously.

"Well, Michael, I'm thinking you and Maurice look a bit alike. Maybe you've been picturing yourself in his place . . . while you 'check files.'"

"Don't get her into trouble!"

His plea confused her. Frowning, Charity perched on the curving edge of his console. "Why would I get Sylvia in trouble? Maurice could complain as easily as I could. Unless—" Michael paled as she paused, causing a spurt of adrenaline to warm her veins. "Unless you've been letting her in here to watch with you?"

The moment she said it, Charity knew it was true. How else could the masseuse have known about her jumping wineglass? She doubted there were cameras in B.G.'s rooms, but Sylvia could have heard her and Eric discussing the incident in hers.

"It was only a couple times," Michael begged. "Sylvia deserves a treat now and then. I don't think Mr. Grantham and Mr. Berne really even see her. Most of the time, they treat her like furniture."

"That may be," Charity said, "but breaking Mosswood's security isn't your call."

Listening to herself, Charity could hardly believe her ears. Never mind she didn't like the thought of Sylvia watching her unawares, Charity sounded as prissy as an old school marm. Despite her consternation, she was grateful when the prissiness did its job.

"I know," Michael said, his head hanging. "Please don't report me."

If he'd been part of the game, this might have been an invitation to torment him more formally. Instead, Charity was obliged to make a real-life choice. She knew how persuasive Sylvia could be, even if B.G. didn't. Maybe it was a female thing, or maybe bigwigs never realized the mischief littlewigs could get into. From the corner of her eye, she saw Sylvia tear herself off Maurice while he shot impressively into the air—not much help to her decision, though she hoped he didn't end up regretting his pleasure.

"If I keep this to myself," she said, "you have to promise never to do it again."

"Absolutely," he said, a little too readily.

"I mean it." In a fit of ingenuity, she grabbed what had to be the key to the room from a hook. She shook it warningly in his direction. "I can check up on you unannounced."

Michael swore he'd never dream of breaking his word. This was the best job he'd ever had. He didn't want to risk losing it. Charity believed him . . . up to a point. His promise would wear off eventually, especially if Sylvia wanted it to.

I ought to tell B.G., she thought, then shook her head. She didn't care how that Svengali tried to remake her. Not for anyone would Charity Wills become a tattletale.

After her cowardly reaction to getting lost, Charity felt the need to reassert her nerve. One outfit she'd packed suited her purpose perfectly. Bought as an act of defiance after being fired from her waitress job, it included shiny red leggings made of PVC with Stripperella-style laces running up the legs. The things required twenty minutes to put on, and she took satisfaction in being late as a result. Sadly, her backward triumph was spoiled by the fact that dinner had been switched from B.G.'s suite to the dining room. When she reached it, neither he nor Eric were there.

The space she'd been rerouted to was dramatic: the polar opposite of the creepy Elizabethan hall, with sheets of windows and a ceiling so high you could bungie jump off the colorful Dave Chihuly chandelier. Both the table and chairs were clear plastic copies of Louis the Something originals. *Ghost furniture,* she thought, pushing back a shudder. The long line of chairs looked funny with only two seats filled.

"Just us," Maurice said with a smile of lower wattage than usual. A trio of fresh scratches on his neck suggested the scene Charity witnessed might have been recent—that, and the two empty seats between him and Sylvia. "Mr. B and Mr. G had business that couldn't wait."

For the sake of the chauffeur's feelings, Charity hid her dismay. Chances were, he was glad B.G. wasn't there, even if he hadn't minded his previous punishment. Sylvia, the likely instigator of his sin, simply looked grim. She waved her fork in hello, already tucking into a blackened tuna steak.

The food *was* good, but the masseuse ate as if she feared someone would steal her plate, her forearms defending it from either side. Then again, maybe she wasn't supposed to be eating with her and Maurice anymore. Charity considered mentioning her chat with Michael, then decided against it. Sylvia was apt to take her interference as a challenge. Given the volatility of her moods, discretion seemed the better part of valor to Charity.

She finished her dinner with as little talk as she could manage, declining Maurice's invitation to a friendly round of pool. Everything seemed flat without Eric and B.G., the game barely worth thinking about unless they were around.

She didn't regret turning down Maurice until she returned to her room where the quiet and the shadows were the last things she wanted to face. Determined to keep her mind occupied, she showered and dressed in a yellow silk camisole and tap pant set. Her legs were shaved, her skin nicely moisturized. She considered repainting her nails, but they weren't chipped. She sighed loudly when she saw the time. Eight thirty-two. If she wasn't careful, she'd be creeping to the library to get a book. Frankly, she doubted the Sherlock Holmes room would ease her fears.

Since she was little, she'd had an irrational terror of ghosts. One of her mother's boyfriends found out about the phobia and decided it would be fun to pretend every creak in his old Massachusetts farmhouse was the shade of his dead grandma. Charity had been twelve, old enough to act as if she thought the taunts idiotic. Nonetheless, her mother's failure to step in, coupled with the fact that she'd laughed along, had left a scar. A stranger guessed she was afraid. Why couldn't Charity's mom?

To this day, she couldn't watch a commercial for a horror movie without wanting to switch it off.

"I am a quantum being," she recited as she sat in the center of her bed hugging her knees. "I spit at ghosts."

It was a measure of how upside down her world was that this mantra made her feel better.

"I am a quantum being," she said again to the ceiling. "I am unbelievably brave and wonderful."

Unfortunately, when she flopped back on the pillows, she was still lonely.

"If I am a quantum being," she said more sternly, "my astonishing mental powers will call Eric to my room."

She nearly choked on a gasp when a knock sounded on her door. "Who is it?" she said, having failed to see the person cross her window wall.

"It's Eric. Who are you talking to in there?"

She jumped off the bed with her cheeks gone hot and her heart pounding. She told herself not to be silly. Eric had already been at the door. No way could her words have called him. Nonetheless, she turned the knob with a sweaty hand. Eric peered at her curiously as he walked in.

"I was talking to myself," she said. "Like any self-respecting nut."

"Glad to hear it. I wouldn't want to think you were getting into trouble with someone else." He held up a small, handled bag stuffed with tissue. "I brought you a present—in case you were thinking I was neglecting my duties as your keeper."

"A present!" She plopped on the bed and held out her hands. Grinning, Eric handed her the gift.

"Let's see," she said, digging through the wrapping. "Pink velvet wrist cuffs—very feminine—some sort of minty-smelling rub, and—wow—a gorgeous pair of evening gloves!"

"B.G. picked those."

"B.G. has good taste—not that I could doubt it with you around."

With an endearing grimace of denial, Eric sat beside her. "I noticed you liked being bound. I thought you might enjoy a variation on the theme."

"Just to keep me revved, right?"

"Yes, just that for tonight."

They looked at each other, blue eyes to gray, the electricity between them abruptly strong. She knew they were both remembering this morning—being skin to skin, straining in unison for one more explosive climax.

Impulse had her touching his knee. "You know what I feel is more than the game."

His gaze had dropped to follow his finger beneath the slippery strap of her camisole. The tease made the tips of her breasts tighten. Reluctantly, he looked up. "It's always more than the game. People can't help being human."

"Does it always feel like this?"

"No," he admitted, catching his breath when she slid her

hand up his thigh. He was hard already. A long, firm ridge met the press of her palm. She wanted him to say more than *no,* but he bent to kiss her instead, the roughness of his mouth, the slightly less-controlled passion a pleasant contrast to B.G.

"Would you like to do this here?" he asked once he had her pulse tripping. "Or would you prefer I take you somewhere else?"

Your room, she wanted to say, but his earlier silence made it impossible. "Here's good," she said, "or anywhere there won't be ghosts."

The words slipped out unthinkingly. Eric looked startled.

"I thought I heard one," she explained. "When I was lost in the hall with the big stag head."

His hands molded soothingly over her shoulders. He appeared to be deciding what to say. "We've had guests get spooked before," he said carefully. "Mosswood can be an intimidating place, but it's always turned out to be a squirrel or something sneaking in from outside."

"That's what I was hoping." She didn't mention it must have been a giant squirrel with petticoats. She couldn't confess that to Eric, though she suspected she'd have told B.G. He wouldn't have talked to her as if the wrong response would shatter her fragile grip on reality.

"Maybe I should distract you?" Eric suggested. "Take your mind off your fears?"

He seemed a bit too eager to get her off the topic of ghosts. Not liking it much herself, she slid her arms around his neck willingly. Her mood improved the moment he pulled her close. His kiss was delicious. The problem was, as their clinch grew enthusiastic, she felt as if she'd time-traveled back to high school and was being forced to act like the goody two-shoes she never was, squirming in her little panties without any hope of relief.

Eric was better at this delayed gratification stuff than she was, but soon even he needed more than groping her through her clothes. "I want to take this off," he panted, tugging the hem of her camisole.

Charity was too breathless to do more than nod and lift her arms. She let him peel it off, followed by the tap pants. Then, with two spots of color blazing in his cheeks, he held out the evening gloves. She could tell the thought of seeing her in them pushed a few buttons. When he spoke, his voice was hoarse.

"Put these on first, please. The cuffs need to go on top."

Licks of fire danced along her skin. She wanted to be tied again, wanted him to do anything and everything he could think of—not that she intended to give in without bargaining.

"Take off your belt," she said, "and open your pants. I want to see how much you like watching me pull these on."

He stared at her, then did as she asked in jerky motions. The belt buckle clanked and was tossed away. Reaching into his tight white briefs, he settled his heavy erection onto the waistband, his balls bulging impressively behind the cloth. The forward thrust of his shaft was aggressive, even just sitting there. Watching it, she was reminded of the technolunk with his foreskin caught on his glans. The memory sent more heat cascading to her sex. Without being told, Eric unbuttoned his shirt as well. His six-pack was worth an ogle, but even better was the way his muscles flicked like a horse's at the touch of her eyes.

"You are so hot," she said, unable to hold back a grin. "I could just eat you up."

His lungs worked faster as she turned the donning of the gloves into a reverse strip-tease, first the left hand and then the right. Their hems reached above her elbows—a smooth, form-fitting clasp. One by one, she pushed the fingers snug.

Naked except for this, she wondered if she looked like a

lady now. Looking like one was all she could hope for, but with Eric's reaction as a reward, she figured it would do.

"Good," he said, a smoky breath of sound. "Now you're ready for the rub. Sit on your heels and flatten your hands on your thighs."

"I'd rather touch you. I'd rather hold your cock in my glove."

His erection jumped, but he shook his head. "Later," he said. "First I'm going to prepare you."

As she accommodated his request, she had the sense that they could happily exchange orders like this all night, shifting control back and forth, getting more excited as they went along. Her nipples tingled as he opened the jar of ointment, then grew hot when he smoothed it around. Their circles plumped beneath the mint-infused emollient. The scent was too distinctive not to recognize.

"This is what B.G. used on you."

"Yes," he said. Her reminder had his pupils expanding until no more than a ring of iris remained—the blue that sweetened his gray. "It won't numb you out. It's safe to use on other things."

He dipped his finger into the jar, then dragged a line of heat from her breastbone to her navel. There he circled, wet his lips, and asked permission with his eyes.

He wanted to rub her between her legs.

"Yes," she said. "Go ahead."

He took the hood of her clitoris between his finger and thumb, working in the ointment. After all their teasing, the direct stimulation came as a shock. "There," he said, "that should make you feel nice and hot."

It made her feel nice and crazy, the minty stuff sensitizing every nerve the sexual hot button had. Suddenly she understood how men could think of their penises as separate from themselves.

"That's enough," she gasped when his gentle rubbing

threatened to get too good. Her pussy was so wet she felt ready to overflow. To her relief, he lightened his touch, now only drawing the pad of one finger around her outer labia.

"You're beautiful," he said, his erection too stiff to do more than vibrate. "All flushed and peeping out."

"I'll bet," she panted. "I feel twice as big as normal."

He kissed her as gently as B.G. would have, reaching behind her for the pink velvet cuffs.

"Wait," she said, stealing his line. "Let me touch you."

He shook his head.

"Yes," she insisted, stroking the glove down his face. "I won't be able to once you tie me up."

"I'm in charge."

His words were soft, but her response was even more so. "*We're* in charge. Together we make it better for each other. Come on, Eric." She rose on her knees to lick the lobe of his ear, drawing a tiny shiver from his shoulders. "Let me rub this satin up and down your prick."

He laughed at the word, then eased back. "Do it lightly," he said: his compromise.

"Very," she agreed.

"And slowly."

"As slowly as I can."

She clasped him quivering in her hand, then did the one impersonation she could pull off. "You're so big, Mr. President," she said girlishly. "I think I might need two hands."

"Jeez," he said, recognizing her Marilyn voice.

That's it, she thought. *That's the button that explains his fascination for these gloves.*

"Could I kiss you?" she lisped, delighted with the success of her guess. "I know it's disrespectful, you being such an important man, but I'd really like to taste that little bead of cum."

A shudder was her only answer. She bent, her breasts

brushing his thighs, the very tip of her tongue curling out. The crown of him was smooth as silk.

"Oh, God," he breathed, the words shaking.

"Yes, Mr. President?"

He put his hands behind her head. "Suck the tip," he said. "Just that. Hold the rest of me with your gloves."

She did it, the gentlest, slowest blow job she'd ever given, one that wasn't supposed to end in climax. Even so, she couldn't draw it out very long. Each time she stroked him, he jerked. He seemed to like the brush of the gloves as much as that of her tongue. After far too few minutes, she sat up to let both their excitement ease. He was really breathing hard now, his hair clinging to his face with sweat. She pushed a lock of it back.

"I've been meaning to ask you," she said. "About B.G. He seems to have totally Olympic sexual control. So I'm wondering, this morning, how did you make him come first?"

Eric blinked rapidly. "How?"

Her question had been idle, designed to keep the tension between them going. When he failed to answer immediately, she wanted the secret for real. She slid her warm, satin-covered palms inside his open shirt. The fabric rasped enticingly on his hair.

"Yes," she said, the pleasure of touching him zinging straight to her sex. "I'd be curious to hear your method for defeating the great genius."

Thirteen

Eric hesitated.

"You don't have to tell me," she said, her grin fading. "I understand if it's too private."

He covered her hands where they pressed his chest. The gloves—where they weren't damp from his sweat—were deliciously slippery. "No," he said. "It's fine."

She smiled and bit her lip at the same time. "Your heart's beating faster. This story must be good."

"I . . . threatened him. Told him you and I would join forces to overpower him. I, uh, believe I made some mention of you using a dildo on him."

Her fingers had unconsciously drawn up, like a cat preparing to knead a sleeping spot. "And he liked that idea?"

"Apparently."

His voice was threadier than he expected. If she'd thought his pulse had quickened before, it was slamming now. His head was actually light.

She looked down at her gloves, her lashes dark and glamorous, then up at him. "We should do it," she said decisively.

"What?" The word might have been dragged out of him.

"We should team up to overpower him. Don't act so

shocked," she added as he sucked a breath. "You know this idea has done more than cross your mind."

To prove it, she dropped one hand to cup his balls. The pressure, light though it was, was enough to provoke a curse.

"He might not like it," he said, reaching for reason. "People sometimes have fantasies they don't really want to play out."

Charity smiled as she trailed two fingers up his under-ridge. "I suspect we'll be able to tell if he's enjoying himself. Be a sport, Eric. It isn't good for anyone to have his way all the time. I think your buddy needs to give up being the boss for once."

Eric shuddered as her fingers plucked at his quivering tip. Too sensitized to be played with, he pulled her hand away by the wrist. He couldn't believe he was considering going along. His body could believe, though. His erection felt overfull, and his skin hummed from scalp to toe.

Do it, ordered his libido. *You'll be sorry if you don't.*

"We'd have to give him a safeword."

"Sure. 'The crow flies at midnight.' "

He had to laugh. "That's not a safeword."

"Whatever," she said with a flippant shrug, her beautiful, naked shoulders going up and down. "You have to admit it'd be hard to say by accident."

Eric wasn't ready to admit anything . . . except that he couldn't walk away from this chance.

"We're coming in," Eric said into the speakerphone outside B.G.'s door.

B.G. thought this a peculiar method for requesting entry. He exited the file that contained the last security report, shut his laptop, and stared for a moment at the entrance to his suite. He was willing to swear Charity was honest. Their background check on her had been thorough. In no way, shape, or form could she be a candidate for intrigue. She possessed neither the experience nor the contacts.

The solution with the highest degree of probability was one he didn't especially want to face, in part because it meant his judgment was not as good as he believed. If his suspicions were true, he'd yet to figure out how the trick had been managed. But that was for his team to discover. If he tried to investigate the matter directly, he'd simply alert the person to the fact that the jig was up.

In spite of knowing his team was qualified to handle such situations, he remained off-kilter. He'd been so ever since Eric broke the news of his sister's call, as if the atoms he was made of were trying to form new orbits. His long hot shower—usually a cure-all—had not helped. He found it highly disconcerting to have to set aside their play for an unsuspected and, for now, inexplicable threat.

B.G. hadn't lied to Eric. His research thus far was useless. Nonetheless, if someone had discovered his secret project, he'd have to shut down, for no other reason than to prevent less-skilled hands from doing inadvertent harm. This was a remedy he was reluctant to enact. He hated the thought of walking away from a challenge. Better to think the Feds were being paranoid. It had happened before, after all—especially when the scientist in question didn't fit their mold for how trustworthy citizens behaved. To the men in suits' way of thinking, people like B.G. would always bear watching.

"B.G.," Eric's voice said more insistently. "Open up."

At this demand, a shiver—simultaneously delicate and sensual—slid like rainwater down his neck.

He shook it off as he rose to answer the door, his white terrycloth robe brushing his shins. Eric and Charity entered as soon as he stepped back.

Unlike him, they were wrapped in thin silk kimonos of earthen brown. The pattern of each was different, but the knots in the belts appeared identical. B.G. had read that

strongly attracted lovers often exhibited a "twinning" effect, one that caused them to dress in similar fashion or unconsciously mimic each other's body language.

It seemed this effect was making itself felt on Eric and
Charity. The pair formed a visually united front.

"What's this about?" B.G. asked. "You look as if you're
about to stage a coup." Not entirely joking, he was unable
to resist a primal urge to fold his arms defensively across his
chest.

When Charity did the same a second later, his heart gave
a little lurch. "Denial isn't the only thing that gets people
off," she said. "The question is, do you trust us?"

"Trust you?"

"To look out for your pleasure. To be sure you aren't hurt."

"I—" Momentarily speechless, he turned to Eric. His old
friend offered an unexpectedly sweet, slow smile. B.G. had
never seen him wear quite that expression. It was . . . open,
sure of itself, and very fond. If Charity brought this out in
him, B.G. had chosen his path better than he knew.

"Yes," Eric said. "Do you trust us?"

B.G. examined him up and down, wondering what else
might be different about his friend. He noticed something
stuffed in the pocket of Eric's robe, something his hand was
playing with.

"B.G.?" Eric prodded.

He met Eric's dark gray eyes. "Yes," he said before he
knew he would. "I trust you implicitly."

It was no more than the truth, yet when Charity stepped
forward to take his hands, the gentle pressure she put on his
fingers spurred a touch of fear.

He was letting her turn everything upside down.

"You're ours," she said. "We're going to take care of you."

"You can choose where," Eric put in. "If you like."

B.G. didn't know why his heart was in his throat. This was
nothing like Eric had threatened to do this morning—no

harshness, no violence, just a soft insistence on having their way. He knew he could stop it any time he wished.

"Here," he said. "In my bedroom."

"In your bedroom," Charity purred, drawing out the words. "What a convenient choice."

She tugged him toward his four-poster bed with what felt like tottering steps. He sat on the mattress before his knees gave out.

"You do the honors," Eric said, tossing her a bundle of pink velvet cloth. B.G.'s mind quickly identified what it was. Cuffs. Quilted inside. With long, trailing ties. They must have been what Eric was playing with in his pocket.

Charity caught them neatly to her chest. "Thank you, Mr. President."

Eric chuckled at what B.G. assumed was a private joke. "No more of that. I don't need to pretend to be anyone here but me."

Her eyes glowed at Eric. Then she turned to him. "Where do you keep your personal toys?"

The part of him that always maintained control considered not answering. He couldn't see how this break with tradition would further his plans. He wanted it to play out, though, more than he'd known he could. To have the two of them take him, to give himself over to their lead was an invitation he could not refuse.

"There's a cabinet," he said, "hidden in the wall above my headboard."

He sounded calm. She'd give him that. Only his eyes betrayed a hint of nervousness. They followed her, glittering, as she grabbed a mahogany bedpost and jumped onto the mattress. Pretty plaster flowers adorned a section of his wall, like she'd seen in pictures of chateaux in France. She ran her fingers across them, expecting one to trigger the release.

"The next one," Eric and B.G. said in unison.

"Turn it," B.G. finished. "To the right."

Turning the plaster rose caused a section of the wall to swing silently to the side. The recess behind it was shelved, lacquered in Chinese red, and lit up.

"Cool," said Charity, appreciating the mechanism's cleverness. She stood on tiptoe to peer at the upper shelf. "And look, what a fine collection of dildos!"

Feeling a bit like Goldilocks, she began pulling them out. "Too big," she said, tossing the first one to the mattress's foot. The next had attachments she wouldn't have known what to do with. "Too complicated. Yeesh. Too *green*."

"That one's jade," Eric said, the darker note that had entered his tone telling her to back up.

She considered her would-be discard more carefully. Its stone was very smooth, almost translucent in the subdued light. Not too large, she thought. Plus, the handle on the bottom could have been designed to fit her hand. She enjoyed the way both Eric and B.G. hissed through their teeth when she slapped the shaft against her palm.

Either she was threatening a valuable piece of erotic art, or they were imagining that slap against their own skin.

"This jade isn't brittle, is it?" she asked to be sure the latter was the case.

"Oh, no," B.G. assured her. "If it were, it would have cracked by now."

Eric and B.G. exchanged smiling glances. "Old favorite then?" she suggested.

"A good fit," Eric said, "and easy to maneuver."

"Good. Then it shouldn't be too hard for me."

"Oh, boy," B.G. said with a breathy laugh.

Charity totally loved being able to shake him up, though she didn't want to give this away. "Okay," she said briskly. "Let's get you tied."

She took stock of her surroundings with what she hoped looked like a practiced eye. Even though she was standing on the coverlet, the bed was extremely stable, probably bolted to the floor. The mattress creaked, but nothing else. The canopy, a rich silver and blue brocade, draped a similarly sturdy frame. Overhead, thick wood slats formed a lattice stretching overhead.

"I'll attach you here," she said, pointing to its center. " 'Cause we definitely want access to you all around."

"Thoughtful," B.G. said with a small, wry smile.

Charity decided if he was amused, he didn't completely get who was boss. "Take off his robe," she said to Eric by way of fixing this. "And anything else he's got underneath."

He had nothing underneath, of course, nothing but smoothly muscled skin. Someday she'd get him to explain how he removed his body hair without leaving stubble. For now, she let him off with offering his wrist. The simple act of wrapping the cuff around his wristbone had soft bursts of heat rolling through her sex.

He offered his second hand just as obediently. She stood in front of him to secure his arms above his head. As she did, her breasts brushed his chest through her robe. The ointment Eric had rubbed on them kept her nipples tight. Struggling not to get distracted, she left enough play in the ties so B.G. could kneel.

"How about a bolster for his knees?" Eric suggested, holding one out.

"Why, thank you," Charity said. "That's most helpful."

B.G. snorted at them, but Charity took the sound with a grain of salt. The great B.G. Grantham wasn't as cool as he pretended. His cheeks were flushed, and his fingers opened and closed compulsively on the long pink ties. These little betrayals spurred her appetite for bigger ones.

She let her eyes drift to his erection, just as a man might stare at a woman's breast. He looked good as he was, ready, but she was convinced she could do better.

"Comfortable?" she asked, one finger tapping her chin.

"Quite," he answered, but she thought his jaw looked tense.

"Ties not too tight? Room not too cool?"

"I'll start a fire," Eric offered before B.G. could respond. Wood had been laid already, and he soon had it crackling. B.G. watched him work with fascinated eyes. Charity knew he hadn't missed this shift in who Eric answered to. This, more than anything, seemed to rock him back.

"Better?" she asked when Eric returned.

B.G. could only nod. She knew how he felt as if she were inside him: the nervous excitement, the weird sense of complete freedom. Emotion closed her throat, a sympathy so potent it could have been love. She hadn't anticipated how much she'd want to give him this gift. Temporarily speechless herself, she laid her hand flat against his chest. His muscles were spread and lifted by the position of his arms. She could see what swimming did for his physique, how it sleeked and tightened everything. His skin was smooth as velvet, hot as sunbaked stone. Beneath his ribs, his heart was beating fast.

"We've unnerved you," she said. "I hope you're not afraid."

Slowly he shook his head.

Eric murmured something blasphemous, obviously enthralled by his response.

"We're going to pleasure you," she said, making her voice even softer. "You won't have to do a thing. On the other hand . . ." She began to circle him, dragging her fingers around his narrow hips. "If I can't inspire you to fight at least a little, I might feel as if I've failed."

He was shorter than her now. She had to lean down to breathe the last part into his ear.

"Fight?" he whispered back.

His bottom clenched, inviting her, daring her. Surely he had to have guessed what they planned. Rather than answer in words, she underscored her meaning with a brisk, hard spank.

"Charity!" he exclaimed, sounding genuinely shocked.

"Sylvia took more than that," she said with a touch of scorn, plunging into her role with unexpected ease. "And Eric told me he promised you I'd do this."

"Eric . . . promised . . . a lot of things."

She adored the way his chest heaved for air. "Your safeword is 'green,'" she snapped, adding another smack. "Say it and everything stops."

"Got it," he gasped. "Won't say it by mistake."

She had to laugh at the pure joyous triumph of taking charge.

Charity was a revelation, a strange, ferocious force of nature. She knelt behind him now, steadily smacking his buttocks with her hot cupped palm. His skin blazed with every blow, the sensation spreading like wildfire. The strength she used sent the deep, tingling vibrations straight through his cock. Eric never would have hit him as hard as this. Considering how gentle B.G. was himself, Eric wouldn't have dared.

B.G. groaned in a reaction he could not control.

"There," she said, fiercely approving as she caught him beneath one cheek. "Feel what it's like to surrender."

He thought he might weep, despite being unable to think of a reason for doing so. Like his body, his emotions seemed to be rocketing off their tracks.

She smacked his other cheek, then up and down the backs of his thighs. He was hot all over, pulsing, as if his borders were expanding and contracting unpredictably.

"Sweet," she crooned, the sound as blurry as a dream. "Sweet, sweet Benjamin."

A sob caught without warning inside his throat.

She stopped then, laying her face against the small of his back. When she kissed his buttock, her lips felt cool.

"That's enough," she said, murmuring it against the blaze. "Now you need to feel something nice."

He opened his eyes, only realizing then that they'd been closed. Eric knelt in front of him, smiling. Was the look in his eyes amusement? Wonder? B.G.'s judgment was too jangled to say. All he knew was when Eric clasped his face and touched their lips together, no gesture had ever been that sweet. His kiss was as gentle as Charity had been rough, the contrast perfect, as if they'd planned it between them ahead of time. Maybe they had planned it, or maybe they'd grown so attuned it happened naturally.

Which possibility was more unsettling, B.G. could not have said.

He moaned as Eric's mouth pulled away on a last, slow lick.

"I'm going to help her take you," he said from an inch away. "She's never used a dildo on a man before."

The disclosure that he would be her first struck a small erotic blow, one too many on top of the rest. B.G. couldn't answer, either in praise or protest. He was a fair hand at biofeedback and meditation, plus a few methods of physical control he'd invented for himself. All his tools were useless now. He couldn't call on a single one. He *felt*—no more than that—as if feeling were a state of being as real as liquid or gas. He was at their mercy. If they wanted him to come, he would.

He shuddered as Eric instructed Charity on the proper lubrication of the toy.

"The key is to go slow," he said. "That jade can't sense where it's going, so you need to give him plenty of time to relax. Don't push against resistance. Wait until the shaft slides in naturally."

The words alone elicited a gasp of desire. Charity kissed

B.G.'s nape before she started, a tender press she followed with a nip. The way the bite streaked through him had him bowing his head.

Nothing in him resisted her. It seemed as if nothing could. The jade slid into him inch by inch and then was still. The pressure felt good. Too good. He wanted to groan, but the sound stuck in his throat.

"Good," Eric said. "Now, remember, the first inch is loaded with nerves and, after that, he'll feel the friction most over his prostate, which is toward the front. Don't overdo it, though. The longer this lasts, the better his climax will be."

"Can I move it now?" she asked, the question hushed.

"Not yet," Eric said. "Wait until I start."

His words revealed an important truth: Charity wasn't completely in charge; they really were doing this together. Physically, Eric could have overwhelmed B.G. at any time. Emotionally, neither he nor Charity could succeed alone.

As B.G. tried to absorb this, Eric came back around him, sitting on his heels with his knees spread in a V. He was close enough that B.G. could feel his breath on his groin.

"Sh," he said, rubbing B.G.'s hip as he shivered. "You're not still cold, are you?"

"No," B.G. gasped, all he could get out.

He wasn't cold, but he was glad when Charity wrapped her warm, soft body against his side. He needed the extra bracing when Eric lowered his head to his cock. Eric's mouth was wet and strong, the drag of lips and tongue a very welcome pressure.

He'd believed nothing could surpass it, but then the smooth jade form pulled back inside him, and everything came clear. This was what he had been waiting for, what he had feared: when pleasure stole his very will. His head fell back on Charity's shoulder as his fingers twisted uncontrollably in his bonds. Without even thinking, he wound the slack in the ties around his wrists. He was lifting his knees off the bolster, the effort as necessary as breath. The beams of the canopy creaked as he swayed.

"That's it," she said into his ear as she pushed the toy back in. "Show me how you fight."

Maybe he was fighting. Maybe this was the best he could do. Eric was taking him deeper into his mouth, his hand coming around to help Charity. With his guidance, her handling of the dildo became more deft, the sensations it roused more intense. Whether she knew it or not, she was catching his prostate with every slide. B.G. made a sound, a half-swallowed cry. Her legs straddled his hip, parting the front of her robe. He could feel how wet she was, how soft and feminine. Her nipples pressed him through the silk. He should have come. His balls were tight with it, his cock aching in surges with his pulse.

Someone pinched his nipple, and he didn't know who it was.

"Twist it," Eric's voice buzzed against his crown. "He likes that."

The twist made him gulp for air, made him twitch and jolt inside Eric's mouth. He swayed, but it was the world that seemed to tilt. Charity was kissing her way down his side, bending farther and farther forward, sucking hard enough to leave marks. He cried out as the dildo moved faster.

When she fit her head next to Eric's, he knew he was gone. She didn't even have to suck the side of his scrotum that she could reach. When she did, though, when she did, she caught the first burst of lightning that was his climax and sent it supernova. The orgasm literally blinded him, light exploding behind his eyes as ecstasy tried to turn his body inside out. He came so hard he couldn't breathe until it was over, his ribs squeezing far too hard against his lungs.

"Lord," he said when he finally could draw in air.

Eric had released him, and Charity sat back as well, grinning up at him in a manner that was both bashful and pleased. He couldn't resist the combination. He twisted around to kiss her until he had to stop for breath again.

When he let her go, Eric was holding her hand.

❧

B.G. looked, well, *dazed* was the only word Eric could think of—not unhappy, but as if he wasn't sure what had happened.

"You okay?" Eric said.

B.G. was staring at his hand. Until that moment, Eric hadn't realized he'd reached for Charity. The gesture had been too natural to think about.

Now he dropped her fingers. That, oddly enough, felt awkward.

"Let me get you out of these cuffs," Eric said, rising to cover the strangeness. The ties were hard to undo. The pressure B.G. had exerted had pulled them tight, reminding Eric how unaccustomed he was to being on the receiving end of bondage. When his friend rolled his head around his shoulders, Eric worried he'd grown uncomfortable with the delay.

"I could cut them," he offered.

"No need," B.G. said with a cryptic smile that was more like his usual. "I can wait."

He rubbed his wrists when he was finally free. Eric's brows went up at the welts. "You chafed yourself."

"It's all right," B.G. said, then grinned full out. "You could say I wasn't thinking."

Eric was already swinging off the bed. "I'll get something to put on that. Something cool."

As he rummaged through the bathroom cabinet, he heard Charity speak to B.G.

"*Are* you okay?"

"Yes," he said, warmth and indulgence coloring his voice. "If we freaked you out . . ."

"Only in a good way."

When Eric returned with the antiseptic, Charity was sitting on the bed while B.G. stood beside it. B.G. was squeezing her shoulder reassuringly. She looked past him to Eric, and his steps faltered. Her expression was just a smile, but something in it made him stop.

She loves me, Eric thought, too stunned to react. She might not know it herself, and who knew how long it would last, but in that instant, she loved him.

He'd known there was a chance this might happen, but he'd never guessed it would strike him like a thunderbolt.

"I . . . found a spray," he said, holding it out.

Charity hopped up to take it from him. "I'll do it. This kind of thing is girls' work."

B.G. offered her his hands as trustingly as he had before, but Eric could tell he'd mastered himself again. He watched the top of Charity's head as she fixed him up.

"Should we stay?" she asked.

"Stay?" This startled B.G. The hand she'd just finished spraying jerked back.

"Yeah," she said. "Like a sleepover."

B.G. touched her hair, then met her gaze when it rose. In that moment, Eric saw his friend as if he were a stranger— a dignified, supremely isolated stranger. Eric wondered if anyone had ever related to him as easily as Charity.

He hadn't himself. He'd always been in awe of the great genius, always slightly subordinate. All at once, that seemed a terrible mistake.

"We'd like to stay," he said as he stepped forward.

Only B.G.'s head turned. The light from the fire played over the planes of his face, his inscrutable eyes as dark as ink. Eric sensed the turning of his inner wheels, though what B.G. was thinking he alone knew.

"You should then," he said after the slightest hesitation. "Both of you should stay."

Fourteen

They had a second round, sort of. Eric rolled her beneath him on B.G.'s bed, thrusting slowly and smoothly into her. He was steel-hard from waiting, from the things they'd seen and done to B.G., and Charity almost melted at the feel of him gliding in. She supposed the straightforward, missionary-style lovemaking was all his body could handle. She could tell he was into it. His jaw was bunched, and his gaze never left hers. Those gray eyes of his were intense, their focus as arousing as anything that came before. Despite the attention, she knew he was far from oblivious to his friend.

B.G. stretched out beside them with his head propped on one hand—lazy, catlike, and more than close enough to touch. Somehow she knew he wouldn't, an understanding Eric seemed to share.

B.G. was there to watch.

The arrangement was strange but sexy. B.G. appeared to be memorizing what Eric did, maybe figuring out what Eric had found she liked. The tempting conclusion was that he meant to use the knowledge to take back the advantage some people might have said he'd lost.

Except he didn't act disadvantaged. He acted interested.

When Eric made her come strongly enough to arch up, all he did was smile.

The vulnerability she'd seen in him before seemed as much a dream as Mosswood's ghosts.

He waited until Eric shuddered in climax, then touched the curve of his lower back. "Sleep," he said, sliding a hand to his flank.

Eric hung over her on his elbows, trembling from the force of his long-delayed release. A bead of sweat rolled off the tip of his nose. "I'm awake," he said, but his eyes were drifting even then.

"It's all right," B.G. assured him. "I'll handle the post-coital cuddle and chat."

"I knew it!" Charity snickered. "It does take two men to treat a woman right."

Eric mumbled something and withdrew, already so relaxed he had to secure the rubber with one hand. He tossed it into a trash container whose location he must have been familiar with.

"Thanks," he said, perhaps to them both, after which he kissed her crookedly on the cheek. Then, as only a man would, he rolled over and conked out, without—so far as she could tell—even thinking about a shower.

Charity thought about it, and settled for a quick turn under the spray and a rubdown with a steaming towel. B.G.'s bathroom was luxurious. He'd abandoned his French theme for a more monolithic, modern style. The same rammed earth walls that graced her bedroom were present here. The floors were sealed concrete, allowing the multi-headed shower to remain open. Intrigued by this glimpse of B.G.'s most private retreat, she poked around enough to find doors leading to a sauna and a Jacuzzi.

Apparently, living the high life kept you clean.

Despite her dawdling, her host was sitting up when she returned. He lifted an arm for her and smiled, making it impossible to do anything but snuggle into his hold. Not that she had any particular urge to resist. Eric was on the other side, sleeping like a baby. B.G. had pulled the sheet over him, and now he pulled it over her. The pillows behind them were soft as clouds.

As if they'd done this every night for years, his fingers combed gently, soothingly through her hair.

"This is nice," she said, feeling both peaceful and oddly alert.

"Yes, it is," B.G. agreed. "Almost nice enough to make a man believe other people can make him happy."

Charity craned her head up from his chest. "Are you saying they can't?"

"Strictly speaking, as emotional entities, human beings are self-contained. We believe other people's actions cause us to be happy—or miserable, as the case may be—but it is our thoughts about their actions that create the hormonal responses we interpret as happiness."

This mouthful made Charity think she and Eric really had rattled him—either that or put him too much at ease. B.G. hadn't brought out his geek-speak for a while.

"So every man is an island?" she tried to ask intelligently.

"Only from a Newtonian perspective, where people are viewed as discrete objects. The quantum view would say we exist in a continuous energy soup, where people—indeed, all forms of matter—are merely areas of higher vibrational concentration that act and are acted upon as would be expected of solid things. Because this solidity is an illusion, our brain waves have no trouble radiating outward, thus conveying our thoughts to the universe. We seem as though we're separate, but we are not."

Charity couldn't help laughing. "B.G., either man is an island or a soup. You can't have it both ways."

"Yes, I can. Both views are valid within their own context. Moreover, they lead to the same conclusion. If we are

self-contained, no one can 'make' us happy. If we are con-
centrations of waves within a continuum, then we attract
happiness-inspiring events by strengthening our focus on
that emotion. Joy draws joy, and misery more cause for the
same. Either way, we are responsible for our own state."

If she hadn't been lying against him, she was convinced he
would have crossed his arms. Then again, with a philosophy
like that, he needed to be tough. To take his premise to its
logical conclusion, every experience he encountered would be
of his own making. He'd have no one to blame for anything
but himself—which seemed pretty harsh, if you asked her.

Amused by such extremism, she patted the hard, flat
muscle of his right pec. "All right, Mr. Genius, have it both
ways. But if one person could make another person happy,
I'd be honored to have given it a shot for you."

She'd actually rendered him speechless. His mouth
gaped slightly, and he stared at her with suspiciously tear-
bright eyes.

"Well," he said, blinking himself back into composure.
"That's . . . that's very kind."

She hid her smile by laying her cheek against his chest.
"No problem. Apart from the hopping wineglasses and the
ghosts, you've made me happy yourself."

"Ghosts?"

"Oh, yeah. I forgot to tell you. This afternoon I thought
I heard one down in your creepy Elizabethan hall. Sounded
like a gown sweeping the floor."

His hand stilled on her hair, then moved again. "Probably a squirrel," he said, relaxing beneath her. "They're always getting in."

B.G. didn't sound as if he believed this. In fact, he
sounded as if he knew differently. Charity opened her mouth
to call him on the lie, then decided she'd rather let his denial stand. If he had reason to believe in ghosts, she didn't
want to know.

* * *

TRUE to form for her new-and-improved quantum self, Charity woke before either of the men.

The skylight in B.G.'s sitting room announced a watery gray morning. Without a clock, or instructions on how to find one, Charity had no idea if it was time to get up.

Her stomach settled the issue by rumbling.

Somehow she'd ended up in the middle of the bed. When she squirmed out from between the two warm male bodies, B.G. grumbled in his sleep and immediately snuggled closer to Eric.

The move made her smile even though it was insulting to be so easily replaced. But who cared about that? She'd be twice as popular when she came back. It was a well-known fact of Seattle life that you couldn't judge a new lover until you'd seen him before coffee.

B.G.'s cook helped her in her mission by loading a trolley with Spanish omelets, quartered oranges, and a big pot of espresso. Feeling extremely pleased with her haul, Charity pushed it into B.G.'s bedroom.

"Food," Eric groaned into his pillow.

B.G. rolled onto his back and covered his eyes with his arm. His bedhead was less comical than Eric's, but his face was definitely morning pale. He cleared his throat before he spoke. "Tell me there's coffee."

"There is," she said. "Freshly made." She tipped the lid of the steaming pot and let the scent waft out. "Mm. Smells like double roast."

Eyes still closed, B.G. held out his hand. "Please," he said. "Black."

"What'll you give me for it?"

"My first-born child."

"As far as I know, you don't have one."

From the way his eyes slitted open, she decided she'd

pushed him past his pre-coffee edge. "Never mind," she said, passing over a cup. "I'll collect my favor later on."

He inhaled, then swallowed, then let out an addict's sigh. Eric was more interested in food, but as she set a laden bed tray over his lap, he was equally appreciative.

"You're a goddess," he said, his mouth full of hot omelet.

"Yes, I am." Charity perched beside his hip. "Though Mrs. Alvarez deserves some credit."

Feeling pleasantly wifelike, she filled B.G.'s cup again, then helped herself to Eric's toast.

"Sorry 'bout crumbs," Eric said, but B.G. waved away the concern. He looked less pallid, even if his nose was buried in his cup.

"Keeps the maids from getting bored," he said, and all Charity could think was, *Must be nice!*

When he'd sucked down his second cup, he turned to her. She wasn't prepared for his next question. "Tell me, Charity," he said. "How many foreign nationals have you seduced?"

"B.G.," Eric chided.

"I'm sorry," B.G. said. "The way she bargained with that coffee made her seem sly. I decided it would be irresponsible not to ask."

"I dated a Canadian skier once," she offered, though she didn't understand why he needed to know.

"Canada." He rubbed his chin musingly. "No. That wouldn't do it."

"Do what?"

"Nothing." B.G. gave her one of his semi-goofy, all-sweet smiles. "We shall have no negative talk this morning. Unless"—he pressed the side of a finger to his mouth—"you didn't by chance accept gifts from the skier worth more than a hundred dollars?"

"Uh," she said, now thoroughly confused. "The most I got was a bunch of roses. In fact, now that I think back, he gave me a bunch of roses with the wrong girlfriend's name on the card. He sent both at the same time and got them mixed up."

"Not good."

"Not good at all—though it was kind of funny to think of him having two girls mad at him at once, all because he couldn't be original."

"Spontaneity can be a challenge for some men." B.G. wagged his head as if this was his problem, too. Maybe it was. B.G. sure did have a thing for pre-planning.

"I know what we could do," she said, "if you're feeling like you're in a rut."

"Oh, God," Eric said, seeming amused.

She pushed his thigh. "Get your mind out of the gutter. I'm thinking we could go bowling."

"Hm," said B.G. "Mosswood has many amenities, but I regret to inform you a bowling alley is not among them."

"No, let's *go* bowling. Off the estate. I'm sure I saw some lanes in one of the towns on our drive here. We should do it, B.G. Everybody needs an occasional break from mind-blowing sex."

This inspired a grin. "You know," B.G. said, "I don't believe I've ever bowled in my life."

"All the better. I'll mop the floor with you. Ooh!" She jostled Eric's coffee by bouncing on the bed. "Can we take Maurice? I know Sylvia is in the doghouse, but I bet Maurice knows which holes to stick his fingers in."

"And then some," Eric quipped while steadying his cup.

B.G.'s eyes were wide. "You want my chauffeur to join us?"

"Sure." The more she thought about it, the better the idea seemed. "Isn't Maurice an important part of your quantum soup? You wouldn't want to neglect your potatoes."

"No, indeed," the great scientist said. "Neglecting my potatoes would be a grave oversight."

*   *   *

Bowling was a total blast—even though, contrary to her expectations, Maurice turned out to have two left thumbs. B.G. did fine once he started plotting trajectories, but it was Eric who surprised them all, getting spares and strikes nearly every time. It took all Charity's math to remember how to keep score.

"Played in a league at college," he said with a secret glint in his eye.

"A ringer!" B.G. exclaimed, obviously enjoying his friend's triumph. "Give him a handicap!"

Soon after they arrived, the lane beside them was taken by a group of teens. With B.G.'s photograph a staple in high school science texts, it was only a matter of time before they started glancing his way. When they figured out who he was, they insisted on treating him to greasy pizza, which he ate with great relish, using the pepperoni to give an impromptu demonstration about the nature of what he called the "multi-branching multi-verse," where reality split according to whether you ate the slice or put it down.

"Dude!" said one of the teens when he started in on multi-dimensions. Apparently, B.G. Grantham was a hero to the high school set. The only brighter moment was when Maurice was recognized from his wrestling days. "Bad Mo," as he'd been known, redeemed his gutter balls by signing autographs all around. Blushing, he drew the line at signing one girl's bra.

All in all, it was a day for the record books.

"Hah!" Charity crowed as she and Eric walked companionably to her room. "Who says you can't make other people happy?"

"Certainly not me."

They were at her door, swinging hands in a way that was both delaying tactic and whimsy. B.G. had wandered off, murmuring something vague about "seeing to business." Charity wanted Eric to stay, but was it too much to ask?

They'd spent an awful lot of time together. Maybe even an erotic keeper needed time off. For that matter, she ought to be needing time off herself. She'd never been one to want to be joined at the hip with a man.

Of course, it wasn't her hips that were most interested. From the glow in Eric's eyes, she wasn't the only one whose sex drive had recovered since the night before.

If she put the moves on him, was the best she could hope for more teasing? She wasn't sure she was up for that. Maybe not asking was better than having to hold back.

Unable to decide, she dropped her gaze to watch her feet shuffle on the floor. "It was nice of B.G. to buy us all new shoes," she said, admiring the red and cream leather.

Eric pulled her hands to his chest, letting them rest lightly on his shirt. "I suspect the thought of all the feet that had been in the rentals before us gave him the shakes. Plus, he might want to see you in those again."

"Hoo, baby," she said with a laugh. "Your friend has some weird kinks."

"He's not the only one."

"No, he's not. Last night was fun."

The crinkles around his warm gray eyes did dangerous things to her heart. She had to brace herself when his thumbs rubbed tingling circles under her palms.

"More than fun," he said. "And today was good, too." He drew a breath as if he needed courage. "That was a really nice thing you did."

Even though she craved it, his approval embarrassed her. She shrugged crookedly. "It was only bowling."

"It wasn't only bowling. You got him out of the house. You reminded him he can have fun in the real world. I confess, it wouldn't have occurred to me to do that. I wouldn't have expected him to let me."

"Why not? He's not your boss twenty-four-seven. When it comes right down to it, he's your friend."

This time, Eric shrugged. "Friendships have dynamics. I guess that's ours."

"That's dopey. You told me he doesn't like to be coddled. If you think he's getting too hermity, you should speak up." Eric's hands rose to smooth her hair, but Charity wasn't in the mood to be soothed. "Screw the rules, anyway. Why can't we just be people?"

He smiled, seeming to know she meant more than the rules that applied to him and B.G. "We're still people even with the rules."

"Yeah, but with the rules, you can't always tell what's real and what's play."

He lowered his head to kiss her, starting soft and ending deep. Her knees went wobbly within seconds. All too soon, he pulled away, her shoulders braced in his hands. "This is real."

It might have been real, but it was just a kiss. Even the huskiness in his voice didn't tell her what she wanted to find out. She already knew he was attracted to her. The question was, did he *like* her? Did he think she was good enough for more than games? The funny thing was, for a moment, he was looking into her eyes as if he longed to know the same thing.

"I should go," he said, sounding reluctant. "You were up early. You'll want to rest."

"Right," she said, stepping back awkwardly. "Thanks."

She clenched her jaw as she turned, determined to hide both her hurt and her sense of stupidity. Being too direct seemed not to be her problem now.

❧

Dolt, Eric thought, watching her back go stiff. He hadn't meant for her to feel rejected. He'd meant for the things he'd seen in her eyes the night before to be said out loud.

Not that he had any right to want her to admit she loved him. It wasn't like he knew what to say back.

A man who could be jealous of both her and B.G. hardly qualified as clear in his mind.

"Charity," he said, his hand reaching toward her arm. She turned back halfway, the look in her eyes cautious. He willed his tone to be soft. "I'm glad you're here. I'm glad you're shaking things up."

Her smile wasn't as sure of itself as it could have been. "Good," she said over her shoulder. "I'll see what else I can shake up tonight."

His blood pumped faster at the promise. He had no doubt she meant what she said.

B.G. slapped off the view screen, walked four steps toward his favorite chair, and picked up a glass of partially drunk pinot noir. He was distantly aware of his face being boiling hot.

Eric and Charity thought he was a hermit. Today's excursion had been about pity, not friendship.

He clenched his hand around the stem of the glass. He had no one to blame but himself for this unwanted knowledge. He shouldn't have watched them. He should have turned away the moment he saw their interaction was personal. He should have remembered how easily people forgot the presence of cameras. If nothing else, that stupid *Real World* show should have taught him that.

Without taking a sip, he put down the wine and sat. The bowling shoes pinched his feet. Maybe rentals would have been better. Maybe a normal person wouldn't have cared about a few old germs.

Honestly, though, what was Eric thinking? Why didn't he verbalize his sentiments? Anyone could see Charity was smitten, but B.G. knew women needed words. If Charity didn't get them, she wouldn't feel secure enough to give hers back. The exchange of emotional confidences was a crucial stage in developing a relationship!

Anger made for a more comfortable heat than humiliation. Letting it rise, B.G. toed off his shoes and kicked them across the rug.

They were idiots, the pair of them. B.G. wasn't romantic, and he had no trouble picturing them happy, the solution as clear as any scientific theorem he'd ever solved. He shifted in his seat as the picture rose. Eric and Charity would buy a little Craftsman-style home on the slopes of Queen Anne Hill. They'd sit on the porch each morning, drinking coffee and taking in the view. B.G. would visit them for holidays—platonically, of course, because they'd be married by then. Naturally his daydream wouldn't match reality point for point—one couldn't give dictation to the universe—but he knew his instincts were sound.

Those two fit each other: Eric's responsibility, Charity's wildness, the way they worked as a team. Although the game had gone off the rails of late, its basic structure heightened their reactions admirably. B.G. shouldn't have had any difficulty nudging them together. He'd proved his methods for success too many times to doubt them now.

He worried his lower lip between his finger and thumb, despite knowing how little this agitation would help his cause. He hoped he hadn't been mistaken in introducing his methods to Charity. She seemed to be making progress, but perhaps her long habit of doubt was obstructive.

Let it go, he thought, closing his eyes and forcing a slower breath. If his confidence remained firm, the universe would do the job for him. Serendipity worked better than human will.

When he'd pushed away his frustration, his hurt remained. It didn't matter. He *was* a creature of habit—a hermit, as they had said. He'd always be more comfortable here than out in the world. He'd made his peace with that—more than made his peace, he'd turned it into an asset.

His calm was an asset, too, letting his mind roam free. The answer already existed in the quantum realm. He would find it if he relaxed.

Hermit or not, Charity wasn't the only one who could shake things up.

"Have you seen this?" Sylvia demanded.

She pushed off the wall outside Charity's room to flap a sheet of folded stationery in her face. Clearly, she'd been lying in wait for Charity to return from her swim.

Just as clearly, she'd spent the wait fuming.

Reluctant to open her door and allow the other woman to continue her rant inside, Charity took the letter from her hand. Her brows went up as she read.

"It sounds like B.G. has given up on enforcing the rules. 'Until further notice, guests and staff may form whatever personal arrangements they choose without said arrangements negatively impacting the terms of their employment.'" Charity looked from the neatly printed letter to Sylvia's white-faced rage. "Well, I don't know why he did it, but I admit I also don't know why you're mad. How can this be a bad thing?"

"He didn't tell me," Sylvia said. "This"—she tapped the paper—"was taped to your door. I had to hear the news through Michael."

"The surveillance guy?"

"Yes. He's support staff like I am, though *he* rates a notice." Her mouth twisted to one side. "Apparently, the high and mighty B.G. Grantham no longer cares what I do."

"I'm sure he values your skills. Maybe he overlooked your copy because, um, your responsibilities changed recently."

Sylvia glared at the reminder, causing Charity to pull her terrycloth robe closer to her neck.

"He's a capitalist pig," Sylvia snapped, "changing the rules to suit himself."

"I thought you liked him."

"I do!" she said, then pressed her fist to her mouth. "Most of the time."

In spite of her annoyance, Charity softened when she saw the other woman's eyes well up. Sylvia was a drama queen, and odd to boot, but nobody liked feeling slighted. Hoping to calm her, she put her hand to Sylvia's impressively hard bicep. "Can't you make the best of it? Have your fun and ignore the rest? I mean, now you can see Michael all you want without sneaking around."

Charity realized sneaking around might be part of the appeal, but she didn't expect Sylvia's abruptly glacial regard. "Michael told me you walked in on him," she said. "He told me you guessed he was screening surveillance tapes for me."

"I didn't tattle to B.G., if that's what you're getting at. I only asked him not to do it again."

Sylvia continued to stare, her arms now folded across her chest, her expression measuring. Her slender fingers tapped her elbows. When she forgot to frown, she was one of the loveliest women Charity had ever seen: a true sculpted ice princess. She could understand how a man's better judgment might be dazzled.

Finally, Sylvia stopped tapping. "I'm sorry," she said. "I shouldn't be mad at you. You're only trying to be nice. It's simply that Michael isn't the point."

"He's cute," Charity said. "And smart at his job."

At this, Sylvia rubbed her lower lip. "Do you want him?" she asked. "Michael enjoys being dominated. It makes him quite excitable."

Charity couldn't help it: The thought of accepting flashed through her mind. If Eric or B.G. wanted to watch, she might have been more inclined to bite, but she got the distinct impression that wasn't what Sylvia was suggesting. Either this was Sylvia's idea of a friendly gesture, or she was hoping to participate.

"Um, my, plate is kind of full right now."

"Yes," Sylvia said with an expression she couldn't read. "I guess it is. You're welcome to change your mind, you know. I have no hold on him."

From what she'd seen, Charity doubted that. Michael was as obsessed with the blonde masseuse as a man could be.

"I appreciate the offer," she said, hoping to avoid insult.

"Hmpf," Sylvia snorted and spun away. She was wearing tight black leather jeans, and her little fanny twitched as she walked. As if she knew Charity was watching, she wagged one finger in the air. "You're also welcome to change your mind about me."

She said this without turning, but Charity still did her best to hide her reaction—just in case the masseuse had eyes in back of her head. Pretty or not, pitiable or not, Sylvia wasn't someone she wanted to tangle with . . . on any basis.

She shook her head, then noticed she'd unknowingly crumpled B.G.'s letter in half. Here was another mystery. Did B.G.'s change of heart mean she'd passed a test or failed one? Would suspending the game increase or decrease the closeness between the three of them? Most of all, what did she really want to happen?

Unable to answer, she turned to open her door. Working herself into a state would do her no more good than it had Sylvia. Rather than jump to conclusions, she could ask B.G. what he meant.

For all she knew, he'd simply decided bowling was better than sex.

Fifteen

Steam rolled through B.G.'s private sauna like Hollywood horror fog. B.G.'s and Eric's backs were propped in opposite corners, their legs stretched down the same cedar bench. With the ease of long association, their knees lolled together lazily.

"You're sure about this?" Eric asked, the tension from his talk with Charity nearly sweated out. His tension at B.G.'s decision was a different matter. That cohabited just fine with the oppressive heat. "You want to throw the rules out the window. No more waiting. Everyone can ask for what they want and say 'yes' or 'no' as they please."

"Everyone could always say 'yes' or 'no.'" B.G.'s eyes were closed, his hands folded loosely across his flat belly. Like Eric, his hips were wrapped in a towel. Despite the sweat beading on his face, he looked ready to fall asleep.

"Just tell me why," Eric said, unaccountably frustrated. It wasn't his job to be annoyed—or pleased—by B.G.'s choices.

"Perhaps I think our guest has the right to know the difference between what each of us truly feels and what we do for the game." B.G.'s eyelids tipped halfway up, but between the clouds of vapor and his boss's talent for concealment, Eric couldn't read his emotions.

"You heard us talking," he said, guessing that much.

"Yes," B.G. admitted.

"Shit." Eric sat up and pressed his fists to his thighs. "You heard what we said about you not getting out enough."

"Yes, but that has nothing to do with this."

"The hell it doesn't. You've got to be a little angry and hurt."

B.G. closed his eyes again. "If I am, it's my concern."

"You're pissed at us. You want to push us away."

"If I wanted to push you away, why would I make it possible for us to be together without limits?"

"I don't know." Eric swung his feet onto the sealed-concrete floor. "Maybe Charity makes you uncomfortable. Maybe you're hoping you'll get tired of her if you can have her all you want."

"Does that scenario seem likely?"

"No, but I'm not you."

B.G. seemed to like this answer, surly though it was. "It's an experiment," he said with a gentle smile. "I want to observe the effects of this change. You know I'm always interested in human behavior."

"Charity isn't your guinea pig!"

B.G. drew his finger and thumb down either side of his grin. "Why do you assume I'm experimenting on her?"

Eric had no answer. How could he when B.G. kept the majority of his thought processes to himself? Stymied, he settled back into his corner, his knees drawn closer to his chest. Sometimes it really ticked him that he didn't understand better this man he loved.

"You don't have to stay with me," B.G. said. "I'm perfectly fine on my own."

"Are you kicking me out?"

"Of course I'm not. I merely thought you'd want to spend time with her now that you don't have to hold back."

"People always hold something back," Eric retorted. "It's human nature—as you should know."

B.G. laid his hand on Eric's ankle. His fingers were slick with sweat, his expression watchful and calm. "Maybe you're afraid of what would happen if you opened up."

Eric twisted away and got to his feet. If that wasn't the pot calling the kettle black! "Fine," he said. "Since you're so eager to get rid of me, I'll go screw our 'guest' senseless."

"I'll never be eager to get rid of you. I love you very much."

Eric raked his hair back and growled, then bent to kiss his infuriating boss. "I'll see you later," he said, sweeping his hand down B.G.'s cheek in a rough caress. "Leave the cameras off."

"Yes," B.G. agreed. "I believe I've learned my lesson with regards to that."

It might have been Eric's imagination, but he thought B.G. looked wistful when he drew back.

❧

Ironically, Eric had to resort to the cameras to find Charity. She turned up in the last place Michael checked: the V-shaped glass catwalk overhanging B.G.'s ultramodern living room. Equipped with earphones and a player hooked to a belt, she was gyrating up and down the walk like a madwoman, full out, dancing the way she lived. When she swung her body around one of the strong steel cables that held it up, Eric's heart lurched in his chest.

God help him, she was the Evel Knievel of pole dancing.

The bridge was too well engineered to sway, but that didn't stop Eric's dizziness. He put his hand on the surveillance console to steady himself. The file entry mentioning her exotic dancing dug its metaphoric elbow into his back. Her head bopped energetically, her hips rolling like her spine was made of rubber. The Joffrey might not have hired her, but no one could fault her confidence.

"Wow," Michael breathed as she did two blood-freezing walkovers in a row. "She could get paid for that."

"She did. Briefly." Eric swallowed, distracted by the way Charity filled her bright-blue jogbra and shorts—tight, boy-style shorts that made her butt look cute enough to bite. He shook himself back to where he was. "You can shut this down now. Sorry for dragging you from your book."

Michael turned to look at him. "You're sure I shouldn't leave the cameras on? The system is completely programmed. It can stay on autopilot."

"No need," Eric said. "Security will keep whatever they need running. You can take a break until you hear differently from B.G. or me."

"If you say so." Michael sounded unsure, but Eric didn't bother worrying about his doubt. For as long as the game was suspended, they were all entitled to privacy.

<hr>

"You want to come down from there?" Eric shouted from the highly polished marble floor.

Fortunately, Charity heard him through his cupped hands. "No way," she laughed. "You come up."

Eric sighed and took the enclosed stairway, trudging reluctantly up each narrow tread. He supposed he should have been grateful she didn't volunteer to bungee jump down, but he was clammy by the time he forced himself to step onto the translucent, green-tinted glass.

The thirty-foot peaked ceiling made the room feel like a barn.

"Oh, man," Charity said, instantly noting his shaky state. She pulled off her earphones and rushed forward. "Sorry. You should have said you were afraid of heights."

"It's not that bad," he denied even as he let her help him sit on the floor. He felt better as soon as he took a death grip on one of the railing's struts. When Charity sat facing him, her knees bumping his, that was better, too.

He told himself it was only his imagination that the room was tilting like a ship at sea.

"Wow." Her hand rubbed a comforting circle on his thigh. "You look as pale as one of my ghosts. How can you stand walking in Seattle?"

"I make a concerted effort not to look down the street. Weirdly enough, it's okay when I'm in a car." He managed to meet her gaze. "B.G. doesn't know, and please don't tell him. I didn't discover I had this problem until I came out here. I'm sure I'll get used to it eventually."

"How long have you been here?"

He rubbed his nose and laughed. "Three years."

"So when you say 'eventually,' you mean it."

"I'm hoping for the best."

He appreciated both the humor and the understanding in her eyes. Charity was pretty good at not judging.

"Do you want to go down now?" she offered after a bit.

"Oh, no," he said, his voice a fraction higher than usual. "I'm fine. Well, actually, I need a few minutes to recover from coming up."

She bent over the hand that wasn't gripping the strut and gave his knuckles a laughing kiss. "Can I ask you a question? If it wouldn't distract you from holding on?"

"Believe me, nothing could do that. What do you want to know?"

"How exactly did you end up working for B.G.? I know you're friends, but it seems out of the ordinary for someone of your background."

"Ah, my silver spoon rears its ugly head again." He smiled at her wince of apology, not so much dreading this as resigned. "You really want to know?"

"If you don't mind."

"I don't mind. At this point, I guess you have the right to ask. I warn you, though, it's not a flattering story. In fact, it's a period of my life I'd just as soon forget."

"Don't tell me you got fired!"

He shook his head at her disbelief. "No. But quite possibly I should have been."

"What did you do?"

"My job," he said and released his breath heavily. She'd left her hand on top of his. He turned it so their fingers twined. "I was director of communications for an Internet start-up called FineEats.com. As my mother likes to put it, 'Bernes don't sit on their bums,' so I'd been working for a while, but this was my first big-deal management job since graduation. We were going to deliver gourmet groceries to people who ordered them online. Have our own fleet of trucks with pictures of brie and caviar on the side.

"The president was the father of an old school buddy of mine, and he went out of his way to recruit me. Big salary. Stock options. I was flattered—not to mention eager to sink my teeth into the challenge. I was responsible for getting our message across to the media and, through them, to the purchasers of our shares. Let me tell you, I was good at that."

"So far I'm not seeing why anyone would fire you. I take it something went wrong."

Forgetting he needed to hold on, he rubbed his second hand across hers. "What went wrong was that the bankers decided our burn rate wasn't high enough."

"'Burn rate' is how fast you go through the money?"

"Right. They wanted us to spend more, borrow more, and give the investors they'd lined up more opportunities to collect interest. That was how things worked in those days. Everybody wanted another Yahoo! or Amazon. Nobody took you seriously unless you spent big.

"As a result, they pressured our president to expand into

areas he didn't understand, areas our employees didn't have the expertise or the numbers to support. What would have been a great small company turned into a giant mess, and my job became lying about the fact that, behind the smoke and mirrors, we had gone to crap. Because of me, because I was so freaking good at what I did, there was virtually nothing left to salvage by the time the SEC stepped in."

"Were you charged with anything?"

Eric closed his eyes and shook his head, the motion dizzying. "I had a certain amount of deniability. After a point, I knew what I was telling people wasn't true, but I hadn't been informed officially that it was a lie. Fortunately for me, B.G. stepped in. I hadn't been in touch with him in years. I don't know how he heard I was in trouble. He pulled some strings and arranged for me to give evidence in exchange for immunity. In the end, I had the unique privilege of not only betraying my fellow employees' trust—a few of whom are still unemployed—but I got to rat out my bosses as well. Then I walked away scot-free."

Overwhelmed, he rubbed his face. "I thought if I just kept saying everything was great, if I just kept those plates spinning in the air, I could buy the company enough time to turn itself around. Instead, I made things worse.

"I had friends at that place. Good friends. They wouldn't speak to me after that. Not to explain, not to hear my offers to help them out with money—which, I guess, it didn't help that I still had. All the times we'd spent working late, the dreams, the endless boxes of pizza, might as well have been shared with strangers."

"Okay," Charity said after a pause. "I think I understand this. Even though you lied for what you thought was a good reason, you feel guilty for doing it. You also feel guilty for telling the truth. Then, to top this guilt fest off, you think you ought to take responsibility for the fact that, in three long years, a few young, smart people didn't pull themselves together and move on. Finally, you're convinced it would somehow help if you were suffering as much as them."

Eric was too startled to take offense. "You forgot to mention my sins of pride."

"Oh, yeah. That's where part of the reason you lie is because you're ashamed to admit you joined a team with a losing coach. I bet you'd been hoping to outdo your overachieving big sister with your success."

Her insight into his character was enough to shock him, but to his amazement, she was grinning.

"You're enjoying this," he said. "You like hearing that I messed up."

"I am small enough to admit it . . . or maybe it's big enough. Anyway, yes, I'm glad to hear you're human. I admire the fact that you feel this bad about what you did, even if I think your guilt is kind of useless. If you really want to help people who are out of jobs, you'd start a new company and hire them. As for the suits you ratted out . . ." Charity blew a raspberry through her lips. "People like that always land on their feet. Chances are, they're dashing somebody else's dreams as we speak."

"You can't make me out to be the good guy," Eric protested. "My own sister thought I was too compromised to warn when she caught wind that the investigation was coming down. If it hadn't been for B.G., I would have been screwed."

Charity reached forward to squeeze his wrists. "I know I don't have a sibling, but from what I've heard, they're not the most objective judges of character. B.G. thinks you're a good guy, and so do I. You're just not a perfect guy, which bugs you I suspect, but them's the breaks."

"Yeah, them's the breaks." Her estimation depressed him, but also carried a certain relief. He wasn't perfect, and that was okay with Charity. He didn't resist when she pulled his hands onto her knees.

"I take it B.G. hired you after that."

"I couldn't face trying anywhere else. Right or wrong, I was a bit infamous after my bosses were led away in cuffs."

"I can see how that could happen. Of course, working for B.G. has its perks."

His smile felt creaky and new. He'd come here to make love to her. Instead, he felt as if she'd loosened a chain he'd had around his neck. His gratitude was alarming, his sense of connection. He stared into her soft violet eyes with a helpless tightening in his gut, the same helpless tightening dozens of males must have experienced ever since she hit puberty.

"You know," he said, his voice rough with emotion even though he tried to keep it light, "you're pretty smart for a girl who thinks she can't survive Harvard."

Charity gave her head a haughty toss. "I am a quantum being. You never know what I'll manage next."

⊱⊰

He was smiling, but it wasn't at her joke. The respect in his eyes made her feel funny. She'd worried he might be angry with her for being blunt.

"So," she said.

"So," he answered, his mouth curving farther up. When his fingers drew feathery scratches on her bare knees, a squeeze of desire streaked to her groin. Beyond the catwalk, a bank of modern windows filled the room with drizzly light. Eric's lashes dropped, fans of silver-brown that shielded his gaze. Happily for her, not everything was shielded. The blood rising to his cheeks implied a common interest.

"Um," she said, squirming a little, "since we can do what we like for now, would it be too much to hope you'd been a bit Boy Scout-y on your way here?"

He looked at her with such affection, her pulse began to skip.

"No," he said, "it wouldn't be too much to hope." He

patted his pocket, which crinkled promisingly. "Considering how hot you look in that outfit, I'm reluctant to ask you to peel out of it, but I really wish you would."

"Here?" She gestured to their perch so far above the ground. "Won't you be nervous?"

Her voice was breathy, his deceptively casual. Had it not been for the bulge rising in his trousers, she might have felt insecure.

"Maybe making love to you up here will effect a cure."

"A cure for something anyway."

"Yes, indeed." He rolled forward on his knees, the motion quick and predatory. "A cure for something very big."

She leaned back from him instinctively, the woman in her responding to the implicit carnal threat—not that she minded him crowding her. Recovering without much effort, she pulled the racerback bra over her head.

He was close enough that she heard the rush of air through his nose.

"Shorts, too," he said, beginning to empty the contents of his pocket.

To take the shorts off, she had to rise. She nearly stumbled when four foil-wrapped condoms were joined by a tube of lubricant.

"Optimistic," she said.

His eyes tilted with amusement as he helped her drag the stretchy shorts down her legs. "I've noticed a tendency for overindulgence when I'm with you."

"All the same, four is a lot."

He laughed and kissed her belly. "Maybe," he whispered against her navel ring, "my eyes are bigger than my . . . stomach."

When he flipped her piercing with the tip of his tongue, a tremor snaked down her spine. Feeling her reaction, his hands tightened on her hips. He used the hold to tug her to her knees, the evidence that he was plenty big enough brushing past her abdomen. With one arm to support her back and the other lifting her rear, he took her mouth in a deep, tight kiss.

For long, yummy moments, she let him have his way.

"You're still wearing your clothes," she pointed out when she could bear to interrupt the kiss.

"Take them off," he said. "I want you to make me naked."

She was happy to oblige, button by button and piece by piece, running her hands over each stretch of skin she bared. His chest was wonderfully solid, its hair curly and warm. That on his arms was silky, on his legs crisp, and on his groin—where it surrounded his upcurved cock—it was the roughest of all. She was glad he didn't shave like B.G. It would have been a shame to hide how masculine he was.

She even loved when his stubbled cheeks scratched back and forth across her breasts.

He said her name between soft, sucking kisses, his hands gently cupping her shoulder blades. "Oh, Charity, how could anyone get enough of you?"

She wouldn't have told him even if she knew. She sighed with pleasure as he laid her back and claimed her mouth again. The glass of the catwalk was cool beneath her, a shocking contrast to the heat of his big body. She gripped his buttocks to pull him closer, reveling in the way it made his muscles clench.

"Not like this," he said, pushing gently back from her hold. "I'd like to take you the way I couldn't that first time."

Her skin seemed to pulse in tandem with her heart. She hadn't forgotten lying on her bed with him behind her, telling her the story of his first sex with B.G. Now he was on his knees, thighs spread, sex hard, his phallic skin so richly red the color needed a different name. Without a word, she reached out, drew the circle of her fingers down his silken shaft, then turned onto her belly.

"Charity . . ." he breathed, clearly shaken by her compliance.

"I'm yours," she said, meaning it more than she'd ever meant anything. "You can take me any way you want."

He sucked in a breath but didn't answer. Instead, he pressed his mouth to the dip where the top of her buttocks met her spine. From there, he trailed slow, wet kisses down the backs of her legs. Her ankles merited a gentle bite. She tensed but couldn't contain a moan when he reached her feet. The pressure of his thumbs did magical things to her arches. When he massaged the pads beneath her toes, tingles swept straight from there to her groin. Surprised by the strength of the effect, she had to gasp.

"Just what I love," he chuckled darkly. "A girl with sensitive feet."

By the time he kissed a return path up her spine, she was more than a little wet, her body writhing restlessly on the glass. He made a prop for her hips with his rolled-up trousers, still pleasantly warm from his wearing them. Satisfied with her position, he lowered his weight over her. He must have sheathed himself at some point. His latex-covered crown teased the tip of her clit, slipping with embarrassing ease in her arousal.

"Nice," he growled, the sound thrilling through her as he eased the broad, curved head just inside her sheath.

"I thought—"

"Sh," he said, hushing her confusion with a kiss just beneath her ear. "That's for later. When you're relaxed."

She liked his method for inducing it. He filled her smoothly, thickly, in a single, breath-stealing stroke.

Now inside her, his pulse beat as steady as a metronome.

"Oh, boy," she said and felt him smile into her hair.

His hands slid up her arms to twine their fingers into fists. She wondered if his eyes were closed, if he dared look through the glass to the gallerylike room below. Then she simply wondered when he would move. She sighed in relief when he did.

"Tell me when you need me to rub you," he said. "I'd like to warm you up a bit before you come."

She was warm already, but not crazy enough to rush. He felt too good pushing steadily in and out, growing harder by the second. He almost made her climax from that, seeming to know exactly where she was sensitive. Before he'd always been a little out of control. Now his experience was on display. When he finally did help her over with his hand, her orgasm was explosive.

He held her up for it, tilting her perfectly against his hips.

"Good," he praised next to her ear. "Let's see if you can't do that once or twice more."

He had a surprise to ensure it. He released his hold on the softness between her legs, fumbled in the breast pocket of his discarded shirt, then brought his hand back with what felt like flexible rubber thimbles covering each of his fingertips.

"What—" she had time to say just as the thimbles began to buzz. Then she couldn't speak at all.

"Battery-powered massage aid," he said, amusement warming his voice. "B.G.'s friends at Scarlet Creations want to call it the Handy Kit."

"Um," she said, arching her back uncontrollably as he slid his fingers into a different, even more effective position. That he was inside her at the same time, rigid and throbbing, perfected the sensations.

He chuckled at her reaction, finding all her good spots—the ones that liked a light touch and the ones that liked a hard press—each buzzing finger spreading the pleasure until she had to cry out with the sweet, building sharpness. It broke in what felt like handfuls of orgasms all at once.

"Your turn," she slurred in the boneless aftermath. "I swear I'm relaxed enough."

He pulled out and switched condoms, the second noticeably thicker than the first. Despite her lassitude, she was able to crane her head just far enough to watch him lube up.

"I love that," she said in sleepy enjoyment. "Someday you'll have to let me watch you jack off. Maybe you could use that Handy Kit on yourself."

"I'll keep that in mind," he said, the words arousingly tight. "And maybe you'll return the favor for me."

She'd prepared herself to tolerate what he did next. This particular pleasure seemed better suited to men. All the same, when his well-oiled thumbs found a set of nerves she hadn't known she'd had, she couldn't help but jerk.

Her body was suddenly a lot more eager than she'd expected.

"Everything all right?" he asked.

"Um, yes," she said, wriggling a little. "That feels good."

He heard her surprise, and it made him laugh. "You haven't done this before, have you?"

She shook her head and bit her lip.

"I'm glad." He leaned closer. "They say women remember all their first times."

She didn't think she could forget anything he did, but the way he groaned when he eased inside was memorable. He seemed bigger this way. Harder. The pressure was strange for a moment, but it quickly turned interesting. Once he was fully in, the tremors that went through him felt electric. He was so worked up, he had to stop for a bit.

"This will be slow," he warned. "I want to be certain you aren't hurt."

She saw little danger of that, not with his caution. Each stroke was a slow journey, one that spread and multiplied the sensations that gripped her sex. Her craving for an orgasm was soon frighteningly strong.

"Touch me," she said, fumbling for his hand. "Put your fingers inside me."

She didn't want the toy that time, just his naked touch. Seeming to know this, he slid two fingers into her as gently as he thrust. His care couldn't save her from her emotions.

Without warning, she was overwhelmed. It was as if he *owned* her now, as if she'd given him possession of more than her body. He lifted her backward as she shook, tipping her up until she sat on his lap. His second hand came around her to cup her breast.

She couldn't speak; she could only gasp for breath as he pushed into her from both sides. His thumb caught her clitoris beneath its pad. Pleasure streaked up her nerves.

"That's it," he said, feeling her quiver. "Be sweet for me. Be wet. I've wanted you so bad, Charity. Oh, God, you feel good."

She climaxed beneath his hand, her cry coming out a sob. As long as he'd waited, this was too much for Eric. He didn't even have to thrust again. She felt him swell inside her and then he went over, too. His pleasure was hard and long, nearly silent but intense. When it finished, he took a minute to loosen his grip. Unfortunately for her, the end of their lovemaking didn't stop her hormonal storm.

"Don't cry," he crooned, pulling out of her and turning her around. "It's all right, sweetheart. It's all right."

Embarrassed, she dragged the back of her hand across her cheek. "Sorry. I don't know why I'm being a drip."

"Because trusting me to do this is a big deal."

"I liked it," she admitted.

He laughed and kissed the next tear away. "I know you liked it. I was there. I'm very grateful and very glad."

She played with one of the curls matted on his chest. "You made it easy. You were nice."

"You're easy to be nice to."

His words fell sweetly on her ear, maybe too sweetly. Rather than steal a glance at his expression, she let her fingers drift down his midsection. "There's still two condoms left."

"So there are." He bent to nuzzle her neck. "What do you say we find a shower and see how well they work wet?"

She nodded, happy but shy. Now that she could ask for

anything, she found it strangely difficult to speak. She hesitated, then plunged ahead. "We could see if B.G.'s shower is available."

"We could," he agreed.

From the warmth of his expression, she sensed she'd suggested the perfect thing.

Sixteen

The next two weeks were the closest thing to heaven Charity had ever known. What worries she might have had failed to gain the slightest grip on her mind. Did Eric care for her beyond a temporary fondness? Would he want her in his life once she returned to her own? And what did it say about her character that she was increasingly drawn to B.G.?

These questions seemed unimportant in the face of having two strong, sexy men cater to her erotic whims. Her memories alone would supply her fantasies for years. It might not be enlightened to admit, but one halfway decent lover boosted a girl's ego. A pair of really good ones shot hers into the stratosphere. Between the two of them, she felt wonderfully spoiled and wonderfully motivated to spoil them back.

This, she thought, was a glimpse of the very best she could be. She was holding her own with them in bed and out—as if B.G.'s magic wand had been waved over her brain. She'd never be as smart as him but, for the moment, she felt smart enough.

With that rarity to buoy her, nothing could dampen her high spirits, not even the realization that she was recklessly close to falling in love with both men. She was simply too happy to count the potential cost.

By the end of the second week, she was grinning everywhere she went, her body as sleek and relaxed as frequent lovemaking could make it. Her thoughts were relaxed, too. The more she practiced B.G.'s eccentric brand of positive thinking, the more it changed her mood—until she felt very pleasantly unflappable. She was beginning to hope she'd put her ghost-phobia behind her.

"I am a quantum sex kitten," she teased herself, tossing an apple she'd nabbed from Mrs. Alvarez. "I am a hot little bundle of happy things."

On the final toss, the fruit bounced off her fingertips. She'd been walking down the corridor to her room, weighing the possible benefits of a pre-dinner nap—an important consideration when so few nights were taken up by sleep. When her snack rolled to a stop at the door to B.G.'s romance library, she realized she might kick off her rest with some light reading.

Who knew what new fantasies she might pick up? It seemed smart to have a few stockpiled with the chance for their fulfillment so close at hand.

She bent to scoop up her apple, then opened the door. The possibility of finding someone inside was the furthest thing from her mind. As a result, when the figure at the window turned, it nearly stopped her heart.

"B.G.!" she exclaimed, her hand to her throat. "I'm sorry. I didn't mean to intrude."

"You're not." Before she could withdraw, he pulled one ice-cream-parlor chair out from under a lace-draped table. "I was thinking of having tea."

Because he obviously meant her to take the seat, she did. "Tea sounds nice."

"And biscotti," he mused, sitting opposite. He didn't move to call for either, merely smiled at her in his gently interested way. Charity fought a twinge of awkwardness. Despite all she'd done with Eric and B.G., she hadn't spent much time with her host alone. He seemed comfortable among the room's frills, not less masculine but oblivious to any threat to his identity.

Scrounging for conversation, she nodded at the colorful paperbacks on the shelves. "Do you read these books?"

"Occasionally." He stroked the tablecloth idly. "I like having a window into women's minds."

"I guess you're not a serious romantic then."

He shrugged one lean shoulder. "More serious than some. Less serious than others."

Charity laughed. "There's a nice, committed answer."

He propped his chin on his hand, a rueful slant entering his smile. "I thought you'd have noticed by now that commitment isn't my middle name."

"You sure? Because you seem pretty committed to your work, not to mention loyal to your friends."

"That's a different species of commitment than women write about in these books."

"Well, I admit I haven't read them all, but from what I have read, I suspect their idea of commitment isn't all that far off from yours. You never know, you might find a happily ever after someday yourself."

B.G. shuddered comically, as if to say, *God forbid*. Since his eyes were sad, she let the matter drop. She had mixed feelings about commitment herself, her mother having spent way too much energy chasing her increasingly inappropriate "soul mates."

So what if she and Eric—and B.G., for that matter— were ships passing in the night? Maybe being really excellent ships was nothing to sneeze at.

Eric and B.G. were one-in-a-million guys. Charity had dated enough of the others to know that for sure. If she'd met them under different circumstances, if they'd been pursuing

more traditional romantic goals, Eric could have counted on
her to keep her hands off B.G. What she couldn't have promised was that a daydream or two featuring the handsome
physicist would never have crossed her mind. Though she'd
come to know B.G. better, he was still a deep, dark, sexy
mystery.

Her reality being what it was, it seemed silly to waste
the chance to investigate.

"I've noticed something," she said, slipping her fingers
between his on the lacy cloth. "You haven't approached me
alone since you set aside the rules."

In a heartbeat, B.G.'s gaze turned from mild to keen.
The full force of his attention prickled her skin like an electric buzz. It took a moment before he spoke. "I thought you
enjoyed the three of us together."

"I do. I'm just wondering if the question you once asked
me still stands."

She knew he'd remember what she meant. A mind like
his held on to everything. What she hadn't guessed was that
when he answered, his voice would be rough and shy.

"You implied you wouldn't be intimate with me until I
was desperate."

"Maybe I don't want desperation. Maybe I want you."

He blinked at her as if his brain was temporarily stuck,
his fingers withdrawing an inch from hers. "You want me
for now, you mean."

Again that roughness brushed the nerves of her ear.

"Isn't now enough?"

At her question, his head jerked slightly back. She felt
like a fencer scoring a touch, knowing she'd caught him out
even though she couldn't say how.

"Yes," he said slowly, standing as he did. "I suppose now
couldn't hurt."

*   *   *

B.G. knew what he was doing was dangerous. Every move he'd made lately seemed not to accomplish what he was aiming for. The last thing he'd expected when he dropped the rules was that Eric and Charity would want to spend time with him. Mind you, he wasn't complaining. These last few weeks had been quite rewarding. He had laughed more and relaxed more and certainly been pleasured more than he could remember happening before. With them, a simple evening before the fire became an angel's boon. Their company was addictive, and therein lay the rub.

He had to prepare himself to let them go. Without being caught interfering, he had to coax Eric to pursue what B.G. knew he wanted: to commit himself, as Charity put it, and claim his personal happy ending.

Accepting Charity's offer seemed unlikely to bring this about, unless a childish thing like jealousy could get Eric off his sticking point.

More likely, if Charity had sex with him on her own, without their threesome's inherent charm, she'd see once and for all whom she preferred.

"Here?" he said.

She smiled at his question, the expression softening her already feminine face. "Anywhere is good, cowboy, as long as you're comfortable."

He liked the endearment. She could tell by the way he ducked his head and smiled to himself. She didn't have long to wait before he moved. He knelt before her chair, initiating a seduction as unique as he was. A bright-yellow pleated skirt covered her thighs, a flippy, cheery thing that suited her mood. B.G.'s hands warmed her knees, then slid under the cloth. His fingers drew teasing circles on her inner thighs.

"That tickles," she said.

He smiled but couldn't resist giving an order. "Don't talk," he said, kissing one knee to soften the words. "I want you to listen through the silence."

She listened as he disrobed her: to the rustle and slide of the skirt, the pop of her shirt buttons, the snap of her bra, the soft thunk her shoes made on the carpet as he set them carefully aside. His deliberation fascinated her, especially when he turned it on himself. She knew how lovely he looked naked. She hadn't known how lovely he'd look stripping. She especially loved that under all that calmness, his cock was high and ready.

She didn't try to touch him, just let him sweep her up in his arms and carry her to an overstuffed pink loveseat. Springs creaked beneath her as he set her down. When he took the seat beside her, his knee bumped hers. His hand slid down the curve of her side. The caress was so polite she wanted to laugh. Apart from being naked, they could have been Victorians in a scented bower. Just so, the lovers of days gone by might have listened for the sounds of quickened respiration or sought the evidence of a deepened blush. B.G. leaned forward and gave her both, his breath rushing soft as butterflies across her cheek.

Thus he began his Kiss.

It deserved a capital letter, at least in her mind, demonstrating as nothing else could how much he'd adjusted his natural style for her and Eric. This kiss was gentleness itself, a blind man's exploration of the planes and curves of her face. Her brows were praised, then her temples, then the tingling tip of her nose. Long minutes of enchantment passed before he settled his mouth over hers, and even then it spoke subtly. Desire was there, and tenderness, and a selfless patience she wasn't sure she'd ever understand. Bit by bit, his kiss erased her awkwardness, arousing her in slow motion until each soft pulse of feeling shook her body.

He *knew* her, as old-fashioned people liked to say, without their flesh becoming one.

Hoping to bring that part of the process closer, she swung onto his lap. Even with her eagerness, she found herself moving slower than normal.

The sensation was worth savoring. As she slid to him, one knee to either side of his hips, his erection brushed her belly, as strong and heated as his kiss was soft. She dragged her nails along his scalp until his head fell back. When it came up again, his dark eyes glowed.

"Candy dish," he said, the only words he'd spoken since they'd begun.

The dish sat on the table to her left. She removed its flowery ceramic lid to find a selection of wrapped condoms. *Candy, indeed.* Grinning, she opened one. The silence increased her anticipation as she rolled the sheath down his stiffened shaft. His tip was already sticky. She pinched the latex lightly against it for the pleasure of making him gasp.

She almost had him. He drew a breath as if to speak but then held back.

She rose onto her shins, impatient to have him inside her once and for all. B.G. stopped her before they engaged, gripping her waist and lifting her even as he came to his feet. He was stronger than she expected. Hitching her up against him seemed effortless.

She clung to him, watching his gleaming eyes for some hint of what would come next.

He looked at her lips and licked his own. He carried her past the tea table and a tufted pink footstool. She clutched his shoulders and tried not to hyperventilate, her efforts obvious enough to make the corners of his mouth turn up.

When he thunked her back against the wall beside the gilt-framed portrait of some bewigged Regency rake, she knew they'd reached his goal.

If they hadn't, she doubted he'd have used any force at all.

Pinned by his weight, she trembled just like a romantic heroine. His gaze dropped to her breasts, then to the place where her pubis rolled against the muscles of his waist. She was squeezing him so tightly, it wasn't easy for him to pull his hips back. That done, he widened her thighs, pressed his cock down with his thumb, and eased himself into her cleft.

She moaned at the slow, thick entry, at the lengthy withdrawal and return. Now that he was taking her, he held her trapped to the wall, the velvet flocking on the paper soft behind her back. She would have added her strength to his if she'd been able, but his hold on her hips prevented her from taking any more than he gave. *He* moved her. *He* chose his penetration and angle. It was a bondage of the simplest sort, that of superior male force. It was also a kind bondage, nothing he did remotely capable of causing hurt.

She wanted it to last forever, but even the great B.G. had his limits.

She knew when he reached them. The change in his breathing would have been another man's curse of pleasure; the tightening of his buttocks, someone else's groan.

As she struggled to stay silent, she sank her teeth into her lower lip. Finally, she gave up.

"Please," she whispered, needing the end as much as she needed breath.

The word went through him like a slap, but even then he didn't speak. He thrust a little higher inside her, a little stronger, his hands hard on her softness. Another minute passed at this pace, during which he held her an aching fraction from orgasm, until she was literally panting for it. His eyes squeezed shut at the sound, and his jaw clenched hard enough to click. He sped up the one bit more she needed. Her body tightened and reached. Then, as if a huge quantum hand had gripped them both, the climax burst like heat lightning, flashing over them at the same instant, triggering one rolling burst of feeling after another.

At the end, a single sound broke low in his throat.

She thought it might have been her name, but she wasn't in any condition to say. Her own voice had been stolen by pleasure, her ears nearly deafened by the rushing of her blood. She came until her bones felt limp.

When her tremors stopped, he touched his lips to hers again.

For no reason she could explain, his kiss felt like an apology.

B.G. rested his chin atop her head, his arms still locked beneath her hips. Her weight was a burden he felt strangely comforted to support.

This isn't good, he thought, his mind having trouble constructing more than these simple words. Yes, joining one's body to another's tended to affect one emotionally, but his chest was almost too tight to breathe. He wanted to weep the way he had the night she spanked him—which seemed a less than appropriate reaction.

He couldn't be falling in love with her. That would be perverse.

"You're all right," he said, unintentionally making it more order than question.

"Yes," she said, noticeably disconcerted by his tone.

He uncoupled them as gently as he could and set her on her feet. The prophylactic took only a moment to strip and toss in the trash. Charity touched his subsiding shaft as if to soothe him while he fell. One fingertip traced a heavy vein, the gesture intimate enough to unsettle him.

"Well," he said. Truly naked now, he patted her bare shoulder. She was so warm, so soft . . . A flush as fine as French rosé glowed on the slope of her breasts. Her nipples shook with tiny aftershocks of excitement. In spite of his recent satisfaction, his body began to reverse course. In that moment, he knew true regret.

He couldn't take her again. One more coupling like that just might brand her on his heart. His hopes for the future did not include pining after what wasn't his.

With an effort, he pulled his attention back to his brain. "I should go. I have some correspondence I need to see to."

He gathered his clothes as quickly as he could, pausing only to put on his pants. Considering his omission of undergarments, not to mention his agitated state, he was lucky he didn't do himself harm. Charity watched in silence, her gaze like weighted fire.

"B.G." Her voice stopped him at the door. "Are you really that uncomfortable without your rules?"

This was the same accusation Eric had made. From her, at this particular time, the arrow struck a trifle too close to home.

"I'm fine," he said, his hand resting on the lintel for support. "I have some work to do."

She let him leave without further challenge. For that, he was appallingly relieved.

Charity tried not to feel rejected, but B.G. might as well have poked his finger into the bubble of her happiness. With each step she took toward her room, her spirits sank.

She'd thought . . . she'd hoped she'd be able to keep B.G. and Eric for a while. Not forever, but a while. Now—just like those times when her mother's man-chasing ways had made her the new kid in school—she'd have to fight to be liked again. She'd have to start all over from scratch.

She didn't understand how what they'd shared could make B.G. want to run. To her, their lovemaking had been amazing, a truly special touching of souls . . . unless her soul was too shallow to be worth touching.

She'd been kidding herself, apparently, about being new and improved.

"Stupid," she said, pushing her door shut behind her. The hinges were designed not to slam, or she would have reveled in the noise. Everything she'd feared was true. She was an overemotional, shallow, stupid floozie just like her mom.

"Stop it," she ordered, swiping at the tears that had sprung to the corners of her eyes. She was blowing this all out of proportion. She was letting B.G.'s reaction make her unhappy when he could have had a thousand reasons for what he did. For all she knew, her guess about the rules being his safety blanket was on the mark.

Maybe B.G. wanted to get away from her because he liked what they shared too much. The man might be a genius, but she'd long since learned anyone with a Y chromosome could act dumb occasionally.

She flung herself onto the bed and wrapped the comforter around her, still feeling crummy but more in control. Determined to pull herself together, she forced her breathing to calm.

She was what she was. If God or the universe or whatever ran this world couldn't manage to love her, with or without improvement, they weren't worth worrying about.

Ri-ight, said a sneering inner voice. *You don't care if you're loved.*

"Crap," she said and threw a pillow against the wall.

The outburst didn't make her feel better, but she tried to pretend it did. She'd had a boyfriend once, a hippie throwback who'd taught her to meditate. The habit hadn't taken, but she still half-remembered how. She breathed in, then out, holding the air and slowly releasing it. The room was shadowed, the sun setting on the other side of the house. The courtyard garden looked weedy and sinister. In spite of being prone to the creeps, she was damned if she was going to get up and turn on the light. If she *wasn't* a quantum being, if her thoughts had no reality-altering power, her fear of ghosts couldn't attract them to her.

This conclusion didn't prevent her neck from tightening at the sound of footsteps dragging down the hall. A full-body tingle swept her skin. Those weren't Eric's footsteps, or B.G.'s; they scuffed along the slate too much for that.

She became aware that the room was icy. Silence had spread through the house around the shuffling sound, descending without warning like a cotton fog. No clocks ticked. No voices spoke. Nothing moved but the approach of the strange footsteps.

Charity breathed faster, her head gone oddly light. The sensation was so trancelike that when she noticed she could see her breath turn to white clouds, she couldn't get her mind to process why that was wrong. The door began glowing around its edges an instant before it was shoved.

That's when she discovered she was paralyzed.

A figure moved through the light, familiar but shadowy.

"Stupid," it said with a sneer of supreme disgust. Then tried to slam the bedroom door.

Oh, my God, Charity thought as the figure covered its face.

It looked just like her. It stood there, trembling: a picture of Misery struggling not to cry.

"Stop it," it said, and wiped the tears away. It looked so angry Charity was proud.

Be angry, she thought. *Stupid Y chromosome.*

But the figure wasn't mad at B.G. It was heartbroken, staring forlornly into space like it didn't care if the world ended.

Poor thing, Charity thought. *She needs to snap out of that.*

Then her double flung herself onto the bed and into the very space Charity occupied. Every hair she had stood on end. The other wrapped the comforter around herself, just as Charity had done before. The other blew out her tension. The other forced her breathing to calm.

I am what I am, Charity heard her think—and all the

rest that followed. Though she'd conceived those words herself, they seemed alien.

She was outside her thoughts. Or maybe she was bigger
than what her brain could contain. Maybe the ideas that flitted
through her conscious mind were only the tip of the iceberg of
who she was. It was the kind of revelation you had when you
were stoned, but stoned wasn't how she felt. This was a different level of altered state, one in which she was absolutely alert.
Her atoms seemed spread to the distant corners of the cosmos,
intertwined with everything. If she was quiet, she could feel
each line of energy being tugged by the lines it crossed, a huge
radiating net of awareness. She was conscious of being terrified, but the emotion seemed not just removed but irrelevant.

I am a quantum being, she thought as her double threw the
pillow against the wall.

The spell, or whatever it was, broke the instant the pillow hit.

The double disappeared. Charity was alone.

"Holy cow," she gasped, covered in a clammy sweat. She
had to brace her hands on the mattress to keep upright.
Then she heard it: the slow, scuffing drag of feet coming
down the hall. Her feet. Approaching the room again.

"Fuck," she said, then muttered a hasty prayer. The vapor
of her breath came out winter-white.

This time, before the door could open, she mustered her
will and screamed.

B.G. was at the turning of the passage to his private wing
when he heard Charity's cry. A thousand possible causes
whirled through his mind as he raced to her room.

Despite his haste, Eric was there before him, on the bed
hugging her tight. Charity was crying and clinging back.
The pang B.G. experienced was ironic. He'd been thinking

about jealousy, and here it was. He simply hadn't expected it to be his.

"What is it?" he asked, taking a seat on the edge of the futon. "Why did you scream?"

It took a few tries to sort out her tale of ghostly doubles and events going round in loops. She seemed embarrassed by her hysteria but unable to rein it in. When she explained that a long-ago boyfriend of her mother had instilled this panic by trying to convince her his house had ghosts, B.G.'s temper snapped.

"That's outrageous!" he exclaimed. "Bad plumbing is my guess. For goodness sake, the vast majority of supposed spectral phenomena turn out to be nothing more than clanking pipes."

"B.G.," Eric said cautioningly.

"But it's a travesty. Terrorizing a twelve-year-old. How could her mother condone it?"

"I don't know," Eric said, evidently trying to send a message with his eyes. "The point is, you certainly wouldn't want to suggest to Charity that *you* believe in ghosts."

"Oh," he said, suddenly wishing he'd caught on right away. For that matter, he wished Charity had divulged this story earlier. He would have done a number of things differently. Hoping to undo the damage, he called on his most confident professorial demeanor. "I have absolutely no hard scientific evidence to support the existence of conscious ghosts."

For some reason, this declaration inspired a laugh. "Thank you," Charity said, "but that still doesn't explain what I saw. It was like that movie *Groundhog Day*. I thought it was going to play over and over to infinity."

At her resurgent sniffle, Eric patted her back while B.G. tried not to feel useless. It didn't help that this was his fault. It broke his heart to see those tears staining her cheeks.

"It might not have been a true time loop," he said, offering her a fresh tissue.

This was not the right thing to say.

"What the hell else would you call it?" She snatched the tissue, blew her nose, then looked abashed. "Sorry. I'm not mad at you."

That was debatable, but B.G. chose to act as if he believed her. "Strong electromagnetic fields have been shown to affect the temporal lobe of the brain, which can, in turn, produce hallucinations. What you saw could have been a waking dream."

In his desire to be helpful, he had spoken incautiously. When Eric turned to stare at him, B.G. feared his old friend was assembling the pieces of a picture he'd hoped to keep indistinct.

"Strong electromagnetic fields?" Eric repeated. "Correct me if I'm wrong, but you're not talking about the kind of EM field you find around a hair dryer."

"No," B.G. admitted.

"Hell, B.G., what have you been playing with?"

B.G.'s shoulders tensed defensively. "I shut the project down when your sister told us about the trouble. The fields should have dissipated by now."

Eric's face was grim. "Exactly what did you shut down?"

B.G. hesitated, then decided he couldn't make the situation worse—and Charity probably had a right to know. "I'll show you," he said. "Both of you. But you must swear never to go there alone."

Charity spoke through the crumpled tissue she'd pressed to her nose. "If whatever it is caused whatever that was, you have my solemn oath. I'd just as soon not revisit *The Twilight Zone.*"

B.G. appreciated her stab at humor. He hoped she could hold on to it through the rest.

Seventeen

She could walk, but barely. Though the threat she'd faced wasn't physical, her knees were still quivering. Too much adrenaline, she supposed. As she stepped away from the bed, her legs almost gave out.

Eric's hand flashed to her elbow. "We should do this later. You're in no state for sightseeing."

Part of her wanted to give in, but she knew if she let herself, she'd never overcome her fear. "I want to go," she said. "I need to see whatever made this happen."

"You need new clothes," B.G. put in. "Those are soaked."

Clarity glanced down at them in surprise. She'd assumed she was clammy from sweating, but no sweat could get clothes this evenly wet.

"It was cold," she said slowly. "Right before it happened, the room went cold as ice."

B.G. nodded. "Probably a change of vibration due to the energy field. That can lead to heat transfer and condensation." He fingered the strap of her form-fitting ribbed tank top. Material that had once been light green was now dark. "Maybe what happened here wasn't in your mind."

"You know," Charity said, "you could at least pretend to

be a little more sympathetic and a little less scientifically intrigued."

She'd meant to tease, but hurt slipped into his eyes before he could hide it. "My apologies," he said, looking away. "Sometimes I forget other people aren't experiments."

Charity clucked her tongue. "I know better than to believe that. I also know you can't help being interested." She rubbed his sleeve when she wasn't sure her reassurance got through. "I'm putting on a robe. I'll be right out."

Not knowing where they were going, she grabbed a pair of jeans as well. When she emerged from the bathroom, the men were standing awkwardly side by side—her guys, as she'd begun to refer to them in her mind. She doubted they'd said a word while she was gone.

"Shoes," B.G. advised, and she laced on a pair of Nikes.

If *just do it* ever needed to be her motto, now was the time.

Walking through the house was different with B.G. Once they passed into the below-ground section, the lights no longer turned on for him. Eric and Charity were following a few steps behind him, and a small but definite lag marked the time it took for them to trigger the sensors.

"Something wrong with your wiring?" Eric asked, noting the delay.

Too preoccupied to answer, B.G. shook his head. He looked as worried as Charity had ever seen him. Given that this was the Great Inscrutable B.G., his expression would have passed for mildly concerned on anyone else.

"He's made himself invisible," Charity deduced. "Programmed the system not to announce his presence. I bet there are no cameras down here. He can creep around all he wants without being seen."

B.G. raised a brow but didn't deny her guess.

Eric pulled her closer to his side, his arm warm and protective around her back. "Is it much farther?"

"No," B.G. said. They had reached an open archway under which stood a small marquetry table. A bronze statuette of a Grecian woman with an urn sat on its patterned wood. Even when the lights were on, this hall was murky. Whatever lay behind the arch was hidden by the dark.

Charity watched while B.G. touched something on the statue to release a hidden drawer in the table.

"Night vision goggles," he said, handing over a pair.

They looked small to Charity. The lenses were the size of swim goggles, set into a flexible metal band—perhaps an improvement on previous technology that B.G. had given his two cents to. When she put them on, the world turned ghostly green. However they worked, they gave off a barely audible, high-pitched hum.

"Isn't this a bit cloak and dagger?" Eric asked as he settled his goggles on his nose.

"Apparently not," B.G. said drolly.

Charity assumed his answer had to do with whatever "trouble" had led him to shut down his secret project. She hadn't been listening closely at the time, but now she wondered what Eric's uptight sister had to do with it.

"This way," B.G. said, gesturing them into the glowing dark. "Stay close to me, please. As long as you're within three feet of me, you won't set off the detectors."

They bunched together like kids creeping through a haunted house. The comparison amused her, but her humor faded as soon as the first suit of armor clued her in on where they were going. She sighed loudly enough for Eric to squeeze her shoulder. It figured this would involve revisiting her last scene of terror.

The glassy-eyed staghead didn't look any better in the goggles' unearthly light.

"Sorry," B.G. said as she gritted her teeth against complaining. When he pulled aside a tapestry, however, with a distinctive swishing noise, her tolerance gave out.

"You were the ghost I heard! Why didn't you tell me? You could have saved me from being afraid."

"I was hoping you'd believe the story about the squirrel."

She was muttering a curse when Eric wrapped her in his arms from behind. "We can argue about this later. Let B.G. open the door so we can move where we aren't in danger of being heard."

The door had a hidden panel that scanned B.G.'s hand and retina prints. That checked, the steel-backed, pressure-sealed wood swung inward to reveal a descending concrete corridor. The air inside was cool and still. It smelled familiar, but the scent wasn't one she could pin down. When the door closed behind them, the overhead lights went on. They pulled off their goggles.

"Wow," Eric said, taking in the nuclear bunker view. "When did you build all this?"

"Construction finished the year before you came. Getting permits for the equipment was a challenge, but I managed to keep as few people as possible in the loop."

B.G. tipped his head to indicate they should walk. They continued for what felt like a quarter-mile, all of it sloping down. On the way they passed two fire extinguishers and three riveted metal doors, one labeled "Emergency Shelter" that was striped in eye-catching slants of yellow and black. Charity's nerves weren't comforted by the suggestion that emergencies might occur. A hundred feet farther, the next door was similarly striped. To Charity's relief, it only said "Observation Deck."

B.G. unlocked it, and they went in.

The room was crammed with equipment Charity wouldn't have known how to recognize. Electrical cords tangled into nests on the floor, and a half-dozen white lab coats hung from pegs on the wall. A double-thick, wire-reinforced square of glass overlooked a void as black and featureless as a cave. B.G. picked between the cords, stepped around a worn-looking rolling chair, and threw a large wall switch. With a hollow clanking noise, the lights beyond the window went on.

"Holy shit," Charity breathed.

The observation deck overlooked a concrete pit the size of a pleasure yacht. Sitting down inside it was a huge machine. It resembled sewer pipes connected at their joints by brightly colored boxes, forming a ring that encircled more rows of equipment. Computers, she suspected, though they weren't the kind she was used to seeing—more like tall metal cabinets. Another, smaller circle of piping made a loop above the one beneath.

Too amazed to be afraid, she stepped closer to the window for a better look. "What the hell is that?"

Eric came up beside her. "Unless I wasted my time leafing through all those issues of *Discover,* that is Benjamin Grantham's personal synchrotron."

Despite knowing the answer, he sounded as stupefied as she felt. Charity rubbed the tip of her nose. "Can I ask what's a synchrotron?"

"It's a particle accelerator," B.G. supplied. "We use it to speed up streams of subatomic particles with powerful electromagnetic pulses. When the streams of particles go fast enough, we extract a few and smash them together. Most scientists study the smaller particles that are produced, but I'm more interested in side effects."

"Like time loops."

"Yes," he said, "most of the induced phenomena involve the warping of ordinary time. That's because the radiations emitted by the collisions are traveling at the speed of light. As Einstein predicted in his theory of relativity, this means that—from our perspective—those waves of released energy have infinite mass, infinite energy, and no size whatsoever. They're also free from the limits of linear time. In essence, we're yanking a bit of pure, undigested quantum stuff into our dimension."

He had joined her and Eric as he spoke. Now he curled his palm around her nape where her robe's silk collar folded down. At the sweep of his thumb beneath her hair, Charity shivered—but not from fear. This was the sort of shiver she thought she might have experienced if Einstein himself had shaken her hand. Naturally, she had no way of judging if B.G. was as smart as that, but to her he was. For the first time, she felt privileged for having been able to see what she had. Scary or not, she'd been admitted into an elite circle. She'd witnessed what other people only wondered about.

She turned to gaze at B.G.'s profile: the long nose, the soulful eyes, the wonderfully sensitive mouth.

I love him, she thought, giving up her denial. She didn't know whether to swear or laugh, especially since this must mean she loved Eric, too. The knots both men put in her stomach were pretty darn similar.

"Someone must have noticed this weird stuff before," she said aloud. "You can't be the only one."

"Mostly civilians," B.G. acknowledged. "Unfortunately, if an ordinary citizen claims to have seen something from the future or the past, or if they're in a situation where their experience of time is anomalous, their stories are generally dismissed as quaint—no more real than a folk legend. Naturally, scientists who work in subatomic facilities prefer to pretend the phenomena don't exist. Reluctant as they are to admit their work might be interfering with the space-time continuum, they're hardly going to go in search of proof. They'd rather not, as you put it, step into *The Twilight Zone.*"

"But nobody's gotten hurt working here?"

"We've only been able to elicit small occurrences—less dramatic than what you've seen yourself. Changes in brain activity. Altered states that produce what may be no more than hallucinations. We document everything, of course, and try to repeat the effect, but thus far the process has been chaotic. The smallest change in initial conditions, and we get no results at all." B.G. scratched his head in frustration. "We did have a lab tech win some money in the lottery when he fell asleep at his desk and dreamed the right number. I have to admit, though, we haven't validated that as a true precognitive event."

Charity put her hand to her breast. "You have a 'we.' That's nice."

"Of course I do. I can't run all this by myself."

"Speaking of which," Eric said. "Your employees . . . ?"

"Cleared," B.G. assured him.

"Cleared of what?" Charity asked.

B.G. looked at her, furrowed his brow, then appeared to make up his mind. "They've been cleared of security risks. According to Eric's sister, who works at the Treasury Department, someone at the CIA thinks we have a spy."

The conclusion Charity jumped to came quickly, but she hesitated before airing it. "Don't you think . . . I mean, unless you know some reason why it can't be true, don't you think the spy is probably Sylvia?"

B.G. sighed. "I expect you're correct, although I'm loathe to believe it. Being emotionally awkward and inept at getting close to people scarcely makes one a spy. In truth, it's hard to imagine the spymaster who'd hire her. On top of which, I approached *her* about coming here in the first place, under circumstances I don't believe could have been set up. Back then, I didn't ask for more than a cursory report on her because—ironic as it may turn out to be—I thought I could trust my judgment. She'd been at that spa for a year, a spa I'd only visited once before. I'd be willing to bet she's genuinely kinky. It's difficult to fake liking what she does."

He shook his head regretfully. "I suppose those arguments don't matter now. My security team is going over her background with a fine-toothed comb. So far they've come up empty, but rest assured if there's anything to find, they will. In the meantime, unless Sylvia does something overtly suspicious, I'm going to treat her as I normally would."

Charity worried her lower lip, suddenly pricked by guilt. "Would having an accomplice count as suspicious?"

"An accomplice?" This came from both Eric and B.G.

"I kind of found out by accident. That camera guy, Michael, is totally obsessed with her. He's been earning sexual favors by privately screening tapes for her."

She had to fight not to quail when B.G. turned stern. "Why didn't you tell me this right away?"

"For the same reason you didn't tell me you were looking for a spy. I didn't think you needed to know. I'm no tattletale. Anyway, Michael promised he wouldn't do it again. I nabbed the key so I could double-check."

"God," said Eric to the ceiling, though he looked more exasperated than angry.

"You probably shouldn't be too mad at him," she added. "Sylvia has a knack for playing on people's sympathies. He thought he was giving her a treat to make up for being snubbed by, uh, you two."

"Mainly me, I suspect," B.G. said. "It seems Sylvia wasn't my only ill-considered hiring choice."

"He didn't—"

"I know." B.G.'s hand settled on her shoulder. "He didn't mean any harm."

Charity had a knee-jerk urge to plead for Michael not to get sacked. Instead, she asked the question she dreaded the answer to. "Could Sylvia have found out anything important?"

B.G. blew out a heavy breath. "I don't think so. We keep our data isolated on the servers here, and we haven't had any breaches. I'd be more concerned if she were gone. Because she's not, she may still be trying to discover how to locate and gain access to the lab."

This sounded reasonable to Charity. "She did seem like she was hoping to buddy up to me. Maybe she thought I could help her find it—which I would have said was a waste of time, except here I am."

"Here you are," B.G. agreed and, in spite of everything, he broke into a beatific smile.

"We have to look into this," Eric interrupted uncomfortably.

"I think we have to do more than look." B.G. dug a phone from one of the cluttered desks and pressed a two-button code. "Seal the estate," he said to whoever answered. "And call your local law enforcement contacts. We have a situation that precludes letting anyone leave the grounds."

When he hung up with no more words than that, Charity knew they were finished with playing games.

They forgot to put on their goggles and bunch together on the way out, but it didn't matter. The tapestry that hid the tunnel door had been pulled aside, and the lights were already on. Like a nightmare called up by her fears, Sylvia stood outside in black leather pants and bustier. Despite her beauty and the fetishy vibe to her clothes, she came off as precisely the sort of female badass Charity hoped not to meet in a dark alley.

Shit, she thought, freezing in her tracks. She wished she were wearing anything but this stupid ankle-length robe and jeans . . . and that was before she noticed the gun.

There wasn't a curseword big enough to express her dismay at that.

"Out," Sylvia barked, using the firearm to gesture. "Line up against the wall."

B.G. stepped forward instead, rubbing his temple like an absentminded professor. Not so absentminded, Charity didn't think. When he moved, the door to the lab automatically swung shut.

Now that she was listening for it, Charity could hear the mechanism lock.

"Stop!" Sylvia ordered. "I want you against the wall!"

B.G. stopped but didn't back up. "What are you doing here?" he asked, sounding confused.

Charity would have thought the answer was obvious, but Sylvia was eager enough to explain. She tossed her head and did her best to look down her nose. "Michael was kind enough to inform me of the lockdown. He worried I'd be afraid. I figured this was my last chance to move."

"And you knew we'd be here because . . . ?"

This made Sylvia run her tongue across her grin. "I suggested he install infrared cameras down here. So we wouldn't miss anyone 'getting busy' anywhere." Her gun arm came out a little straighter. "You see what happens when you forget that little people have power?"

"Where is Michael?" Eric asked. "Is he all right?"

Sylvia seemed not to notice he'd stepped up beside B.G. "He's a bit tied up at the moment. He became upset when he realized I hadn't befriended him for sex."

"Why are you doing this?" Charity asked—as she realized the object seemed to be to keep Sylvia talking.

Sylvia turned to her, her eyes as blank and cold as chips of green ice. Looking into that odd, disconnected gaze, Charity knew whatever she thought she'd understood about the masseuse, it hadn't been the whole story. Sylvia was silent for so long, Charity thought she wouldn't answer.

"I'm doing this to keep the Americans from controlling this discovery all by themselves," she said at last. "They really can't be trusted, you know. Look at the trouble they cause in the world. Surely even you can see they need to be kept in check."

"I'm, uh, not very political," Charity said.

"No." Sylvia's gaze raked her up and down. "I guess you wouldn't be."

"Not to sound trite, Sylvia," B.G. put in, "but you really can't get away with this. If the house isn't surrounded, it will be soon."

"That *would* be a problem," Sylvia said, "if I didn't know there has to be a secret exit from your lab, to allow your employees in and out without being seen. I'm betting you didn't tell your guards to barricade that." With an ominous click, she released the gun's safety. Her hand was shaking, a fine, nervous tremor. Unfortunately, it wasn't shaking enough to suggest she'd miss. "Open the door, B.G. I want to see your real playroom."

"I'm sorry, Sylvia." B.G. sounded truly regretful. "What you want doesn't matter very much to me."

She shot him so quickly and with so little noise that Charity didn't realize it had happened until B.G. staggered back with a burst of red flowering on his sleeve. Sylvia had hit his upper arm. Eric moved as if to rush her, but B.G. restrained him even as he bled. For her part, Charity couldn't contain a cry of fear. Sylvia had both hands on the gun butt now, and her eyes were locked on B.G.'s.

"Let me into that lab," she said, dark and low.

"You know I can't, Sylvia. My research mustn't fall into the wrong hands."

Without warning, her face went crimson. "Yours are the wrong hands!" she shouted. "Yours, yours, yours!"

Charity's heart was threatening to choke her throat. She moved closer without thinking. Sylvia was out of control. Her forearm muscles were corded up. She was going to shoot B.G. again, maybe somewhere crucial. "Sylvia—" she began.

She didn't get a chance to say another word, helpful or otherwise. With a noise that sounded like a snarl, Sylvia grabbed her wrist, spun her back against her chest, and shoved the gun beneath her jaw.

"How about her!" Sylvia demanded. "Would you open the door for your precious Charity?"

Don't, Charity tried to mouth, but B.G. wasn't watching. Instead, he was shuffling forward toward Sylvia, his right hand clamped to his wounded arm. Sylvia backed up so he couldn't reach her, but the move distracted her from noticing Eric was edging away.

Yes, Charity thought. *Go get help.*

"You should give up," B.G. was saying in his calmest, gentlest voice. The only sign he'd been shot was his slightly ragged breathing. "Let us get you some help. If you keep this up, you know you'll fail. It's impossible for it to end any other way."

A shiver slid down Charity's spine followed by a more general wash of cold. Behind her, Sylvia shuddered, too. The same indefinable scent that had filled the tunnel to the lab tickled her nose, except that now it seemed to be rolling off of B.G. Was he trying to distract Sylvia, or could he be attempting to coax the quantum dimension to nudge events in his favor? If he was, Charity's fear could only get in the way. She reached for confidence instead.

"He's right," she said as clearly as she could with the muzzle jamming into her neck. "I know you're angry, but fighting B.G. is pointless. He always gets what he wants. Somehow, some way, he'll get his way this time, too. Maybe the gun will misfire or your hand will shake. Maybe the power will suddenly go out. However it happens, you'll be caught."

It might have been her imagination, but the lights appeared to flicker just a tiny bit.

"Shut up," Sylvia snapped. "You think you're better than me. You think you can split them up and pick the one you want. But they'll always love each other more than you. You're nothing to them but a stupid slut."

Everything she said might have been true, but Charity had never felt less stupid. Slightly taller than Charity, Sylvia had leaned down to hiss the insult in her ear, tilting the gun away as she did. Though this wasn't the break Charity had been picturing, she wasn't at all surprised when a weight crashed into them from behind, driving them helplessly to the floor.

Even as the air rushed from her lungs beneath the impact of two bodies, Charity grinned. The pistol flew from Sylvia's hand as if it had been thrown. B.G. nabbed it and then the weight lifted from her back.

"Son of a bitch," Sylvia cursed, leaping for Eric.

At once the pair were grappling across the hall, rolling around too wildly for B.G. to get a clear target. Charity managed to sit up, but all she could do was watch. Sylvia was out for blood, scratching and biting anything she could reach. Eric seemed to be trying to subdue her without causing injuries. This, and his underlying lack of craziness, put him at a disadvantage. As they struggled, one of the suits of armor toppled over them with a crash. Eric's head came up with a gash.

Charity had recovered just enough air to gasp.

"Damn it," B.G. exclaimed. "Stop being a gentleman!"

"Fine," Eric said and knocked Sylvia unconscious with a single, well-cocked blow from his elbow.

Even though she'd been trying to gouge out his eyes, he winced as she crumpled.

"Thank you," B.G. huffed. "I thought I was going to have to stand here forever and bleed to death."

"You deserve to," Eric panted, just as furious. It was the first time Charity had seen either of them angry. "What were you two planning to do, use your amazing 'mind power' to hypnotize her into submission?"

"We gave you an opening."

"You gave me an accident!"

The argument seemed likely to continue—a release of tension, Charity supposed—but just then what was probably B.G.'s security team, plus a bunch of government commando guys, pounded into the paneled hall wearing camouflage and thick-soled boots. There were at least a dozen of each sort, and the rifles they carried were enough to make her lungs hitch in shock. Charity pulled her knees to her chest and tried to look harmless. One of the armed men, possibly a medic, knelt immediately beside Sylvia. She'd begun to come around but must have been knocked out of her right mind— assuming she still had one. She was moaning something about B.G. having missed his chance.

"Would have done anything for you," she swore. "Would have given up the whole mission."

Her words sparked a prick of sympathy. Apparently, Sylvia had been hoping to get between Eric and B.G. herself.

While the first medic tried to settle her, another saw to B.G. The rest of the soldier guys fanned out. In spite of everything, Charity found their discipline impressive. As the rival captains finished muttering into their headsets that the area was secure, a vaguely familiar woman in a conservative but kind of cute suit stepped with finicky precision through the testosterone-laden crowd.

Her attention detoured to where Charity was huddled on the floor, then moved dismissively on.

She stopped in front of Eric.

Blood trickled from his eyebrow to his ear, and his hair stuck out in tufts like it always did first thing in the morning. Sylvia had also managed to rip his shirt open. Charity couldn't help enjoying the view of his abs, but the woman seemed horrified.

"Good Lord," Dana said, taking in his disarray. "What have you gotten yourself into now?"

Eighteen

B.G. found Charity in her room, tucking her provocative outfits into a carryall. Her movements were slow—sleepy, he might have said—as if her attention wasn't all there, as if against all logic she was in no hurry to leave Mosswood. He didn't know whether to be relieved or sorry she'd figured out she couldn't stay—not with Uncle Sam taking up residence in preparation for going over B.G.'s lab with a microscope.

Catching the spy hadn't been enough.

At least he knew what had put the CIA on alert—despite having no intention of revealing it to Charity. It seemed that Maurice, his chauffeur, had been telling ghost stories in a local bar, swearing he'd seen people in old-fashioned dress flitting through the halls. B.G. sincerely doubted these "ghosts" were anything more than recordings of past events that had been imprinted on his antiques, harmless things with no more reality than photographs. The experiments going on beneath Mosswood might have triggered them to replay, but of course Maurice knew nothing of that project. He hadn't realized what a red flag his stories would send up, coming as they did from the house of a physicist known to be probing the nature of time.

When B.G.'s watchers intercepted the same not-so-tall tale through less savory channels, they concluded they weren't the only country with their eye on B.G.'s progress. Worse, the added detail in the second account led them to believe their competitors had an inside track. Maurice hadn't uttered a peep about glassware moving by itself.

Conspiracy theories were built on such small coincidences. His meeting Sylvia at the spa in Victoria turned out not to have been one of them. His security team redeemed themselves by discovering she'd been visiting a number of places B.G. had been known to go—with the hope of some-day bumping into him. Such patience required that she sup-port herself until she found him, and how better than at an establishment he'd patronized? To B.G., this seemed an in-efficient method for orchestrating an encounter, but it had worked, so who was he to cast aspersions? Certainly he was not the infallible judge of character he'd thought.

Eventually, B.G. was sure he'd find out how a masseuse from Geneva got mixed up with an international faction who'd wanted to steal his work. Sadly, there would always be people in the world who wanted access to secrets they hadn't the faintest concept how to use. As to that, he expected there were a few in his own government.

His contacts at the FBI—whose job it actually was to protect sensitive technology—told him they hadn't been consulted on what they called "this cowboy operation." For whatever reason, the CIA appeared to have hared off on its own. Now, provokingly, he'd have to deal with both intelli-gence arms.

With a silent inner sigh, he smoothed Charity's hair be-hind her ear. "Your interview go okay?"

She turned when he touched her, still moving as if she were underwater, letting a pair of strappy red stilettos fall to the bed. "It was fine. Your lawyer was very helpful. He didn't let the CIA guys bully me into answering anything they didn't really need to know."

"That's Samuel's job."

"And he did it super good." She laid one hand on his ribs, her warmth a poignant shock. "I'm sorry your house is being overrun. I know you value your privacy."

"I have more lawyers, plus a few friends in high places. I expect we'll be able to minimize the intrusion. Sometimes one hand—or branch of government, in this case—truly doesn't want the other to know what it's doing."

"Convenient," she said, her little smile awkward.

When she dropped her gaze, he clasped her shoulders to bring it up again. His arm hurt beneath its bandage where the bullet had strafed his flesh, but the pain was curiously welcome. He was alive. They all were. "I want you to know I wouldn't have let Sylvia shoot you. I'd have opened the door before it came to that. I'd have tried to find some other way to keep my research safe. I chose my strategy because I believed she thought of you, on some level, as someone who understood her. I believed she wouldn't hurt someone who'd given her such pleasure."

Charity hunched one shoulder embarrassedly. "It's funny how, in the end, the person Sylvia wanted most was the one she couldn't have. Those games of yours are pretty smart."

Not smart enough, he thought. Or maybe too smart for their own good. He ran the back of his fingers down her cheek. He didn't expect what she said next.

"I tried to tell you not to," she said, her eyes earnest.

"Not to—?"

"Not to let her scare you into unlocking the lab. I mouthed *don't,* but you were looking at her."

"Ah," he said, stunned and not stunned at the same time. "That was very brave."

Charity wrinkled her nose at the praise. "I wasn't really thinking about it. I only knew your project was dangerous and not just anybody should play with it—especially before you've got it more figured out."

He smiled, touched by her modesty and her trust.

"Can I ask you something?" she asked shyly.

"Of course."

"When you told Sylvia she was doomed to fail, were you trying to pull a quantum trick?"

"I think you must have known I was, or you wouldn't have done your best to help."

"Well, I thought so but I wasn't sure."

"Be sure," he said, cupping her face. "You're usually smarter than you realize."

Her eyes went bright, such beautiful eyes that the old adage about drowning gained new credence. "Boy," she exclaimed, "am I going to miss you!"

His throat closed on his offer to stay in touch, to never lose touch in the first place. Those words weren't meant to be vocalized. Charity wasn't for him. Maybe no one was. His misjudgment of Sylvia—and Michael—showed how poorly suited he was for any relationship. That being so, he knew he should let Charity go. Perversely, his thumbs seemed bent on tracing the arch of her brows. Finally, once they'd slid down her cheekbones, he was able to let them fall. "Eric will want to see you before you leave."

"Assuming his sister hasn't sent him screaming into the woods."

"Dana does have a gift for assuming the worst."

"She's intimidating," Charity said with a mock shiver. "I think Eric was going to introduce us, but my nerves were totally not up for that."

Then she surprised him by pulling him into a hug.

"Thank you," she said, her cheek pressed tightly to his chest. "For everything."

He brought his hands slowly to her back, flattening them just beneath the planes of her shoulder blades. He thought how much he loved the curve of her here, the combination of strength and femininity. He stared at the model of chaos hanging over her bed. He wondered if she'd noticed the program had played through to reveal its final form, a pattern chaos theorists called the "strange attractor." However messy and unpredictable the path the light-blip drew seemed in the beginning, because of the rules it followed, it always traveled on the surface of this previously invisible form, etching it out bit by bit until it shone clear. The strange attractor for this computer model resembled a complicated open flower, rotating slowly through the virtual three dimensions of the flat screen.

Charity was the flower, he thought. Maybe she had been all along, not needing to be fixed so much as shown her true image.

"I've transferred the money you'll need for school into your account," he said.

"I'm not worried about that." She looked up at him without releasing her embrace, her crooked half-smile tugging his prematurely aching heart. "I'm worried you're going to forget me way too soon."

Rather than let her guess how close to the edge his emotions were, he cradled her head back against him. "I expect," he said lightly, "that there's precious little chance of that."

"You're leaving," Eric said.

Charity looked up from zipping her bag. She wasn't ready for this. She'd barely pulled herself together after saying good-bye to B.G. Eric stood in her doorway, his forehead carrying the same pinch of worry it had the day he'd whisked her away from Future-Tech. He'd seemed untouchable then, a privileged golden boy who'd deigned to descend from the heights. He was dearer to her now, less perfect but more real.

His bruises from the fight did funny things to her womanly instincts. She couldn't decide whether to say "poor baby" or jump his bones.

She wasn't looking forward to missing him.

"Yep," she said, forcing herself to smile. "Time to leave B.G.'s magic kingdom behind."

Eric opened his mouth, closed it, then rubbed the groove on his brow—which did nothing to erase it. The only communication he managed was a gusty sigh.

"You okay?" she asked.

His shoulders went up and down. "You mean aside from spending the last half-hour with my sister, listening to her lecture me on everything that's wrong with my life?" Clearly not expecting an answer, he came to her bed and flipped the handles of her carryall back and forth. "She wangled her way in here, you know: to prove that whatever *I* was involved with, *she* was on the right side."

"She probably was worried about you a little."

"I know," he said and puffed out the hollows of his cheeks. "Sorry. I didn't come here to complain. I came to make sure you were all right."

"I am." Her hand found its way to the middle button of his shirt. The cloth was blue, a complement to his soft gray eyes—and much safer to focus on. "Did . . . was your sister able to tell you how Sylvia got involved in trying to steal B.G.'s work?"

"They don't know yet. They'll question her, I'm sure. Dana did say she'd tell me if she heard before I did." He pressed his lips together and shook his head. "Those things Sylvia said, about forgetting the little people—we did treat her a bit like a convenience."

"You mean, like an employee?" When he began to object, Charity pressed her fingers to his mouth. "Look, Eric, I know your mom instilled you full of values. If we were saints, I suppose every one of us would have treated Sylvia like our

best friend. If we had, maybe she would have given up her
plan, or maybe she would have gotten away with even more.
The thing is, you can't take the blame for her choices. You
can only decide how you want to act from now on."

"Right," he said and shook himself determinedly.

He was such a hopeless Galahad, bruises and all, that
Charity couldn't help teasing. "You so want to be perfect,"
she said. "I can tell."

"I wouldn't mind," he admitted with a sheepish laugh. He
watched his shoe scuff the floor before looking up. "I guess
you'll be glad to be home again, after all this disruption."

He was a boy then, as easy to read and as shy. His gaze
searched hers, ashamed to admit he was fishing for assurances.
In that moment, his silver spoon couldn't have mattered less.
He and Charity were more alike than they were different.

It could work between us, she thought, the knowledge
tightening her vocal chords.

She smoothed her hands across the expensive cotton that
draped his chest. "I'll remember everything that happened
here all my life. Being here was the best time I ever had."

"Me, too," he whispered.

The hushed confession broke whatever hold he had on
himself. He took her face in his hands and kissed her, his
palms covering her ears, his hunger making him rough. Her
pulse began to race in a whole new way. As many times as
he'd done this, the magic of having him need her never
dulled. This time, that need seemed especially sharp. His
teeth bumped hers before his tongue curled inside to taste.

Then he cinched his arms beneath her buttocks and
lifted her off her feet. Like her, he must have feared this time
would be their last.

"Shower," he said, already moving toward it. "Take off
your clothes."

His order called to her recklessness. *What the hell,* she
thought. *Why hold back now?* She peeled her shirt over her

head even as he carried her inside. She was bare beneath it, her nipples tight. She shuddered with enjoyment when he dragged his face across her breasts. His whiskers were slightly scratchy, his mouth gentle. With her hipbones balanced on his belly, he pulled her in to suckle. Burying her fingers in his hair was sheer heaven. Her head fell back at the combined sensations, her own hair brushing her shoulders.

They both moaned at the same time.

When he set her on the tile, his gaze burned like silver flame. "Do you want me?" he asked, the question gruff. "Do you want me to take you hard?"

"Harder than hard," she said, and his eyelids closed with his attempt to master his reaction.

She couldn't say he succeeded. They tore out of their clothes at record speed, leaving them where they fell. Charity's panties ringed a wall sconce, and Eric's briefs landed in the trash. She ripped off his shirt herself, scattering buttons across the floor. Luckily for their lustful lack of coordination, the shower was a glassless, open design. Eric cranked the multiple spouts to hot, his erection bouncing with eagerness. She wanted to grab it, to worship it with her hands, but instead she stopped to watch.

She shook her head at herself, taking in all that beautiful, flushed muscle. His arms. His chest. His lovely long, strong legs. Surely he was too fine to even think of leaving behind.

"What?" he asked, noting her look.

"I was remembering how yummy I thought you were the first time I saw you at Future-Tech."

The comment might have been the only thing that could make him pause. "Yummy, eh?"

With lifted brows and a suggestive grin, he looked pointedly at his cock, now nearly vertical. Charity knew an invitation when she saw one. She pulled him under the spray, laced their hands together, and sank to her knees. Despite the warm deluge, his shaft stretched longer.

"Watch that," she warned teasingly. "You're more than a mouthful as it is."

"Take what you can," he said. His moan as she did came out an octave lower.

With her fingers gripped bruisingly tight by his, she slipped him in and out between her lips, his thickness pushing across her tongue and palate with hot vitality. She worked his shaft with all the skill she possessed, sucking and licking him all around, stimulating his hottest spots, wanting to give him more pleasure than he'd ever be able to forget. She suspected he tried to hold back, but soon his hips began to roll at her helplessly. With her hands unable to steady him, this was the only way to get more pressure. She knew he was watching what she did from the way he groaned. Her mouth made him shine as much as the shower.

Hoping to make him crazy, she teased the tip of her tongue into his slit.

"Charity," he gasped. "Wait."

She sat back on her heels and laughed. "Always with the waiting. I thought you wanted to take me hard."

His eyes went dark, taking in her words, taking in the sight of her body kneeling on the floor. "I do," he said. "Always."

He retrieved a condom from a silver canister by the sink, opening the wrapper with his teeth and rolling it on with telling winces of sensitivity. He was ready to roll then, and she was eager to let him, but all he did was reach for the soap and gesture her up.

He lathered her from head to toe—long, slow minutes of loving her with his hands until she thought she'd scream with frustration.

"Me, too," she finally demanded, sticking out her hand and trying to hold her little brain together as his palms squeezed and slipped their way repeatedly up her breasts.

She gasped as he pinched her nipples between his fingers. "I want to soap you."

"Here." He hauled her tight against his front. "Now you can."

Their bodies slid together in the lubrication of the foam: cock to hip, breasts to chest. Eric's hard, cobble-firm abs jerked in and out with his breath. Embraced too tightly to soap his front, she lathered his broad, tapering back. Then, when his hands slid around her buttocks and between her legs, she lost the soap forever to the floor.

It was hard to mind. He was kissing her again, with wonderful whimpering noises, stealing what scraps were left of her power to think. She could barely kiss him back and breathe at the same time. Too desperate to be gentle, he crowded her against the wall with a solid thud.

A shelf built into the corner bumped her side. Eric knew what it was for as well as she did. He shifted her toward it with the two of them still squeezed together. Her sex was so wet, he couldn't miss her readiness against the muscle of his thigh. His erection pulsed as if it knew where it was going. Groaning, he hitched her off the tiles and onto the support.

It was just the right height for the tip of him to nudge her gate.

"Spread your legs," he growled. "Wide."

Evidently, he didn't want her gripping his waist with her thighs. He pushed her knees against the adjoining walls and shoved inside her with her spread open, penetrating as easily as if her pussy had been soaped, too. His size, his thickness didn't matter. In one sumptuous stroke, he filled her to her brim. The effect was beyond good. If he hadn't been holding her in place, it would have been an invitation to go wild. As it was, her head rolled against the tiles, her body tightening greedily on his length.

"God." He drew a long, shaky breath. "Okay, now hold on."

Her fingers gripped his shoulders as his hips drew back.

"Go," she begged, trying to ensure he really would. "Go."

He thrust as strongly as he'd promised—swift, deep strokes of pure, directed force that hit her just hard enough, just fast enough to send her moaning over the edge. He had more control than she did. Though he swelled inside her, he didn't come.

"Again," he said, his every muscle tight with resolve. "Go over for me again."

She grabbed for the nearest shower head and held on. One hand would have to be enough to praise the parts of him she could reach.

It seemed to be. He twitched inspiringly at her caresses, but he was tireless, his skin gone red from the heat pounding over him inside and out. He thrust hard enough that the wetness of her skin squeaked against the tile. He gripped her bottom more securely. She didn't care that she might end up sore. The pressure of him inside her was incredible, and the spray shut them into a private erotic world. Only him. Only her. Only the rise of sensation and need. She cocked her hips to help him go deeper, an assistance that made him grunt.

"Yes," she moaned, stroking his bunched-up jaw. "All the way."

He didn't let up as he turned his head to nip her hand. Instead, he wedged his palm between their bellies, his thumb reaching down to rub her clit. He knew exactly how to get her, how to press her whole pubis until the feeling shot to her core. She gasped his name into the pounding water, her body clutching his in a long, tight orgasm.

This, at last, brought the human out of the machine.

"Love you," he groaned, urging her knees up his sides as his thrusts shifted into high gear. "Love you, Charity. I . . . love . . . you."

He came between the words, breaking them, his body

hunching closer with bursts of release. His hand cupped her soaking hair against her neck.

He sighed, his eyelids smooth and closed.

He had let more out than his climax.

Shaken in more ways than one, Charity pressed her head to his shoulder and hugged his back. The water ran down their bodies like a hard, tropical rain. Even a day ago, his saying he loved her would have been the dearest desire of her heart. Now she fought to remember the fragile lessons she'd learned in the last few hours.

He didn't take long to sense something was wrong. He set her down carefully, reaching past her to turn off the jets. The loss of the noise came as a shock. Dripping water joined their breathing to echo through the steam-filled room.

Her failure to return his declaration grew more obvious by the second.

He tilted his head to one side. "I did say that out loud, right?"

She had to smile at how cute he was. "Yes."

"Good, because I meant to. I love you, Charity. I know we can't stay at Mosswood, but I want you to move into my condo downtown. I don't want you going back to your old life."

She was reluctant to shake her head for fear of it hurting him. "I can't go back to my old life no matter what. For that, I'd have to be the same person I was before."

He studied her, his hands sliding restlessly up her wet arms. "I think you love me, too," he said at last. "Maybe I'm wrong, but I think you do."

"I think you're right."

"Then—?"

It was hard to face his question, but she made herself. Ironically, the grip he had on her was steadying. "All my life," she said, "I've had boyfriends. I told myself I wasn't like my mom because I didn't jump whenever they said 'boo,' but maybe—in my own way—I needed them as much as she needed hers. Men made me feel powerful when nothing else could."

"I'm not them," he said. "You and I would be different."

She feathered a touch across the purpling puffiness by his eye. The medics had put three stitches where the falling suit of armor had gashed his skin. He didn't wince at the contact. He was too focused on her for that.

"Tell me," he said. "Make me understand."

"I'll try. I'm only beginning to understand myself. I'm afraid—" She gathered her words as well as she could. "I can't rely on someone else to make me think I'm growing up. Even if I'm in love. Even if he's the best boyfriend on the planet. Having you and B.G. like me—boy, was that good for my self-esteem! Unfortunately, the minute something happened to make me think I hadn't really changed, just like that, every bit of my confidence caved. My fancy new image of myself was a house of cards. Until I learn to stand on my own two feet, that's all it can be."

Eric had looked at the floor while he was listening. Now, when his lashes lifted, his eyes were bloodshot.

"Jesus," he said with a shaky exhalation. "I wish I didn't know what you were talking about."

"But you do."

"If I didn't, I would have spent my life running through my trust fund. I wouldn't have tried to be anything."

His understanding made her love him even more, made her feel grateful and heartbroken. How could he doubt himself? So what if he'd failed in business once? He should try again, as many times as it took. He could do anything. Be anything. The reminder that this was his line—and B.G.'s—made emotion sting behind her eyes. The feeling must have been catching. As she fought back her own upwelling of sentiment, a tear joined the water beaded on his cheek. He laughed in embarrassment, but he didn't wipe it away. When he spoke, he brought all his famous persuasion to bear.

"Don't leave Seattle," he said quietly. "Forget what I said about Harvard. The University of Washington is a perfectly good school. Later—"

"I can't let myself live for later. That's just another crutch."

He tightened his mouth and stepped back. Her shoulders were abruptly cold, and she had to struggle not to shiver. She reminded herself she was doing the right thing.

"I can wait for you if I want to," he said, or maybe threatened. "That's my choice."

Her heart full, she put her hands on his chest and kissed him, lip to lip, balancing on tiptoe.

"It's my choice," he repeated, and she prayed this soul-sweet promise wouldn't screw her up.

Nineteen

Out of politeness, Eric offered to let B.G. stay with him while the government's special agents went through his house. To his surprise, his friend accepted.

"You sure you don't want to oversee what corners they're poking into?"

"No," B.G. denied, despite seeming uneasy at the idea. "Between my lawyers and the head of my lab, they ought to be kept within tolerable bounds. Besides, it might be better that I'm not there to give permission for incursions beyond the limits of their warrant."

So B.G. and Eric drove back to Seattle together. It was a sparkling day, clear and pleasantly hot, the kind of day that drove the natives outdoors in hordes. Eric passed up the loan of B.G.'s Rolls in favor of his own dented but beloved Porsche, a leftover from his heyday working in PR. Family money had afforded him many luxuries, but this toy he'd bought on his own. The feel of the sleek, powerful machine was a comfort to his overstretched emotions. This car couldn't reject him, couldn't claim it needed "space to find itself." When Eric gave it the gas, it simply went.

With his hands skimming pleasantly over the wheel and

the sun beating on his back, he decided he'd see if his old squash partner's criminally neglected 1930 Isotta Fraschini was still available for sale. Getting the old classic car running would at least keep him occupied. Eric would need something to do—and who knew for how long?

However things turned out with Charity, he was pretty sure he couldn't go back to playing keeper for B.G.'s games. His heart had developed some very exclusive preferences as to where it wanted his body to go. He couldn't even be sorry. Obstacles aside, Charity was a wonderful object of desire.

To Eric's relief—since he hadn't decided how to broach his long-term plans—B.G. proved able to entertain himself. He filled his days with walks around the city, long phone conferences with his lawyers, and just as long periods where he shut himself in the guest room Eric had given him to use as an office. Eric assumed he was working, though B.G. didn't say.

While Eric was glad his friend was getting out, he hoped all this activity wasn't meant to prove anything to him. B.G. even dated—former lovers, apparently, about whom Eric had known nothing. They were attractive society types, men and women both, who arrived at Eric's door in glossy evening dress. None returned with him at the end of the night, and few appeared more than once, but Eric knew that omission ruled out little.

B.G. was jumping back into circulation with a vengeance.

Despite the pinch of annoyance this caused—why should B.G. be sexually active when Eric was going without?—the pair slipped into a relatively easy roommate relationship.

They shared a bed—usually—ate breakfast together—always—and traded sections of the *Post-Intelligencer* like an old married couple. On the nights B.G. didn't go out, they rented movies and ate popcorn. Any differences in their neatness levels were erased by the Merry Maids. Eric in particular missed Mrs. Alvarez, but both were happy enough with take-out. Conveniently, B.G. had discovered a garage on one of his walks where Eric could lease a bay to work on his cars, now up to a fleet of three. If Eric broke down and bought the Studebaker he'd been eyeing, he'd have to sell one of his fix-ups and admit this hobby was turning into a business. B.G. liked to tease that Eric was on the verge of becoming a used car salesman.

All in all, for a pair who'd never lived in quarters this close, Eric thought they were managing famously.

Except for one complaint.

B.G. wouldn't stop talking about Charity. The slimmest excuse was enough to launch a recitation of her many fine qualities. Day in and out, Eric's attention was directed to the clothes she would have looked good in, the comments she might have made, plus countless mentions of marvels she'd actually performed.

Did Eric remember when Mrs. Alvarez took a day off, and Charity burned a whole loaf of toast trying to feed them?

What about the time she beat Maurice in a game of strip pool?

And surely he recalled that cute noise she sometimes made at climax. Would Eric call it more of a hiccup or a cry? B.G. couldn't decide, but it always struck him as if pleasure had caught her by surprise.

If that weren't enough, B.G. also felt compelled to share the periodic progress reports he received from her assigned tutor. Charity was working hard, the tutor said. Never asked for help beyond what was fair. Even impressed a few of her professors with her knack for laying out an argument. Most tormenting, at least to Eric, she hadn't left the area. As he'd suggested, she'd applied to the University of Washington. She still lived in her old apartment. He could have walked there on his lunch hour. For that matter, he could have jogged there any lonely midnight he felt the urge.

For someone who was trying to respect Charity's wishes and stay away, these reminders that she was close were little better than torture. How the hell did Eric know how long it took to stand on your own two feet? Until Charity got in touch with him was his guess.

Finally, one Sunday morning he blew up.

"Call Charity yourself," he snapped, "if it means that fucking much to you."

Eric's tone was harsher than he'd intended, the product of too many nights spent aching for Charity's touch. B.G. stiffened on hearing it and retreated to the guest room, where he remained in what Eric interpreted as accusatory silence for the next two hours.

Damn, Eric thought.

He was going to have to apologize.

He knocked softly on the door before opening it, but B.G. didn't notice. He was in the swiveling chair with his back to Eric. His laptop was out, and he was watching a DVD with the attached earphones. Eric assumed it was a movie until he got close. Then he saw it was a recording from Mosswood, one he hadn't known was made, of the night he and Charity teamed up to tie B.G. to his bed, and Charity spanked him while Eric sucked him off.

As soon as he recognized the scene, blood rushed in equal measures to his head and groin: arousal, self-consciousness, and most of all awareness. The camera must have been hidden in the headboard. It had a straight-on view of B.G.'s face. The utter, helpless pleasure of his expression, the devastation of his normal boundaries, told Eric something he should have guessed long ago.

"Shit," he said, too surprised to guard his words. "You're in love with her, too."

B.G. snapped the laptop shut and spun the chair around.

For a moment, neither of them said a word. Eric couldn't remember having seen his friend at such a loss before. B.G. looked guilty, of all things, as if what Eric had caught him doing was wrong.

Eric knew what that was like. From the beginning, his attraction to Charity had felt disloyal. Now his dismay did. Lord, what a fuckup this was. Against all logic, against all fairness, Eric wanted both B.G. and Charity to love *him*.

B.G. tugged off the earphones. "I suppose I needn't say you should have knocked, since you probably did."

"Yes . . . B.G., did Michael have access to this recording?"

B.G. shook his head. "No. This was just for me."

"Just for you." Eric squeezed one hand above his eyes, trying to find words that wouldn't make this worse. "Why didn't you say something? Why have you been pushing me at Charity when you have feelings for her yourself?"

"You chose her."

"That doesn't mean I own her! Look, it's not like I'm trying to recruit competition. I suspect I've got plenty of that as it is. But if you love her—"

"I don't love her." B.G.'s denial was as swift as it was unconvincing, a fact he read in Eric's dubiously lifted brows. "I only brought the one disc. I haven't been watching it all this time. I was intrigued by her effect on me."

Eric snorted. "For you, 'intrigued' is as good as in love."

"I think you and Charity make an excellent match. I'm not trying to get between you."

"Yeah, well, maybe you should be." Eric sat on the guest room's double bed and leaned shakily over his knees. He felt pole-axed by this discovery, flattened out like a cartoon coyote. B.G. was in love with Charity, and rather than pursue her, he'd decided to keep his feelings secret.

"Do you still love me?" he asked, needing an affirmative more than he had any right to.

B.G. looked genuinely shocked. "Why do you think I'm doing this? Why do you think I hoped you'd fall for her from the start?"

"You love me, and you hoped I'd fall in love with someone else? B.G., I know you're the genius, but that's crazy."

"Let me tell you a story," B.G. said.

"Oh, God." Eric pressed his aching head with both hands.

"You'll like this story," B.G. said, "or at least Charity would."

"Fine." Eric tried to pull a bit of patience into his voice. "Tell me this story that explains why you think I should fall in love, but for you it's not allowed."

B.G. frowned at him. "Are you going to listen?"

"I am," Eric said. "I always listen to everyone."

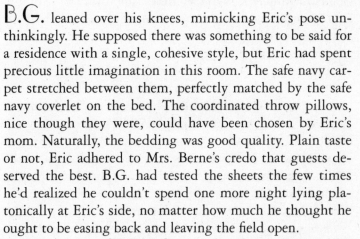

B.G. leaned over his knees, mimicking Eric's pose un-thinkingly. He supposed there was something to be said for a residence with a single, cohesive style, but Eric had spent precious little imagination in this room. The safe navy carpet stretched between them, perfectly matched by the safe navy coverlet on the bed. The coordinated throw pillows, nice though they were, could have been chosen by Eric's mom. Naturally, the bedding was good quality. Plain taste or not, Eric adhered to Mrs. Berne's credo that guests deserved the best. B.G. had tested the sheets the few times he'd realized he couldn't spend one more night lying pla-tonically at Eric's side, no matter how much he thought he ought to be easing back and leaving the field open.

Eric was part of B.G.'s life, a very good part. Letting him go wasn't easy. Now B.G. felt caught between worlds, his personal electrons unable to decide which quantum leap to make. This way lay happiness, that way misery, and be-tween them hung all his dreams for his dearest friend.

"Speak," Eric said, a laugh in his voice, "or forever hold your peace."

B.G. almost changed his mind at Eric's choice of words.

"Go on," Eric said, seeing the doubts in his eyes.

"This is a story from before we met. I'm not certain you

know what my life was like, what *I* was like back then. I'm
not telling you this to elicit pity, but I didn't have a single
friend my own age. Home schooling was part of the problem, although I blamed my intelligence. The other children
were jealous, I reasoned, and in any case, were too stupid to
interest me. I only interacted with adults, most of them
professors in the college where my mother worked. I told
myself these adults were my friends, but in truth I knew
they were not. They were friendly, yes, and often took time
to have academic conversations. Part of me, however, couldn't
help but observe that the relationships they had with their
peers were different from the relationship they had with me.
Even though I was smart, they thought of me as a child. So
it was that at the age of eight I was obliged to learn a lesson
I resisted with all my might."

"Should I ask?" Eric said, his look so kind B.G. had to
avert his gaze.

"The lesson was that I didn't have friends because of *me*.
Whoever caused the first injury, myself or some neighborhood child, the situation persisted because I was angry and
insecure and spent all my energy trying to prove I was superior to these small people with whom I didn't know how to
communicate. It wasn't their responsibility to rise to my
level. It was mine to open myself to theirs."

"I don't know, B.G. That's a pretty big lesson for an
eight-year-old."

"Too big for me, I assure you. I was at the park one day
with the brand-new dirt bike my mother had bought me in
the hope that it would help me fit in. Because I couldn't
ride, this hope was ill-founded, but you know how she is.
My mother's thought processes—while well meaning—have
never been overly linear. For my part, I figured I could simply wheel the bike around and make myself seem more appealing to children my age."

"And that didn't work?"

"Well, I did succeed in gathering a crowd, but the members of my chronological peer group were not as stupid as I'd assumed. One of them thought to request that I do a trick. A wheelie, as I recall. When I refused—with impressive dignity, I thought—he stole my bike and rode off. I was angry enough to fight by then, but since three of the thief's compadres remained, I got myself soundly thrashed."

Eric slid off the bed and sat on the rug, the toe of his loafer nudging B.G.'s ankle. "Bummer," he said, "as Charity would comment if she were here."

"Yes," B.G. agreed. "Getting beat up was a big bummer. Little did I realize it was also the most normal childhood interaction I'd experienced to date—not that the knowledge would have cheered me then. Furious and nearly blind with tears, I stumped to the center of the park, where a small wooden bench sat beneath a big willow tree. There, shielded from my tormentors, I vowed I'd never speak to a child again. I didn't need them. I didn't need anyone.

"This is when things get strange. Even though the park was normally crowded, from that point on, no one interrupted what happened, nor can I recall a single noise beyond the ones I made. No birds. No cars. No barking dogs. It was as if I'd been enclosed in my own bubble. The very breeze ceased to blow.

"It is possible I was crying too hard to notice the woman's appearance, but suddenly one was sitting on the opposite end of the bench. My memory of her is extremely vivid. She was dressed in a clean khaki coverall, something a janitor might have worn, although she didn't look like one. She was pretty in a quiet way, with deep red hair you don't often see. As it happens, her eyes were very like Charity's—a lavender so rich they were almost violet. I remember thinking it odd that their expression could be both kind and cool.

" 'It's your doing,' she said before I could speak. 'Your conditions cannot change unless you change yourself.'

"Assuming she'd witnessed my humiliation, I responded rather rudely.

" 'Anger is pointless,' she said just as calmly as before. 'It stands in the way of what you want.'

"No doubt I should have realized something odd was happening, but my temper had shot past the breaking point. 'I don't want to be a freak!' I shouted. 'I don't want the other kids to call me names!'

" 'Well, but you are a freak, Benjamin,' she said, 'and in your heart of hearts, I don't think you want to change. You enjoy being smarter. Your second concern, however, is within your power to address. If you work at liking other children, really work at it instead of always focusing that brain of yours on their flaws, some of them—the ones who are truly suited to be your companions—will begin liking you back.'

"It gave me a start to hear a stranger use my name, but I was something of a celebrity in our neighborhood and I concluded she knew me from that.

" 'You're talking crap,' I said with eight-year-old hubris.

" 'Suit yourself.' She shrugged with an elan I wished I could imitate. 'But a true scientist wouldn't dismiss my claim without a test.'

" 'It's bullshit,' I insisted. 'Touchy-feely New Age crap.'

"She smiled in a knowing way that truly pricked my rage. 'When your mother hears what has happened,' she said, 'she's going to try to help you again, and this time her attempt will have a greater probability of success. If you make a good-faith effort to go along, what happens next will set you on the path to getting everything you want and more.'

"At this further insult to my good sense, I jumped up, fully intending to storm off. Before I got more than a step, the strangest part of the whole strange encounter occurred. The woman touched my arm. She didn't grab it or try to hold me, she simply laid her palm on my skin. Instantly, I felt as if someone were pouring a strong electrical current through my body. My hair floated straight up on my scalp, and my feet seemed to be magnetized to the grass. I couldn't have lifted them to save my life.

" 'I'm putting the proof in your pocket,' she said. 'When you look at it tomorrow, you'll know.' "

"What was the proof?" Eric asked, his voice hoarse enough that he needed to clear his throat.

In spite of himself, B.G. smiled. "Well, I didn't know yet. First I had to go home, where I deliberately refused to tell my mother about the theft of my bike. That, so I thought, would thwart my uninvited soothsayer."

"And did it?"

"Not in the least. That night at the market, three separate people told my mother what had happened, having heard the story through the neighborhood rumor mill. Because my mother was upset, on her way out she crashed her car into the bumper of the very woman she'd been considering asking for help, a woman she didn't know very well but who had a son just my age."

"Oh," Eric said with a shiver big enough to see.

"Yes, 'oh.' Normally your mother didn't shop at that market. She came that night as an expedient when her cook ran out of Tabasco in the middle of a barbecue. Fortunately for me, despite her dented car, your mother had a firm belief in instilling a sense of duty in her children and more or less ordered you to teach me to ride my bike."

"Jeez." Eric scrubbed his hand across his hair. "Mom never told me that part of the story."

"I only pieced it together later. At the time, I wasn't inclined to go along. I told my mother thanks but no thanks. Then, the next morning, I felt something crinkle in the pocket of the jeans I'd worn the day before. Pulling it out, I discovered the folded cover of a copy of *Science Weekly* magazine, the issue for the third week of November. As this was the first of April, you may imagine it caught my attention. I was aware that magazines had lead times, but surely not so far ahead. Most interesting of all, the address label was for our house.

"Still too stubborn to be convinced, I decided this was, nonetheless, enough evidence in the stranger's favor to take her advice seriously—to 'test her claim' as she put it. I agreed to my mother's request to meet with you and to try to be amenable. To my surprise, I found myself liking you very much. Even though you didn't take to me right away, you, my old friend, were the politest eight-year-old I'd ever met. Not once did you call me a name or lose patience with my awkwardness. When you finally did warm up to me, I was so caught up in the singular pleasure of having a same-age friend that the mystery of the magazine cover went completely out of my head. I didn't think of it again until the third week of November arrived. I chanced to be the one who took in the mail and, lo and behold, our issue of *Science Weekly* had its front cover torn off. When I dug through my room and found the cover from the stranger, the pattern of the tear marks matched perfectly."

"Wow," Eric said. "That is extremely weird. Did you ever find an explanation?"

"I did not, although that doesn't prove none exists. I suppose these days some would call my stranger an angel. My personal feeling, with which you are welcome to disagree, is that she was from the future, a time traveler who, for whatever reason, wished me to choose my current path—or at least not stay on the road I was on. Who knows? I might have remained too resentful to achieve anything useful."

"A time traveler," Eric said, sounding dazed. "So you think your secret project might turn out to be something."

"Or something that leads to something. Perhaps my theories will be the foundation on which others build. What really matters, for the moment anyway, is that believing this interpretation, as well as the other things the stranger said, inspired me to change the direction of my life. I have made friends who have been—as my stranger promised—good companions. I owe her, and you, more than I can ever repay."

"Is that what you think? That you have to give Charity up because you *owe* me?" Eric rolled forward far enough to put his hands on B.G.'s knees. "Even if you did owe me—which you don't—that's a debt I'd never, ever collect. You've given me too much. Hell, you might have saved me from doing time. If you love Charity, show her the respect of letting *her* choose."

"But she should choose you. You're the one she'll be happy with."

"Forgive me, B.G., but you're an idiot. How can you believe in time travel and that freaking mind power stuff, but not that you could make one ordinary girl happy? I mean, that's a blind spot the size of Mt. Rainier!"

"I know myself," B.G. said, his jaw and throat feeling as if they were in a vise. Doubts about his visitor from the future he'd expected, but not a debate on this. He drew his hands into stubborn fists. "I know how I am about relationships. I guard myself. I keep myself from connecting the way you and Charity can."

"Oh, really? You keep yourself from connecting. That's why you love her. That's why, for the sake of our friendship, you're willing to sacrifice someone you really want in your life. Because you're so fucking bad at connecting."

"Look what happened with Sylvia!"

Eric actually laughed. "Sylvia chose her own path. You are not bad at connecting. You're just afraid. And that, as your time traveling stranger would say, is pointless. It stands in the way of what you want."

"You don't understand."

"I do. I just don't 'understand' the way you want me to."

"Eric, I think you've—"

"Shush already. You've done enough thinking. I'm going to have to fix this for both of us."

"*You're* going to—"

Eric kissed whatever he'd meant to say back into B.G.'s mouth, the only sure way to silence him. Naturally, Eric enjoyed it. He didn't think he'd ever kissed B.G. for more than seconds without getting worked up. B.G. didn't fare much better, but as soon as a longing groan rumbled from his chest, Eric pushed back.

Enough, he thought. It was time for someone with common sense to take charge of this romantic mess.

"You're going to wait until I fix this," he said, his voice husky but firm. "You're going to lock up that little black book of yours and take a dose of your own medicine."

B.G. crossed his arms and tilted his brows.

"Forget it," Eric said flatly. "You're not snowing me with that I-know-everything pose. Just once, you're going to trust *me* to know best for *you.*"

Twenty

The afternoon held a nip of winter as Charity stepped off the bus in the steep residential area near her apartment. The clouds hung low and surly, and the air—cool though it was—possessed a skin-caressing softness only an incipient drizzle could bring. It was classic Seattle weather, guaranteed to make people sigh for sunnier states.

Charity slung her heavy knapsack over her shoulder, girded her thighs to hike up the nearest hill, and let her mouth curve into a grin.

The last few months had been the best and worst of her life. She'd spent more nights crying alone into her pillow and more days feeling satisfied with herself than she would have thought possible. As of today, she'd survived her first semester at the University of Washington without being late to a single class. Best of all, thanks to the adorably nerdy labgirl B.G. loaned her as a tutor, her grades were a squeak short of As. She'd had precisely one date to interrupt her studies, and that had been an accident—a teaching assistant had invited her to what she thought was a lunch meeting to discuss a future paper. She'd put him off as politely as she could and learned a valuable lesson in the process.

Academics were people just like her. They might have
started out with a better education, but some of them for sure
didn't have her sense.

The realization was quite freeing.

Life was good, she thought. Not perfect, but more than
promising enough to let herself enjoy the pleasure of entertaining possibilities. She'd come a long way and had no reason to think she wouldn't go further still.

She regretted nothing. Never mind her tear-stained pillow; she wouldn't have undone her time with Eric or B.G.
or the silly jumping wineglass for anything. Truthfully, at
that instant, if she could have pushed a button to make it
happen, she would.

Just as she had the thought, a small brown bird swooped
across her path, so low and close the breeze from its wings
brushed her jeans. Her pulse skittered at its passage, but
almost at once she laughed. Maybe the universe was sending a sign that this moment, with its little punch of emotion, was the one that reached back to that dinner to make
time skip.

She was huffing pleasantly when she reached her apartment's cracked cement steps, the fatigue in her muscles as
satisfying as her state of mind. "I am a quantum toughgirl,"
she murmured humorously to herself.

Her smile slipped from her face when she saw the car.
Parked in front of her building, it was a classic convertible
from before the second World War. Obviously in cherry condition, it had red leather upholstery, a long cream-colored
hood, and a winged lady for an ornament. What looked like
lightning bolts shot across the shiny chrome grill. The car
was, she thought, thoroughly cool. It was not, however, what
set her heart to hammering against her ribs.

That honor belonged to the car's driver, who'd slipped
from behind the wheel and was resting his hips on the
swooping fender with the very sexiest casual ease.

"Eric," she said, his name coming out breathy. "I almost didn't recognize you in those clothes."

He wore black sweatpants and a snug gray T-shirt that did nothing to hide his impressive upper body. From the bulging of his arms as he braced his weight on the hood, he'd spent some time in a gym since she last saw him. He wasn't bulkier, just a bit more ripped. His sweatpants were loose at least, but the way his long legs were crossed drew her attention to the mouth-watering heft of what hung between.

Charity swallowed and tried to smile brightly.

"I hope it's okay to be here," he said, his eyes as gray as ash in the gloomy light. His gaze was very steady, as if he might be working to appear calm. Working or not, he was doing better than Charity.

His lips were even more kissable than she recalled.

"It's fine," she said, waving her hand. "Perfectly natural for you and B.G. to want to check up on how I'm doing."

"Actually—" Eric pushed off the car and prowled forward. "We're hoping you'll spend some time with us on your break."

His scent reached her before he did, along with a thousand erotic memories. The shower. B.G.'s bedroom. Being taken in a leather harness in a small black room. Charity's mouth was dry. She tried to keep her gaze on his, rather than let it drop to the situation she was pretty sure was developing in his pants.

"On my break?" she repeated. To her dismay, the final word was a squeak.

Hearing it, Eric smiled and tugged a waving lock of her hair. Immediately, the blush she'd been trying to pray into oblivion seared across her face. Even worse, a sluice of hot, creamy moisture wet her panties.

"I missed you," he said in a low, growling tone that made her body clench on another gush. "I missed you so much I guarantee I'll go insane if I have to wait until you graduate to see you again."

"Really?" Her eyes were losing their battle. His sweat-pants hung temptingly low on his hips, the drawstring knotted sloppily. Seemingly by themselves, her hands had found their way to his waist. Unfortunately, she wasn't pushing him away.

That being so, she couldn't blame Eric for leaning down.

"Really," he said into her ear. "In fact, I think I'll go insane if I don't get you somewhere really private, really soon."

Charity gasped as his teeth pressed gently, slowly, into the skin between her neck and shoulder where her oversize V-neck sweater was slipping down. The bite couldn't be mistaken for anything but a sexual claim—and a primitive one at that. His hands slid down her arms to urge her to touch the warm, bare skin beneath his T-shirt. When he pulled back, she was completely at a loss for breath.

The gleam in his eyes said he knew exactly what he'd done.

"I'm assuming," he went on, "that you're interested in getting together."

She snorted, because of course she was. "Just a visit?" she asked, peering up at him through her lashes.

He shrugged, the gleam in his eye sharpening. "A visit's a place to start."

"Here?"

Though he joined her in glancing up the old brick building to her window, he made no move toward the door.

"I'm ready enough for here," he said, "as you might have guessed, but that wouldn't be fair to B.G. He's been missing you, too, you see, and I insisted he go cold turkey until I coaxed you back."

"You're playing the game again?" She wasn't sure how she felt about that. Excited? Disappointed? A bit of both?

Eric shook his head before she could settle on an answer.

"No games," he said. "We want you to come because you want to spend time with us."

She thought for all of two seconds.

"I do," she said, "but I'm making no promises."

Her coming was a kind of promise, no matter what she said. Eric opened the passenger side door and held her elbow to help her in. Seeing her slide into the car he'd restored with his own two hands offered a satisfaction that leading her to B.G.'s limo couldn't have matched.

When she said, "This is *sweet,*" and cruised her palms across the dash, she might as well have been stroking him. He had to adjust himself before he could sit.

"I fixed her up," he said after clearing his throat. "I think restoring old cars is going to be my new business."

"Ah-ha. Ready to try your hand at being a boss."

"Only the boss of me," he said, secretly pleased by her approval. "At least for now."

It seemed too soon to mention that Maurice had been dropping hints about helping out, but Eric certainly didn't mind when she cooed some more as he drove, wriggling around to check out all the details. His occasional glimpse of her jean-clad derriere provided a welcome distraction from the giddy drop to Puget Sound. She was dressed in her official student uniform—jeans, sweater, a long white shirt underneath with the tails trailing. The clothes were indistinguishable from thousands of others' except for the delectable way she filled them out. Entertained by the New Her, he passed the car dealerships and the Space Needle, then headed south on Second, through downtown toward his building.

"B.G. is at your place?" she asked.

"He's been staying with me since you left." He turned his head to check how she reacted. She seemed accepting but nervous. He hoped he was doing the right thing. B.G. was the one who was usually sure about everything. *Believe it and you can do it,* was his motto. Eric was the worrier, always had been and maybe always would be. He'd employed more will than confidence to convince B.G. to go along with his plan. Chances were, in fact, that he'd convinced B.G. because B.G. had wanted to be convinced. If Eric's idea worked, it could be the most rewarding turning point of their lives.

If it didn't . . .

Eric gnawed his lip and eased the Isotta down the ramp to his garage.

If it didn't work, he supposed he'd survive, but he hoped it wouldn't come to that. Falling in love with Charity had taught him life could be a hell of a lot better than surviving.

Charity's first thought on entering Eric's twelfth-floor condominium was, *Wow, this place is big.* Her second was, *Boy, does he like navy.* Apart from the blond wood floor—so new it still smelled of sawdust—navy was the only color in the place. The modern L-shaped couch, the Danish-looking side chairs, even the starkly designed display boxes on the wall were midnight blue. A scattering of throw pillows bore black-and-white zebra prints. She liked the effect, though—apart from the zebra prints—it wasn't what she would have chosen.

"Nice view," she said, turning toward the floor-to-ceiling windows, all of which were shielded by thin vertical blinds.

Eric put his hand on her shoulder, maybe to anchor himself. "City and sound," he said, then made a face. "This was the lowest floor I could get."

She laughed, remembering how much she'd liked being with him when he loosened up. "I guess our encounter on B.G.'s catwalk didn't cure your problem."

"No." His fingers found the curve of her neck, his eyes soft and smiling as he traced her tendons to her collarbone. "If you wanted, I'd be willing to try again."

"And try and try," she quipped. Her skin was tingling where he'd touched it, a tide of emotion rising helplessly in her chest. No matter what she'd thought, she hadn't left him behind. She'd carried him in her heart all along.

Eric's expression changed as he read her look. "Charity," he murmured, clearly the prelude to something more intimate.

"Try and try what?" B.G. asked with perfect timing, padding out from a back room.

Ridiculously, her emotions surged just as much at seeing him.

He was carrying a yellow legal pad and pen, and he looked more approachable than she'd ever seen him. His sweatpants were a mirror image of Eric's except in gray. He had also forgone a shirt, which gave her an eyeful of his lean physique. Even allowing for this uncustomary show of skin, he looked different: sexier, less ethereal.

Having spent the last few months with him, Eric was less dazzled. He gestured toward the pad and pen. "Why are you working?"

"My brain doesn't turn off at my convenience. I had an idea for a new synchrotron experiment."

"You let your hair grow back," Charity interrupted, suddenly realizing what was new. His pecs were furry, a nice black haze that narrowed beneath his sternum before diving under his waistband.

"Er, yes," he said, rubbing his chest. "I hope you don't object."

His unsureness made her close the distance between them, made her draw him into a hug and press her cheek to the manly fuzz. "I like," she said. "Very much."

He hugged her back more tightly than she expected, the pad he'd been carrying poking her back. "Charity," he said into her hair. "It's good to see you again."

Maybe it was silly, but she couldn't make herself let go. Instead, she held him and swayed, letting out a sigh when his hand curved behind her neck. Considering all they'd been through, it was funny how safe she felt in his arms.

"Where are the candles?" Eric asked. Some men might have been jealous at her greeting B.G. this warmly, but he sounded as if he were about to laugh. B.G. inhaled sharply and pushed back.

"Shit," he said. "I forgot." He plunged his narrow hands into his ink-black hair. "And the champagne!"

"Guys," Charity scolded. "This is me. You don't have to lay out a big seduction scene. Honestly, having both of you in one room is seduction enough."

"We wanted to create a conducive mood," B.G. explained. "Because we . . . we—" He shot a pleading glance at Eric.

"Because we have important things to tell you, B.G. in particular." Obviously still amused, Eric waved him on. "Go ahead. Tell Charity what you want to say."

B.G.'s grimace was so comical Charity had to laugh. "Sorry," she said, her hand in front of her mouth. "I feel like a shopkeeper, and you're the kid whose mother is about to make him apologize for stealing a pack of gum."

"It's not a matter of 'making' me." B.G. pulled his shoulders straighter in affront. "Eric has been kind enough to provide me with an opportunity to confess that I love you."

Charity had been braced to stifle more laughter at whatever he had to say. Instead, her jaw dropped like it had turned to lead. She'd known B.G. was fond of her in his eccentric way, but *love* her? When she reached out to steady herself, Eric took her arm.

"Furthermore," B.G. said, pressing stiffly onward, "both Eric and I would be grateful if you would make room for us in your life—assuming you don't wish to choose between us or, um, avoid us altogether in your quest for independence. As to that, for myself, I should like to express my belief that you are standing on your own two feet and, mostly likely, always have been. There are, after all, only your feet under your legs."

For a moment, Charity was too choked up to speak.

"That," she said, her vision sheening with tears, "is the nicest weird thing anyone's ever told me."

"I could repeat the part about my loving you, if that seems more appropriate."

Eric hugged her shoulders, but it was B.G. he reassured. "She liked all the parts," he said. "You done good."

"Well. Then." B.G. set his pad and pen on a shiny black end table. "Perhaps you'd care to enlighten us about your feelings."

His tone was endearingly defensive.

"I love you right back," she said, her voice gone thick. "I love you both."

"But?" B.G. prompted.

Now she let herself grin. "There is no 'but.' I survived my first semester. I didn't date—okay, except for going out with girlfriends, but I was always in before midnight. I wasn't late. I almost got *A*s—which wasn't as hard as I expected because, let me tell you, college is a lot more interesting than high school! Anyway, I think I'm ready to be with you guys." Overwhelmed with emotion, she crossed her hands atop her heart. "My guys."

"So you'll move in?" Eric said. "You can have your own room, your own bathroom, if you like."

"You know the way to a woman's heart." She turned to squeeze the muscle of his shoulder. "I'll move in, but if my grades go south, that's the end of that."

Eric laughed and bent to kiss her forehead, his eyes sparkling like stars. "B.G. would never let that happen. He'll positive-think you onto the dean's list."

"Nonsense," B.G. said. "She has to do that herself."

He had stepped to where she could see him, and over Eric's shoulder their gazes met. She felt as if their souls were looking at each other, though what they said was in a language she didn't know. All the same, some communication was exchanged. Suddenly, the air was heavy and hot. A flush moved over B.G.'s face, and Eric's hand slid into her hair. The pulse at his wrist was noticeably quick. Her attraction to B.G. had attracted him. The lust that fisted inside her as a result would have frightened her if it hadn't been these men she felt it for.

She knew they wouldn't leave it unsatisfied.

"Do I have to do *everything* myself?" she asked. "Because, considering my self-imposed no-dating policy, that's what I've been stuck with all semester."

Eric groaned at her implication and buried his face in her neck.

"Oh, no," B.G. assured her softly. "I think the two of us can help you out quite a bit."

Eric's bedroom was a variation on the rest of the apartment's theme. The walls were matte black, the bedclothes dusty blue, and the carpet a textured cream. Navy sheers draped the broad windows, almost but not quite blocking out the view. Above the bed, which was very low to the ground, a single picture held pride of place, an eerily lovely black-and-white photo of an old growth maple encased in ice—probably captured after a storm.

Once she got over the initial shock of the black walls, Charity decided it was one of the most peaceful rooms she'd ever been in. Seeing it made her realize this man she loved had depths she hadn't explored.

At the moment, of course, she was most interested in exploring the king-size bed. The goosedown coverlet at its foot seemed especially inviting.

"Wait," Eric and B.G. said as she moved forward.

Then both of them laughed.

"We want to undress you," Eric said. "Bit by bit."

"Bit by bit quickly," Charity urged. "It's been months."

Despite her words, they didn't hurry much, though she supposed the process of getting her naked might have seemed quick to them. She had to admit it was pleasant to watch them work in coordinated silence, to shiver beneath the gentle caresses of their hands, to hear the changes in their breathing as the different parts of her appeared.

Being treated like this, a girl could get to thinking she was a goddess.

When her clothes were gone down to the last sock, Eric knelt at her feet. "Beautiful," he said, his touch feathering up the back of her calves.

B.G. nuzzled her hair aside to kiss her nape. His hands smoothed circles around her hips as the ridge behind his zipper brushed her bottom. That they were dressed and she was naked made her feel vulnerable.

"Tell us what you want," B.G. murmured against her vertebrae. "Let us be your servants."

Eric leaned close enough to lick her belly. She knew, if she let him, that wouldn't be all he tasted.

Before she lost the will, she slipped from between them and sat cross-legged on the bed.

"Undress each other," she said. "I want to look at you."

To her amusement, this they did quickly, with a good bit more cursing and less grace than they'd spent on her. It hardly mattered to her enjoyment. They were beautiful specimens of their sex, both muscular—even if B.G. was leaner—and both imposingly aroused. The sight of their erections made her lick her lips, but they didn't do more than brush each other as they undressed, a restraint she had plenty of sympathy for. When both were bare and panting, Eric looked at her, then at B.G., then pulled his partner into a deep open-mouthed kiss.

B.G. hesitated a second, then kissed him back, groaning as he gave in to the pleasure. The sound slid through her like molten gold, pooling low and heavy between her legs. She gasped at the force with which their arms wrapped each other's backs, at the clenching of their well-developed sinews. Their intensity told her they hadn't been playing much while she was gone, that they were close to desperate. She could have watched for longer, especially when they began to slide their cocks together side by side. Somewhat to her disappointment, as soon as the friction got enthusiastic, they broke apart and turned in unison to her. Both their faces were dark.

"Who do you want inside you?" B.G. asked raggedly. "You can have us both if you want, but one of us has to go first."

Hardly aware of what she was asking, she glanced at Eric. He was rubbing his palm across his diaphragm as if he wished he were rubbing something else. He was certainly ready; his erection was huge, the tip taut and red. When the three of them had played at Mosswood, Eric had usually been the one to take her. It had seemed more comfortable for everyone. Now that she knew B.G. loved her, she wondered if "comfort" was really what that arrangement had been about. Maybe B.G. had conceded that intimacy to his friend because he thought he didn't have the right to push himself forward.

As if he could read her mind, Eric smiled and gave her a tiny nod. His friend was more important than his hard-on.

"You," she said to B.G. "You take me the way you want."

∼⁂∼

He wanted to be slow and suave, but the minute she said *you,* desire rolled like an avalanche through his body and shut off his brain. He pushed her down on the bed and took her mouth like the marauder he'd never known he could be. Her thighs came up on either side of his waist, soft, warm, hugging him as tightly as he hugged her. He couldn't keep from grinding his erection against her abdomen, even when it made him swell dangerously.

The sound of his moans embarrassed him, but the sound of hers wouldn't let him stop. He loved her. He loved her and Eric, and they were all going to fuck each other like madpeople.

If Eric hadn't flipped the condom wrapper against his ear, he would have forgotten it entirely.

"Let me," Charity said, a plea whose power to gratify was only exceeded by the careful motions of her hands.

He had to sit back to give her room to work. Now muscles tightened all over his body as she got him sheathed.

"There," she said, patting his hip. "All ready to rock and roll."

He kissed her because he had to, kissed her until she trembled as hard as him, kissed her until her arms clutched him back. When Eric sat on the bed beside them, B.G.'s excitement increased. Eric's heat was palpable, the sound of his shallow respiration sexier than a moan. B.G. had to stop kissing Charity then because he couldn't catch his breath. She must have known Eric was there, but she looked only at him, her palm petting his cheek, her eyes big and shining.

"I love you," she whispered. "You have your own place in my heart, and it's just as important as his."

He couldn't doubt her. He understood exactly how she felt.

"Ditto," he said, or tried to. He was sounding a tad asthmatic at the time.

She must have understood him, because she laughed.

"Are you ready?" he asked, and she nodded with endearing eagerness.

As he lowered himself back into position between her legs, Eric sat close enough that his naked hip pressed Charity's shoulder. His erection was high and pulsing, each snaking vein etched by a master pen.

"He is pretty," Charity said, noting B.G.'s distraction.

At the comment, Eric's cock gave a little bounce, clearly liking both their attention. B.G. felt as if he were acting on his friend's desires as much as his own. He pressed forward automatically, only stopping when her folds closed around his crown. At this singular pleasure, B.G. remembered he didn't want to rush.

Neither, apparently, did Eric. "I want to feel you go inside her . . . if that's all right."

"Be our guest," B.G. rasped back. "I don't believe either of us would complain."

Eric eased his arm between their bodies, brushing Charity's pubic curls along the way. When he reached the softness of her cleft, she twitched, then gushed against B.G.'s tip.

It was too much. Eric had bullied him into going without for too long. Doubly held by her body and by the circle of Eric's finger and thumb, B.G. pressed smoothly inside. The sensation of engulfment was exquisite, not only because here was this soft, wet, sexy woman, but because the soft, wet, sexy woman was her: a woman he loved and was loved by in return. What a gift that was. What a rare miracle.

B.G.'s eyelids drifted shut as shudders of bliss rolled down his spine. Eric must have known how close he was to losing control. His hold tightened painfully on his base, calming the warnings of imminence.

All of them stopped then, breath held, muscles tight, none of them wanting this treat curtailed. Charity was the first to relax.

"I think you can let B.G. go now," she said softly to Eric. "I think he's ready to move."

B.G. moved the moment Eric released him, deeply in and deeply out, savoring every millimeter of every stroke. He loved the way Charity squirmed beneath him, growing stronger and wilder in her impatience. To torture a woman with slowness was his idea of paradise, her sighs of longing his favorite accolade.

He reduced her—finally, wonderfully—to growling with frustration and amusement. She rolled their clinched bodies over, the bed so big they were in no danger of falling off. When the rotation finished with her on top, he was still inside her, a victory she seemed to enjoy.

B.G. grinned back at her, stretching his spine and arching his neck, letting his cock flex deeply into her sheath. She made a very sexy picture straddling him. She planted her hands on his chest as if to hold him down.

"You like this," she said, her pussy giving a delicious, grasping pull. "You like it when I ravish you."

B.G. was dizzy with the truth of what she claimed. He wanted to say a prayer that he could know this pleasure all his life.

"Maybe," he said instead. He placed his hands at the bend of her thighs and gripped, anchoring her firmly at the bottom of her stroke. "And maybe I like giving Eric a chance to play."

≈≫≪≈

Eric had been stroking Charity's hair before she rolled, but he moved behind her at B.G.'s cue. That they'd planned this part ahead of time was clear. Eric retrieved a bottle she hadn't noticed lying on the bed. It sloshed when he tipped it, then again when he set it down. Even without touching her, his body seemed to vibrate against her back. The hands he dropped to her shoulders were warm and oiled. When they began to knead her, she knew she was a goner.

"Ooh," she said, never having gotten a massage *while* she was having sex. Eric knew just how hard to press and where, finding all the knots she'd picked up studying.

If Sylvia hadn't been jettisoned already, Charity would have suggested B.G. let her go.

"Oh, boy," she said as Eric's thumbs cruised down her spine, her hips rocking languorously on B.G.'s cock. "This has got to be nirvana."

Eric didn't stop with her spine. Oil was dribbled down her front and rubbed in until she felt as relaxed as if she'd been baking beneath a Caribbean sun. His motions behind her were like the ebb and wash of the waves. His erection slid in the oil, over her curves and between her cheeks, making her buttocks tingle with his passage.

Eric didn't push inside, but he hardly needed to to send her libido into ultra-high gear. She noticed his whole body this way, rather than just his cock. He rubbed her with his hands, with his arms, with the warm, crinkly hair of his chest. All of him became a sex organ to her.

Later, she thought with a private smile, *we'll try out the rest of the arrangements.*

Seeming enthralled, B.G. watched everything Eric did: every pull of her tight, shiny nipples, every bunching of the muscles in his thighs. Her own thighs were still imprisoned by B.G.'s hands, and his fingers only tightened as his tension rose. He wasn't thrusting, but his cock was so stiff and full it felt like bone.

After a while, the reclusive physicist bit his lip. "He's not inside you," he whispered, "and after I assured him I wouldn't feel upstaged."

Charity grinned at the way their different minds could follow the same track. "He must not have listened, but he did take me that way back at your house. My first time ever."

The sweat that glittered suddenly on B.G.'s forehead was as arousing as his earlier whisper. "Sorry I missed it. He's good at that."

"Oh, yes," Charity agreed. "Very."

"Next time, I'm definitely watching."

"Hush, you two," Eric said as Charity chuckled. "I'm interested in feeling lots of things tonight." To prove it, he used his fingers to tip down his rigid shaft, gliding its upper surface between her legs until its crown bumped B.G.'s balls.

B.G. and Charity both went *"Ooh."*

Then he slid himself back the other way.

"Now that I have your attention," Eric said, pushing forward with his upper body and, in the process, forcing Charity's down, "I want Charity to thrust in time with me."

At this, B.G. freed his hold on her hips. She could move again, but Eric was controlling how. Each time he slung his pelvis against her buttocks, she was shoved along B.G.'s length. Each time he moved back, she grabbed her chance to rise.

The former boy genius was more than close enough to read her eyes. "You like this," he whispered, echoing her certainty of before. "You like having power *and* being bound."

She was balanced on her forearms and folded legs, with Eric braced above her to protect her from his full weight. Her breasts sat softly on B.G.'s newly hairy chest, her nipples wonderfully sensitive to his texture. To illustrate his point, B.G. cuffed her around her underarms. Mild though the bondage was, the addition of this pleasure to all the others sent her into an altered state.

She . . . surrendered. There was no other word for what happened to her body, no other word to explain her overwhelming sense of trust. She and Eric moved together, breathed together like one person. She could have laughed with joy, but she didn't need to. When B.G. joined their rhythm, when he began pushing upward and flexing to meet their thrusts, she gave up the last of her need to hold herself separate.

She couldn't guard herself, no matter what the future held.

"Faster," B.G. groaned, sounding not at all like his usual self. "Oh, God, please."

Neither she nor Eric could resist his plea. They moved
faster, took B.G. deeper, caught their breath in unison as
B.G. tightened and shuddered and twisted his face and
body in hard release.

"*Yes,*" Eric said as if he were the one who'd burst, and she
had to say it, too.

Their encouragement made B.G. moan, still quivering
with the drawn-out pleasure of a long-denied climax. Eric's
clever fingers found her clit, but it was B.G.'s ecstasy that
pulled hers as if attached by chains. No fear marked her fall.
Her orgasm swooped from soft to strong, from sweating
earth to sparkling sky. Arms held her. Chests warmed her.
Eric crushed her to him as his seed spurted on her back. She
spiked one final time and went limp.

The sound of two men huffing with completion was sweet
indeed.

"Lord," Eric moaned, as if he couldn't believe how good
that had felt.

It took a minute, but he eased off her with a sigh, joints
stiff from tensing up so hard. He collapsed at B.G.'s side,
leaving his other side for her to snuggle up to. The sweat
cooling on her skin made her grateful for his body heat.

"My," B.G. murmured. "That was quite exhilarating."

"Quite," Eric agreed with an affectionate little snort.

"Totally," said Charity, and pulled the comforter over
them all.

Twenty-one

Eric woke with his stomach rumbling and Charity gone from the bed. Night had fallen while they slept the sleep of the well sated. In the light of the bedside clock, he saw B.G. smiling in his dreams. Amused but also touched, Eric pulled the sheet over his shoulder and tiptoed out.

Charity wasn't in the kitchen or the living room. The baths were empty as well, but a quilt was missing from the second guest room. This led him reluctantly to the balcony. Sure enough, her shadow filled the barely used lounge chair. He pushed the sliding window open, held onto the frame, and shivered. The earlier drizzle had become a fog, diffracting the city's lighted windows into stars. Because he couldn't see the ground, this made it seem as if they were higher up than twelve floors. Eric wondered what the chances were that Charity would let him stay where he was.

"Hey," she said, her smile welcoming. "Come share my blanky." She pulled aside a fold, revealing a flash of lovely, soft-nippled breast. "Come on," she said, understanding warm in her eyes. "If I hold this open much longer, I'm going to get perky."

"Or arrested." Despite the possibility, and his phobia, he

was smiling as he squeezed into the pocket of warmth beneath the quilt. There was just enough room on the cushioned cast-iron frame for both their bottoms.

"Mm," she said when she noticed he was naked, too. "Good thing this blanket is big."

"My grandmother quilted it." His voice sounded normal, which was good. Though he was tense, his heart rate was steady. Satisfied he wasn't going to embarrass himself, he tucked Charity's head beneath his chin. As long as no one asked him to make like Spiderman and scale the building, he thought he'd be fine.

"My grandma was a knitter," Charity said as if she knew he needed something else to think about. Her hand settled comfortably at his waist. "She used to compete in national knit-offs. I don't know why, but everything she made was green. My mom was afraid of her, so we didn't see her very often. I did, however, get some really rad Barbie clothes as gifts."

This disclosure seemed to merit one in return. "Grandma Berne was a kleptomaniac."

"No!"

"Yes. We couldn't take her shopping anywhere. And she was strangely obsessed with Hummel figurines. When my sister was fourteen, she was so embarrassed she wanted us to disown her."

"Oh, too funny."

"Mom didn't think so. She was appalled by Dana's 'lack of family feeling.' She made her dust Grandma's collection three months running. Then Grandma decided Dana was her favorite grandchild—she didn't know the visits were a punishment—and started treating her specially. Dana liked that until Grandma left her all the Hummels in her will."

"Even the stolen Hummels?"

"We try not to inquire too closely into that. And Dana's too much of an accountant to throw them out. Some of the old figures have appreciated quite a bit. My dad likes to bait her by giving her new pieces for Christmas—preferably the most mawkish he can find."

Under the blanket, Charity's fingertips stroked his side, tickling pleasantly along his ribs. "Your dad sounds like the one member of your family I might get along with."

Eric rubbed a circle on her back. "Mom would like you, even if I can't promise she wouldn't occasionally put her foot in her mouth. Her family is even richer than Dad's—Rockefeller rich. Marrying Dad brought her down to earth a bit, but sometimes she doesn't understand how regular people live."

Charity's head lifted from his chest, her eyes gone wide. He hoped she understood the significance of him talking about his family. He fully intended that they be part of her life, too.

"Rockefeller rich," she said with a little shake of disbelief. "I can't even imagine."

"Mom's family has a castle in Wales. We spent a few summers there as kids. It was crumbly but pretty fun."

"Huh," she said and fell into a reverie.

Eric let her digest what he'd revealed before he spoke again. "Tell me you didn't come out here because you were having second thoughts."

"About you and B.G.? After tonight? No way! You guys are stuck with me for a while."

"Good," he said, trying to decide if now was the time to admit what he really wanted. She squirmed around and looked at him before he could.

"I was thinking about Sylvia," she said. "What happened to her after I left?"

"Well, eventually she was deported."

"That's it?"

"That's it. They could have charged her with espionage—"

"Or attempted murder!"

"I suppose. But I don't think anyone wanted her talking about what she came to Mosswood for. If she goes back babbling about time-warping machines, most people will assume she's crazy. On the other hand, if a case has been brought against her in U.S. court . . ."

"Someone might take her seriously." Charity sat up straighter on the lounge, a stripe of foggy light reaching through the gap in the quilt. Eric wondered if she realized how beautiful she was—not just a sex kitten, but a beautiful woman with a strong spirit.

Feeling more for her than he knew how to keep inside, he hugged her gently around the waist. "Sylvia had a younger stepbrother," he went on. "Not a blood relation—in fact, their parents might not have been legally married—but they grew up together. From the sounds of it, they weren't exactly brother- and sisterly."

Charity snapped her fingers. "Arne. That's what she called me by mistake when I was spanking her."

"I believe that is his name," Eric said, impressed by her memory. "Anyway, the stepbrother belongs to a radical anti-American student group that sometimes loans their services to more organized factions. I'm not aware of all the twists and turns, but after Sylvia came to America, the stepbrother convinced her to infiltrate B.G.'s household."

"Is anyone trying to shut down the group?"

"They'll be watched," Eric said. "Fortunately for them, they're not terribly effective. Dana says our government is hoping to use them to find the organizers farther up the chain."

"It all seems surreal now."

"Yes, it does."

"Is it terrible of me to hope Sylvia will be okay?"

Eric laughed. "It's not terrible. It's sweet." Wanting her full attention, he laid his hand on her cheek. "There's something I need to tell you, between you and me." He let out his breath, then drew it in. Never mind his nerves. Charity had a right to know what he was planning.

"What is it?" she asked, her hand coming up to touch his wrist. "Why do you look like you're facing a firing squad?"

He shook his head at what he was about to ask. Considering how important he knew her independence was, he really had some damn nerve.

"I don't know when B.G. will want to return to Mosswood," he began, "but I'm hoping to marry you, to make promises to you and have you make them to me. I'd like to keep B.G. if I can, but whatever your feelings on that, I think you ought to know my ultimate goal includes you wearing my ring."

She stared at him unspeaking, then pressed her lips to his with her palms framing either side of his jaw. It was the kiss of a woman with love in her heart. Delicate. Tender. Even a little awed. What it wasn't was a kiss that gave him a clear answer.

"You've decorated really nice in here," she said when she drew back, "but you need some plants. Saw palmettos, I think, and maybe orchids. A few of those Taipei Golds would punch your look right up. I could install them for you. My thumbs have always been green, and now that I've taken some botany classes, I'm actually pretty impressive."

For a moment, her response confused him. What did orchids have to do with getting married? Then the possible implication registered. If her nesting instincts had been engaged . . . Oddly enough, considering how calmly he'd stepped onto this balcony, now his heart was galloping.

"Does this urge to landscape my apartment signify a 'yes'?"

Charity smiled and drew one finger down the center of his mouth. "It signifies a promise to think about it, and a thank you, and possibly a great big 'wow.'"

"You're not going to tell me I'd have to give up B.G.?"

Her grin held an unmistakable hint of Cheshire cat.

"Oh, no," she assured him, her hand trailing down his

torso to his waiting cock. The moment she touched it, it began to swell. "You see, I'm hoping to keep B.G., too."

In the living room, out of their sight, B.G. chuckled silently around a slice of cold pizza. What an interesting development. He could have everything he wanted without a twinge of guilt: his friend happy, himself *connected*, not to mention the added benefit that Charity would have all the support and guidance she needed to achieve her full potential. He wondered if she was serious about botany. An admirable field of study. Why, plants were nearly as fascinating as particles!

Even with his I.Q., B.G. couldn't have imagined a more agreeable ending.

As he watched his friends' caresses turn purposeful, he counted his blessings that he wasn't the only one who knew how to dream.

About the Author

Emma Holly lives in Minnesota where the winters are long and people will use any excuse to warm up. According to Emma, humanity's best inventions are hot showers, the printing press, coffee, chocolate, and bicycle shorts for men. She can be reached at emma@emmaholly.com or P.O. Box 2591, Minneapolis, MN 55402-0591.